THE LATE GREAT WIZARD

SARA HANOVER

DAW BOOKS, INC.

DONALD A. WOLLHEIM, FOUNDER
375 Hudson Street, New York, NY 10014
ELIZABETH R. WOLLHEIM
SHEILA E. GILBERT
PUBLISHERS
www.dawbooks.com

Dedicated to the most excellent friends anyone could wish for –
The Savages of New Zealand – Mike and Joy
and
Nina and George Conasch of Dural, Australia
With many thanks for their generous spirits and their warm
hospitality over the years.

ACKNOWLEDGMENTS

With many thanks to my publishers who are also my friends, Sheila Gilbert and Betsy Wollheim of DAW Books, and the entire hard-working staff. Also to the staff of Penguin Random House, who work equally hard.

With appreciation to the Orange County Fictionaires, a workshop group of writers and poets, for their insight and support and the privilege of participating.

And special gratitude to my "first daughters" and "first readers" Dr. Maureen J. Salsitz and Jessica Greening Ervin, MBA, who have always been my cheerleaders as well as critiquers, and who have made most of my work possible.

CHAPTER ONE

NOT A DAY went by that I didn't wonder if my father was dead or alive.

I tried not to think about it, but the gray day brought the memories back, and I waited for the low roll of thunder as I stood on the sidewalk outside campus (go Skyhawk CC!), my field hockey gear over one shoulder and my backpack dangling from my hand. Summer had nearly finished up and I was well into the fall semester. It wasn't bad at the community college. It just was not what I had planned. Still, with the next hockey season amping up to start in August, I felt like I finally had a handle on things. I had old friends and new, just no father.

I never told my mother exactly what had happened because I'm the reason he went missing.

It started as I sat at the kitchen table, finishing up my college applications to four different campuses, each one part of my dreams, and had all the paperwork, even the essays, in a nice pile. I opened the checkbook for my college fund and got ready to fill in the last step. He stopped by, smelling of cigarette smoke and stale sweat, courtesy of yet another casino. He hadn't been around much lately.

"What're you up to?"

"Getting ready to mail my applications."

He eyed the stacks, put his hand out and gently closed the checkbook. "Not yet."

"I have deadlines, Dad. These need to get in the mail, with money."

Family members had always told me I was a female copy of him: tall and slender, with soft brown hair and a sprinkling of freckles across my face. I added narrowed eyes as I looked at him. "What do you mean, not yet?"

His eyes, not like mine—I share my mother's snapping blue eyes—had shuttered a little as he hesitated. Then he said slowly, "The account is closed."

"What?!"

"Closed. Empty. Kaput."

I remember jumping to my feet. "What did you do?" My chair slammed to the floor, and the neighbors would have heard it and the shouting that followed, but the storm had closed in, a storm reported to be historic with its downfall of rain and curtains of lightning, thunder with booms of its own. It had shaken the house, but frankly, our home was already falling down.

"I borrowed it. Just for a few days. Until I get even."

I could still hear a hopeful echo to his words but he hadn't gotten it, clearly. Gambling is great when you win. When you don't, you double down out of desperation to catch up, and that's when you lose even more. And he had. "You borrowed enough to close the account? You'll never get even. Grandpa left that money for me, and I've put every cent I've earned into it. You stole it from me!"

"You'll get it back, and more."

"Does Mom know?"

Another house-shaking crash had sounded just overhead. I heard a tree topple in response. I remember thinking there would be branches down in our driveway or backyard, or maybe next door.

He had opened his mouth but I'd known then just like I'd know if he said it now—it would be another lie. A meaningless promise given.

I had lurched to my feet, overturning the table, letters and applications falling everywhere, and screamed, "You ruin everything. Get away from me! Get out of here!"

My father had taken a step back. His gaze ran over my face

and stopped at my fisted hands. Barney, our dog, rushed at him, hackles up and barking loudly but barely audible over the crash and fury of the storm.

I had hardly breathed for the anger running through me. "Mom can't pay the bills. We're behind on everything. What happened to you? Why are you doing this to us? You have to stop. Just stop."

His face had crumpled, barely resembling the father I knew. "I can't stop. Not yet."

"Then leave. We're better off without you."

The sky had clashed, gigantic cymbals, and then everything went quiet for a few seconds. I remember raising my fist again.

He left. Hustled out the door with Barney yapping meanly at his heels, and we never saw him again. Stocks, gone. The mortgage, leveraged and foreclosed. We lost everything.

I was the last person who saw my father alive. And he took my dog and dreams with him.

I eventually got used to people watching us suspiciously as if we'd done away with him, friends and reputation falling away. The world turned, and brought new scandals to draw attention, and I graduated high school early, in hopes of starting over. And I had.

This has been a good week. We haven't discovered anything new, but the consequences just keep coming. Mom still half expects someone named Bruno to show up, threatening to kneecap us if we don't make good on what Dad owes the mob. His disappearance is still under investigation, or we are anyway, and the police always tell us, after a significant pause, "There's been no activity on his credit cards or cell phone. John Graham Andrews is off the grid." As if they expect us to confess we buried him in the backyard.

Now we rent from Great-Aunt April. It's a long way from our old neighborhood, but we pay what both my mom and Great-Aunt April call a pittance. Aunt April is so old she remembers when gasoline was ten cents a gallon, so the current price is like heart attack city to her. Still, she helped. That's what family is for, evidently, renting you rundown houses cheaply. Never mind that it's a house where doors open and shut unexpectedly, where the keys on the rack by the kitchen jiggle and ring whenever I come into the house, and where books pop off shelves as if trying to get your attention. I think it's because the foundation of the place has slipped a little.

People helped, a little, at first, but Mom and I didn't want pity, and that's what we mostly got. School was worse. Whispers in the hallway and classroom. Sidelong looks. Popular girls pretended to warm up to me because their parents told them they had to, before giving up. I am not easy to make or keep friends with because I always try to figure out the angle. Everyone has one, right? With the guys, it became obvious they thought a pity date ought to put out. I corrected that notion right away.

We kept wondering then who knew what was going on and why they didn't warn us about it. Tired of the stares, I had quit the JV field hockey team. Grades dropped for a quarter until Mom and I had a heart-to-heart about giving up. Rejoined the hockey team and studied even harder. Walked from the school early. I couldn't imagine what my mother went through, but she put her dissertation on hold for nearly two years, which had to hurt her chances of getting the tenure track job she wanted to land. I know the faculty pressure got even stiffer. So I grabbed the community college partial scholarship when offered and here I stood, remembering what I didn't want to, and trying to appreciate what I could.

"What's up, girl?" Jheri pounded a fist on my shoulder and stopped to grin at me when I swung around. I nearly clocked her with my backpack.

"I'm just deciding how fast I want to run to catch the bus." I smiled back at her. Her expression is absolutely infectious, and one I hardly see because she's usually hidden behind a ton of protective goalie gear. Not to mention her curls, always pulled back with a headband.

"You either need a car or a boyfriend with wheels."

I shrugged. "Neither right now."

She pointed a finger at me— "See you next week"—and she hustled off, the fastest moving person I know. The only reason she's the goalie and I'm the striker is because she has the most incredible eyesight and anticipation. If we go to statewide championships next season, it'll be because of Jheri Browning, near impossible to score against. I watched her dark curls bounce off the back of her neck as she disappeared across the campus parking lot.

A small crowd milled about, students here because they can't afford to be anywhere else or don't need a four-year degree. But most of us have plans, so that's a plus. Skyhawk CC is not an extended high school, contrary to some opinions.

Joanna Hashimoto darted past me, her silky black hair tied back in a ponytail. She was also an early grad, and a mystery. Her father owned one of the country-club-and-golf-courses outside town, and she could afford to go anywhere. But Skyhawk has a rep for computer science, and that's her thing, so I guess she's learning what she can on the cheap. I watched her step into a limo steered by a young and handsome driver, and the car glided away.

A boy brushed past, shoulder contact probably not accidental. I didn't turn to look at him, though. A few of those focused brains seemed to be on vacation as a banner fluttered nearby. The topic was the annual Bachelors and Bachelorettes bash for charity, a good thing to be involved in, I guess, but I wasn't interested. The Andrews family is still better left on the sidelines. Half of Richmond can't decide whether we still need sympathy or we're ax murderers, and the other half just doesn't care. The prettier girls in school wheeled about to look at the auction poster and nudged their friends, laughing, while some of the boys strutted to be noticed as potential dates. Seriously? Leave the action to the runway when the bidders are dying to spend money. I peeled my gaze away, waiting for the bus. Evelyn Statler sneaked in from the side and nudged me in the ribs.

"We'll take you home."

I looked at her over my backpack before hanging it off my shoulder. "You driving?"

"Moron," she said affectionately. "No, I'm not driving. Dad says I can't drive anymore until after the election. He doesn't want anything I do to 'impact the voters.'" She shook her head, blond hair swinging.

"Nice." Knowing Evelyn's impulsive nature, I couldn't blame Mr. Statler for blocking her until he made mayor, but I sounded sympathetic. She was more than a frenemy, but not quite a bestie. She's one of the ones who stayed friends, but I couldn't quite decide why. Maybe it's because she doesn't have an agenda. We've known each other forever, though, and still talk to each other, so that's a plus. I thought I'd left her behind, only to find that she was already at Skyhawk CC, doing both high school and college courses concurrently. She challenged her graduation requirements, spending most of her time at Skyhawk now, as ambitious as Joanna but much more subtle about it. Me? I just want to get educated and get out of here.

We waited for their town car to ease up in the circle coming into the parking lot. "You going to the Spring Charity?"

I gave a negative. "Not interested."

"It's a chance to dress up and be normal for a while."

"Trust me, my dressing up is not normal. Besides, it's an auction." I didn't look at her. She'd draw bids. I didn't think I would, and who needed to be humiliated further?

"It's not just an auction. Everyone that gets bid on carries a pouch with a secret number of tokens that can be used at the Monte Carlo tables. It'll be fun! You might be worth a fortune and not know it! And it's for homeless kids."

I rolled my eyes.

"You can go with me," Evelyn offered.

"You're going to have a date."

"True. Do me a solid and weed through the invites, will you?" She changed tactics.

I raised an eyebrow. "You're in college and you're asking me to do your homework?"

"I," Evelyn said firmly, "am making them put their plans for the evening in writing."

"Wow."

"I know. Sort through 'em for me? You have a better sense of character than I do."

"Said the innocent young blonde to the ax murderer."

Evelyn gave a little snort. I knew her type, though. She liked the bad boys. Well, almost bad. She wasn't really into shocking her parents or doing anything that would jeopardize her father's business and political ambitions. She just liked the dangerous look. I scouted the area, looking for my own bad boy.

I spotted the car just around the corner, almost too far away to keep an eye on us. My bad boy is a good guy, a hometown hero, and we don't talk. He's a war hero and returned home to become a cop, one of the youngest ever, and even though strings were probably pulled to get him his new career, he's worked hard at it. I'm nineteen and he's twenty-three, but there's a whole world of experience between us, and his only interest is in the missing person file. Carter Phillips, veteran, policeman, crush, at your service. He has these winsome eyes to die for. I would give anything if he'd just look at me longingly instead of with an earnest expression which normally read case file blah, blah, blah, missing person number blah.

She socked me in the arm again just as her mom pulled up and the town car doors unlocked. "Attention! Ride's here."

"Right."

We piled in.

Mrs. Statler smiled over her shoulder at me. "Tessa! The two of you making plans for the big night?"

"Not exactly," I told her, but I had the feeling she didn't hear me because she responded, "That's nice. It's good to stay engaged in the community."

Evelyn's dad owned two of the big new car dealerships in town, so she always had a nice ride, conventional, hybrid, or all electric. I settled back into the cushions and watched the outskirts of town as we passed by.

Mom stood waiting for me in the driveway with a bicycle and a toddler chariot attached to it, one of those three-wheeled canvas goodies.

Evelyn peered around me. "What in god's name is that?"

"I have no idea." I sidled out of the car while Mrs. Statler said sympathetically, "Tessa, your mother looks good, with your father lost and all. Bless her heart."

In Virginia, that's often said with as much irony as good intentions. She could have gone on, and would have, but I blurted out, "Yeah, thanks," and shut the car door quickly, trying to block Evelyn from getting a clearer view of whatever my mother had planned. She leaned out the window, perfect hair bouncing, and made hand signs of "call me" as I waited on the sidewalk to make sure they pulled away. Aunt April's car sat at the curb next door, and I pondered the many reasons why it might be. Had something finally broken that Mom couldn't repair?

I turned around to face Mom. She's short, curvy, and blonde; I'm like a weed, but at least I share the gaze and the attitude. We can both stop liars in their tracks. I eyed the bike and chariot Mom proudly introduced with a flourish, like a grand prize on a television quiz show. "What's this?"

"This is a month's rent."

"You paid that much for it? And why?"

"Aunt April picked it up at a garage sale." Mom beamed at the bicycle with cart and back at me. "I've signed you up for Meals by Wheels."

"What? And whatever for?"

"Aunt April has dear friends nearby that use the service, and the regular driver is out for a few months with a broken ankle, so she hoped you could step in. She's giving us a financial pass while you do. We could use the funds for the new gear you need for next season."

"Or I can just get a part-time job, but I think the operative word here is: driver. As in, usually comes with a car."

"We could really use the break on the rent, honey." Mom didn't look directly at me, just ran her fingers over the handlebar of the bike. She didn't like asking any more than I liked hearing her do it. "Meals programs are important. You can always use community service on your resume. She's hard to say no to. You'll have killer legs, I promise."

So family was not only responsible for renting haunted, rickety houses but committing your life to a program involving hungry old people. I opened my mouth to object, but the designer of this humiliation came out of the house, my great-aunt herself.

She smiled. She no longer had freckles but age spots, hidden slightly by a softly blushed powder, and her eyebrows had been drawn in brown over gray hairs, but she walked proud and confidently with the Andrews height, and put a hand on the contraption. I still remember the day when she only got one eyebrow drawn in and took us out to lunch, with me sitting across the booth and wondering if I should tell her about the missing brow. We loved her, but she could be vain, and silence is the better part of valor. I checked quickly to see if her make-up had gone lopsided again, but it hadn't.

"What do you think, Tessa?"

She had appealing brown eyes that I could see Dad had inherited, though Aunt April walked as though she had a yardstick for a spine. Dad's had disappeared, probably ripped out by a casino somewhere.

I eyed the bicycle dubiously. "This is a good idea?"

"A great idea. The regular on the route at this end of town can't drive or deliver for two to three months. It's only ten houses here that we couldn't get covered, so I thought you would be perfect as a substitute. It shouldn't interfere with classes or your hockey practice. You'll love the ladies. I play cards with most of them." She gave me a quick hug. Was it a rule that older women had to smell of lavender?

"Thanks, Aunt April. For thinking of me and—this—" Whatever it was. A bike and chariot? Bariot?

She shook a finger at me. "Don't get in trouble with the professor. Your mother knows him. She needs all the allies she can get at the university!" With that she walked off, got in her car, and left.

I sighed at Mom, but we were now a team. We had each other's backs and stuff. "Will you promise not to sign me up for anything else without asking first? If something just happens along?"

"Deal." She stuck out her hand and we shook on it.

"Annnd I don't have to ride this to campus."

"Nope."

I inhaled thankfully. "Now what about this professor?"

"Oh, that would be Dr. Brandard. He's a smart and tough old codger. You'll like him."

One hoped.

I caved too fast, but it's just the two of us against the world.

While Mrs. Statler pitied me having lost my father, we knew we had the better end of that bargain. Except for my dog. I really missed Barney and his Golden Retriever goodness.

I ducked the auction for days, but Evelyn had me firmly fixed as her "handler." This rather bizarre job title meant each of her prospective dates gave me the written invitation so I could vet the guy and his proposed evening. It's vicarious, but something of a life.

As for the hungry old people, the job did have perks. They appreciated company more than the food. I'd already been given a hand-knit winter sweater (and it's only spring!) and two bottles of toilette water: one rosewater, and the other my Mom tells me is lilac. They are marvelously oblivious to the Internet and have heard far more scandalous gossip in their lives than my father up and leaving. Everyone seemed happy to see me except for that grumpy old professor who lived a block over and two blocks down, the last delivery on my little route. He could have been the first, but I made him the last. It's difficult to explain why except to say that my day was almost done when I got to the professor's, so I could put up with just about anything when I got there. He had a bristly mustache under his nose and out of each of his ears, of the salt and pepper color variation. He did not look like Albert Einstein, although he was probably just as intelligent and eccentric. I don't say that because my mom also taught and had a professional connection with him, so I had to be on my good behavior regardless of his temperament. Her position in academia was tough enough without my complicating it further. I'd been told that Brandard could be a good influence, although he showed no inclination to be one.

The first time I dropped off the professor's dinner, he came to the screen door and blustered at me in a semi-British accent about my trying to poison him in the manner of the Mycenaeans. He exhaled gustily. "Where's the regular driver?"

"I'm the substitute," I said, and proceeded to tell him if he didn't want it, I wouldn't come back, but since the Bronze Age of Greece was long gone, taking the Mycenaeans with it, I was more likely to poison him in the medieval tradition of Lucrezia

Borgia, her being a woman after my own heart. That put a sparkle in his eye.

"You know your history."

"A little bit." I loved history, fostered by my mom's interest, but I wasn't about to encourage him to go on about it. I had things to do, and I'd already discovered that lonely old people could talk your ears off. I left the covered dinner on his front step, took my insulated envelope, which smelled, slightly fermented, of boiled cabbage, and bicycled home. The Meals by Wheels in this area is a Monday-Wednesday-Friday deal, as the funding didn't allow it to offer a full week of meals. When I returned, the door was closed and stayed that way. I didn't see him for at least two weeks, when he deigned to show himself in person again.

My meals had already been dropped off and stood stacked on our front porch like a convention of wayward pizzas, each in their own special insulated envelope. It wasn't pizza though, which I suspected would have a greater reception on my delivery route just for the variety. It smelled like something with cooked cabbage again by its potent odor. Maybe meatloaf. Regardless of what it was, my job was to get them delivered still warm and by five o'clock because old people dine insanely early before watching TV and going to bed.

He sat waiting on the stoop for me. He wore a tweed waistcoat like Mole from *The Wind in the Willows*. I knew the book well, having read it after it pitched itself off after me, at least twice, from Aunt April's highest shelf. He stood up as I put the kickstand down on my bike. Waving his pipe, he said, "Follow me. If I must eat, I intend to do so in style," and he led me around to his backyard. We passed the economical but serviceable Corolla sitting on his driveway. Spiderwebs hung about the sagging tires, and the car looked as if it hadn't moved in a good three years. I took note that it may be available if I asked nicely. The city bus was not all it could be.

The houses in this part of town tended to all be frame and a little bit of stucco or brick, with spindly wooden garages at the rear. His had two canopied windows in front, looking out like

benevolent eyes onto the street. Spacious yards lined the back
of the houses in the neighborhood, most of which had gone
wild. The professor's ran more to a cultivated ruin, meaning
someone mowed and edged it once in a while. We passed an
herb garden, a few fruit trees with green fruit waiting to ripen
in the summer sun, and through a maze that spanned the rear,
where he ducked under an arbor and trellis. He pointed his
pipe stem at it as he went. "Crafted of redwood. All but imper-
vious to rot, pests, and fire. Remember that if you ever need to
secret and protect anything. Redwood is a good guardian."

Which made absolutely no sense to me, but he had a table
and three chairs under the arbor in the shade as he sat down,
waiting for me to deposit his dinner. So I did. Redwood is not
common to Virginia—we use a lot of pine—and it looked perfectly ordinary despite the professor's endorsement. Two of the
chairs were people-sized, normal that is, but the third looked
as if something gargantuan could, and did, sit in it, as it showed
wear. Dinner proved to be a chicken fillet with potatoes au gra-
tin and a leafy spinach salad with a little plastic tub of vinai-
grette dressing. No cabbage. I thought maybe the aroma was
ingrained into the delivery envelopes. He sniffed at each portion, nodded his approval and said, "You'll stay."

Stay and what? But I sat down cautiously on the edge of the
picnic chair. He must have noticed the quizzical look and
added, "To make sure this doesn't poison me."

I quirked an eyebrow and decided silence was my best response. Halfway through his chicken fillet, the professor commented that I had a smart mouth.

"I hope you mean educated."

"Precisely." He sliced his meat neatly into small cubes, easily
chewed and swallowed. I wondered if it was OCD or if it had
become a habit of his age. He waved his knife. "What brings
you to bring my meals?"

"Charity work looks good on scholarship applications.
There's always another semester to pay for."

I must have had an edge to my voice. He looked up. "And you
have something against that?"

"Oh, no. I'm all for scholarships, but I had intended to work this summer. Aunt April signed me up for this freebie, so I'm stuck with it for a while."

"Ah. Until she forgets about its importance."

"Actually, until your regular's leg heals enough that she can drive again." I toed a clump of grass.

He speared a limp spinach leaf. "You look familiar."

I doubted my face had changed much from the local newspaper photos about the disappearance, asking for local help, and I knew it hadn't from the Internet gossip that kept circulating because someone had updated it. I didn't know who it was, but when I caught them . . . I smiled instead. "Probably do."

"I have it. You're the unfortunate young woman whose father went missing."

I nodded. "Him and the family dog." I shifted in my chair.

"Your father and I had a brief business deal. It did not end well." He eyed another bit of spinach. "I should probably discuss that with your mother, however."

"There's probably nothing she can do. He's brought us a lot of grief."

He nodded sympathetically. "If only grief were a finite thing."

I stood up, sliding the meal carrier under my elbow. "Enjoy your dinner, Professor Brandard," and left.

It was a little trickier getting out of the arbor than it had been getting in. Who knew? I felt as though I'd hacked my way out of a jungle by the time I emerged. The sun threatened to settle low in the sky. I scurried off and flung a look back at the redwood arbor, arched innocently over a third of the professor's yard, and wondered. I could see no sign of him or the picnic set buried in its depths. I stood on tiptoe. I knew he was there but could not see him.

The following week, he greeted me warmly and left me with a saying about a man's home being his castle and the threshold as the moat against all evil. Running water the same. I had no idea what he meant by that, except the turkey hash that I carried on his dinner tray looked menacing, and I passed it over to him with misgivings. He seemed terribly grateful for it though. Dark circles bruised the wrinkled skin under his eyes and one hand shook a bit as he balanced the tray.

I took a step away, and then back toward him. "Are you all right?"

"All right? All right? By all the gods in all their heavens, I am fit! Fit as any man who thinks and walks on two feet, and never think I'm not!" His mustache vibrated with indignity.

I hurried away as those words and more boomed after me, as though I had insulted every bone, all 200 and some, in his body.

He'd been afraid. Of what? Aging? Although I had no idea of the professor's age, I knew that he was older than anyone else on my route, but still capable. I had studied Aunt April enough to know that incapability could be a worry. I decided to apologize next time I saw him, although in a roundabout way. I didn't want to face that thundering anger again.

More days passed and the meals had been taken, but I didn't see him. I gathered my nerve to ring the doorbell and apologize face-to-face next time.

My offering didn't smell auspicious when my deliveries were dropped off. Maybe cooked cabbage was a generational thing and older people loved it more than I did, but it certainly seemed to be a staple. I peeked into a tray. Aha. Brussels sprouts. Fake, miniature cabbage. I felt only a tiny bit better as I went about my route and deliveries.

Mrs. Romero, she of the lilac water, had a baggie of oatmeal raisin cookies waiting for me. I took one and thanked her, but left the rest. "All that bicycling won't do me any good if I'm munching on delicious cookies," I told her. She dimpled as she smiled and took the goodie bag back. Even her hands had dimples.

As soon as I was out of sight, I spit out the rest of the cookie. Good lord, had she put in a handful of salt instead of a tea-spoon? I was still sucking down my water bottle when I arrived at Mrs. Sherman's, she of the rosewater cologne, eight deliveries later. Mrs. Sherman was next to last, and she felt her dinner tray carefully to make certain it was still warm enough. She smiled thinly. "That'll do."

"Good! Because between you and me, I don't know how these things will stay warm in the winter." I eyed the old Pontiac sitting in her driveway, lightly driven and all but abandoned, like the professor's car. Maybe I could arrange a payment plan. Not that I intended to keep working the meals program, but Aunt April hadn't told me yet if I could bail from deliveries.

Her yarn and knitting needles fell off the small corner table and we both bent to retrieve them.

"Oh, be careful! Those needles are quite sharp. Antique, you know," she told me. "Made from bone."

"Really?"

"Oh yes. Bone and, if you had money in those days, even ivory. I must say, I'm glad ivory isn't used for such things today. Let me put these away." She hurried to the kitchen and then to her craft room by the front bedroom. She made another trip to the kitchen and brought something back with her. She pressed a wax paper package into my hand. "Homemade fudge."

"Oh, you shouldn't have!" Not after Mrs. Romero, she really shouldn't have.

"It's a family recipe," she said. Mrs. Sherman had red hair. Texas red, my mom called it fondly, and bright blue eyes. "Trust me."

I took a wary nibble. Milk chocolate melted on my tongue, the first thing that could take away the memory of that block of salt. "Oh, my."

"See? Just a few pieces. Wouldn't want to add too many curves to that figure of yours, Tessa."

I licked my lips. "Thanks, Mrs. Sherman!" I waved and trotted back to my cruiser. You win some and you lose some.

At the professor's house, his Corolla had gone missing, leaving big tire ruts in his grass and stone driveway as though it had been dragged away reluctantly. I parked my bike thoughtfully as another car stood at the curb. He had visitors. I'd learned that some of the seniors I served were very keen not to let their friends and relatives know they were on a food program. Professor Brandard might be embarrassed as well, so I went to the side kitchen door framed by an arch with wisteria vine in purple bloom. I balanced in hesitation, not quite able to trespass. He hadn't looked well, he needed good nutrition, and, well, I had signed on for this gig. Or my aunt had, but we both had good intentions. The moment of heaviness keeping me not quite in, not quite out passed. Quietly as I could, I went inside, deposited his meal in the oven, and put it on low to keep it warm. I'd telephone back and let him know. It was NOT my fault that I then overheard the voices.

I froze in place.

"Mortimer, good chap, I'm having a terrible day. They came and took my car today. What are you doing sitting on my steps?" Brisk and almost British, my Professor.

"They've hauled my wife away." Mortimer had a low, rusty voice that rumbled in that heavy, heart-pounding bass range which people roll their car windows down for, thinking everyone should appreciate it.

"Really? What good fortune. Not like my car. Neighbors reported it derelict and now I have to get it back. Wish I had luck like you do, but you always did fall in the muck and come out smelling like roses! Now that you're in, tell me all about it and have a spot of something bracing while you do." The floor creaked dreadfully and I realized they must be standing just inside the foyer. I had barely missed running into them. The professor sounded incredibly cheerful despite his terrible day. "However did you manage something so clever as to have her done away with?"

"I didn't, they did, and she won't like it. She'll be wanting me to come get her." Mortimer sounded far less cheerful about his missing wife than the professor.

"Ah. Umm. Awkward. Do you think you can manage it?"

"Not without your help." An Eeyore of a man, whoever he was.

Another hmmm sound. "Called her name three times?"

"Of course. Didn't help. She's still missing."

"Do you think that's wise then? Meddling with the affairs of others? If they wanted to haul her in, it's because they wanted her kept. Confined and all that. Could cause a lot of trouble to go wading in and upsetting plans and all. Not to mention my retirement. I'm scattered all over, you know, don't know if I can help properly."

"They may have taken her to leverage me or force a judgment. Bribery to let her go. I won't stand for that. I'm afraid she's going to cause a lot of trouble if I don't retrieve her."

"True. Wouldn't put it past her, I wouldn't. Mortimer, perhaps this is a good time to translocate."

Translocate? Was that a word? Did he just tell the man to move without his spouse? I leaned a bit closer.

The voice I tagged as Mortimer's let out a long and resigned sign before answering, "Can't do that. I'm attached to her, you know. Don't want to go without her. She's my wife, after all. She needs finding. I have my duties and law to uphold, and I won't abandon my position or Goldie. I know you can find her, if you wished. You could find anyone." I could hear the floorboards moaning under a shuffled step as if something ponderous moved upon them. Was this the big guy that sometimes sat in the ginormous chair in the backyard? And if the professor could locate anyone, how about looking for my father? Not that we wanted him back, but his being found would make our lives easier. I listened more closely.

"And that's exactly what's being counted on. Wives do that, you know. Bit of sugar with the tart, fluttery eyelashes, soft lips, delectable curves and then, when you've fallen, they put their hooks in. Hooks, talons, whatever, and they go in deep."

"Don't make it sound like that."

"Mortimer! What did you expect when you married a harpy? Hooks, that's what!"

"Can't help it, Professor. I love her in my own way, and I think she loves me too." A muffled noise, rather like a sniffle, followed by a honk as he blew his nose.

A long pause. "It's like that, then, is it?"

"It's Malender—"

"No. No names. Especially not *his*. Wait. You haven't mentioned me to her, have you? Or anyone? I'm just an old friend, aren't I?"

"Never said your name. Not Brennus Morcant Brandard, not once."

"Then it's not a trap for me. Just the old love-and-marriage dilemma for you, Morty. I suggest, however, that we not stand in the foyer and talk about this. Little pitchers have big ears and all, and the study, which is warded, is a much better place to make plans. Here's two glasses for you to carry, and I've got a bottle in hand, and off you go." The floor squeaked and moaned a bit as the two walked off.

I jumped as sudden warmth flooded over my scalp before centering on my ears. I rubbed them, the skin as hot to my touch as if they had been burning and I'd been caught. I wasn't sorry for listening—what if the professor did have a knack for finding missing people? And what a mouthful for a name! Foot over careful foot, I inched my way to the kitchen's screen door and edged out carefully. As I closed it silently in its frame, the professor peeked out from the foyer's depths. Our eyes met. His sparkled darkly. Without knowing why, I put my finger to my lips and hurried away without a sound.

That was my first month or so of knowing the professor.

The second month I set him on fire.

CHAPTER TWO

A HOT LATE spring night found me half-asleep when my cell phone rang. I twisted around, strangling in my sheets, furious at the nitwit who ignored phone etiquette, which says after nine pm, you text. Preferably, you mainly text. I managed to pick it up halfway through the second ring.

Static buzzed in my ear. "Help," gasped the professor. "No time. Fire." And the line went dead.

I flew out of bed to get to my jeans, t-shirt, and sneakers. I snagged my hoodie as I raced out the door.

It might have been faster by bike, but I didn't even think of it until I skidded around his corner and could smell the smoke and see the orange flames licking into the night sky. The darkened street lamps stood unlit, just useless columns. Why were they out? Was all electrical out? One house's windows blossomed from gray to golden yellow as I sprinted past it, so no. I yelled "Call 911!" to the night sky and anyone who could hear as I streaked past. As I drew closer to Professor Brandard's, a tornado of fire and red embers funneled upward. Smoke filled my throat. The house was toast. The neighbors could be saved, but that wouldn't help the professor any. I stood in despair and wondered what he thought I could do. And what I possibly could have done, because I could see the spout of flame centered from the kitchen. Had he forgotten I'd left yet another meal warming for him? I'd called. Was this my fault? I'd set him aflame! I circled down the driveway and hoped to see

Brandard perched on a pair of suitcases or boxes, anything he might have wrestled out the back door, and waiting for me.

No one. And nothing. The old-fashioned sun porch that ran across the back of the house hadn't caught yet. I ran up the back steps, tearing at the screened walls riddled with dry rot, bringing them down. Splinters and ragged screen tore across my fingers. I lurched across the deck to the back door where I lifted my foot to try TV Cop 101 on it, and actually managed to kick it in with a loud bang. Air sucked in with a whoosh as I staggered back and flattened myself, prepared for the back draft. Flames renewed by the influx of fresh air shot out with a roar. Sparks encircled my head like a swarm of lightning bugs. The flames sucked back in as I rolled away, but I could feel their intense heat on my face as I looked through the doorframe. Nothing but a barbecue was going on inside. My heart fluttered for a minute. He couldn't still be inside, helpless. He'd called!

"Professor Brandard!"

No answer, nothing but the growing roar of fire and the sound of glass windows cracking and exploding under the heat. Beams groaned and threatened to give way as flame ate away their centers.

Where were the firemen?

I leaped off the sun porch through the ragged hole I'd made, the fire providing illumination over the moonless and lightless night. The whole house keened with a voice of unworldly noise that sent a chill up the back of my neck as I remembered the professor's place with its quaint identity: A craftsman styling with an upper story. An umbrella stand in the foyer for "bumbershoots." Lace curtains across the kitchen windows and framing the door to the wisteria trellis. A built-in sideboard in the foyer gleaming with dark oil polish and littered with knickknacks I couldn't begin to identify, nor had the professor ever let me linger long enough to get a good look at them. Had he died trying to sweep his memorabilia into some duffel so he could haul it outside? Was he buried in books from his library? Digging up floorboards in the upstairs bedroom to retrieve bundles of cash he wouldn't entrust to the banks? Hiding in the porcelain claw-foot bathtub down the hall in hopes it would protect him?

True, I didn't know if he had a claw-foot bathtub on the second floor. We did. But Great-Aunt April hadn't put much money into updating the plumbing. As if awakened by my thoughts, his house pipes began to make a furious thumping noise, as if water heated beyond the boiling point was using fists in an attempt to break out.

Did I hear sirens coming closer?

Maybe he had made it outside into the tall, dew-soaked green yard. If not outside, then he was nowhere safe, and I couldn't possibly help him. I darted back into the night, coughing and spitting out the taste of the fire. The redwood arch? He'd said it wouldn't burn. I doubted that, but . . .

I halted in the middle of the yard. Something rustled in the hedge near the maze. Neighborhood cat? No, it sounded like something large. Much larger. I peered hopefully toward the noisy shrubbery.

"Professor? Professor Brandard?" The smoke throttled my voice down and only a whisper husked out. I barely heard myself, but the something had heard me. It stopped moving.

"Professor, are you all right?" I sounded like a habitual smoker from one of those warning commercials. What had the professor said to Mortimer? Three times was the charm? I coughed to clear my throat. "Professor Brandard!"

The smoke thinned. The hedge made a furious rustling noise as a being rose out of it. All six foot something of him stood, naked as the day he was born, only a few branches of the hedge hiding strategic spots. My jaw dropped open at the sight of him. A broad shoulder, wavy hair of red gold, or maybe it was a reflection from the fire that tinted it, eyes of bluish-green with sooty eyelashes framing them, and a dimpled cheek. I couldn't breathe for a moment.

I clamped my mouth shut.

I had no idea what to do when a snarling, shouting voice carried from the front yard, interrupting my jagged train of thought. "Holy shit and bloody balls of hell!" More curses and fury filled the air, and impulse hit. Hide!

I dove headfirst over the hedge and dragged nature boy down by the arm to the ground with me. No firefighter I ever heard of talked like that, and I didn't want to meet the enraged man who did.

"You didn't behead 'im? I told you 'e had to be beheaded if things went wrong! If 'e dropped dead on the lot of you, you 'ad to take care of him!" A voice accented by the cockney side of London boomed through the crackle of the fire.

Nature boy started to get up. I pulled him back down, shrugged off my hoodie, and knotted it around his waist. He blinked at me and then, I swear, blushed even as two someones whined in protest to the yeller. One I could hear but not comprehend and the other declared, "Nuttin' could live in that."

"Nuttin' could live in that?" the furious speaker mocked in a voice I could only understand because my mom and I were huge fans of Ricky Gervais and Eddie Izzard. I kept my hand firmly on nature boy's arm. Now was no time to have an argument over whether or not we should have a meet and greet with these guys.

Was it possible they had started the fire? If I hadn't? And they were way too excited about taking the heads off of people.

"I told the lot of you to bring me th' 'ead."

"He's old. How could he git outta dat?"

"He's a wizard, damn your 'ide. 'Ow do you think he GOT so bloody old?"

Seriously? I could tell from the voices they were moving down the driveway and headed into our backyard. I eyed the corner, unsure if we could hop the fence and move fast enough to make a clean getaway or not, the maze being what it was. Especially if nature boy couldn't run in bare, tender feet. I sneaked a look at them. Not a mark on 'em, as if he'd just hatched out of an egg. He looked back at me, worried. Maybe he had some survival instincts, after all.

They continued to rail at one another, as if they had absolutely no worry a neighbor might hear them. Indeed, with the fuss and roar of the disintegrating house at their sides and backs, they might not be heard. But I could catch every word now. I didn't understand half of it coming from the two minions. I did decipher "password, got us in a'right" and "cornered 'im in th' library like you said" and something that sounded like "wouldna tell us a thing" followed by an enthusiastic "so we tortured 'im like ewe said" ending with "an' then the bloody corpse set itself on fire, ran off, and 'alf the house went up!"

The argument continued on, unabated. The leader kept yelling, "The freaking corpse ran off on you?!! I told you t' cut off 'is 'ead!" and they kept yelling back, "No, ye dint and he was a bloody shish kabob." Following came a lot of swear words I did know that sounded a bit quaint in their accents. I decided I had to make a decoy move. I pointed nature boy to the arbor. "Crawl in there and hide. I'll come back for you. The redwood should . . . keep you safe." What did I know? But I thought it might. He didn't budge.

I leaned over and put my mouth close to his ear. "Can you understand me?"

He gave a slow nod. He smelled like cedar and juniper, bracing and good. Well, cedar, juniper and smoke, but I figured the smoke was a temporary scent. I put my hand on his shoulder. His skin was warm under my chilled hand and he flinched a bit at my touch, and then steadied himself, his dimple flashing.

"Stay down. Wait for me. I'll be back for you. Got that?" If any of this was real, if I wasn't having a doozy of a nightmare.

A shake of the head.

"You understand me?"

A nod.

"But you don't agree with me."

A nod.

"Well, see, I'm dressed and you're not, so I have the potential to be a faster runner."

A beat, and then a slow nod.

Good. Too many heroes can spoil the plan. I gave him a little nudge in the right direction as I gathered my legs under me for a running start.

Then Mr. Cockney Foulmouthed and his minions strolled into sight. We froze behind the hedge. The leader wore a dapper suit. His cohorts looked scruffy, like chimney sweeps. I longed for the cute-and-trying-to-be-evil-but-failing Pixar villain and henchmen. These three just plain looked nasty. Unhappy, I froze in place, listening for potential help. Why weren't Richmond's finest here yet?

I was even less happy when Mr. Cockney drew himself up with another oath that I had no hope of understanding, so riddled with venom it was, and he pulled his hand out of his pocket and shot the minion he screamed at. But not with a gun. I swear he just pointed a finger. A blast erupted and enveloped the ragged man.

The being threw his hands up in the air, shrieking in pain and agony as blue flaming heat consumed him from the soles of his feet, eating slowly but steadily upward.

"You absolute idiot. He's a phoenix wizard! There's no way 'e could be dead!" Mr. Cockney yelled into the hapless face of the poor thing burning in front of him. "I needed those relics, I did. The antiques, you scurvy bastard. And you gave me nothing but this!" And he shook his hand toward the thick of the fire. His captive disappeared in a final POOF! The wailing cut short. I shrank back, a bad taste filling the back of my throat and awfulness scratching across my eyes. What a horrible way to go. Not to mention impossible. I could hardly breathe.

"Bloody coward. Can't take criticism, never could. He'll be back." Mr. Cockney pivoted to look his other follower, who promptly squealed and cowered, in the eye.

Sirens filled the air with a vengeance. The noise of the house fire even died back a little, as if knowing its end came near. Mr. Cockney grabbed his other thug by the shoulder of an ill-fitting shirt, turned about on his heel, and disappeared from view into the billowing smoke that poured out of the house and over the grounds.

I shut my mouth again, tightly. Lies and liars, I am more than familiar with. This situation, not so much. I turned to look at nature boy, who huddled unhappily. I elbowed him, because it seemed wise to do so. "Go hide. I'm coming with you."

He nodded and began to crawl his way through the hedge and toward the arbor. I started after him and found myself entangled in something. It smelled of soot and fire. I held rags up to the fire's reflection. Burned to char and dangling threads, but . . . but . . . I could almost recognize them as the professor's beloved tweed waistcoat, and that tangled snake across my ankles resembled the last of a pair of trousers. My eyes followed the new kid, and a few thoughts traded places back and forth in my head. One of which, I swear, was how I was going to get us out of there. That, and where nature boy had come from, and what the villain and his henchmen could have wanted of the professor. And, finally, what was worth death and reincarnation?

Pending answers and explanations, I could grab clothes from the closet in the spare room, where Mom had moved all of Dad's stuff, condensing him down into a few boxes. He'd always been a tall, spare man. I thought a pair of his jeans might fit, and a shirt couldn't hurt, and maybe some of his old Converse sneakers were still thrown in the back. Not the good ones, Mom had given those away, but the ratty pair with a hole at each little toe. I seriously think she kept those not because of Dad but because it had been Barney who'd chewed those two holes.

I caught up with my thoughts. "Stay here. Back to the original plan. I'm going to get you some clothes. Keep your head down. Don't let the firemen or anyone else see you."

He looked intensely at me, almost as if he were processing a foreign language, before nodding.

I made my way through the arbor with no difficulty this time, even finding a convenient hole, which allowed me to wiggle through and practically fall over the neighbor's fence. I got home, packed, and ran back in a flash as the house had given over to clouds of billowing smoke and bursting flames.

I watched, calculating how to get back to nature boy. Men in yellow jackets swarmed the roof, axing great holes in it for the water to get in more effectively. If anything had made it through the fire, the water damage would destroy it. I squeezed through the neighbor's fence again, hoping no one spotted a slim shadow among the bright lights and loud voices of the men fighting the blaze, but that only took me so far. Precautionary hoses were deployed to both sides as well as the main house, and they had the conflagration confined to what was left of the professor's home. And they had onlookers. Not just the neighbors ogling their efforts, but on one side of the driveway, the cockney-accented leader of nothing good carried on a conversation with a police officer. He'd snagged none other than my very good Bad Boy, Carter Phillips. The tall and short pair of them surveyed the area with more than casual curiosity. I might get by one but not both. The short guy walked off, to look over the driveway and garage again. I chose my captor and, replacing my smile with a worried frown, drew up to Carter's side. I swear I could hardly breathe. Must have been the smoke. My messenger bag of clothing goodies banged my side.

"It looks awful."

He glanced down at me and the corner of his mouth quirked. He had a cleft chin but it wasn't centered, it was off to his left side. Maybe it was a scar from his military days. His dark curls blended into the midnight sky but his hazel eyes studied me. "It is. I heard you were here earlier."

Who knew? I swallowed. "I was. Ran home to tell Mom I couldn't find the professor and came back. Did he get out?"

Carter shook his head. "Not that we can tell." He had a strong nose and jawline to add to everything else. Despite that, he wasn't handsome as much as a commanding presence. Really. Mostly because he caught and held my attention closely. Very closely. He took up my hand and I couldn't hide the wince. Turning it over, he traced the raw marks and splinters still in my fingertips. "You tried to get in the back? We thought he might have clawed his way out."

No hiding it. I shook my head. "I did it. I couldn't get an answer. I think he was already gone by then. I tried . . . I just . . . I can't . . . what a horrible way . . ." Smoke still scratched at my throat and I didn't have to push much to have tears brimming in my eyes.

He grabbed up my hands and searched them for injury, rubbing his fingertips gently over minor scratches before he let go. "You need to stay out of the way." Carter folded my arm over his and walked me deep into the yard. I could feel attention burning into our backs. "That was a foolish thing, trying to get in. You leave a fire to the professionals." He let me go as someone called him and, despite the fact I felt terribly alone suddenly, I awaited a chance to escape. As soon as Carter turned to walk away in answer to an inquiry from a fireman, and the night shadows were thick enough, I ducked away into the garden and through the hole into the arbor.

Nature boy waited for me, squeezing as much of his body as he could into my hoodie-become-kilt. I threw him my bag and presented my back, listening to the sounds of him wiggling into the jeans and shoes. I turned around when I heard him zip up and considered him. This was so not good for my mother and me. First my father disappearing, and now Professor Brandard. We were connected. *I was connected.* I mean, I was fairly sure they weren't going to find a body in the destruction inside the house. I knew my mythology. I knew what the hell a phoenix is, dying only to be reborn out of fire and ashes. So did Mr. Cockney. I also know a con when I hear one. Addict in the family, remember? Back to those lying liars. One couldn't be true and the other wouldn't be.

I grabbed nature boy's arm to steer him out of the arbor toward the corner before me. He gave me a puzzled look before letting me.

"We're going home," I told him. "And then you're going to tell me exactly what we're going to do about the late, great wizard."

CHAPTER THREE

THE DOOR TO MY HOUSE opened with a flood of golden light, motes spinning out like a flurry of yellow snowflakes. A cookbook fell off the kitchen shelf around the corner in greeting. Nature boy paused and I touched his elbow. "Go on," I instructed.

My mother loomed in front of us, her face creased with concern. "What is it? I heard you run out. It's the middle of the night. What happened, and who is this?" She blinked, distracted, as she recognized the clothing he wore. "Please, come in."

"Fire," I told her, as if she couldn't smell it on the two of us and hadn't heard all the trucks and emergency vehicles. "The professor's."

"Oh, no. That's where it was?" She stood aside, folding her robe across her and belting it into place.

"This is my mom, Mary, and this is the, the professor's nephew. Grandnephew. He got out, but the professor . . ." An unexpected choke stopped me. Smoke still in my throat or something. "He didn't."

"Oh, Tessa. I'm sorry."

Nature boy ducked his head as he eased past her in the doorway.

I shimmied past her, too, and headed toward the kitchen. I needed a tall, cold drink of water or, wow, iced tea. No need for sleep tonight, anyway.

As nature boy took a seat on the tall stool by the counter, I asked quietly, "What do I call you?"

He looked down at his shoes, my dad's ratty old sneakers, in thought. He shrugged.

"How about Brian? Keep it in the family."

He nodded.

Naturally. What else would I call him? I peered into his eyes. In the kitchen light they were still neither blue nor green but a mix of both. A phoenix wizard. Give me a break. I didn't see anything illuminating in there. I looked down at his shoes, too, complete with Barney-chewed air holes. The professor might have been harboring someone at his house, a grad student or someone. There were no such things as wizards. Maybe they meant a genius in his field, like a wizard of numbers, a savant. Right? Or maybe just an old con man. Of course, that didn't explain how I could think he might have burned away into a brand-new version of himself, but I could chalk that up to something toxic in the fumes. Heaven knew what the professor had stored in all his various jars. Events might have Mr. Cockney freaked but not me. Not quite. I stored that aside for the moment.

Brian kicked me in the side of my foot. My gaze bolted upward. Mom stood over me saying, "Tessa, honey, are you all right?" She put my tea in front of me.

"Ever stop to think and couldn't get started again?" I threw her a quick grin.

She gave a slight laugh. "It's been a tough night."

If she only knew. I wrapped my hands around the glass and found the soreness in them anew. I rubbed my hands up and down against the icy condensation to soothe my fingers.

Brian gulped down the tea my mother had set in front of him, and she poured him a second. Her hand rested on his shoulder a minute. "It must be a great shock."

He nodded. His dimple deepened.

"Were you here for the summer?"

He tilted his head a bit, like he listened to something the rest of us couldn't hear. He spoke very deliberately and slowly. "Something like that." He paused. "Sorry. That sounded rude."

It also didn't sound a bit like the professor, more like Brian was channeling . . . me. I quirked an eyebrow at him, out of my mom's field of vision. He drank some more tea before adding, "I barely got out myself. An old house like that, filled with clutter, you know? It just went up. Tessa found me in the backyard, only place I could think of to go." He spread his arms. "My things are trashed. She found me some clothes. How can I ever thank you?" He *was* channeling me. Or my thoughts, which was even scarier. I tried not to stare.

"By staying here tonight, at least, and for the next couple of days. We'll help however we can. Do you need to call anyone?"

He beetled his eyebrows. "My parents aren't available. There must be someone. I have to think." He drained the glass again.

"Let me go make up the spare room." Color tinged my mother's face. I knew that it was nothing special and cluttered with moving boxes we'd never quite emptied or stored away. There was, however, a twin bed under them, which had probably been there since the seventies. She disappeared up the back stairs, and I didn't say anything until I heard footfalls on the floors above us. My cell phone buzzed impatiently in my pocket. I took it out and thumbed up the text message. Evelyn: *Everyone says your mom black widow did the professor in.*

Gossip at the speed of sound. I narrowed my eyes and tapped back: *Untrue and unkewl.* Then I dropped my phone back in my pocket. Who needs enemies when you have frenemies?

The doorbell rang. Police keeping tabs on us, especially since I'd ducked out on Detective OMG Carter? I yelled, "I'll get it," and motioned for Brian to stay where he was.

Good thing because I opened the door a crack to find myself face-to-face with the bad guy of the week. He stank of smoke. If I hadn't heard him earlier that night, I'd still have guessed English. He had an apple-cheeked complexion, dark eyes that fairly snapped at me, and needed a bowler hat to go with his dialect. He looked up expectantly as light from the house fell over him. Of course he had good reason to wonder what I'd been up to, all dressed and wearing eau de disaster, just like him.

"Mmmm. Can I help you?"

He smiled and tugged on the corner of his suit jacket. I swear a puff of smoke wafted out. "Sorry for my intrusion on your late evening. You 'eard the sirens?" Accent there, but much more cultured.

"Oh, we did. Fire around the corner, I understand."

He made a tsking sound. "Indeed. Bad business, that. I'm making inquiries around the neighborhood, going 'ouse to house. We think there might have been a survivor, disoriented and frightened. Seen anyone about?" The smile on his thin lips did not warm his flint dark eyes or deepen the blush of his ruddy cheeks.

"I don't think so. Did the professor make it out?"

He shook his head and put a finger to the side of his nose. "We, and the authorities, are not quite sure. Too hot to go in yet. The victim possibly had a guest or visitor. Anyone you might have seen would be helpful."

Interesting. Male or female, young or old—he had no idea who he was actually looking for. That could give me an advantage down the line. "No one comes to mind, Mr. . . . ah . . ."

"Steptoe. Simon Steptoe, at your service." I think he clicked his heels. "Give me a shout if you spot anyone. Shock is a terrible thing. They could be wandering around without a coherent thought. I'm here to 'elp."

Sure he was. Off with his head! "I understand." I started to close the door.

His hard-shod foot stopped me. "It's important that you let me, us, know. This survivor might need help or medical attention. They might even have an involvement," he added conspiratorially. "Accidental or deliberate, there have been some terrible events this evening. There might be other inquiries. Don't answer them. Avoid the man named Malender if you can."

You would know. "Noted." I put the toe of my sneaker to his shoe to start to push it out of the way.

He resisted, lips thinning in that almost smile. "It would be advantageous to let me know if you run across anyone. Just as it might be detrimental to forget to advise me." His look dropped to my shoes and fastened there for a long moment. I didn't think humility had anything to do with it.

My shoes. Ash and water runoff from the fire. Shoe prints

stomped in the bent and dewy grass. My shoes and Brian's. Was he comparing evidence mentally?

His gaze snapped back to mine. "It would be most helpful if you would remember me and what I've said." He brought his hand up and a business card flicked into his fingers. I did not take it.

"And you would be Miss . . ."

I had no intention of filling in the blank. I pushed on my door and it gave way slowly, reluctantly, shutting on his last words, but I think he said, "Just call my name."

I was so not about to. I backed away from the door quietly, listening to see if he still stood there on the other side, listening as well. As if I might have turned around and shouted, "Hey, Brian, that guy is looking for you!" Finally I heard the clomp of hard-soled shoes on the steps, and he was gone.

Mom's voice floated down the stairs. "Who was at the door, hon?"

"Nobody, really. Just making sure we knew about the fire and that everything's under control."

"How nice of the fire department. Be ready in a bit up here." Her footsteps dimmed and I heard a very faint sneeze. Dusty work, evidently.

Brian had his head on the counter, dozing, when I returned. He rubbed the heel of his hand across his tired eyes.

"Are you all right?"

"All right? Of course I am. Fit as ever."

I felt as if I had been slapped in the face by Professor Brandard. Déjà vu. I let it pass for the moment. It was more than a bit disconcerting to think that this handsome guy had a crusty old professor hiding out in him somewhere.

"That was a Simon Steptoe," I told him.

"Ah. Simon." Brian sighed. "I think I know of him." Had they known each other then, once upon a time? What else did he know that he wasn't saying? What sort of con game had he and the professor been playing at?

Why not ask? Leaning forward on my elbows, I said, "What's going on?"

I thought I saw an echo of the old professorial gleam spark

in Brian's pretty eyes. "I'm not sure yet, myself. What do you think is happening? Besides a fire."

And there it was, that faint British accent of his own. If he meant to mimic the professor, he was spot on. And if he didn't, if he actually was the professor, reincarnated, he was even creepier. Brandard and Steptoe. How well, if at all, had those two known each other? Were they mortal enemies or something? Beheading sounded like a serious rift between friends.

How could what I was thinking even be true? I needed to examine the evidence or have my own head examined. But what evidence? I'd left the only real trace of the professor, his clothing in rags, in the backyard shrubs. The only thing I had now was nature boy—er, Brian—himself, and he certainly wasn't volunteering much.

I skewed my lips. His answering a question with a question of his own or an indefinite was not what I had in mind. I repeated, "What's going on?" Before he answered (or, more correctly, evaded the answer again), I tacked on a third "What's going on?" Third time's the charm, right?

He bit off a muttered curse. He tugged on a lock of red-gold hair. He folded a lip between his upper and lower teeth and chewed on it thoughtfully. "It seems I am compelled to answer, even though I have few facts. I am uncertain as to all the details. Steptoe showed up with his goons and wanted information I wouldn't give him. There was only one way out when they were done with me, and I took it."

"You set yourself on fire?"

"My recollections are spotty. I can't tell you much more. The house went up in flames, assuredly."

This was the professor talking, all the way. I wondered if there really were two people in that body, or two very clever people behind it. "I heard him call you a phoenix wizard."

"If I am, I barely know anything. I need help. Lots of help." He swirled the melting ice cubes around the bottom of his drink. "I don't even know where to start, Tessa."

I scratched my chin. "There's not much left of the house. If you had anything in there, it's probably gone."

"Do you think a wizard leaves stuff lying around willy-nilly?" Brian stopped. "It's habit to scatter the instruments of one's power far and wide." His eyes widened. "That much I know!" He shot to his feet. "All is not lost. Well, it's lost but I should be able to retrieve it once the memory comes back."

"Do you have an app for that?"

"A what? Oh. Not exactly." He tapped his foot. "I think that I might have been depending upon my friends and so forth."

"To jog your memory?"

He sighed.

"I've gone along with this about as far as I think I can."

He shook his beautiful, handsome head. I watched carefully, determined not to fall for either Brian or the professor, and failing a little. Those eyes. "I was a recluse out of necessity. Now, I realize that might be what dooms me."

"Whatever." I stood up and he sat down. "You need friends. I can solve that." I wasn't sure I wanted to, nor how I would explain it to my mother, but the footsteps overhead had slowed and she'd be returning any minute now, her chores done. I had an idea and decided to run with it. This would be about the third really colossally stupid thing I was going to do tonight and, after all, again, that magic thrice.

I went to the front door. Brian trailed after me. I took a deep breath and without opening the door, I called, "Mortimer."

Silence.

"Mortimer."

Still silent but now it had a kind of expectant quality. As though something unseen listened. "Mortimer!"

"What are you doing?"

"I'm calling for the only friend I know you've got besides me." The house fire had been a big show. Surely Steptoe and I and a few curious neighbors hadn't been the only ones watching it.

A deep vibration. The house quivered. I thought of the tyrannosaurus rex approaching in *Jurassic Park*.

Another thrum. Closer. The house shook. And again, seriously, this time echoed by the groan of the front porch stoop. Another shock as if a pile driver had hit the porch. The front door boomed.

I opened it to find a short, maybe five-foot-tall man glaring at me. He was nearly as wide as he was tall, so it wasn't likely anyone would look at him and think, oh, he could have been a jockey. Frankly, anything on four hooves would have taken a look at him, whinnied, and raced away in terror. He looked as if he'd been carved from granite, or maybe stepped down off Mt. Rushmore. He had a billy goat goatee of yellow-white hair that might have been blond hair going white or white hair stained yellow, hard to tell. He had silvery hair on his head and deep coffee-brown eyes. His nose arched from a brow that could have belonged to a big-horned sheep that was used to knocking heads against immovable objects, and his hands were like shovels. He wore a plaid suit, the pattern stretched wide.

"Mortimer?"

He frowned. "Aye." His glance aimed behind me. "Professor?"

"Dead," said Brian.

"I see." Mortimer's craggy face creased in thought. He didn't seem surprised.

Nature boy nudged me aside a little. "I might need your help as well as your friendship."

"So it's come to that."

"It appears to have."

"You told me you'd retired. You'd broken things apart. That's why you couldn't aid me and my wife. You did try, but you weren't successful."

"I can imagine. I couldn't help that, but I need you now."

Mortimer shifted his weight uneasily to throw his java-colored glance at me, and the whole porch creaked. I remembered that heavy-duty, use-scarred patio chair in the professor's arbor and realized that Mortimer must have indeed been the one who sat there.

Another thought popped out. "What do you weigh?"

Brian waved a quizzical finger at my interruption.

"I thought it might be important. In case the porch collapses or something."

Mortimer drew himself up. His whitish goatee wagged. "I am an Iron Dwarf. Stone and metal are my elements." He paused before adding, "As they were my father's and my grandfather's before. Wood bows before me as it is intended to do. However, that being said, your porch seems sound enough."

Wizards, beheaders, and dwarves, oh my. "Okay." I realized he still stood on the complaining wood. Did he have to be invited in? Outside of general courtesy, that is.

From upstairs, I could hear my mother. "Tessa. Do we have more company?"

"Mmmm. Yeah." I looked at Mortimer, wondering how to explain him. How to keep Mom from being overly curious and hospitable. Inspiration came to me about the same time she skipped down the stairs and appeared in the foyer. She looked poised and a trifle baffled. I didn't want her to ask me too many questions. "Mom. This is Bruno. Well, his name is Mortimer, but . . ." and I let my words trail off. My implication that one of dad's bill collectors had finally showed up hung in the air between us.

She paled.

"Please call me Morty, ma'am," the man rumbled. "I am sorry to be here so late."

"Actually," and my mother sighed, "I think you're rather past due. Well, come in. Late or not, I won't leave you standing outside. Iced tea?"

Morty waggled a bushy eyebrow at me as he came in and I shrugged. He looked like he could be a mob collection agent, after all. Why not trade on it?

We took the convention back to the kitchen.

I whispered to Morty as I passed him, "Follow my lead. She thinks you're a debt collector. For, like, the mob."

He answered with a noncommittal grunt.

Mom not only found iced tea but lemon icebox cookies. She fanned them across a plate and put them in front of everyone. I thought our two guests might be shy, but they filled both hands before I could blink twice.

"So, Mr. Mortimer. It is more than passing late. I appreciate the fact you came in person, but really." My mother looked at him, and her expression could have melted the coldest heart.

He swallowed the cookie in his right fist. "The night is best for visits like this, ma'am, and in person, if you understand my meaning."

"Well, yes. But what if I'd decided to call the police rather than answer the door."

He set his free hand down heavily on the kitchen table. "Best not to involve the authorities in matters like ours. It could be embarrassing for all."

Hell, he needed no hints on how to play this from me!

My mother put her chin up. "I've lost the ability to be humiliated by my husband's activities."

"Have you now?" Mortimer wet his whistle. "Then I've no need to beat around the bush or be delicate. You know what my job is."

"I haven't the money. I don't know how much he owed your . . . organization . . . but he left me with nothing. You're going to have to tell your boss to cut his losses."

Mortimer put his now-empty glass down sharply on the counter. "Tell him what?"

I could see a quiver run through my mother. She straightened one leg as if she thought to lock her knee in place. "Let me make myself clear. My husband gambled. I had no knowledge of it. And then he chose to disappear. I've paid off what I can and there is nothing left. The only thing I haven't lost so far is my job."

"We wouldn't want that now, would we?" Mortimer cornered the market on menacing insinuation.

She put her hand up and then dropped it. "I refuse. Threaten if you must. I won't budge any more. He's gone, and if you want to drain every drop from him, find him and go do it. His matters are none of my concern, not any more."

Mortimer turned a little stiffly to eye me. "And what about you?"

"What she said."

"There are still places in the world where a pretty young woman is worth something." Mortimer eyed me, and then licked the icing off his last cookie before popping it in his mouth.

He gave me the creeps with that bit. My mom picked up the iced tea pitcher as if she might bash him across the head with it to give me a running start, but she coolly refilled his glass instead.

I opened my mouth but Morty interrupted me. "Luckily, my employer understands your position. A bird in the hand is worth two in the bush and so forth. I've been asked to come and assess the situation to see what the possibilities are and then return with a report. You may even find me of some help if an unpleasant barbarian happens by. Not all of us in collection are as civilized as I am. This is the twenty-first century, and we realize we have an image to be concerned with. Not all collectors ask first and listen. There are circumstances here which should be looked into." He gave a nod. "See you in the morning."

"Morning?"

"We are agreed." He gave a little half bow to me as well and said, "I'll let myself out."

The house moaned as he trod through it and the front door shut solidly behind him.

My mother pushed the cookie plate around the counter a moment before picking it up and putting it in the sink. She made a small, stifled noise that hurt me to hear. "Tessa, I don't want you to have to deal with this man."

"I don't mind, Mom. He actually seems kind of reasonable."

"Nevertheless."

"Mom, you can't take time off work. Classes are winding up for me but it's busier for you. I can give him the runaround better than you can."

She brushed the back of her hand past the tip of her nose. Her blonde perkiness had definitely paled.

"I can deal," I repeated firmly. Besides, I knew what Mortimer was really going to be up to. I hoped.

Brian stood to gather the empty glasses and brought them to her. "Mrs. Andrews—"

"Mary."

"Mary. Perhaps it would be better if I find someplace else to go."

"Nonsense! Your house burned down. I've made the guest room up for you and we, more than most, know what it is to have lost everything." She brushed her hair from her face. "It can't get much later, so I suggest we all get what rest we can. Tomorrow we'll help you figure out your next steps."

He nodded and, making grateful noises, started up the back stairs. Another of Aunt April's old house eccentricities—it had servant stairs from the kitchen and a sweeping staircase from the foyer or front parlor. I finished helping clear the kitchen. Maybe I shouldn't have brought Morty in publicly. I had just brought more hurt in, and my mother didn't deserve that. I went up the stairs slowly.

Brian waited for me in a dark corner of the hallway.

"Mortimer. Why can't I remember much about him? Did I not have friends? I've lost everything, but what I've lost most is myself." My brash, irascible professor sounded as if he could drown in grief. I thought that I understood what he might be going through. I put my hand on his arm.

"He used to sit in the arbor with you."

He frowned. "Yes. Yes, he did." Then a glow spread over his face. "Tessa. The arbor. I've hidden something in the arbor. I can't remember what but—" He waved his hands. "I remember something."

"You told me the redwood was a good guardian."

"Yes. Yes, I must have."

"You can't go after it."

"We can't leave it to chance that Steptoe won't find it!"

"You're not going." I grabbed my backup hoodie from my closet. "You go occupy the guest room till I get back." I stopped at the top of the stairs. "Any idea what it is I'm looking for?"

He shook his head sadly.

I shrugged. "I'll handle it."

It might only be trouble, but I was bound to find something.

CHAPTER FOUR

THE ORANGE GLOW surrounding the professor's house had subsided, dimmed by the billowing smoke, which was the natural response of fire to water being poured on it. Most of the excitement and neighbors had evaporated, and I could hear the firemen as they shouted out progress to one another. They seemed to be down to hot spots now, dousing them liberally whenever they found one as they raked through the debris.

I thought the evening had me covered and hidden, but a hand fell on my shoulder as I ventured closer.

I jumped.

Carter Phillips said, about four inches above my ear, "We don't believe he got out."

"No?"

"I'm sorry."

I twisted around to meet his expression. "We were too late. We were all too late! All these nosy neighbors," I waved a hand, "and which one of them dialed 911 before they came running out to see?" I clenched my teeth a moment. He'd called me first. Why hadn't I called emergency myself? I'd run instead. And arrived just as late. Even if he'd reincarnated as Brian, he wasn't the same. Not at all.

"It's not your fault."

I crossed my arms over my chest.

Detective Phillips persisted. "You can't blame yourself."

"Well, I'm not. I mean, I am because I couldn't get to him—

but I'm angry too. Nobody deserves to die like this and yet he had to. It's selfish of me, but I didn't want to lose him. He was kind of a friend. More than that, really, but . . . and I had to know him. The town already thinks we're ax murderers and now this."

"No one thinks you had anything to do with this. Or your mother."

"Checked your Twitter feed lately?" Thanks to Evelyn, I was fairly certain the news and rumors were flying about. Richmond, Virginia was the hotbed of free speech after all, where the church where Patrick Henry gave his famous Revolutionary War spiel still stood, and tweets were nothing if not free speech. Frequent, irresponsible, ignorant, and often inflammatory, but free. I might not agree with anything that was being said, but I'd been raised to fight for the right to say it.

Carter looked as if there were something more he wanted to add, but his jaw tightened and that off-center cleft twitched. I wondered again if he'd been born with it or if it had been carved by his duty in Afghanistan. He was just old enough that we hadn't shared time in middle or high school together. I had no memory of him before he'd come back home a hero of sorts, becoming a policeman and then a detective in record time. Not that he wasn't qualified, but Richmond had found a way to thank him for his service. He was good at what he did, too. Everyone said so. Even when he was haunting our footsteps when Dad disappeared. He'd been both persistent and kind. Not to mention devastatingly good-looking. I turned my head away, not wanting to stare at him, but wanting to memorize his face at the same time.

Before either of us could say anything else, I spotted Steptoe and his sidekick lurking on the other side of the street. Again? I needed to catch a break. No one seemed to notice or block their way as they wove around the workers and hoses and policemen. They paced the pavement like hounds searching for a scent, Steptoe particularly with his head up. I could almost see his nostrils flaring as he waved a hand, talking to the two on his heels. I sidled sideways a step to keep Carter between us. It worked so successfully in the direction I wanted to go that I repeated it. Carter followed.

Another hundred sidles and I'd make it to the arbor. Maybe by the Fourth of July.

"You really shouldn't be here. They're trying to mop up, and then the investigators will move in when it's cool enough."

"Is that how it works?" I tried the wide-eyed and interested look. I tried another step. Ninety-nine more to go.

"If it's property damage only, they'd fence it off and wait a day or two for the site to be stone cold. Since they're looking for remains, they want to get in as soon as possible." He hesitated and then continued, "To verify things."

Things. Meaning the crispy critter that had once been Professor Brandard. That's what they called thoroughly burned corpses. If they found one. The shudder that ran through me wasn't faked. I couldn't wrap my mind around the idea that Brian might have hatched out of the fiery egg of the professor. Or had his body warped and twisted and heaved like a werewolf undergoing transformation until he morphed into nature boy? The image sent chills all over my body, and a late night breeze grew stronger, sending the smoke away from us, clearing the scene and making me all the more visible. Worse, Steptoe seemed intrigued by something in our direction. His head turned slowly but inexorably our way. Did he sense distress? Evil? Me?

I took another step, backward and into the shadows. "I brought him meals all the time. Mom knew him at the university. Can I just . . . just sit . . . and watch for a while?" And maybe hide under a table.

Carter shook his head. "Tessa, you don't want to see him if they find him and bring him out. There won't be anything recognizable. It's not something I—" He cleared his throat. "Or your mother—would want you seeing."

"Please. I'll just sit in the arbor and wait for a while." Not to mention hide from Steptoe and his thugs. He'd either recruited another one from somewhere, or the original had reformed. I rubbed the bridge of my nose. My head began to hurt from all the impossibilities.

"I didn't realize the two of you were so close."

Oh, but he had some idea. He'd tailed my bicycle runs at

least once. He knew I spent more time here than necessary for simply dropping off the food and leaving. He didn't know about tonight's phone call, but he might if they decided to look through the phone records. Unless the call hadn't exactly gone through by telephone. Brian had seemed a little vague about that. I looked up at him through my eyelashes. "We talked a lot. They all do, sometimes. I think they get lonely, you know? Mrs. Sherman even knitted me a sweater."

"Wow."

I leaned in a little. "It's a little freaky looking but I didn't want to hurt her feelings. I figure I've got the next Christmas ugly sweater contest nailed."

He laughed.

"He used to like to eat at the patio table out there. He'd tell me things. You know, once a teacher, always a teacher." I sighed. "I saw the smoke and panicked. I ran over, to find all this. I can't believe he's gone."

Another sidestep to the arbor.

Carter looked down at me, an expression I didn't recognize fleeting across his face. "Five minutes to say good-bye, then I'm taking you home. It's nearly dawn."

Hallelujah. I forced a quiet, "I know."

He escorted me to the arbor, tall enough that he had to duck slightly as he stepped underneath the redwood arch and greenery. I threw a backward glance and saw that Steptoe seemed not to have caught sight of me as I disappeared into the greenery depths. Now that I was in, all I had to do was figure out how to get rid of my sentry, but it looked like he was glued in place. I wished there was a way to get him to leave without making him suspicious. I sat down in the third chair, which showed little wear, and stared first at the professor's preferred seat, and then at the massive, worn-out chair which must have held Morty's density. I reached out and traced a finger over the arm of that chair. Carter watched thoughtfully. Was he wondering how this would affect me, after having lost my dad? Had the professor been a substitute father figure? More a grumpy old uncle figure, but I know I was wondering. Why me? Why did he reach out to me for help? I didn't have an answer. That was part of what made me angry. I felt inadequate. Even helping nature boy wouldn't make up for that, entirely.

A faint query came from outside and Carter stepped through to answer. He looked back at me. "I'll be back in a few; we're setting up a final perimeter now." And he was gone.

I wondered if I got two more wishes or if I'd already met my limit.

I threw myself on my knees to examine the chairs and table. Nothing met my eye. If the professor had put anything here, it was well and truly hidden. The underside of the table yielded nothing but a butterfly chrysalis, waiting to open.

I stood back up and eyed the trellis. Thin and spindly plaited redwood strips, where nothing secreted along their woven ribbons met my eyes. Where then? And what just what had Brian remembered? What could possibly be hidden here?

Morty's distressed wood chair stared blankly and unhelpfully back at me. Gouges and notches danced before my tired eyes, marching in and out of a jagged pattern in the wood grain. A pattern. I threw myself into Morty's throne and ran my tender fingers over the wood.

Definitely a pattern. And the left arm was thicker intentionally.

I leaned close to stare at it, the arbor's long shadows thinning as the night faded a little.

A Chinese box. The professor had inlaid a Chinese puzzle box into the arm of the chair. It wrapped around underneath the sturdy arm, but I could trace its outline, revealing it to me. Press here. There and. . . . so!

A panel slid open. If it contained a treasure, it wasn't much bigger than a stick of gum. I explored with my fingertips and a key fell into my hand.

"Tessa?"

I slammed the panel shut and jumped to my feet. Carter leaned into the arbor. "We're fencing the property off. I have to clear you out of here. They haven't found anything, but they intend to keep looking."

He kept his body protectively between me and the smoking wreckage of the professor's former life as he walked me home.

I didn't see Steptoe and prayed he hadn't seen me as I grasped the key tightly in my fist.

Whatever the professor intended to do with his new life, he was going to have to unlock his old one first.

At the far corner from the house, Carter's shoulder worn radio buzzed. He tapped it and listened to a burst or two of static. He said, "Be right there," and looked down at me. "Are you all right the rest of the way?"

"Sure."

He patted my shoulder and did an about-face to jog back the way we'd come. I wondered if someone had finally noticed Steptoe lurking or complained about his house-to-house late-night ramblings. A feeling like someone had put their cold hand to the back of my neck touched me, and I kicked into a jog-trot myself, eager to cover that last block to home and relative safety. I yawned and covered my mouth with the back of my hand, glad I hadn't done that in Carter's face. Nothing says "you bore me" like a good, stiff yawn. I made it to the corner house on our block.

The raggedy hedge bushes by Mr. and Mrs. Palmero's lawn rattled in the breeze. They were nearly man-high. The year or so we'd lived in Great-Aunt April's house, he'd spent every weekend on a ladder trimming them neatly with his clippers, but the hedges grew like weeds and never looked manicured or short and tidy. I don't know what kind of hedge plant they were, but I guessed they came from a botanical family that could overtake ancient ruins in a fortnight, never to let them see the light of day again. The Palmeros had a prodigal son who came back from time to time to live with them for a few weeks before taking off again. One weekend I'd had the pleasure of seeing them both up on spindly ladders, clipping their little hearts away in futility. Mr. Palmero had looked tremendously pleased, though. That and sunburnt. Young Palmero had worn a hat, the kind with beer can holders and a straw on either side. I think he might have been using them because the holders were loaded.

The hedges rattled furiously again and growled.

I came to a halt. Growled?

The hedges snarled again and added panting.

I leaped into a headlong sprint for my house. Why wait?

They sprang out of the bushes at my heels and gave chase with happy yelps. Not being able to run while looking back over my shoulder, a talent I'd never developed nor been bullied into learning, I had no idea how many of what. They sounded like dogs, big dogs. Maybe even wolves.

I played striker, usually, on the field hockey team. I knew how to cover ground. How to evade. How to hit for the goal. Now I simply ran until I realized I was leading them straight to my front door. What would I do there? Slam the door in their jaws and call the city dog catcher? I swerved across the street abruptly, running between two parked vehicles, catching my pursuers by surprise. Unable to corner so quickly, one of them fetched up against a car fender and gave a sharp yelp of pain and dismay, followed by snaps and snarls as it was evidently disciplined or driven back into the chase.

I angled to my left, and that gave me a chance to see what ran after me. It wasn't dogs or wolves. But it wasn't NOT dogs or wolves either. They couldn't have been real, even though I saw the spittle fly from their open jaws as their tongues lolled out. They yowled joyously for the hunt, their hound heads low as their four legs drove them across the street and pavement. I could almost see *through* them as though I peered into a mirror. One accidently overran his pack mate and sent him rolling, which he did, doglike, if dogs melted into shadow and then reformed after their legs and paws tangled up momentarily. Solid, melted, solid again.

I let out an *oooff* and ran even faster. I had no intention of letting them catch me to find out if those glistening ivory fangs were real or if I would melt when they bit into me. I didn't know what they were, but I knew I didn't dare find out. Across the street to the Palmeros' again, where I threw myself over the hedges. Well, partly over and somewhat through, with a great crash that drew the attention of someone inside the house . . .

Prodigal son Palmero staggered outside, letting the door bang into place behind him, with muttered curses. He'd left his beer-can drinking hat behind. He flung a squinted-up look at me, his face still rumpled in sleep and unhappiness at being woken up. He punched his hand into my shoulder with a growl of his own.

"Help!"

"What th' hell?"

I tried to dodge past him. He caught at my hoodie and hauled me around, his mouth twisted. "I ought to beat the stuffing out of you." I could smell stale beer on his breath as I shoved his hand aside.

"Mr. Palmero, it's Tessa from down the street."

"Like I care. It ain't even dawn yet!" He rocked back on his heels, thick and heavy hands ready to slap at me. I ducked away as the hounds burst through the shrubbery. He gave a twist and stood in open-mouthed amazement.

"Run!" I flew past him, down the side of the house.

"Come back here!"

And then the pack of shadow hounds hit him. I heard a shriek and then a smothered cry of pain and then nothing but the growls and snarls and—what kind of noise do wild dogs make when they're tearing their prey apart? Wet, tearing noises. Awful sounds. Sounds that told me I couldn't do anything to save him. I hurdled the leaning, wooden fence at the back of their yard and fell into the Langshures' Olympic-sized pool, which took up nearly the entire lot across the way, minus the house. Ice-cold water shocked me to my eyebrows and I flailed about, disoriented, telling myself I had to swim. Swim!

Hounds boiled over the fence after me. Five. No, six. There was a deck. They swarmed it and stared at me, eyes reflecting a dark, deep red. I could see them better as I tread water, for the Langshures had pool lights on, making the water a clear, beautiful aquamarine. I wondered if they would have to drain the pool and repaint the plaster after my bloody remains were pulled out of the water. The hounds jostled each other aside, loping back and forth and around the pool, hesitating.

They were afraid of the water.

Suddenly happy I hadn't gotten it together and made it out of the pool as quickly as I'd fallen in, I floated in place and watched the pack. As I did, the gray light of dawn began to lighten the night sky. And then I heard one of the Hap family's crazy chickens next door—the kind that lay colored eggs and have feathers that stick out everywhere, even on their feet—start to crow. The Haps weren't great favorites in the neighborhood because their chickens could be noisy, but on the other hand, they liked to give away free eggs. I listened hopefully. Another crow.

The official end of night.

The hounds began to melt into the pool decking. With soft yelps of frustration and unhappiness, they disappeared before my eyes, all but their reddened stares, and then those too vanished. I sculled another few minutes just in case it was a clever trap. My mind whirled on a thought or two, caught, stalled, and then spun away. Improbabilities of the night melted into downright impossibilities as it did.

I pulled myself out of the pool and slogged it back to my house.

Brian met me at the door.

Liars and impossibilities.

"We need to talk," I told him as I went inside.

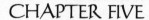

CHAPTER FIVE

"THAT BE A KEY to a box of deposit," intoned Morty. He sat on the strongest piece of furniture in my living room and had a heavy, knotted stick braced across his shoulders, his hands looped lazily about each end. He called it a cudgel and, frankly, it looked as if it could bring any debtor to his knees crying for mercy.

Late morning had brought him back to our doorstep, waking me from what amounted to a long catnap. He had come, he'd explained at the door, to help us search for assets we might not be aware of, still playing his role. I'd let him in as my mother descended halfway down the stairs to listen, hesitated, and then finished the journey.

"Ma'am. I am sorry for the necessity of my return, but my employer feels that there may be assets you're not aware of which can, shall we say, mitigate the situation."

"Assets?"

"Hidden money, goods. Gamblers are like alcoholics, secretive, and many have what they call their 'nut,' or seed money, put aside for a rainy day."

"And you've come to offer your help finding it? So we can hand it over to you?"

"Alas, that would be the end result. It would, however, clear his ledger. I assure you that my employer does not believe in taking a pound of flesh from the innocent. Whatever we find clears the debt. We have no need to enhance our reputation.

May I have leave to assist you in whatever way I can?" Mortimer had really thrown himself into his role as mob collector.

She had rubbed her temple.

"Mom, I can handle this. I know you've got student appointments today."

"I do, but—"

"No buts. I know as much as you do about this whole mess. Go. Do professor work and then get some writing done."

She frowned at me. "This is my job."

"I thought we were a partnership."

"I reluctantly agree with you. Unless this gets too complicated." My mother took one long look at Morty and his cudgel before retreating to the kitchen to make coffee and ready her briefcase.

I'd turned to Morty. "You're too good at this collector business."

The squat man had rubbed the bridge of his nose, which looked like it had been broken once or twice in its history. "I am not unfamiliar with the job." He cast a glance about our house. "I may even have known your father."

"Time is everything," Brian had snapped, and flopped down in his armchair. "This is what Tessa retrieved from the arbor." And then, he had shown Morty the key.

Which the Iron Dwarf had recognized almost immediately, leading us into the current conversation, and just like Mom had beat a retreat to her office, the professor seemed to have disappeared within the depths of nature boy.

Yawning, Brian flipped the key over in his palm. "You're certain? I don't remember what a key like that looks like, let alone what it might unlock." His tousled hair caught stray bits of sun from the windows and seemed to blaze. His dimple accented every word he spoke.

"They have a look to them, those keys. The problem would be to know the bank."

"Safety deposit boxes in a bank then." My mind returned to its lightning quick reflexes.

"It's Saturday. The bank should be open for another two hours. Getting into that won't be hard, but most banks have a sign-in system before you can get into the vault area. That's going to be awkward."

"If we determine what bank." Morty turned his sorrowful eyes on young Brian, who sat curled up rather catlike in the armchair. "Any memory at all might be helpful."

Brian shrugged. "Whatever." He stared at the ceiling, eyebrows knotting deeply, then peered back at us. "I've got nothing."

I tossed a look at him. He'd sunk into his sullen teenage mode, which had proven very unhelpful so far. I couldn't tell if it was his teen body ruling his mind or his cantankerous mind ruling his body, but sulking wasn't solving anything. "That last thing I want," I said pointedly, "is to be on the streets after dark trying to solve your problem."

"I didn't make it your problem."

"Actually, you did. You called for help." I stood up and went to the Richmond phone directory. I could Google what I wanted to know, but the professor seemed more at ease with hard copy. I fanned to the "Bank" page in the book and spread it out on the coffee table. "Read that and see if any gears get jogged."

Brian rolled his eyes. Morty grunted and thrust his cudgel out, shoving the book closer in the other's direction where it couldn't be ignored. With a shrug, Brian leaned out of his chair and began to peruse the pages. I knew it wouldn't be a long read. We had banks, but not a ton of them. After a minute, his finger stabbed downward. "That one just . . . I dunno . . . tugs at me."

I peered over his shoulder. "Greenwood Savings and Loan. Greenwood, redwood. It's worth a try."

My mother's voice floated in from her office. "Greenwood? We have a box there."

My face flushed as my voice had roused her. Still, she offered more information. I barely remembered the bank, but wheeled around. "Do we? Is that where the papers are?"

"Yes. You're on that account too. Remember? We put the birth certificates and Grandma's brooch watch in there." She paused. "Your father could very well have kept a box there too."

I raised my eyebrows. "Thanks, Mom." I looked back to the others and said very quietly, "We're in. I've got ID to get in. We just use the other key when we get inside the vault area."

"Easy," rumbled Morty.

Brian rocked back into his comfy chair and ran his hand through his red-gold hair. "Doubt it." Teenage pessimism. This despite looking like a Celtic god, with two worshippers at his beck and call.

"It's worth a try. Let's do it." I pointed to Brian. "You're going to need a shirt and shoes."

He rolled out of his chair and took the stairs two at a time to retrieve the rest of his clothes. Morty stood with a grunt and a heave, rather like getting a small mountain in motion. The floor barely creaked. My eyebrow twitched. "Did you lose weight overnight?"

"I can lighten myself, when the situation demands it."

"Wow. You've got to teach me that." I grinned. I'd never had a weight problem, but who knew? It might come in handy someday.

I waited at the bottom of the stairs looking up. At nineteen I felt like an overworked mother or something, engaged in the old high school social experiment where they give you a sack of flour or an egg and say, "This is your child. Keep it with you 24/7 for the next week, and nurture it" just to prove if you have an ounce of maternal common sense or not. Well, Brian was my egg. And I hadn't even had him for twenty-four hours yet. I sighed. So far, I couldn't prove any sense, common or not.

Greenwood Bank stood on a shaded street overlooked by the cluster of high-rise office buildings near the river. It looked rather quaint, considering the high-powered backdrop less than half a mile away. The breeze off the river felt good as we got off the bus and stood in the parking lot to observe the bank—the day had grown hot and sticky. A poster rippled as the wind struck it: WARNING: Feral dog packs in area. Exercise caution. Call police.

A photoshopped black and white picture of the younger Palmero bandaged up and minus his beer-drinking hat stared back at me. The poster gave me pause for a long moment. At least he'd survived our little encounter.

"Waiting for the right time?" Morty intoned at my elbow. His deep voice brought me back to the problem at hand.

"It's not like we're breaking in," I said finally.

"Not exactly, no."

Brian stretched. His shirt rippled, suggesting muscles underneath it. He kicked a foot out. "If there's money in it, can I buy new shoes?" His little toe wiggled through the hole in the side.

"It's your money. But I don't suggest stopping to buy anything if we're being pursued." I heaved the strap of my satchel purse up on my shoulder. It was nearly empty, prepared to hold the contents of whatever we found in the safety deposit box. I had stashed my personal goods in my pockets. "Come on."

Brian and I entered the bank, leaving Morty at the front doors, where he squared himself off to keep a lookout, thumping his cudgel on the pavement. Brian bumped a shoulder into me as we passed the building threshold. I turned and looked into his stunning eyes. Not the eyes of the professor but green-blue eyes with a youthful shine. He took my hand.

"Look. Sometimes there's two of me in here, and sometimes there's just me. And the just-me feels pretty bewildered about a lot of things, except for you."

My breath caught in a hitch. "Me?"

"You. I know I can trust you. And, I like to look at you. You're . . ." Brian gestured with his free hand. "You're beautiful."

"Me?" It sounded worth repeating.

"I think so. At least, when it's me thinking. So, I just wanted you to know, I appreciate your help, and I know that you know that. Still, I'm glad it's you."

"It has to be someone, I guess." I moved away, reluctant to take my hand from his and look away from those gorgeous eyes, but we had a job to do. Plus, I needed to be breathing properly. And, he was making me feel guilty about Carter, even though there was no Carter in my life, even though I wanted there to be.

I signed into the vault visitation book and waited for someone to notice us. A woman looked up and put up a finger to let us know she'd be a minute, and smiled at her customer.

"This one's for you," I whispered to Brian. He lifted one shoulder and dropped it.

There's nothing quite like feeling you're the only one making an effort. I waited till the assistant manager drifted over, her nametag proclaiming her to be Betty. I smiled. "I need to get into the family box."

"Of course, of course." She buzzed open the gate and ushered us through the double doors. Inside the inner room the boxes gleamed. Most were ordinary size, though one bank of them on the inside wall held drawers that were positively humongous, and I wondered if the bank doubled as a mausoleum on the side.

I showed her my key: 116. That was legitimately ours. Smiling, she put in her master key, and that was Brian's signal. I pointed at him.

Male: my distraction, female: his.

He doubled over, coughing. Betty turned about. "Oh dear."

"Water," he said. "Pollen. Asthma. Water?"

"Of course, of course, come with me." And she bustled off efficiently, leaving her master key behind when he clutched at her arm and half-leaned his young, virile body against her. I liberated the key ring, found box 66 and promptly used it, and then slipped in the professor's key. It turned, although a little reluctantly, and I felt a tingle through my fingers. The box slid out when I tugged on it.

Nothing much filled it. A small packet of money, maybe a few thousand dollars, tied in a colorful green ribbon. Two rolled up scrolls (Scrolls? Seriously?) as ancient looking as the professor had been. I supposed everyone might have a scroll or two in his background. A coin that was so worn I couldn't tell what nation had issued it, except that it was silver. A few modern papers, folded over and unspectacular looking. And then there were the passports. Five in all. I looked at the most recent one. It was USA official. Current. Embossed. Had all the seals.

And no passport photo, which made it totally illegal. I put that in my jeans pocket, and dumped everything else in my satchel. The worn coin didn't seem to want to go in . . . can't explain it, but it kept trying to twist out of my fingers, so I finally shoved it in with the one passport where it seemed content. I put my wallet and house keys in my jeans too, to hide the bulge, closed the drawer, and went back to the original box just as they reentered the vault. I handed Betty her assistant manager keys, saying to Brian, "Next time, bring your inhaler. Absolutely never go anywhere without it!"

"Gotcha." His gaze dropped on the satchel, which had grown lumpy.

"Are we all done here, then?" Betty smiled brightly at Brian, all but ignoring me. He grinned sheepishly at being called out on his inhaler. He ran his hand through his fine, red-gold curls and she nearly buckled at the knees.

We made a quick exit. Morty caught us both by the elbows on the outside, his great hand squeezing down on my arm.

"We've company," he said grimly.

A tall, stately woman across the street in high-heeled boots pinned her gaze on us, and a pack of red and cream hounds wound round her ankles in the shade of the tree-lined street. We have a lot of hounds in Virginia, but these guys stood out. Maybe it was the woman. I could only be relieved that these weren't the red-eyed shadow dogs of the night before, though she looked formidable too.

"Who is that?"

Brian told us, "That is Remy. She is one of the good guys. Supposedly."

"Good timing on having a memory."

He cleared his throat. "Remy is nothing if not unforgettable." I think he blushed faintly, but which of him felt the heat, I couldn't tell. I scratched the side of my nose. If she was responsible for shadow hounds as well this daytime pack, I didn't think "good guys" applied to her. Twisting out of Morty's hold, I cried, "You're on your own," and sprinted toward the greenbelt running alongside the river, where the St. John's banks ought to put water between them and me, even though the sun didn't seem to bother this pack.

I put my head down and stretched my legs out. I wasn't worried about leaving the two guys behind because I figured I carried what she wanted. I wasn't happy about it, but fairly certain. The hounds gave chase and voice, eerie howling that could easily have been the screech of tires on hot pavement or brakes on speeding cars, lost in the sounds of the inner city. I thought I could hear her driving them after me. I wasn't going to slow down to make sure.

They drew closer with every leap and bound as the satchel bounced on my hip and flank with each pounding step. I could see the greenbelt stretching just ahead of me, lush with springtime. I reached it just as the first hound hit me.

The impact sent us both rolling onto the parkway. The second hound caught my sneaker in his teeth as I tried to get back to my feet and then I was surrounded, kicking and flailing, the air thick with their growls and pants. The hound with my foot in his mouth dropped his chest to the grass and held on. I consider wiggling out of my shoe and decided to stay shod, at least for the moment.

The woman Brian had called Remy stopped at the edge of the grass. She gave a whistle and the other hounds flattened, matching the one with my foot in his mouth. "Hand it over."

"Hand what over?"

"The bag. Everything in it." She put out an elegant, long-fingered hand adorned by two or three sparkling rings that caught the sun as she did, and waited.

I wrapped both hands about the strap of my satchel. "The professor says you're one of the good guys."

"Positions like that can be so relative."

Something dark streaked the sky overhead, but neither of us paid any attention.

"I don't see how. I mean, good is good and bad is bad, right?"

"The world is not, and never has been, simply black and white. But you are smart enough to know that." Remy drew a step closer, avoiding the grass as she did. She had no intention of bogging down in the dirt with the heels of those elegant leather boots. "My comrades should be handling him and his bulky companion right about now."

"Why aren't you still one of his friends?" I wiggled my foot a teensy bit. The hound growled and hunkered down lower to hold on.

"Friend? He called me a friend."

"Yeah."

"It's complicated. That would require more explanation than

would be wise for you to know. He should never have dragged you into his affairs. Put down the bag and walk away now and your life should return to absolute normal."

That made the corner of my mouth turn up. "Lady, my life has been so *not* normal, you couldn't believe it. And that was before I met the professor." I twisted my foot free, catching the hound unaware, and leaped over the dog pack straight at her. I caught her and tumbled her onto the grass and took off running again.

They caught me a second time at the river's edge. I took the bag off my shoulder and slung it in a wide arc, aiming for the water.

Remy cursed and leaped for it, gaining air in a move that any basketball player going in for a dunk would envy. She caught the satchel and whipped it around to embrace it as she landed. She did it without a single hitch in her designer clothing or breaking a sweat under her flawless makeup. The hounds came at me, all tooth and snarl, and she gave a shrill whistle. They heeled smartly and jostled around behind her, eying me. She put up her bejeweled hand and the sun caught me in the eyes, dazzling me. "Tell the old fox that alliances have fallen and been remade. Tell him the game is up. Tell him that the world is not what he hoped and that he can depend on no one. And, above all, warn him away from the great obelisk."

Shadows fell over us and we both looked up. Three midnight-dark crows, or maybe they were ravens, because they were huge, wheeled over us. They crisscrossed back and forth across the sky overhead. Remy paled.

"Remember this. Malender has been listening."

"What?"

She made a gesture pointing upward and the three birds dropped, spiraling to the grass where they lay still as death. Remy toed one and looked up at me. "I did not kill them. He takes the life when he is finished with them."

"And he was finished when we caught him eavesdropping."

"It's one of his ways. Also Devian, but it's Malender that worries me."

"I don't intend to drop like that."

"Yes. I can see why the professor liked you; he always admired a quick wit. Not quick enough, though." She snapped at my eyes, rings catching the sunlight again and flashing right at me. When I blinked and could see again, she was gone.

At least she hadn't wounded me. One feeble point for the so-called good guys. I dropped to one knee to pull in several deep breaths, winded and upset. I'd lost the professor's goods. Well, except for the counterfeit passport. I dug my fingers into the grass, uncertain how I was going to explain the theft. They'd understand if they'd been under attack, too, I thought. Surely.

A scrap of paper blew off the riverbank. It wafted toward me and I caught it. It looked crisp and new, not some piece of trash that had been scuttling about the greenbelt for days or weeks, so I unfolded it. It must have fallen from the purse when I slung it through the air.

Huh. It was a copy of the Meals by Wheels contract. Scribbled on the bottom of it, someone had written, "Professor Brandard, the senior center has found your cane. This is your third notice. Please come and retrieve it or we'll put it in the donation box."

Cane? Him? Even aged and crusty, I'd never seen him with a cane. I refolded the paper and put it in my pockets along with everything else, thankful that I hadn't lost my wallet with my driver's license and ID in it, or my keys. Small triumphs in a disaster.

I got up and started to walk home, hoping to catch a bus along the street. Brian and Morty were waiting for me at the bus stop, both disheveled and sweaty but in one piece. Morty had lost his impressive cudgel, and an angry red mark edged the wrist where he'd carried it on its strap. He shrugged when I glanced at him. They both declined to say what had gone after them.

Brian frowned. "She caught you."

"Yes, and got the satchel. I'm sorry. This is what she took." I described the deposit box contents.

He shook his head as I detailed each one as best I could remember. "Nothing strikes me. Keepsakes perhaps, although the scrolls were undoubtedly important. But they couldn't have been terribly valuable or I would not have kept them in metal.

Magic deteriorates in metal." The professor peered at me through Brian's eyes. "Are you certain that's all you found?"

"Well. There's this and this." I pulled out the passport with the silver coin and the contract.

As he touched the passport, I swear I saw a flare of light, a flash like a static electricity spark that came and went. He opened it. All in good order, its photograph intact, a reasonable likeness considering what most official photos could look like. My jaw dropped. I snapped it shut. I couldn't have been mistaken that it had been blank before but I had no explanation. I had thought to tell him all that Remy had said, but decided I should wait until we were alone. Instead I peeled the edge off one fingernail that had gotten jagged while he opened the contract and read it. Then he read it aloud, one eyebrow arching at Mortimer for an opinion.

Morty rumbled, "Possibly an unimportant item, but you should not be leaving anything behind, Professor. Personal items can be used for tracking."

"No, I shouldn't. I quite agree. But, dude, I have to go to the old folks' center."

Listening to two people in one body at the same time gave me a splitting headache while they decided to rescue the cane. I bet on its being one of the footed ones, hospital issue, as I tagged along behind them. Morty could move when he wanted, rather like a mountainside giving way to a massive but speedy landslide.

The senior center positively bustled on a Saturday afternoon. There was a spirited shuffleboard tournament outside, and inside the rec center, a potluck had begun to assemble. The smell of food leaked out to remind me we'd missed lunch, and Morty's stomach gave a momentous grumble. A pretty, if blue-haired, woman smiled at us from the counter. I wondered if she played cards with Aunt April, and if I should warn her my relative was a card shark. I passed the paper over to her.

"I deliver the professor's meals. Thought I'd get his cane for him."

"Of course, dear. You're Mary Andrews's daughter, I know

your route. It's about time he retrieved it!" She ducked into the back office and came out with a gorgeous hand-carved walking stick. She dimpled as she handed it over to me. "I think he was avoiding us. Several of the girls here are quite taken with him."

I took the cane. Common sense warred in me over whether to tell her the bad news about the fire or not since she seemed not to know. Discretion won. "I'll tell him not to be so shy!"

"Oh, do that!" She waved good-bye cheerily, and Brian made a choked noise behind me. Morty thumped him on his back as he steered him outside.

Once there, Brian grabbed the cane. He rubbed his hands up and down its length, holding it in front of him. He looked up, a fierce gleam in his eyes. "This is no crutch for a feeble gentleman. This is my blasting rod!"

I hustled him past the shuffleboard courts and parking lot and into a quick walk home before anyone could notice us, opting not to wait for a bus. Morty huffed and puffed behind us as the blocks passed. Once there, I shut the front door on us, before saying, "What do you mean, blasting rod?" Mom's car no longer stood in the driveway, so we seemed to be alone.

"Beleaguered as we have been, you couldn't have found anything more perfect." Grinning ear to ear, Brian swung around on us, pointing the cane. "It's a wand, a defensive and offense weapon, just what we need! Nothing better."

"It's a cane, a walking stick. A nice one. But it is what it is." I crossed my arms as my mind balked, finally, at the improbability of Professor Brandard. Despite hounds that melted in the sunlight and those that didn't, and the mutterings between these two, and menacing Steptoe, I still had my doubts about the whole realm of magic. I had no idea what to make of Remy, other than I hoped I'd look that good when I got older. And as for hefty Mortimer, he could call himself an Iron Dwarf if he wanted to, but that didn't make him one. The professor had needed some help, I'd helped him. I was done. Enough of the charades. My mom and I were up to our necks in trying to survive my dad's disappearance and didn't need more drama. The professor's surviving relative had to step up and tell the truth about what happened instead of sneaking around.

I narrowed my eyes at him. "This is as far as I go. One suspicious disappearance in the family is enough. I have no intention of being on the hook for a second."

"Whatever do you mean?" Brian turned on his heel to peer at me closely, as if just remembering I was in the same room and possibly dangerous.

"I think she means," said Morty, "that her credulity is strained. She wants answers."

I nodded to him. The man might be thick as a rock but he wasn't as dense intellectually. "Look. Both Remy and Steptoe have told us this Malender is coming and that doesn't look good. What or who is a Malender?"

"Attention we don't want," Morty grumbled.

Brian reacted more vividly. "We are beset," the professor roared, "by enemies and idiots! This is my perdition rod."

"Perdition?" I tried not to roll my eyes.

"Perdition!" He turned heel, aimed the tip of the cane at an inoffensive urn in our foyer and yelled, "Avaunt!"

The urn shattered into pieces and Brian dropped like a stone, out cold.

CHAPTER SIX

"AVAUNT? WHAT IN the name of sleeping angels did he just do?" My own knees felt like they might buckle.

Before either Morty or I could move, the front doorbell rang. I moved to it, looking out the peephole into Carter Phillips's intriguing off-center chin cleft. He ducked down to eye level in time to see me peering out at him. Caught.

I waved at Morty. "Get him up."

"What?"

"On his feet. Get. Him. Up." I put my hand on the doorknob. "Now, please!" My ears rang with my words and I cleared my throat. When did I start sounding like a dictator? I opened the door, slowly.

"Tessa."

"Detective Phillips."

We traded looks.

Carter said slowly, "Are you all right? Is there a problem?"

"Did you want me to have a problem?"

He tilted his head. "I heard there was an incident earlier today and your purse was stolen." He eased toward the doorway opening as if he might come in. He smelled like leather and pine and something else I couldn't name but found enticing. I hesitated. Not that I didn't want him in my presence, but now did not seem like an opportune time.

I made an offering. "I did lose an old purse, but it was mostly empty, so no harm, no foul, right? Maybe someone else needed it more."

"You gave chase. According to witnesses."

I wondered just how much his witnesses had seen and what they had told him, because I had been chased and then lost the satchel. So much for reliable statements. I retreated. "Whatever."

"You don't want me to take a theft report?"

"I'm pretty sure it's long gone by now and not worth the effort." And I was certain I didn't want Mr. Detective to find a handful of dubious passports and cash inside it if he did retrieve it somehow.

His gaze went over the length of my body, taking inventory as if he wanted to know for himself there'd been no harm. My face warmed. I wondered if he took note of the tooth marks in my sneaker and casually hooked it behind me, standing with flamingo grace on one foot.

"You look all right."

I stifled the impulse to return, "I look *good!*" and nodded instead, reminding myself that he was on the wrong side of the law. But that didn't take away the impact his eyes were having on my breathing ability.

Carter straightened up to ask, "Do you mind if I come in?"

"Of course not." I stepped back to let him in, and bellowed, "Detective Phillips is here!"

He winced before his eyes took in the sight of Morty shouldering Brian on his feet and swaying as they walked into the living room. Well, Morty walked. Brian just dragged his feet.

"I correct myself. Is everyone here all right? And who is that?"

My mother barged in the scene, saying, "It's nice to know I can be gone for a few hours and the world, if not Aunt April's vase, stays in one piece," as she took in Brian being seated, or rather dropped, onto the couch by Morty as his eyes fluttered open. She set down her briefcase and sweater, shaking her head in sympathy. "It was a long night and the stress of knowing his uncle is gone for certain is just taking its toll. Carter, this is

Brandard's great-nephew." She leaned over him. "Brian, perhaps you'd like to go upstairs and lay down for a bit?"

"I didn't know the professor had relatives visiting."

"I didn't either," I returned truthfully to Carter.

"Can you verify your relationship?" Carter studied Brian, who still looked woozy but was making attempts at alertness by widening his eyes, rather like an adorable, wonky baby owl.

Between eye openings, he mumbled, "Everything burned up at the old man's."

"Family elsewhere?"

"Not readily available. They're working in a remote area of Peru."

"Archaeologists?"

"Herbalists. Looking for native species of plants for new medicines, that kind of thing." His verbal ability came back in a rush. Brian bolstered himself on the couch, mental acuity working even if it looked like his limbs were still noodles.

"Tessa?"

I shrugged at Carter. "News to me. I'd like to, but I can't really vouch for him. I found him in the professor's backyard, pretty much in shock." He stared at me for a long moment, and my face heated a little because although I'd been there off and on all night, he clearly remembered I'd been alone, as far as he knew.

Morty cleared his throat. "I'm an old family friend. It's been many years since I've seen Brian, but he is the professor's grand-nephew. Now if you were to ask me if he was in the will or anything, that I couldn't be telling you. But he is family, come to visit." He shifted his weight as if squaring himself off. The house responded to that with an alarming crack and pop at the joints.

"And you are?"

"Mortimer Broadstone. I've known the professor for decades."

"My condolences for your loss."

Morty nodded solemnly while Brian inched a bit taller on the sofa and shook his head to clear it.

"All right then. I'll make a note in my reports. If we need to talk to you, we'll find you here." It wasn't a question. Brian nodded in response and my mother folded her hands as if satisfied as well.

"You'll have a cold drink, Detective?"

"No, ma'am. I'll take a rain check on that." He dipped his strong chin at me and let himself out. The door made a satisfying thud behind him.

Not that there was tension in the room, but I don't think anyone breathed for a minute or two, and then we sighed collectively. My mother took up residence in an armchair. She crossed her legs and pinned Mortimer with her bright blue gaze. "What have you involved my daughter in?"

"Nothing, really."

"Really? Who broke Aunt April's vase? Just goofing around, the three of you?"

"They said it was magic." My voice broke a little, and I realized I sounded petulant.

"Magic. Seriously."

I pointed at the blasting stick. "That destroyed Aunt April's vase."

"Well, not really," Brian offered. "A bit of sleight of hand gone wrong—"

"What?!" Mom slashed a hand through the air for silence. I shut my mouth and crossed my arms, feeling deeply offended. "You. And you." She pointed at Brian, who immediately tried to look innocent, and then at Mortimer, whose jaws clenched at the sight of her index finger. "I think I know a con when I hear one, and you've gone and involved Tessa."

Morty's beard quivered as he rumbled lowly, "Madam, I assure you. I am most certainly what I say I am. Those are the robes I wear in this life. But I am more than that, and so is the lad here." He leaned forward. "We are the very embodiment of the magic that this world tries its best to ignore. And yes, we pull the con, but only to hide the truth."

My mother went pale. My jaw fell back open.

"I break rules talking to you squarely, but the two of you deserve it. You've extended courtesy to strangers and I must do the same. I have little liking for lies, whoever tells me them. I represent the rule of law among my house and my people, and that binds me to a standard. I would tell you more if I could, but I am held back. However. You can put whatever trust in me that you must, and I will honor it." Mortimer put his hands on the table in front of him and shoved himself upward. The table and his chair and the floor all gave voice to his movement. "Hide in your denials if you wish and tell yourself this is part of a game, but you are wrong, and if you persist in thinking that way, your ignorance could very well doom you."

My voice squeaked slightly. "Doom?"

Brian rubbed his temple. "As in destruction and despair and death."

My mother straightened up. "It's good to know where we stand." Her slightly strained gaze fell upon Brian. "Just who are you, then?"

"Brian. I'm a new body, raised from the . . . ermmm . . . re-arranged molecules of Professor Brandard's old body."

"Reincarnation."

"Rather similar."

"And just where is the professor?"

"Dead. Mostly. He resides in me like a, hmm, second personality. And a crusty one at that."

"He haunts you." I watched Brian across the table, as did Mortimer, his immense brows lowered heavily on his face.

"Oh, it's rather more than that. It's like I have two souls. One of them goes absentee a lot, and I think if I can get my memory back, he goes to rest permanently, having passed his power and teachings onto me."

My mother's voice stayed sharp. "So this is magic. Not a stage magician? An illusionist?"

"Nothing like that. Like a shaman or . . . or Merlin!" A smile shot across Brian's face. "Yes, exactly like Merlin."

"But you're not him."

"Well, noooo. Not him, no."

"One of his brothers."

Brian hung his head, defeated. "Not that, either. Just a worker of magic."

"Once a great worker," Morty intoned. "In a spot of trouble, lately."

This was nothing new to me, but I could see shock waves rippling across my mother's face. Of course, I had two days' head start on her. A stray thought tickled my brain. If Brian was a phoenix wizard, and Morty was what he was, could his wife Goldie actually be a harpy? My mind throbbed and I decided to ignore that thought. For now. I touched the back of her hand. "It'll be all right, Mom."

She glanced at me and back at the two men. "And you had to involve Tessa." She shook her head. "I can't believe you. If the professor resides in you, how do I know him?"

"I was, for a very brief time, on your dissertation committee. How is your paper on magic realism and its necessity in pop culture coming along?" The professor watched her from Brian's eyes.

My mother swallowed, very tightly. Then her jaw relaxed. "Why my daughter?"

"I needed a friend. Immediately. I had a feeling she would answer my call."

"Next time call 911 first and leave it at that. I'll accept magic, conditionally, for now. After all, the belief in it and its spirituality is a thread woven deeply into the human conscience. As you so aptly reminded me." She heaved a sigh, and turned slightly toward Mortimer. "Then you're not here to claim a pound of flesh?"

He shook his head. "I have, once or twice, called in debts when they infringe upon your culture, but I am, among my people, an arbitrator and a judge. I could swear an oath of truthfulness, upon the Eye of Nimora, if you wished." His gaze flickered slightly, for some reason.

"No need. And what might your people be?"

"I'm an Iron Dwarf." He sat back, his plaid suit jacket straining at his shoulders, looking every bit what he proclaimed.

My mother looked as if she considered that, and then she shook her head quickly. "So, what do we do now that Tessa no longer has to lie to me?"

"We eat dinner and make plans."

Brian licked his lips quickly. "Could we have pizza? It's been a long time since I've had a gut that could digest it."

"Pizza it is. Tessa—"

"Got it." And I did.

While we waited for the delivery, we looked over the perdition rod, mourned the untimely demise of Aunt April's hallway vase, and tried to decide what we should do next. I kept running my fingers over the carving on the cane's handle. Rather than etched inward, it was contoured outward, like a stamped sculpture. I remembered the arm on the professor's redwood chair and its secret panel. I spoke up when the thought wouldn't leave my mind. "I think this is a key. Insert it, embed it, and it will open a secret panel."

"What?" Mortimer had his great hand wrapped around a dewy mug of sweet tea, which he had grumbled wasn't ale but would do in passing. He stared at me.

"The professor has a liking for secret panels. I'd say this carving fits into a depression somewhere."

"Somewhere, lass, is an almighty big destination."

"No, wait." Brian scooted forward on his chair. He'd been doodling with pen and paper, since Mom thought he should record his random thoughts in case his memory might be developing even more holes. "She's right. You found the key in the patio chair, right?"

"I did."

"One panel, one key, is not a lot to base a pattern upon." My mom eyed me.

"True. And even if I'm right, it's useless if the panel was in the house. I mean, it's all gone now. Nothing left but wet ash and char. Pretty disgusting."

"Wouldn't be in the house," Brian countered. "Too close. Not hidden enough."

"True that," Morty rumbled. "He told me he'd scattered his goods far and about. Said he couldn't help me find my wife because of it." My mouth opened to debate how we could determine where to look, but the doorbell rang and the arrival of dinner put other discussions on hold.

After dinner, our minds got lazy while our bodies digested

the better part of two pizzas—I mean, Morty practically totaled an entire extra-large all by himself—and we sat around trying to think of what the professor had done with his magical regalia upon retirement. I'd related everything I'd heard to date, much to my mother's distress and the others' fascination.

When my mother yawned behind her hand, I got up. "I'll clean this up." She hadn't slept really well in years. I tried not to let her know that I noticed it, but she worried me. As much as I worried her, I suppose. I gathered everything up and left to Morty's vibrating bass tones quizzing Brian without much success, back door banging at my heels and garbage cans beckoning in the moonlight.

Steptoe caught me taking out the trash. I always knew there was a good reason not to do chores, especially the icky ones. He blocked my path, still imbued with the faint odor of smoke despite seeming to have showered and shaved, and he smiled at me. It was a thin-lipped expression that did not warm his face or his eyes, immediately making me suspect. But then, I'd already had dealings with him and suspected him of a lot.

"You're in grave trouble if you continue to harbor him," he said without preamble.

"Him who?"

"Our boy." Simon picked a bit of nonexistent lint off his lapel. "I presume he is a lad, although I can't be certain of what age. I also presume that he is likely to be in the middle of puberty, or perhaps even a bit older."

"Why?"

"Why? Because Professor Brandard was an accomplished wizard, and he would scarcely translocate himself into a body that could not bear the stress and strain of the situation he anticipated. This situation. A time of crisis like this one." His words slipped in and out of his accent.

"No, I meant . . . why would I be in trouble? If I harbored anyone."

"Ah." Simon Steptoe laced the fingers of his hands together and gave his knuckles a quick crack. "Because the boy isn't stable. He's not quite incendiary, not yet . . . but he will be. Until he finishes the ritual of the phoenix, he's very, very dangerous.

Things could, and will, go up in flame around him." He freed his hands and traced his index finger through my hair, tucking a strand behind my ear. "And you, dove, would not look good scorched."

Or without a head. I ducked away from his hand. "If I was helping someone, there isn't a lot you can do about it."

"Not just I. I imagine Remy and one or two of the other Guardians have been about. I thought I spotted her on the out-skirts of town earlier." He paused thoughtfully, a faint crease forming between his eyes. "Tell your professor, if you do see him, that tides have turned. Yes, indeed. Friends may no longer be friends, and enemies, well, there are possibilities there, too." He leaned forward, nearly nose to nose with me. "Tell him that Malender has awakened and is coming our way. None of us want that. NONE of us. If you turn the new boy over to me, I can assist—"

"You wanted to behead him!"

"Ah. Yes. I thought other ears had 'eard me." He pressed a finger to his lips. "Mmmmm. Most unsavory sounding. But my orders were to behead the man if he dropped dead on us, to prevent the conflagration that, ultimately, ensued anyway. His head is all that was needed for his successful reincarnation. He'd have been saved, and the house too. All intentions went willy-nilly thanks to the incompetence of my assistants. He willed himself into a phoenix state and, rather like a flash bomb, nearly took all of us with him. And it could happen again. Will happen, unless he gets the aid he needs. I stand ready to assist him. As I said, enemies are not necessarily still at odds with him. You will tell him, won't you?"

"If, and it's a long if, I see anyone who fits your description, I might. I wouldn't count on it, though."

His gaze dropped to my sneakered feet. The corner of his mouth stretched in a genuine smile that did bring a spark to his eyes. "Your shoe is a bit gnawed. I see you've already met Remy and her hunt. She proves my point rather well, actually. She used to be one of Professor Brandard's staunchest allies. The Guardians appear to be a bit off him now. Society politics, it seems." He dropped his voice a little. "They were lovers, once.

Now, well, she is hunting him and you, too, by the looks of it. I know a hound's bite when I see one."

I put my chin up. "The longer I stand here, the more something stinks. I don't know if it's this bag of garbage I'm lugging around or . . ." I sniffed. Shrugged. "I suggest you leave before I scream or something."

"Then I shall do so. I remain your servant, Miss Tessa Andrews." Steptoe gave a small bow. "Just call. I believe you know how."

He turned about and moved so rapidly into a set of shadows that I could almost think he disappeared on the spot. I didn't though. I unwound the strand of hair he'd touched and found a business card tucked there, behind my ear, like a magic trick. I shoved it into the back pocket of my jeans. When we got through this, the professor was going to owe me. Like my next few years of college or something.

I found the trash can and violently threw the heavy plastic bag into it, beaning and scaring the heck out of a raccoon perched in the bottom of the container. It chattered at me balefully as it climbed out and ran off.

At least something respected me. And with that thought, another great thought followed.

They were waiting for me at the kitchen table. Brian and Morty had evidently helped my mom with the rest of the kitchen cleanup, and they all held expectant gazes. I plopped down. I decided to pass along regards later. "Sorry I took a while. I was chasing raccoons."

"I should get another dog."

"What if Barney comes home? He'll be heartbroken!"

My mom gave me a faint smile. "I think he'd have made it back already if he could." Reaching across the table, she patted my arm.

Morty cleared his throat, sounding like a rock polisher. "We seem to be at a loss as to our next move."

I glanced at Brian. He looked pale and drawn, nothing like the hearty teen I'd found in the professor's backyard. He'd just downed the better half of a large pizza. How could he look so weakened? Did he walk a tenuous line between being mortal and catching on fire again? Had Steptoe buried a little bit of the truth in the discussion we'd just had? What was the advice when lying? Stay as close to the truth as possible to make the lie successful?

I took a deep breath and put my thought out there. "It's obvious. We have to go where we were promised trouble. Remy said to stay away from the great obelisk."

Brian locked gazes with me. Something moved through his eyes. "That's it. She was either warning me off in her new role as my enemy or she was giving me a hint in her old, familiar role as friend and guardian. Either way, that's exactly where we have to go!"

"Which great obelisk?"

I tilted my head. "There's only one great one in this part of the world. We call it the Washington Monument."

CHAPTER SEVEN

MY PHONE CHIMED GENTLY and I pulled it off the nightstand to see Evelyn texting me. My head had hit the pillow when everyone else's did—well, I don't know if Morty's hit a pillow or the whole damn floor because the house shook and had aftershocks for a good twenty minutes after—but I hadn't gotten to sleep yet. I read the screen with one eye open, hoping if I kept the other eye closed I might have a chance of falling back to being nearly asleep.

Invites???

I groaned. Somewhere in the depths of my backpack, I had a fistful of them I'd totally forgotten, and a promise was a promise. I scrunched a foot out from under the covers and hung it over the side of my bed, fishing with my toes until I found a canvas strap and hoisted up my backpack onto the covers. I thumbed back *Wait a min* and put the phone aside while diving into the depths of the bag. Hockey clothes—ew, totally forgot about them, too—I needed to drop them into a speed wash tonight and hope the machine didn't wake everyone up. I shuffled downstairs, threw a few things into the washer, and set it up, phone screen lighting my movements from my pajama pocket and hands dealing through the various envelopes.

Funny what a difference handwriting makes. Or even the ability to print decently. The educated side of me wanted to toss the bad ones aside immediately, but I pushed that impulse down. At least the guy hadn't made his mom address the invite!

We'd already tossed two out that had been handled that way. Still squinting with one eye, I trudged back to my room with possibilities in one hand and ughs in the other.

I opened the most intriguing one first, naturally, sliding soft lavender colored paper out of its matching envelope. A delicate branch of cherry blossoms decorated the upper left-hand corner and, as I scanned to the bottom, it was no surprise to see that Joanna Hashimoto had penned it. Joanna had never been close to us, but her father was backing Evelyn's father in the election. So the invite hadn't been shocking. Well, it was and wasn't. That the letter seemed almost an art project wasn't startling, I had seen Joanna's papers over the years and always admired the serene beauty of them—but that she'd sent this to Evelyn, well. That opened both my eyes. I scrubbed the lazy one a bit before focusing on the letter.

Wow. She had planned not only for the night of the auction, but for the day too. Pickup for a light tea lunch cruising down the river, followed by a massage and a custom makeup artist, then dinner at her father's restaurant, which was stellar in all respects, with American and Japanese pavilions (including those delicate paper sliding screened doors to divide a few rooms, I'd heard). The food got raves. The country club with its golf course, restaurant and spa was a sprawling, high-class destination. From dinner, of course, they'd just trot across the greenbelt to the country club meeting rooms where the bash would be held. I'd no idea if Joanna was sending signals or just thought that girls ought to have fun, but Evelyn needed to have a look at this one.

By the time the third yawn hit me, I'd found two other fairly coherent auction plans and set them aside to text her. I led with Joanna. The screen stayed blank for a very long moment, and then Evelyn replied.

Joanna? Really?

I sent back an affirmative and the condensed version of the date.

Got back a lingering: *Hmmmmmm.*

Answered: *Looks fun.*

Another *Hmmmmmm.*

I keyed *Time is running out, you know.* Then I followed up with the other two she might consider, because she'd turned down the twelve I'd sent her over the last few weeks.

I could see on the screen that she was still connected, if quiet. Then she sent *WTH. Drop off Joanna's invite too. Sounds like fun.*

I told her I'd do it in the morning and closed the phone down. My work there was done. I put my head back a minute, trying to imagine myself at the auction. I wasn't even sure I'd ever wanted to go. I remembered daydreaming once that it would awesome to go, knock Carter's socks off, and be the subject of a bidding war, but that had never really been in the cards. As if he'd ever ask. My plans could go up in flames and, unlike a phoenix, stay in ashes. What filled my mind instead whirled round and round in time with the washer downstairs, as if my thoughts were on spin dry. The professor. My dad. Morty. Brian. Steptoe. Remy. And the mysterious don't-mention-his-name Malender. Downstairs, the washer let out a tiny melody letting me know it had finished the job, so I tiptoed down, threw everything in the dryer, and let it rip. Wrinkled in the morning was good enough for me.

I feel asleep thinking of Japanese pavilions with cherry blossoms drifting about and Evelyn tripping over the hem of her too-long kimono while firebirds flew in to carry me off into the horizon. I kept arguing with them until they finally dropped me, and that woke me up.

I hate falling dreams. I don't like the part where your stomach knots up and feels as if it's gone into another dimension. No slingshot roller coasters for me. If I want to scream, all I have to do is venture outside and let Steptoe pop out of nowhere again.

I fluffed my pillow up. Downstairs, a very low rumble sounded now and then, so deep in tone it sounded primal, as if the tectonic plates of the earth had shifted, and I realized Morty must be snoring. It was kind of comforting, almost like a white noise barrier against the deep night. I settled back in, intent on making it all the way till dawn when another, furtive, very quiet sound caught the edge of my hearing.

I hadn't been listening, honest, but identified the unexpected: crying, soft and muffled, from my mother's bedroom. We'd been through a lot together, but she rarely cried. I lay very still, hoping the sounds would stop.

They didn't.

I slid my feet to the floor, cool and solid under me, and then got the rest of me out of bed as silently as I could. There are floorboards that creak in the hallway, but they can be avoided if you take the right steps, easy to remember on the faded pattern of the worn carpet. Nearly threadbare, its royal red and blue oriental pattern was a mere shadow of what it used to be, but Evelyn and I had discovered a pathway over it that kept it silent. You know, just in case. I traced the way, stopping every now and then to see if my target still showed distress. She did.

Finally, at the door, I took a deep breath. Knocked and opened it anyway, edging inside. "Mom?"

The noise halted and then she said, "I'm all right, honey. Go back to bed."

Instead I went and perched on the corner of her mattress. "It's not all right."

She gave a little, choked laugh, blew her nose and turned on the small bedside lamp. It cast a very faint glow into the dark of the room. I smiled at her face.

My mom cries like a movie star. Her complexion gets dewy, her eyes brim with wetness, and the tears flow in exquisite streams down her cheeks to her chin. She still looks awesome. I, on the other hand, cry ugly. Blotchy, red, bloated disgusting ugly. My freckles pop out. Luckily for both of us, we rarely resort to tears. She reached out and grasped my hand.

"I'm sorry, Mom. About this whole mess. Tell me and I'll kick 'em to the curb. They can do what they want on their own."

"It's not that."

"Sure it is. It's wicked strange, and I've decided I don't want to be in the middle of a Harry Potter book. It's not all it's cracked up to be. You're worried and that's not right."

"Well, I am a little worried."

"See?" I squeezed her hand back. "In the morning, I'll pack

them up and tell them where to go, politely. Like to Washington and stuff. I can't handle the weird stuff either."

"You can't?"

I shook my head vigorously.

"I thought you were solidly in the camp declaring that magic is just science that hasn't been discovered yet."

"That's a saying?"

She inclined her head.

"Wow. Still, if you'd seen what I've seen . . ." I stopped dead at that one, deciding that shadow hounds in a pack and raven eavesdroppers weren't going to make her feel any better. Nor would knowing whatever had been big enough and bad enough to do in Morty's heavy cudgel. "I'm sorry if I worried you. I'll let them go on this thing on their own."

"If that's what you want, but that's not why I'm . . ." She sniffed and waved her hand clutching a soggy tissue.

"Then why?"

"I miss your father. I know, I know—" She held my hand tighter to keep me from turning away. "You asked. The least you can do is listen."

My back had gone stiff. "Right."

"Seeing those clothes of his walking around again just reminded me of when we were both young, and I could trust him."

I had to do something but without any clear idea of what, I decided to give her a fresh tissue. She took it with a sigh.

"What would you do if he came back?"

I shrugged. "What would you do?"

"Make sure he was clean and sober. I guess that's the phrase, even with gambling."

"He'd have to be! He can't ruin everything all over again."

"We wouldn't let him," Mom told me. "This time we'd know." She squirmed around in the bed until she sat next to me.

"I don't know. What if he's not really even? . . ."

"Still alive?"

I nodded, a miserable knot of something holding back the rest of my words.

"I'd like to say that I'm one of those people who'd somehow

know if their loved one is gone or not, but I'm not, and I'm not sure anyone really is."

"Seems impossible, huh?"

"It does. It's a difficult world out there. Anything can happen." She blew her nose again, softly, daintily. It made me grin and she put an elbow to my ribs. "I can't help it if *you're* snotty."

"Yeah, well. It's DNA." I scratched my head. "The professor mentioned he'd had 'a dealing' with Dad."

"Really?" She set her jaw and thought hard. "I don't think they even knew—no, wait. There was that big cross-college society meeting about three years ago. The professor—doctor, really—was giving one of the talks. It was a fundraiser, very academic, a little stuffy. I was very intimidated, but your dad and Brandard got on like a house on fire."

"Don't say that."

"What? Oh. No." Her face pinked. "You know what I mean. They talked for quite a while. Your dad valued pragmatic intelligence, you know."

"The professor is a wizard. How pragmatic is that?"

"You never know. Maybe that's what it takes to make magic." She smiled a little and dabbed at her nose again. "I'd forgotten that."

"Morty says the professor is very good at finding things. And people."

She looked at me. "Really."

"Besides our friendship, that's one of the reasons I decided to help him. I was going to ask, before all this—" I waved my hand.

"Do you think it will do any good?"

I shrugged. "And if it does, is it something we want?"

"I really love your father, Tessa. How about you?"

"I did. The other dad."

"It's the same dad."

I shook my head, hard. "No. Not at all."

She squeezed my hand again. "It's more complicated than that."

I stood up. "It shouldn't be. Giving everything you've got for the people you love shouldn't be complicated at all." I uncurled my hand from hers. "Anyway, unless you tell me not to go, I've got a big day planned for tomorrow."

"Ditching school?"

"That'll be the start. Missing a class now and then is practically a college tradition." Silence followed me as I went to the door and left.

CHAPTER EIGHT

WE BOUGHT FOUR round-trip train tickets online. Morty slapped a black credit card on the desk next to the computer. The name on it: Broadstone Family Enterprises, holder Mortimer Broadstone, and I didn't hesitate to get the better seats. I'd raised an eyebrow at him.

He'd waggled one of his back at me. "It helps," he commented, "to know where the jewels hide in the depths of the earth. We Iron Dwarves are rarely poor."

That boggled my mind a bit. "You'd have to know the current worth."

"Aye, and be prepared to sit on your stashes a bit. Wouldn't do to flood the market." He scooped up the card and returned it to its protective folder before stowing it away in a heavy, tooled leather wallet. The RF folder impressed me, too. This guy lived in the present, unlike the professor. It made me wonder how his wife had gotten stolen. And why he'd depended more on Brandard to get her back rather than conventional means.

Mom got up early, too, and caught me in the kitchen making two pots, one of fresh-brewed coffee and the other of steeping tea. The mingled aromas cheered the kitchen up despite an early mist of dank-smelling fog creeping around the edge of the yard.

"I'm staying," she told me. "With all the cuts in everyone's budget, I can't afford to look like an unsteady faculty member. No missing classes for me until I catch cholera or something. You will be careful?"

I poured her a bracing cup. "Of all of us, I think I'm the fastest runner, and I intend to maintain that reputation. Remember, I'm a hockey striker, I know how to intimidate my way to the goal."

"Good." She put in a dollop of honey and whisked the amber goodness about until it dissolved before she put the cup to her lips and sipped gently at it. "Tessa, thank you. I needed this."

"Must be the Tory blood in us. Stubborn and persistent, rather like the French Canadians. Revolution or not, we still want our tea."

She laughed. "Something like that, although I wouldn't bandy that story about here in Richmond." She wrapped her slender hands about the cup. "Do you really believe their story?"

"I don't know. It's like finding out that the aliens have landed and there's been one living next door to you for years. Although Palmero the younger has always been kind of freaky, so maybe that one's true, too."

The rack of copper pans over the stove began to sway back and forth rhythmically. We both looked at it, and looked away again. It clattered to a stop.

"Do you believe in magic?" She hid part of her expression behind her teacup.

"Not quite yet. I mean, I've encountered some things I definitely can't explain, but I'm not ready to rearrange reality yet. I keep asking myself, how can that be? Sometimes I tell myself it's more on the order of mental energy like telekinesis and stuff. You know, science that can't be proved yet either."

"Too bad."

I quirked a look at my mother. She smiled over the lip of her teacup. "Really. Everyone should have a touch of magic in his or her life. The great mystery. An intrigue. An unknowable you might want to chase down for the reveal. Some things will always be beyond you, but there are those you might be able to unravel. Why give up on the impossible at such a young age?"

"I gave up on the hope I could fill an inside straight."

"There's that, of course, and knowing what we do of your father, I can't blame you. But this is a different kind of gambling, this is magical. Spiritual," she put in, as if words had failed her.

There was that word again. I shrugged. "I do the best I can," I offered. I added, for a second time, "I vow I'll be careful, and I definitely have my running shoes on."

She glanced down. "A little bit worse for wear."

"There was this hound dog—"

"I don't want to know."

"You really don't."

She leaned over and hugged me, hard. Then she stood up, gathered her leather satchel from the old oak buffet in her office, and left for work.

Morty already had his phone out and was punching in numbers. "I'll have a car here for us. An SUV," he added, evidently in response to something he'd seen on my face. I swear, it wasn't fear. Exactly.

Brian entered the kitchen with his mouth stretched in an enormous yawn. "I don't know which one, but one of us is not getting enough sleep."

"Which one?"

He jabbed a thumb at his chest. "Me or the professor."

"Oh-kay."

His hand curled immediately around a coffee mug, and he began to mix his milk and sugar into the pour. "I sleep, or try to, but the professor is awake, trying to remember. His mind is like a squirrel in a cage, going around and around. Every once in a while, he finds a nut of information he wants me to know and shoves it into my mind. It wakes me up. Sometimes it even hurts." He sat down with a long-suffering sigh.

"Would you rather be ignorant then?" Morty leaned against the threshold in the kitchen, which groaned faintly as he did.

"It's not like I have the option. I'm here. I want to live. It seems that the only way I can do that is to know who I was, and quickly. I just wish it didn't make my head throb."

I slid a plate holding a waffle covered in peanut butter and the syrup bottle in front of him. "Eat. We're leaving in fifteen minutes." I watched him try to decide which hand to use with the fork. The professor had been markedly right-handed, like most of us. Or had he? Had he grown up in an era when natural left-handers were forced to become righties because of superstition?

While I struggled with that, Brian sighed and grabbed the utensil in his right hand, the syrup bottle in his left, and laid waste to the waffle.

"Is it that bad? Being two in one?" Frankly, the thought horrified me. Brian's strapping beauty definitely caught my eye, but I could almost hear the professor word for word sometimes when he talked. That creeped me out.

Brian thought about it with a mouth crammed full. He swallowed. "When he comes to the front and takes over, I mostly go to sleep. He can be pushy that way. He's resting now because he had a busy night. The idea of going to Washington riled him up."

"I can't imagine why."

"Because he wants to know what it is we're looking for and he has no recollection. He's frustrated. I think that once we get there, his mind will thaw. I mean, it's like looking for the exact word for something but every time you try to think of that word, it just slips away." Brian waved his fork around before stopping long enough to lick the peanut butter off it.

"He needs to chill then."

"No kidding, huh? He's smart but stuffy."

Morty made a sound, which might have led to words, but the toaster popped up again, and he dedicated himself to filling his plate with fresh waffles and snagging the syrup out of Brian's hand.

"Whereas you talk like me. Sometimes."

"I listen. I learn. It's all about survival."

"Ever wonder how many times you've done this before?"

Brian scooped up some syrup with the side of his finger and licked it clean. "Now that seems rather personal."

"And hello, Professor."

Brian's eyes gleamed. "Hello indeed, young Tessa. Been making plans?"

"Trying to. You and your teen body need to eat so we can leave."

He licked the corner of his mouth tentatively. "We appear to have been in the process. I'll try to get our speed up, however."

"You do that." I crossed the room and busied myself with a bowl of cereal, trying not to look as creeped out as I felt. Truth to tell, if and when the time came that Brian's phoenix ritual could be finished, I might lose the professor altogether. I knew I'd miss him. And what if he held a chance to find out what happened to my father? Would he pass that on to Brian, or was that a talent only the experienced could develop? What if the chance to find my dad disappeared forever on the day the professor did? The thought bothered me so much I almost forgot to pour milk over my crispy pops, breakfast of field hockey champions.

Our car was a bright (ruby red) and shiny SUV, almost new, and we gave Morty the front seat while we settled in the back. I swear the vehicle settled as if its springs no longer existed.

I tapped Morty on the shoulder. "What do you drive at home?"

"A World War Two Jeep. We have a graveyard of them for parts. A little rugged, but they take to the roads and get me where I need to be."

That and maybe his own brand of magic. I'd seen no sign of any jeep, vintage or otherwise, when he'd appeared at our house. Then again, I *had* summoned him. Maybe it was worth leaving him behind, getting to where we were going, and trying that bit again.

Brian sat rubbing the cane nervously between his palms as if he might drill a hole in the floorboards. I reached over and stopped him.

"Sorry."

"Nervous?"

"Never been on a train before. Or in a car." Voice down, he looked out the window and quickly looked back.

"The professor has."

"Mmmm. Sometimes we just aren't that meshed." He took a little gulp. "So how far are we going?"

"Train station is about another ten minutes, and the train trip itself should be about three hours. You can sleep but the countryside is pretty. We might even go through a little bit of spring rain. We'll get there just in time to think about lunch and order a car from the station to the mall."

"The mall. Isn't that a shopping place?"

"Not this one. It's the great park where the monuments are, and green lawns, and a great big serenity pool. More trees. Lots of stonework. The Lincoln Memorial and stuff."

"Ah." He had stopped rubbing the cane but now he gripped it so hard his knuckles stood out whitely.

"Close your eyes. Lean back. Let the professor do the thinking for a while."

"I would but—" Brian swallowed. "His thinking is even scarier than this trip."

"Oh." He must be calculating the various dangers and traps we might run into. I patted his knee. "He can worry for all of us, then. I'm enjoying the day off classes."

And then it hit me.

The invites. I told Evelyn I'd drop them off. I leaned over and frantically went through my backpack. Yup, I had at least stowed them where they were supposed to be. "Detour! I need to make a stop!"

Morty and the driver both twitched in their seats. "How much of a detour?"

"Got to swing by the campus. It's only four blocks that away." I pointed my fingers out the window.

The driver, a stoic-looking guy who probably spent his free time trying to audition as a zombie for *The Walking Dead*'s local filming crews, turned his head to Morty for permission.

"Will we have time?"

"Oh, yeah. I planned for that."

"As she wishes then." Morty settled back with a ponderous movement of his shoulders.

The driver knew the college and turned neatly down a side street.

Various classes were in session so the walk to Evelyn's morning session seemed deserted. She always sat in the back, and she looked up from her desk/chair as I peeked in. I waved the invites and stuffed them into her book bag and backed out without irritating the lecturing professor too much, or so I hoped.

Brian waited by the SUV door to hand me up. "Everything okay?"

"So far."

And it went smoothly to the station. Brian was only slightly whiter than a sheet of paper when we emerged. I handed the tickets out.

Morty read his briefly. "We go here, then?"

"That's the plan. I'll go get your refund."

He nodded before wrapping his heavy hand around Brian's elbow and steering him in the general direction they meant to go. I watched them and tried to ignore the tickling feeling at the back of my neck, as if someone eyed me.

I let the two of them sit at the platform while I took his credit card and the ticket meant for Mom back to the window to return it. After a few moments of stark terror, Brian seemed to relax and enjoy the activity around him. I turned on the heel of my sneaker casually, to scan the crowd before leaving them on their own. It wasn't extremely busy, as the early commuter trains had left hours ago, but a steady stream of people milled about. I don't know what I expected to see but nothing caught my attention, except a tall figure, casual rock band t-shirt and jeans, who went around a corner about the time I thought I saw him. Carter Phillips? It couldn't be. I took a couple of steps in that direction but the fleeting vision moved beyond my range. I shrugged to myself. Imagination, though if it was, civilian clothes took years off the guy. He had looked almost normal. I shot a last look at Morty, who nodded at me and shooed me off. He and Brian sat more or less calmly on a bench, waiting. It was I who clutched the black credit card as if my life depended on it until I got to the service window.

I pushed the printout toward the ticket agent. "We had a cancellation. I'd like to get reimbursed for this ticket, back onto the credit card."

An elegant, long-fingered hand closed over mine and drew it back, twitching the ticket from my possession. "I'm late, dear, but I'm here. No need for that."

The ticket agent yelled next and I got shoved aside, only to swing about to face Remy.

"You can't have that. That's . . . that's theft."

"Trust me, you'd never be able to prove it." Remy stowed her stolen ticket away in a purse that looked terribly familiar. "What did I tell you about the obelisk?"

"Not to go."

"But here we are."

"Did you think we'd listen?"

"Oh, I knew you would, and head right there." Remy smiled, and she looked even prettier when she did. I wanted to take a picture and march into a beauty salon and ask to be made to look just like her. I blinked, hard, and that feeling went away. She continued, "I'm going to follow and do whatever I can to make certain nothing disastrous happens."

"I'd say from the professor's point of view, it can't get much worse."

She drew me aside from the crowd. "It can." An open newspaper covered the pavement under our feet, footsteps marking it where passersby had trod over it, and she pointed down.

MYSTERIOUS DIE-OFF OF FISH ON THE TIDE
Thousands of bodies found drifting.

I read the headline three times. "Stranger than fiction?"

Her lips closed into a line before she said, "We talked about this."

"That—that's him? Drawing power?"

"And that means he's here. He made the coast. Before, he was extending his reach. Now . . ." her voice trailed off.

"Are you following to help us or him?"

"The Society would like not to have to take sides."

"Oh, come on!"

Remy made a face. "Professor Brandard has always been independent, outside our purview and struggle, set on neither helping us nor hindering us, and we have returned those favors. But now." She stopped dead in her tracks. Or words. Whatever.

"It's too dangerous."

"Precisely. Some members of our Society have always been favorable to the dark side of power, and our body appears to be fracturing."

"That's what you meant by old alliances and stuff."

"Yes. Unfortunately."

"So which half is telling you what to do?"

One side of her curved mouth smiled at that. "Tessa . . . it is Tessa, isn't it? No one tells me what to do."

She was taller than me. Much, much prettier and wiser than me, but she didn't intimidate me like she had at first. "I bet," I told Remy, "that someone is making some pretty strong suggestions."

She bent forward. "I'll be on the train. We shall see what we shall see."

And she whirled away, disappearing into the crowd, even as the loudspeaker called out our route and boarding information. I hurried to catch up with Morty and Brian, still unsure of where Remy stood in the scheme of things. We boarded, and although I expected the shocks on the train car to sag or complain at Morty's weight, they didn't. This must be one of those times when he managed his size. As I found a seat and took it, I decided that Remy wanted her alliances foggy so that she could observe and make whatever choices she had to make when it was most advantageous. No sense to decide to jump over the cliff before reaching it.

Brian buried himself in magazines someone had left in the seat pocket until he relaxed enough to join in seeing the sights. After storing his returned credit card carefully, Morty settled into a kind of half slumber without the oceanic deep whale calls of the evening before, and I just watched the trees whipping by and tried not to think of a tide of pale, belly-up fish bodies floating onto the shore.

After a while, thinking of all that salt water made me thirsty, and I planned a trip to the dining and vending car. I took orders from the two of them and said, "I've got this, but you're not getting beer or ale, I'm underage. Soda for all of us."

Morty grumbled and waved me on. Brian looked at me.

"Need company?"

I shook my head. He grinned, making his dimple wink, picked up a magazine, and went back to learning about Fantasy League Football.

The train swayed from side to side but barely noticeably as I made my way through three passenger cars. I didn't see Remy, although I wasn't sure if I could, even if I stared right at her. If magic was that magical.

I had just about decided the jury was still out on that when a voice with a strong cockney accent spoke just behind my shoulder while I stood at the drink counter. I jumped and a hand reached out to steady me as I came down.

"Steady, luv. Car is full o' people. Might get yourself trampled." Steptoe smiled broadly as I spun around.

"What are you doing here?"

"Ah, well that." He put a finger alongside his nose. "Would be tellin'."

I didn't even try not to roll my eyes.

"A'right. I put a little burr onto your jumper."

"My jumper? A burr?"

He cleared his throat. "Hoodie that would be. And a tiny patch of a tracker."

"On my hoodie."

"That's whut I said." He was smiling again. "I thought you lot might be movin' about, travelin' a spot here and there, and it might be useful t' know whereabouts." He lowered his voice a tad. "Remy is hereabouts too."

"That, I know."

"Do you? Oh, good. Th' lot of you are sharper than I thought."

"And I read about the tide and the dead fish."

"Ah. Even sharper!"

I decided not to take credit for that one. "Remy pointed it out."

"Did she, now? More helpful than I figured she'd be."

My turn at the counter was near. "I think everyone is still trying to figure out which side to be on."

"Don't doubt that, not a bit. Safer that way."

"For you or me?"

"Both o' us, both." He pointed behind me. "Order up."

I ordered four Cokes and pushed one into Steptoe's hand as I left. He trailed at my elbow.

"Well, now, that's a right gesture. Good on ya."

"Thanks." I sipped at my straw. Chilled sugar and caffeine rushed down my throat like a blessing while I pondered his friendly demeanor. "Got any burrs you could lend me? Protective ones, maybe?"

His coal-dark eyes measured the thoughts flowing through his mind. "Throw m' luck in wi' you?"

"You've already suggested as much."

"True that. I might have a few pebbles." He felt around in his natty suit coat pocket for a second and pulled out three pebbles. He poured them into my free hand. "Defensive but a bit of a flash-bang, if you get my drift. Use one at a time. Don't be wasting them." He closed my fingers around them. "An' don't be tellin' Remy. I'm circumspect about that lady."

"So am I. And thanks."

He lifted his drink. "A trade for a kindness." Steptoe winked. "Magic works that way."

He spun about and headed for the other end of the train car, leaving me thinking: Did it now? Did that mean Remy owed me something for the train ticket?

They reached eagerly for their cold drinks when I got back to the seats. I sat down gingerly with mine, having filled each and every one to the last frothy drop I could get in the waxed cups.

"News," I announced. "Remy and Steptoe are both on the train."

"Both! That's calamitous."

"Not necessarily. Both seem to be on the helpful side."

Brian stared at me with the hurt look a puppy has when he'd been told no. He folded his arms and looked stoically out the window.

"She betrayed him once," Morty offered.

Brian snorted. "More than once." He turned about again. "She's a beautiful woman who convinced a . . . a mature man that she loved him, when obviously she did not."

"Now then." Morty cleared his throat, yellow-white goatee waggling a bit. "By then she'd cast her lot with the Society and you hadn't joined it with her, and she was pressured by that."

"I found her with another man."

"As I recollect, you told me she was training with another wizard, and that sort of circumstance was to be expected. She wanted to climb ranks and take you with her."

"I didn't mention what kind of training!" Brian's face flushed, and I found myself glad that the professor now inhabited a young body, because if he hadn't, he'd have blown a gasket.

I'm no fan of gossip, having been surrounded by it the last few years. I put my hand up. "Can we agree that she was ambitious and acted accordingly?"

Brian made a noise and I took it for agreement, so I wrenched the subject around to Steptoe. "What about Simon?"

"Simon's partnership has always been consistently suspect. He's a minor demon, so that bends him down a certain road."

I sipped my soda to hide the reaction I had to the word *demon*. I swallowed carefully. "I got the feeling he's looking for a bit of redemption."

"Could be, and in fact, that may very well be probable. His actions will judge him louder than his words."

"Okay, then we'll keep an eye on him. Remy pointed out a headline to me, about many dead fish on the tide, and said Malender had come ashore."

Morty shifted on the train's bench, and I thought for a moment that the entire car swayed and hoped it was my imagination. "There is thought to be a great darkness awakening. Malender may well fit that role, and his being about is definitely worrisome. The old professor could have handled him, but now—"

Brian squeezed his eyes shut a moment before opening them wide. "I've got it, already. I screwed up monumentally and now we're all in a jam."

From his words, I knew that the professor had retreated like a coward, leaving his successor holding the bag, and that we wouldn't accomplish much more at the moment.

I looked out the window from my side. "We've got a few hours, might as well rest a bit. Washington is always a busy town."

Despite the caffeine, Brian settled back almost immediately and closed his eyes. I wanted to shake him awake, to look at the country we sped through, but decided he looked like he needed the rest. I left my seat and went up to join Morty, sitting across from him in one of those configurations where the seats faced each other in case the passengers wanted to talk or play cards or whatever. My knees touched his as I did.

"He's out."

Morty nodded. "Good."

I raised an eyebrow. "Did you have something to do with that?"

He turned one of his mittlike hands over. "It is more like a sense. Think of the earth as a vast cradle, holding you safe, rocking you, with its own deep and pulsing heartbeat. Wrap that thought about you and it will carry you away."

"Wow. Which kind of makes sense until you think about earthquakes and avalanches and tornadoes and stuff."

He grunted. "Every dream has nightmares."

"No kidding." I leaned a little forward. "I wanted to tell you I couldn't get your money back on the extra ticket."

"Oh?"

"Remy showed up and kind of took it from me. That's how she got on our train."

"And you let her."

"I know. Shouldn't have but she took me by surprise, and then I didn't think my starting a brawl in the middle of the station would help much."

"True." He considered a moment. "I cannot be certain if her taking the ticket puts her in our debt or not. If you'd given it to her, then certainly."

"And we'd want that?"

"It would give us a certain advantage. That's how hospitality works among our folks. Did you look for Remy when you went for the drinks?"

"Didn't spot her. She's on board somewhere; I haven't seen her since the station. Do you know her as well as the professor?"

"Almost. In our community, alliances once made are often lifelong."

"No wonder he seems bitter. That's a commitment."

"Indeed, but one forged after many years of trust and experience. Remy and Brandard, well, most of us figured that bond would be unbreakable. Not like mine."

"Your wife who was taken?"

A hurt expression went through his eyes, darting by so quickly I almost didn't see it, but I did.

"Who could have done that?"

"I don't know. If I did, I would take their house apart stone by stone, stick by stick, and root by root."

And I had no doubt at all that he could. "Do you think Brian can help?"

He shrugged. "I have hopes. I must do something. The professor—"

I remembered that he had declined at first and must have changed his mind, determining to help Morty. "What is your wife like?"

He stared at me for a long moment as if deciding whether to answer or not. He answered slowly. "She is a strong woman. In her thoughts and actions. She defends herself most vigorously and can be very persuasive if she thinks you are wrong-minded. We knew each other decades before I decided I must make my move, as you would say. When I asked her to marry me, she shook her head. 'I'm a hard woman to love,' she told me. 'All my kin and all yours would agree. I am not a pretty flower to be admired, but a statue of command and decision to take heed by.' So I said to her, taking Germanigold's hand, 'I promise to value your thoughts and deeds as much, if not more, than my own. And stone keeps its promise.' She did not answer then, but in a few years she came to me and said 'Yes.' We sealed our vows with bridal gifts. To prove my love, I gave her the Eye of Nimora." He sat back against the train bench with a heavy sigh.

"The who?"

"Nimora. It's a gem in a setting. It has a power of its own, and that's all I will say about it." He closed his jaw tightly, goatee not wavering.

"That's her name? Germanigold?"

"I've always called her Goldie."

"You've kept your promise."

"No. I let them take her from me! I don't know what kind of battle she fought against them, or how she fares now. I don't know what she thinks—that I let her go or have not come for her yet." His hand curled into a fist. "I haven't forgotten her!"

I could feel his heated emotions, a warm wave enveloping me. I leaned still closer. "Of course not. And she has to know that, from the way you described her. Brian will find her, but if he's not capable, I will help you. We will find her."

"Thank you, lass." He cocked his head slightly. "But what about you? Are you not about finding your father?"

I shuffled a foot. "My mom wants to. I'm still . . . I'm still angry, I guess. He wrecked everything and we, Mom and I, won't get out of this hole for a long time."

"You're sure it was him?"

I narrowed my eyes at Morty's expressionless face and strong brow, like a battering ram. "Considering that everything he did was an inside job, pretty sure."

"Remember, I've heard a bit about his owing and borrowing. I found myself surprised that this man, this man I'd known about for a handful of years, could suddenly and recklessly run up so much debt. Desperately. Even knowing what it could do to his family, and," Morty lowered his chin a bit, pitching his voice lower, "I know that he loved you both. He would get behind a hundred or two but never in the thousands or tens of thousands."

"What are you saying?"

"We live in an electronic age. Identify theft is rampant."

"But." I tried to think. "But wouldn't he have tried to stop it?"

"Most don't find out until the damage has already been done. Mind you, I have no idea if that could have happened. I do know your father had dealings with the professor, and Brandard has a fairly good eye for character."

"You've said that before. Dealings. What kind of deal?"

"That, I couldn't say. I'm not privy to the professor's business. Brandard had connections all over the world, for all that he would bluster and say he was retired."

"Magical business?"

The corner of Morty's mouth pulled back, just a bit. "The business world is full of much smoke and many mirrors, is it not?"

Okay, now he was just being mysterious and irritating. I flung myself back into my seat.

"Whatever."

"We will both be greatly enlightened once the professor is himself again."

I found myself looking over Morty's bulky shoulder at the sleeping young man behind us. "But he won't ever be the same, will he?"

"No. Your blustery, gruff, bent, and aged old professor is gone. But the mind I knew, curious, bright and lightning-quick, aye, that man should come back to us."

"The sooner the better."

Morty patted my knee. "You'll get no argument from me on that." His head turned. "It looks like civilization is nearing."

I followed his gaze. Indeed. The forests had given way to neighborhoods and roads, and in this area, all roads led to the capital.

CHAPTER NINE

THE BUSTLING HUMANITY at the train station in Washington DC swallowed us up as we arrived. I saw no one I recognized, although that tall figure caught the edge of my eyesight again, the one I *knew* couldn't be Carter Phillips even though I kind of lost my breath at that brief glance. He disappeared against the dazzle of white and gold marble, and the din of the place smothered his going. If Remy or Steptoe had followed us off, they'd become undetectable immediately. I'd been to this grand station twice before, both on school trips to the various Smithsonians along the mall, but the destination itself never failed to impress me. Six major rail lines came into this station, with all the life they brought with them, plus the attached building was a mall in and of itself, tall and cavernous in a glorious way, holding a galleria, landing after landing of shops and restaurants. They smelled of good food, leather, fine perfumes, and the press of people. I took a long in and out breath.

Pulling my phone out, I texted my mom that we'd arrived all right, and the weather looked great.

She texted back. *Thanks, and remember to do the adulting.*

I grinned at that. It was her way of worrying about me and telling me to be careful. She was always telling me that I'd assumed the adult role in the family, going around and doing all the door locking at night and other things, admonishing me to let her be the adult. I answered: *We can be adults together!*

The ground vibrated a bit. I turned around to face Morty. "There should be buses, double-decker buses, and private shuttles for tourists at the edge of the parking lot, all waiting for passengers. We ought to be able to hire one."

His broad face smiled. "Then we shouldn't disappoint them."

"I need to find a restroom first."

"Then we shall wait for you." His beard inclined a bit, and I trotted off while he turned to explain a few facts to Brian, who stood at his heels, still a bit pale from the trip. Maybe he was just hungry—again. He seemed to always be hungry. If that was it. If he wasn't fading, somehow, some way, because he wasn't fully transformed. I wondered if he felt as if he were caught between two worlds: the past and this one. He shouldn't be tired. He'd napped more than two hours.

More primal thoughts filled my mind and I hurried to find my destination, the restroom. Once done, I paused near the upstairs banister. From the landing, I had the vantage point overlooking much of the mall's main floor, a shot of the archway to the train station itself, and the streams of people coming in to shop, eat, and mingle. I searched for Remy and saw nothing of her, making me wonder if she carried a Potter-style Cloak of Invisibility. Shouldn't all mages have one? I did see plenty of ordinary people. The crowd skewed mostly my age, and I could hear excited voices echoing upward as the noise dueled with the reports of footsteps. Much of the traffic seemed headed for various dress shops. Ah, the lure of dating. I wondered if Evelyn would pick the "girls' night out" invitation for the spring bash. It sounded rather fun.

"Going shopping or just skipping classes like the rest of the kids?"

I whirled about at the voice in my ear. Long, tall Carter Phillips in a soft cotton t-shirt with that band on it and old jeans stood waiting for an answer. It had been him I'd spotted. Kids. I was one of them it seemed. It made the gap between us loom that much wider. I didn't know if that was a step up from being a Person of Interest or not. I wasn't sure I wanted to find out. Heat simmered up my throat and into my cheeks as I stammered. "Playing tourist. I brought the professor's nephew."

I found a smile.

Carter lifted his chin so that he could look past me. "The hefty guy and Brian?"

"That'll be the two. There isn't much we can do at home until the body is released and the investigation is finished, and Mom and I thought we'd try to take his mind off . . . well, what happened."

He nodded.

"But how did you . . ." I let my question trail off. I had found, over the last few years, that it works much better if you don't question the police. They don't like that. The last few days had rattled my brain enough that I couldn't think of a sideways approach, though, and I shuffled one foot restlessly.

"I seem to have a built-in GPS when it comes to finding you." Carter's eyes smiled, though his mouth stayed neutral.

"Or you put a tracker in my car, but wait—I don't drive."

"If that's what you want to believe."

"Well, if you're not here to arrest me, I have two tourists to round up. Lots to see!"

"Why would I want to arrest you?"

"My father has never turned up and now you've told me the professor's body still hasn't been found."

"And I never said you were anything but a victim." He put his hand on my wrist. "You found Brian at the professor's house, right?"

"Just like I told you. Hiding in the backyard. Poor guy had been asleep when the house went up. Had nothing on but his skivvies, as they say."

"Huh. Did he smell like chemicals or anything unusual?"

"Just smoke. Why?" I frowned at Carter. "You think he might have started it? If he did, he made a poor choice for working clothes."

His jaw tightened a little. "We found an accelerant in the foyer. The arson investigator is a little perplexed because it's only in one, small area, and it's not been identified. Normally accelerant is spread throughout the entire house, for maximum burn and damage."

"Maybe it was just a bottle of brandy or something on the sideboard."

He shook his head. "Different chemical signature. But you don't think Brian could have been involved in anything like that?"

"Never. He's smart, but in a backward sort of way. And naïve."

"Or a good actor."

I shrugged a shoulder. "I think I'd notice. Is the house a total loss?"

"Most of it. One room stayed relatively untouched."

"Upstairs bathroom?" I guessed, thinking of all the porcelain and water pipes.

"No. It looks as if it might have been his library or study."

"Wow." That meant the heart of the professor's home had stayed intact. Or it would until someone else found out about it. I could bet that he'd have looters if word got around. Antique hunters if no one else. "Can Brian go in, rummage around, and salvage what he can?"

"Not possible. The rest of the house is pretty fragile, and we do have an investigation going on."

"Oh. Right." Seriously, what was I thinking in asking permission? It would be better to ask for forgiveness, after the fact. I'd never gotten farther than the threshold to his library, and that musty smell of many, many books shelved about, like a forgotten vault of knowledge and mystery. The thought made my pulse step up and I knew where I wanted to make a beeline to, the minute we got home.

Below, Morty had been casting about and finally saw me up on the second-floor landing. He gave a hearty wave, his hand filled with paper slips, tickets, no doubt.

"I need to go. I think there's a tour that needs its guide."

He leaned over the rail and waved back, to Morty's consternation. I could almost hear the rumbling *humph*. "I'll be in town most of the day, if you need me for any reason."

"Why would I need you?"

His gaze had never left Mortimer Broadstone. "That man is,

as far as I know, a total stranger. If he's bothering you or your mom, you need to tell me."

"Oh, no, no. He is a genuine, longtime friend of the professor. He wants to help with Brian. Mom approves of him." At least, I thought she did.

Carter looked back to me then, assessing my face for a long moment. "But you would ask if you needed assistance."

"The police? Maybe not. But you, yes. Mom calls you a gentleman."

He might have blushed faintly, hard to tell in the mall's lighting, but his eyes crinkled at the corners and his cleft deepened attractively. He tapped the banister railing. "Just a tourist day? No thought of searching for the last known trail of your dad?"

That last part of his question opened my eyes. "What do you mean by last known?"

Carter went stone silent.

"You guys all said there had never been any activity on his credit cards or his phone. That there was no trail."

"That's what we said."

"But you know better."

He shifted his weight.

"You *knew*. All this time. He just didn't fall off the face of the earth."

"He did, eventually. Your not knowing that there had been a trail helped lift some of the suspicion."

I wanted to get up in his face and stopped myself, knowing we could draw a crowd. "Some of the suspicion? Just some? I'm nineteen now. The last two-plus years of my life have been absolute hell because no one believed us that he just walked out and we never heard from him again. Half of them wanted to burn us at the stake and the other half couldn't look at us without dripping pity. My father!"

"Tessa, I'm sorry but it wasn't my call."

"Oh, damnit. I'm not here because I knew something which I never knew, but if you know anything at all, you'd better tell me when I get home or I will go down to the department and raise all sort of holy hell." I shook my finger in his face.

The color in his face rose a little more, making his cleft scar stand out in its paleness. He took my hand in midair, wrapping his much bigger and stronger hand around it. "I'll take that as a promise."

His warmth and strength enveloped my hand, and sent a spark somewhere deep inside, stopping me. Before I could say another anger-filled word, he turned and left, weaving in and out of the crowd, some of them throwing back a curious look at me.

I sagged against the banister. John Graham Andrews hadn't just disappeared. Well, he had, but what—days, weeks, and months? —after he left us. I ignored Morty's vigorous waving at me. We'd had no clue. I straightened. Well, I'd had no clue. I wondered if my mother had had the slightest inkling. She would have told me, right? Partners, right? Just like I immediately told her all about the weirdness surrounding the professor. Maybe that's why she'd never blamed me for his departure. More had been going on than I had ever guessed.

Morty bellowed, "Tessa! Time to go!"

I hustled before he took his agitated bulk to the marble stairway and cracked it or something.

"Remember that?" I murmured to Brian as the shuttle approached the mall and the Washington Monument dominated our view, Morty firmly entrenched in the front passenger seat, his shoulders nearly half the van width. He'd hired a rather new shuttle van, complete with eager driver ("Call me Sam!") but his weight still rocked it.

"How could I forget?" Brian inched closer to the window on his side, taking in the sight.

I stretched my neck to look over his shoulder. The first time my middle school had brought us, the monument was still undergoing repairs for earthquake damage, skirted by a grid of scaffolding and such. It had been impressive then, but stood even more so now, refurbished and cleaned, a spike of majesty into the sky that had almost not been finished being built—twice—despite great plans. It looked different, better and bigger in person, than it did on TV and film shots, which always seemed to size it down. I've been told the Eiffel Tower is the same way, much more massive than in pictures. I hope to check that one out in person someday.

The driver pulled over to a parking lot where, despite its being a weekday, only a few slots were left. I wondered if Remy had parked her broom over to the side. The driver pulled out an iPad reader while we piled out of the vehicle. He'd wait until we wanted to move on, and we had all day, if we needed it. He seemed remarkably disinterested in anything we might have to say, until I spotted the discreet ear pods. Probably hadn't heard a word anyway.

We approached on the footpath, my head going back as I looked up and up. I wasn't sure if the ground moved a bit as Morty strode along it, but I hesitated as we got in line to tour the obelisk. The line wasn't long, by Washington tourist standards, but I could feel Brian, and then Morty, fidget.

Morty's brows settled heavily in his vast face when he finished assessing the monument. "She was gravely wounded," he told me. "I can feel the scars still healing. I would have liked to have been part of the restoration crew, but my second cousin was, and that will have to do."

"You won't, um, that is . . ." I couldn't figure out how to word my worry but Mortimer seemed to be a walking earthquake.

"Don't worry, lass. My presence will only strengthen the tower more. She's made of good stone, both quarries that birthed her." He looked upward at it. "A fine work it is." He put a hand up, palm out, a faint smile highlighting the concentration that creased his expression. "If only th' two of you could hear it speak."

Brian had been carrying his cane but now he let the tip touch the ground, his head tilted to one side. "I think I do."

Their vibes shivered up the back of my neck and I shook them off. "It's easier for me to just read the plaques. The monument is full of them." I pulled the listing we'd printed out from my pocket and smoothed it. "We have a hundred and ninety-four memorial stones to look for in five hundred and fifty-five feet, more or less." Pointedly, at Brian, "Any chance that thing will work like a dowsing rod?"

He rolled it between his palms, waiting a long moment, and then gave me a shrug. He lifted it as if to point, and we all jumped as the cane gave a visible jab in the air, almost lunging out of his hold. He tightened his grip on the cane to hold it back, and it gave a bronco buck of defiance.

I stepped out of the way, sorry I'd said anything.

CHAPTER TEN

MORTY PUT HIS HAND out to steady the cane, moving his sturdy frame to obscure the action. "Don't be drawing attention, lad," he said lowly. To me, he added, "Good idea, that one."

I couldn't tell if that was sarcastic or not. We both looked at the entrance. "We should walk it," he grumbled, "inspect it step by step, though it goes up a fair piece." Brian let out a shiver at the thought.

I shook my head. "You can't. Elevator takes you up, then you go down one floor to see the museum, and then you walk the rest of the way down. Because it's narrow, it's sort of one-way. About eight hundred and ninety steps." I pointed at the cane. "And we'll be locating every step of the way, from the looks of it. That will draw attention, even if there is any room to swing it around."

Morty's bushy eyebrows knotted. "A bit too many people to my way of thinking."

"I don't think they give private tours, if that's your idea. Money can't buy you one of those. Not unless you're the President or something."

"Mayhap not. From the looks of that thing's reaction, whatever we're looking for seems awfully near. It's homed in on a signal of some sort. We need to clear the sheep away if we can, so we can tend to business." His gaze raked the doorway ahead of him. He held a hand out in front of him, not conspicuously but as if he thought perhaps of shaking mine or Brian's. His fingers curved genially, but I could see his knuckles going white and the tendons of his wrists tighten. What was he up to? And just what did he mean by sheep? Although I was pretty sure I knew, I couldn't help listening for baaing.

I could see the concentration spread across him, into the tightness of his shoulders and then the cords of his neck. His square body grew denser and more rigid, as if he might become stone altogether as Morty evidently worked at some making from his talent. Brian reacted with a slight gasp. I could feel it, like an irritating buzz that left me uneasy, but no more than that.

I shifted from one foot to another. "What's going on?"

"The structure," Morty said quietly. "It's got good bones, it does, but the shaft has problems and it's not been fixed properly, not as it should be, not quite yet."

"You mean the elevator? They shut it down for over six months and rebuilt it. And now you're tinkering with it."

"Needs to be pulled out and replaced entirely, I would say. The stone and metal have a stress to them that cannot be fixed unless done that way. Repair alone cannot fix what is wrong with it. It needs a rebuild."

"You're talking millions of dollars, if the inspectors could even tell what might still be wrong with it and decide to replace it. Believe it or not, Washington doesn't have that kind of money. They relied on donations to help with the stonework after the earthquake and hurricane. For the capitol dome, too, I think."

Morty's jaw worked. "I know a foundation that would fund it." He cleared his throat. "And a company well-regarded to do the work."

My jaw dropped slightly as I followed his circular thought. "Out of one pocket and back into another. You wouldn't really make money on a project like that."

He answered me slowly, his concentration growing even more intense. "More or less, but you forget that it will build reputation and that's as valuable as dollars. But it's what needs to be done. I think they need a bit of convincing." As if arm-wrestling some unseen elemental, Morty suddenly twisted his hands about and then dropped them. A heavy thrum vibrated through my eardrums. Deep in my bones, I could feel the agony of the stonework and a groaning twist of the steel and cables that comprised the elevator and its shaft. I rubbed away the disconcerting feeling on my forearms as soon as I felt it, whatever it was, that Morty had wrought. He rocked back on his heels, folding his arms over his chest, finished.

"What did you do?"

"What needed to be done."

"Great. I love a meaningless answer to an important question." I wrinkled my nose at him.

Brian looked at me. "Wait for it."

I had no choice, unsure of what I was waiting for, and gave a silent prayer that it wouldn't be the sudden plunge of the elevator from 800-plus feet above us.

Nothing happened for a while, except for the restless movement of those of us in line, tired of waiting. I could hear the shuffle of feet from beyond the doorway, where those inside waited for their turn to go up. Someone said, "Finally!" and we could hear the power drone as the machinery powered on, with a chug and a ratcheting noise. The elevator car descended with an ever-louder clattering that ended with a loud thump as it hit bottom and its doors whined open. Rangers rushed inward to the distress call of the machinery. A thin smoke veiled the entranceway.

The stream of people who'd been going into the monument suddenly turned on itself, with cries of disappointment. Bodies going every which direction blocked the threshold in chaos.

"Elevator broken again. The landmark is closed."

". . . Thought they fixed that."

"Nine months they took it down, but they're still having trouble. You'd think fixed was fixed. What a waste."

"Can we get our money back?"

Behind them, at the doorway to the vast tower, I could see the park rangers herding visitors out. Whatever Morty had done seemed successful but not too traumatic to tourists. The sheep, as he'd evidently meant, thinned out appropriately, but we couldn't just march in. Not yet. I watched the crowd and spotted what might best be called a distraction. Actually, it seemed a tantrum had just started to wind up for one young lady.

"Come on!"

The two of them followed me closer, behind those who'd been sent out and who began to encircle the rangers with questions and comments (rude even) as the young lady in question finally reached maximum peak in her expression and began to wail.

"Bu-ut it's for schoooool!" Her voice grew higher into the supernatural range until I expected Remy's hounds to appear and join in with their own pitched howls. Two park rangers stepped closer to her elbows. They paid no attention to us as we circled about to the befogged entrance.

"We're sorry, miss, but the monument is closed for repair. We may or may not have it reopened later today."

"I can't come baaaack!" Her voice climbed until human ears could barely detect it without pain.

I felt her dismay even as I waved Morty and Brian into the smoke. "The rangers will give you a note. And trust me. Google will save your life on this one." I smiled optimistically into the glistening red face of the distressed girl, years younger than me and definitely more spoiled, and even surpassing me in the ugly-crier contest. Some adult figures loomed up behind her to lead her away and her voice rose again to ear-bleeding heights.

The crowd, however, had thinned enough that I knew I'd be noticed if I darted into the monument, clearly going in the wrong direction. Hoping the guys were already inside, the rangers pretty certain they'd already gotten everyone out, I slipped my hands into my jeans' pockets, thinking.

My fingers ran into small round objects I'd forgotten I carried. Steptoe's flash-bangs. Were they anywhere near as potent as ones the SWAT teams used? Hopefully not. I just needed a little bit of noise and another curtain of smoke. I fished one out and, while everyone was still watching the debacle with the howling young lady, I pitched it inside the open elevator where it rattled solidly up against the back wall. It erupted with a loud crack-bang and a delightful puff of foul-smelling smoke that quickly filled the interior base of the monument once more. I dove inside, while everyone nearby screamed and darted the other way. Because I could see very little of anything, I fetched up against a solid body that could have been the wall of the monument or an Iron Dwarf. I squinted my eyes to verify it was Morty.

"Well done." He fanned his huge hands as he bent over, clearing the delightful stink and mist away from our corner. Brian let go of the cane and it shot forward like a spear to sink into a single stone in the northwest corner.

I stared before offering, "That's the cornerstone, but it's underground, underneath that block."

Morty barely shook his head. "We'll not be touching that. What the cane seeks is here," and he squatted lower, putting his palm to the crowning marble, his fingers splayed about the tip of the cane. "Hold it steady," he instructed Brian.

Brian's mouth thinned and his jawline tightened as he wrapped both hands about the wood again. I could feel him tensing up, bracing himself against a force that seemed to radiate throughout the walking cane. He groaned. I moved into position behind him, bringing my arms up to embrace his, my hands clasping just ahead of his elbows, spooning his body, feet spread and steady. His coldness surprised me, but he began to warm a little as I wrapped myself around him. I could feel the shivers running through his body. I couldn't see over his shoulder to know what they were doing, but Morty let out a deep "Now!" and then Brian lurched forward as if the marble had given way. A blue bolt lanced the air, and that was about all I saw. He went to his knees with a short and muffled cry. I saw the great piece of marble, hollowed out, laid open as if split in two, and put my hand over my mouth. That shocking blue I'd seen misted for another second and then faded away, sinking into the cane and disappearing. I stared at the cracked marble block. What had they done? Had they corrupted the very foundation of the monument? How could it stand, so weakened? Did we have to run for it and hope for the best?

Morty dropped his hand like an anchor on my shoulder. "It will hold. It has all these years."

"It's been hollow?"

"Aye, but not empty." He pointed.

Brian, still holding the perdition rod in one hand, leaned

forward on his knees and thrust his hand into the massive marble brick, sweeping out a small velvet pouch, two tightly wound scrolls, a candlestick holder, and a half dozen agate marbles that looked like they might be flash-bangs on their own. He swept his fingers over them and made a joyous noise, like a kid in a pack of puppies.

"Success." Morty sounded satisfied.

I stood on one foot and then the other, nervous, pointing. "Can you fix that?"

"Of a certainty. Soon as he's done claiming his goods."

"How nice," another voice put in softly, elegantly. "I so love it when I can get a man to do the dirty work." A low humming sang through the air. Both Morty and Brian froze in place. I managed a half-turn but it was an extremely slow one as the atmosphere tugged at me like quicksand.

Remy glided forward, her motions quick and efficient as she scooped up Brian's treasures and stowed them away in that traitorous leather bag that had once belonged to me. She stuffed a train ticket in my pocket. "Won't be needing the return trip. Thank you, my dear, for all your help and consideration."

I wanted to speak. I wanted to put my foot out and trip her as she turned about. I wanted to grab my purse by the strap and sling her to the ground on her pretentious elbows and butt, to shatter that elegant image, to shock and surprise the unbreakable confidence. Nothing worked the way I wanted, my voice stayed stuck in my throat and my body stayed glued in some very heavy gravity. She'd frozen me as if I'd lost a game of tag. Memory of what Steptoe had said to me bobbed up in my brain like a cork and I grabbed for it, hoping to stop Remy if I could if she did owe me a debt of any kind. I managed a faint gurgle.

Remy looked in my eyes a long moment. "Interesting," she noted. "And commendable. I must remember this. I wonder if the professor had an inkling about you." And then she was gone. A single, clear, ringing note sounded as if something had fallen in her wake.

Paralysis fled. I blinked at the air. "Damnit."

Morty uncoiled slowly and Brian fell over on his side, his

face gone pale again and dotted in perspiration. He curled up, staring in disbelief at his empty hands. "What happened?"

"Remy happened." I bent over to help him to his feet, but he didn't want to stand up. He stayed bent over, combing the ground ineffectively with his nails.

His voice cracked. "Gone! It's all gone!"

"She got everything."

"What?" Morty staggered forward a step and shook himself.

"Lost." He put his face in his hand a moment. "Not only my relics but whatever clues I might have left to lead us on. We're lost."

"Not quite." I went to the corner where I heard the noise, something metallic falling to the floor, and I picked up a thick bronze or gold ring lying among the shards of marble. If it was gold, it was 20 or 24 karat, heavily weighted and dark in color. I dropped it in his palm. "I don't know if she dropped this or if it fell as she was shoving everything into her purse, but there's this."

Brian's eyes lit up and he clenched his fingers tightly over the ring as he threw me a joyous look. "And if anything had to be saved, it would be this. You did this."

"No way. It happened on its own."

He waved his closed fist at me. "No. No, everything of mine that I've needed has come my way because you've been there. Yes, there were items in the stone which would have been nice—very nice—to have, but this," and he opened his hand, palm up, and the heavy gold ring glinted in the low light. "This was the only necessity." With those words, he slipped the ring onto his thumb, the only finger it would have fit, and immediately seemed to stand a bit taller. "You have the luck, Tessa Andrews."

"If we don't get out of here in about five seconds, luck or not, we're going to have the park rangers and possibly the Feds as well." I backed up a step or two as Brian retrieved his cane and Morty knelt by the hollow stone and repaired it as though he held mortar in one hand and sculpted it with the other. When he'd finished, the block of marble looked as if it had never been blasted open or hollow. He grabbed both of us by the crook of our elbows as we stood in openmouthed silence and guided us to the outside.

Rangers frowned at us. "Anyone else in there?"

We shook our heads. "We couldn't see our way out of the smoke. We kept thinking someone would come in and rescue us."

The ranger nearest me started to open his mouth and shut it abruptly, as if realizing we could charge them with neglect. Instead, he muttered, "Stay clear now. It's dangerous."

Coughing and fanning ourselves, we made our way through the onlookers and the federal workers beginning to congregate, arguing about what to do with the elevator system. Brian faked a precarious wobble as we did, and the crowds parted to let us through, more curious about the monument itself. Morty paused long enough to extract a business card and slip it into a suit coat pocket of what appeared to be a supervisor, his deep voice slipping down a notch lower to where it seemed subliminal, saying, "Contact them. You need a total replacement."

With a half-smile mostly hidden by his neat beard, he rejoined us, hurrying Brian to match his massive strides while I loped alongside. We didn't stop until we reached our private shuttle and piled inside as quickly as we could. Brian put his head back against the headrest and closed his eyes for a moment, his energy spent. I looked at him, saw the faint bruises under his eyes, the too-sharp edges of his cheekbones, and realized that every day he lived incomplete took a terrible toll on him. He looked markedly weaker.

"What was that lightning bolt of blue about?"

Morty shifted in the front seat as the driver negotiated the back road of the mall slowly and carefully. "What bolt? What blue?"

"When the cane struck the marble, the air went blue—at least, our side."

Brian just shrugged, his eyes still closed, rubbing his fingers over the thumb ring on his other hand. "I didn't see anything."

Morty shook his head.

"It was right in front of the two of you. How could you have missed it?"

"Perhaps we were busy?" Morty suggested with a bit of a grumble. "Mayhap the smoke from the diversion affected you."

"No, seriously, it looked like a lightning bolt and it lit up the whole base of the monument and then the cane absorbed whatever it was. A charge or something." I nudged Brian.

Brian half-opened one eye. "What?"

"You had to have seen it. Or felt it. One of you. Don't tell me you didn't." No way did I want to think my senses unreliable.

"I am no liar." Morty looked around this time, his big square face glaring.

I put my hand up. "Didn't say you were. Just wondering what I saw." I reached for the cane where Brian had set it on the floor, and put it across our laps to inspect it. "Doesn't look like it got singed or anything." I rotated it. "Whoa."

Both of Brian's eyes flew open. "What?"

"This." I pointed to words burned into the cane and read them aloud: "Pass through the eye of the needle." Brian's face went dead white.

CHAPTER ELEVEN

I SHOVED MY hand up to his shoulder, thinking Brian would face-plant any second, but he took three big gulps and rubbed his fingers over the words instead. "You're right." The gesture brought a tiny bit of color back to his cheeks.

"What do you mean, 'you're right'? How and why could I lie about something like that?" I huffed a little.

Brian shook his head at me. "I wouldn't have seen them."

"Of course you would have! They're right there in front of you."

"No. As you spoke each word, it revealed itself."

I grabbed his chin and turned his face toward me. "Repeat after me: I, Brian, am the wizard here. Maybe late, but definitely great, and you'll be there again."

"Perhaps, perhaps not. Not even half a wizard without my artifacts returned to me, and although you've kept this trip from being an entire disaster, Remy has outwitted us all." Brian still sat there, but the voice spoke as pure professor. "To repeat myself, perhaps on deaf ears or perhaps not—the writing only revealed itself as you spoke its truth."

I shook my head. "It was all there before I read it. You're just tired. Or perhaps Remy got to you a bit."

"To what end?" Morty grumbled.

Brian leaned forward to Morty. "To whatever end she chooses, as usual. I can't say if she's doing the will of the Society or if Malender has caught her up or if she has an agenda of her own.

I will say this: she knows the value of what she's taken from us, and what's missing. She knows that although she's gotten her hands on some valuable scrolls and my passports, she's not taken anything I can't do without. The scrolls are but paper reminders of what I learned once and will regain when the ritual is finished. Whatever she's up to, she knows that I must retrieve far more important objects to revive myself and secure my power."

"In other words, she's not about to give up."

His glance flickered to me. "Precisely."

Not that I ever thought Remy would be a quitter. She struck me as truly tenacious. I tapped the cane. "Any idea where this pertains to? Other than maybe a Biblical verse?"

"Not yet, unfortunately."

"Maybe another obelisk like the Washington Monument?" I tried to nudge Brian's Swiss-cheese memory.

"Not an idea."

The driver turned around, taking his ear pods out, and looked at each of us carefully. This was the man who'd been carefully neutral and uninterested about any of our goings on or conversations, so disinterested we hadn't even bothered whispering or talking in code as he'd listened to his audio book. He cleared his throat. "Don't want to butt in, but the gent who told me to look for you all said you might need a bit of help now and then. Looking for another obelisk? The next most famous one I know is in Central Park. It's near the Metropolitan Museum of Art. Came all the way over from Egypt when people were stealing those things, you know. Cleopatra's Needle they call it."

I think we all blinked. I know I did, and Brian did, and all I saw was the back of Morty's head, but he sat in stunned silence. The driver, whose name I suddenly remembered as Sam, shifted in his seat.

"I used ta drive tourists in New York, too, you know."

Not that we would have any way to know, but now he'd told us.

He'd been so quiet I thought Morty had put an earth hug on him or something. I sat back. "Huh."

"Now, you guys been a good bunch and pay well, too. It's a

three-four hour drive one-way and we'd get there after dark, not much to see then, and traffic and all. But if you're willing to stay over tonight, I can drive everyone tomorrow and bring all of youse back. I even have room for that gent who talks like a chimney sweep, the fella who told me you needed a shuttle."

Steptoe! I leaned as far into the front seat of the shuttle as the seat belt let me. "What about him?"

"Oh, nice guy. Hailed me at the curb, told me you guys would be along in a little bit and want a drive or two. He looked the shuttle over and said it looked in pretty good shape. Some of my fellow drivers, they go for the economy models, or they get used and drive 'em to death. I take care of my ride. He said it showed. He, ah, well he paid me on top of your fee. Said all of youse were doing a little scavenger hunt, like, and mum's the word, but I'd be doing all right by helpin'. And he's been right, so far." Sam reached forward to his console, which looked like a bird or mouse nest had taken up residence in it, and fished around till he pulled out a business card. As he flashed it, he confirmed the name.

"As he told you, mum's the word."

"Oh, yeah. Said I should keep my tongue tied about all this, what might be said and such. Secret society goings on and all, and not to be repeatin' anything I heard. Might be important, he told me, and maybe even a touch dangerous. I don't need dangerous after driving in New York City or Boston—jeez, now that's a town to avoid drivin' in—but I keep quiet all right."

"You certainly do," Morty told him. He bent back toward me. "I don't like that Steptoe's in this."

Morty's jawline tightened while he considered Sam's words.

"He wanted my head," Brian muttered.

"Because he thought you'd immolate everybody and everything around you, and you almost did. He was trying to get to you ahead of that Boss," I said.

"Boss?"

"Malender."

"Oh. They wanted my things. They threatened me."

"From what I heard, they wanted to give you an escort to a safe revival, but you started a fight and it got out of hand. Their view seems to be that the professor needs to be renewed and at top speed to face what is coming."

Morty gave a half snort. "Steptoe's story will change as he deems it profitable, if we are to be generous."

"And if you're not?"

Morty's eyes gleamed at me. "A downright scoundrel." He reached around and tapped the cane. "Seems like we should check that out."

"We'd have to get a couple of rooms. I'll call Mom, but I don't think she'll be too upset."

"Done, then." Shifting forward, Morty must have flashed a smile at the driver. "Any place you can recommend?"

"Just so happens my brother-in-law runs a nice, clean motel in Alexandria, on the outskirts of Old Town. It's on the small side but he should have a couple of rooms available. I'll give him a call." The driver anchored his hands-free device about his ear, put a call through, and five minutes later we had two rooms booked. The shuttle even stopped at a local drugstore so we could get little travel kits of toothpaste, toothbrushes, deodorant, and other things. I sneaked in a big pack of trail mix for late night munchies as well, and Brian threw in a pack of Coca-Cola, neither of which escaped Morty's attention when he slid his credit card through.

We went to lunch at a Chinese place after checking in and asking for recommendations within walking distance. Old Alexandria, outside the main hub of DC, is a hotbed of restaurants, small and quaint, some reasonable and some outrageously expensive. I wondered if we'd see a congressman or two, but if we did, I didn't recognize anybody. I thought they might give themselves away by ducking out of view but no one seemed to care. As for public spectacle, nothing matched the stares we got at lunch. It's hard to beat Mortimer's plaid suit on the march.

Morty insisted on a table with a lazy Susan in the middle, and the hostess took one look at his build and went scurrying for an emperor chair rather than the plain ones we got. Even at that, the cherrywood frame complained a little as he settled into it, but that wasn't the cause of the interest. I suspect it came from the parade of servers, with plate after plate of steaming goodness to be plunked down on the lazy Susan until it could hold no more. Interesting enough but nothing compared to the sight of Morty digging in.

We were all hungry. The smell of fresh-wokked ingredients, a bit of garlic, meats, pepper, ginger and other savory aromas surrounded me as I grabbed my fork and served myself mounds of this, that, and the other. Even so, I couldn't begin to compete with our Iron Dwarf as he inhaled plate after plate, using chopsticks like a pro. Some he ordered refills on, and after others were done he ordered something completely different. Brian ate well too, after a moment's hesitation, pouring tea whenever anyone asked and humming now and then when something delectable went down his throat. I watched him and thought I could detect both the professor and the young man vying for control to enjoy the lunch. I think it might have been Brian, though, who passed on the sea urchins. I joined him on that one.

When Morty slowed down, I looked at him in admiration. "Wow. I have seen our college football team devour a meal. I would love to take a bet on whether you could beat them. I'd make money hand over fist."

"I don't always eat like that, missy. If I did, your refrigerator at home would be bare."

I thought back. "True. Why today?"

"Out of deference to your supplies and the business at hand, I've been on short rations. It seemed advisable to catch up and tuck away what I could for the future."

"Well, I know they're glad." I gestured at the waitstaff.

He smiled. "I shall remember this restaurant for my family's business." The smile faded slowly. His tone became somber. "There were times in the past when food was not gotten so easily."

"Must have been tough."

"It was. We can, when necessary, eat dirt for our nutrients. Not a palatable diet, but doable."

"Dirt?"

"Indeed. Have you not heard of such a thing?"

I had, sort of, as a real oddity and not normal, but I just stared in disbelief.

He nodded. "Rare, I know, but still done."

"Wow. I wouldn't have thought—"

"The necessity has saved our hides more than once. Food and water have a way of growing scarce."

My gaze dropped to my mostly empty plate. "Here's hoping we've all learned better."

"That's the spirit." Morty's broad smile returned as he reached for his wallet.

Mom would have been proud, though, at the broccolini and watercress I devoured, to go with everything else. I begged for a box of char siu bao rolls to take back to the room, their steamed doughy insides filled with smoky sweet barbecued pork, just in case we missed dinner later. Morty ordered two boxes. He laughed at my ear-to-ear grin. He threw in a box of lo mein noodles for Brian, so we all walked back to our rooms satisfied and happy.

Mort stored our leftovers in a tiny refrigerator that looked as if it might hold four bottles of water, tops. Then he turned about and gave me a sorrowful look. "There is something Brian and I need to discuss privately."

"Oh. Ooooh." I headed to the door. "I'll just be next door in my room. Or maybe down at the park square for a bit. Fresh air and all that." Not to mention better for phone privacy since the walls here seemed a bit thin.

"Best if you stay here. The threshold is a ward not passed by many."

"Okay, I'll just be out for about fifteen. I don't have many bars here." I waved my phone at them. "Need to check my email and stuff. Reception is a lot better at the corner park. I caught that when Sam drove us in."

"Knock once on the door when you get back. I don't want to have to worry about you."

"I will."

I heard Morty's low tones vibrate through the door even as I closed it.

The little corner park was more of a side yard for a twelve-story condo building down the street, but I inhabited its bench without remorse. Quiet and lushly green, with a squirrel who eyed me closely before twitching its tail and bounding off in disappointment as I pulled my phone out instead of peanuts. No text messages, but I did have mail, and the longest one by far came from Evelyn. I called Mom first.

"How is Washington?"

"Hot but not humid yet. We found something helpful, but have to go up to New York. The guys are sharing a room and I get one to myself. We're in Alexandria."

"Oh." She sounded wistful. "I used to love to go there on long weekends."

"Maybe in the fall."

"Deal. So, what's in New York?"

"Another obelisk. One in Central Park, looks like."

"You'll miss class again."

"A lab, and he's good for make-ups. I'm getting an A, so I should do all right."

"I'm not happy about all of this."

"Mom." I didn't quite know what I could say.

"It could be worse, I suppose."

"Infinitely worse. Morty could be drinking ale."

She laughed. "He's not driving, is he?"

"Nope, we have a driver and a pretty new SUV." I dropped my voice a little. "Morty has one of those black credit cards."

"Wow. Well, just don't take advantage of him."

"We're not. But it's nice to know he can afford the trip. Gotta go. I'm out walking off the Chinese we had for late lunch."

"All right, honey."

Then I phoned Evelyn. Based on her email, I knew texts would be insufficient.

I could hear her enthusiasm tumbling through the sentences and her oh-my-gawds after almost every period. Over coffee, she and Joanna had elaborated on plans and Joanna had pledged two tall and handsome escorts for the bash itself. And bidders. It sounded fun. I answered her with enthusiasm of my own, even though I knew this auction wasn't for me. Tickets, dress, shoes, and guy all seemed beyond me. Next year, I thought, as I disconnected.

The bench grill felt cool against my back as I put my chin up and studied the sky. It was hot today and would be hotter tomorrow, but we'd be further north. A few white cloud wisps skittered across the blue before shredding away to nothingness. A big cloud of starlings rose, near the airport I guessed, and wheeled around like a dark cloud of their own, heading my way. I didn't see the jet that must have sent them winging up, but I could see their tiny dotted bodies grouped in flying formation.

Suddenly, a few dropped. Just fell out of the sky, little black smudges hardly visible from my position, and the cloud of them flew on toward me without hesitation, tiny wings beating smoothly. Then the flock began to disintegrate, falling right and left, little starling bodies skidding about and dropping inexplicably like rocks, hitting the ground somewhere between there and where I sat.

They'd died, right there in the air, while flying.

I thought of the ravens, listening. Of the schools of dead fish, floating. Of a being named Malender that sucked the life force out of things both great and small.

I jumped to my feet and ran to the motel.

CHAPTER TWELVE

I THREW MYSELF upstairs to the landing and at the motel door but the knob wouldn't budge in my hands. I pounded in alarm.

Brian opened the door enough to peer out, and I slammed him back to get in.

"He's coming!"

"Who is coming?" Morty lumbered to his feet, the mattress springing up, freed, as he did.

"That guy. Malender. The one who sucks the life out of fish and birds and for all I know, has the same planned for us."

"What makes you think that?" Brian ran a hand through his hair in distraction.

"The starlings. A whole cloud of them rose up by the airport and began flying this way. And then they began to drop. Just fell out of the sky by the dozens and hundreds. That can't be good, right? They were flying right at me, from miles away."

"Indeed, that is not good." Morty waited a beat, watching my face.

Brian rubbed the thick gold ring about his thumb. "You and I might be considered a little life for the taking."

"Well, he's not getting mine without a fight. This guy has to have weaknesses or he would have taken the world over by now, right? From what Remy told me, he's been hiding out in Europe or Asia."

"Where things have not been exactly cool and calm."

"So he grows on pain and chaos. Nothing new for a villain."
I crossed my arms. "Will the threshold ward hold him?"

"It could. It goes both ways, however, in that he shouldn't be
able to attack us nor should we try to attack him." The professorial voice went silent as Brian fell to pacing the room in
thought.

"Why not?"

"That would violate the ward. If he forces it, we can retaliate
with all that we're capable of, but we can't strike first."

"Wonderful. America was built on sneak guerilla attacks,
you know. It was the only advantage we had against the British." I put a shoulder against the doorjamb and shoved my
hands into my pocket. Steptoe's ammo rolled against my fingertips. "Or I could outflank him." I eyed the door between our
adjoining rooms, locked as it was meant to be but fully unlock-
able if needed. I pointed at it. "Unlock that for me."

Retreating back to my own room, I took a glance from the
landing as the cries of tiny birds pierced the afternoon. My key
card took a minute to activate the electronic lock and then I
was in. The queen bed looked big and fluffy, the rest of the
plastic wood furniture clean and utilitarian as I bypassed them
all to unlock the suite door from my side and went through.

Brian and Morty both stood there waiting and watching. I
pointed behind me. "That's another threshold, right?"

"It should be."

"Should? Don't you guys have a way of testing these things out?"

"We are known to you as friends and allies. The threshold
wouldn't bother us at all if we tried it, not unless you refused us
entry. Then it might or might not, because you're not a magical
entity."

I stared at Brian. "But earlier you said . . ."

"That was our doorway. It's a little different."

I pointed at the adjoining doorway behind me. "Tell me that
one is a little different, too."

"It should be. Perhaps not from our side but yours."

I nibbled on my bottom lip for a moment. "It had better be,"
I told them finally. "You keep the door unlocked. I'll be in my

room, waiting. Let out a yell when he gets here." As the walls were more on the paper-thin side than rock solid, I figured I'd hear him. Brian looked dubious.

I tilted my head back at him. "He is coming, isn't he?"

"It would appear so. If he gives us a chance, we'll sound the alarm." Morty waved me back into my room, and we prepared to wait.

My room didn't have a TV, or at least not a working one. It had a metal hanger that had been twisted arduously into a kind of antenna, but nothing helped the animated scramble focus. I turned it off, opting for silence over the tortured fizz of sound. A coffee pot sat on part of the bathroom counter, and it looked well stocked. I could have coffee, decaf, hot chocolate, and tea, but only one cup of tea unless I reused the bag. I also had a mountain of salt and pepper. For what, I couldn't guess, but there the packets were, stored in with the others. No refrigerator in my room either. I stared at the salt. That might come in useful.

I took some of my many packets and made a line parallel to the metal runner at the door, wondering if books and movies told any truth at all about the evil-fighting powers of plain salt. Paper bits littered the worn-out carpeting. I picked up as much as I could and it still looked like I'd had a ticker tape parade in there.

I glanced out the door and up to the sky, seeing only a ragged thread of birds that had almost reached Old Alexandria. Could Malender be far behind?

I closed my door carefully, lest I worry Brian and Morty next door that I'd gone wandering. One escapee tiptoeing about on the floor was enough. I prepared uneasily to wait.

Patience is not my strong suit. Evelyn, like a cat, can sit and stare at things no one else can see for hours, without blinking her eyes once. Well, maybe once or twice. I can't. I fidget. Twiddle my toes. Play with my pockets. Hum out of tune. See if I can teach myself Morse code by batting my eyelashes. And that's in the first five minutes. If I can manage to sit still, I invariably fall asleep so my brain can at least dream and avoid the tedium.

I can wait and stalk on the hockey field, though, so I knew I had it in me. Somewhere.

I must have fallen asleep when suddenly I heard "Avaunt!" and realized Brian had loosed his perdition stick on something. Steptoe's ammo came willingly into my hand the moment I dipped into my pocket. I had two left and decided they ought to deter the attacker, at least long enough for Morty and Brian to defend themselves.

Opening my room door stealthily, I leaned out and saw—

What I saw has no description. Maybe if the Invisible Man had gone and rolled in crude oil, so that he loomed large and dark, sticky and damp, outline blurred and drooling to the ground, that might be the image. Maybe not. Because when it turned to look at me directly—and yes, it caught me staring—I saw inside the cloud an image of the Perfect Man, a being so incredibly beautiful it made me want to weep and pull him free from the cloud of evil enveloping him. He wore leather and lace and looked like a cavalier from ancient days, with a carved and perfect face and brilliant jade green eyes, an oily darkness bubbling about him. Only, he was the cloud. I think.

Brian's avaunt had torn away a good chunk of the cloaking on his right flank. Even as I watched, it oozed to fill in, and with every drop that rushed downhill from his shoulder to replace the emptiness on his side I thought of a tiny black bird, pesky but innocent, now distorted into shadow. My stomach clenched.

He made movements with his hands as if he could swim out of that dark cloud, his teeth bared in a ferocious grin, his body struggling with—what? I had no way of knowing.

He thrust his head back and yelled, "I must be free!" The cloud around him parted for the faintest of openings and then clapped shut again, and he turned to face me, his handsomeness creased in anger and frustration, brows knotted together, knifelike creases along the sharp planes of his face.

He billowed toward my direction, one hand with fingers curved in claws. I smiled, hauled out a handful of flash-bangs and threw them right at his feet. He howled in a voice both human and inhuman as they exploded. I heard the crackle of the perdition rod even as I spun away and slammed the door between us.

He came after me. I could hear and feel the thrust of weight on the landing as he came to the door and pounded on it, trying the latch, twisting the electronic panel off it and bending the handle. He would get the door open. I knew it and stood, heart pounding, by the inner door on my side, torn between watching Malender come in and bolting to Morty and Brian.

Inky darkness began to slide under the bottom of the door. My threshold didn't hold it—hadn't a chance. Malender was coming after me and there wasn't a thing I could do about it but run. Sweat and fear trickled down my back and dotted my forehead. Even if I ran, I had no guarantee of safety. The other two might make it, they were magical, but I was just me, Tessa Andrews, as mortal as any starling. Like fingers probing the underside of the door panel, the shadow groped over the threshold. I fetched out my last flash-bang, balanced on the ball of my feet, ready to dart through the suite door when—

The salt stopped it.

The cloud halted abruptly, sizzling and evaporating as it touched my line of white crystals. I lunged for the coffee maker with its tray of condiments where a mound of salt packets still sat waiting, grabbed them, and tore through the door between our rooms. Whoever had brought them into the hotel had a real thing about hoarding salt packets, but that was to our advantage.

Both Morty and Brian swung on me as if to attack.

"Whoa!" I threw up a hand in air, clutching little white packets. "Salt. Salt stops him." I ripped up a few and doctored the suite doorway before leaping to the main door and slathering its threshold with as much salt as I could manage. Torn paper dotted the carpet like snowflakes gone crazy. Brian joined me in assaulting the hoard of salt packets. The door had been wrestled open, as evidenced by the busted frame and the loose way it now hung, temporarily no longer under siege, but Malender would return to it. And, if the hissing and sizzling of his cloud was any indicator, he'd be madder than a boiled owl.

"Get away from there! He's already breached it."

"I can tell. But listen." My hands shook, scattering salt everywhere but where it needed to be as I tore the envelopes open. "It stopped him at my door. It injured him. Just like Brian's bolt got him."

"My rod got him?"

"A big gash in his right flank. And my flash-bangs dazzled him and he went after me then." I looked to Brian. "Can you manage another bolt? I think we've got him discouraged."

Morty grunted. "And that's about the best we can hope to do at the moment. He's weakened by the transit and his enemy is not what he thought it would be, so if we can put him into retreat, we might have a few weeks while he recovers to prepare a better offensive." He muscled the door shut as best he could.

My voice squeaked. "Weeks?"

"Sorry, lass, but that's about the best we can do—Look out!"

The door catapulted open, knocking me on my keister. I scrambled backward, propelled by raging fear. Malender loomed in the doorway, the miasma about him boiling and crackling as it tried to flow over the doorway with its hastily laid dam of salt.

He stood out, distinct from that oily fog, and I thought of his shout for freedom but had no more time than that before the attack.

He shouted three words at Brian, none of which I could translate or grasp, leveling a finger at him. Morty roared back, shielding Brian's body with his own as Malender shot a bolt barehanded, hitting the Iron Dwarf hard enough to rock him back on his heels. Brian stepped out from behind Morty with a shout of "Avaunt!" and the rod fired away.

Malender made a noise like a teakettle on high flame, his cloaking shivering and dancing about him as it melted away, leaving him exposed in the flesh. His handsome visage twisted grotesquely as he faced us. He said a single word and disappeared.

I stayed on the floor. Brian went to one knee, and Morty stood like a pile of bricks for a moment before shaking himself. I realized he must have turned to actual stone a moment before

Malender hit him with his best shot. If he'd been hurt, there seemed to be little actual damage.

"Earth magic?"

Morty nodded to me and stretched each and every limb carefully, like a cat. A big, blocky, thuggish-looking cat.

Brian bent over his cane. His hands stroked it briefly and when he spoke, it was in mourning. "It's done for."

"What?" I scooted near and reached for it. "The words are still here."

"Yes, but it's . . . it's emptied. It won't recharge again."

I took it from him as he let it go reluctantly. It did feel incredibly light in my hold, as though it were made of air and not solid wood. "You don't know that," I protested.

His face twisted in a sad smile. "I know it, and even you should be able to feel it."

"It's different. But maybe it just needs a rest. A magical new battery or something." Sort of like Brian himself, who swayed even as he argued with me.

Morty reached down and pulled me to my feet. "It's the way of things, Tessa. Nothing is permanent, not even stone, although it lasts far longer than most mortal things. The professor gathered a good many relics in his day that had been totally spent of their essence."

"But he kept them."

"Indeed, he did. Retired them to a loving home, he often said."

"As if they were people. But it's not mortal, it's magical. Right?" I looked from expression to expression as Brian got unsteadily to his feet, holding onto what was left of the metal door in its frame. "Right?"

They both went silent and I looked down at the object in my hands. Its etching stared back at me.

I refused to give up. Not after outgunning Malender. Not after tearing up a bazillion salt packets with paper cuts and salt stings in my wounded fingers. "We're going to Cleopatra's Needle. We have to. If this cane exists, it still has work to do."

Brian put a hand over mine. "You have a point. It exists, though barely. It has a mission to finish."

"Then so do we, in the morning." Morty went out on the landing. "In the meantime, it looks as if I need to pay for a new room and a new door."

"Umm," I said. "Make that two new doors. Annnnd salt. A lot more salt. A barrel of it!"

CHAPTER THIRTEEN

TRUE TO HIS WORD, Sam showed up bright and early to drive, at just a yawn past dawn in the morning. He did not look happy as I opened the door to the main room. A recent shower matted down his black and gray curly hair, and bags sagged under his brown eyes, which didn't quite want to meet mine, at first.

"Morning, Sam."

He lowered an eyebrow at me, one eye narrowed, his fingers moving about the rim of his driving cap, around and around. "My brother-in-law says there was lots of commotion here yesterday. A lot of trouble."

"And it looks like he called you either very late or very early." Sam nodded.

Morty eased us all out the door, carrying a plastic bag full of leftover trail mix and Coke cans. "Indeed there was, but now your brother-in-law's establishment has two brand-new security doors and a new LED TV in each room."

"You got him TVs, too?"

Morty smiled. "It seemed the least we could do for the inconvenience."

"I didn't see any new TV." He peered over the freshly vacuumed room.

"Because they're being installed tomorrow."

I think I huffed. I know my lower lip stuck out a little as Brian laughed faintly and jostled my elbow.

Sam considered Morty before giving a sharp nod. "All right

then. My brother-in-law can be hard to please, but it sounds as if you gave a good compensation. Come on, before the traffic gets really bad." He pulled his cap into place.

Already warm, the sun gleamed down, threatening to bring on a truly hot day, with all the humidity it could also provide. I wasn't unhappy to be leaving DC under those conditions, although I would have loved to have just strolled about, taking in the various sights. Maybe the zoo with its pandas. All the tiny but very good restaurants where people-watching was better than TV. According to my newly charged phone, as I rarely leave home without a charger, the weather in the city looked to be ten degrees cooler and much more respectable in dampness. As for people-watching, what could beat New York? Go Big Apple! I hopped in the car with anticipation that Malender, at least, would be left behind, and what more could happen?

Brian solemnly gave me custody of his cane as we settled in the back seat. It rested across my knees with scarcely more weight than a handful of leaves. I ran my fingertip over the ornate carvings and the words etched yesterday, still holding a faint blue cast to my eyes. I wondered why I should have seen what happened while they did not. I told myself it was because both of them had been incredibly busy at the time.

Sam evidently decided his time to be silent had passed, and kept up a running spiel as he negotiated the terrible traffic on the various connections. One or the other of us would speak up now and then to respond to something he asked or said, while the other two would relax. Except Morty snored when he was being tranquil, ruining the overall effect. Brian kept lapsing in and out of professor mode so that I never knew who I was talking to there, and I found it easier to keep up conversation with Sam than with the phoenix wizard sitting next to me. Some things were just odder than others. Not to mention that I tended to cringe whenever I saw a winged creature in the airspace about our moving vehicle while Sam regaled me with stories about near-miss collisions in both New York and Boston. The ones about Boston raised the hair on the back of my neck. No wonder their baseball fans were screwy.

Finally Sam seemed to be talked out. He directed his attention to the highway and said, "You might as well nap too. Seems like you all had a busy night."

Morty was already grinding logs and Brian purring softly, so I put my head back and closed my eyes. I'd slept in my own room, with the door between half-open, and the night hadn't been nearly long enough. Somewhere in my dreams I realized that Steptoe hadn't joined us, because I was running around looking for him. I couldn't decide if his absence was a good thing or a bad thing, and when I woke up, I was still undecided.

The traffic noise rose around us. What would New York be without the sound of car congestion and horns blaring? And the people, moving quickly and with determination down the ranks of sidewalks, to and fro, colorful and different, suited and nonconformist, each and every one. Half expecting to see Steptoe's dapper figure in the crowd, I stared out my window at the migration. The electronic billboards dazzled the eye, though not nearly so much as they would at night. Rolled-up windows kept the smell from hitting us, but it would the minute we stepped out at Central Park. We hit town at midmorning and I knew the skyscrapers around us would be full of people. Yet the sidewalks had not even begun to empty, everyone on a different and busy timetable.

"Okay," Sam told us. "We're here and I'm heading to the museum. You can't miss the needle, it's tall. I'm going to let you off at the stop for the museum. I can't wait there—"

"Why not?" Brian asked.

"It's not legal. Don't worry, I won't get caught dropping youse guys off, but I can't wait there. I'll circle about. When you're ready, head back to the museum and I'll see you there. I'll park there if I can, but not bettin' on it."

"It's a tuck and roll."

Sam grinned at me in the rearview mirror. "Not quite, but it would be nice if you all hurried out."

I picked up the cane and my backpack, ready to unlatch the seat belt and take off. Brian got his feet under him as Sam reached out and shook Morty's shoulder. The snoring had stopped, so I knew the big guy had stopped sleeping a while ago, alert under the radar. He shrugged and sat up higher in his seat.

"Everyone ready?" Without waiting for an answer, Sam took a city corner at breakneck speed, pulled out and stopped with a screech, and we flung our doors open. He left us standing at the curb with the same alacrity.

We watched him drive off with a wave.

"I wonder if that was necessary."

"I think New York driving requires a certain authenticity and showmanship," Morty told Brian.

"You mean street cred."

Brian would have groaned if he'd understood the pun. I settled for an eyebrow waggle from Morty. We all turned about to scan the horizon of Central Park and indeed, the stone obelisk could be seen, at least its pointy top, very easily. It looked small from where we stood but I was certain that was a matter of distance and perspective. As I looked at it, I thought of what Morty had told me about stone and promises. I wondered if he was thinking the same as he cleared his throat twice. I knew that he helped us out of loyalty to the professor but also, no doubt, out of hope that the restoration of his friend would bring help to find Goldie, his missing wife. Time seemed of the essence for both people.

"What are we looking for?"

We hit the pathway into the park. It wound back and forth, determined to take people wandering even if they didn't want to. But it was meant to preserve the greenery, so we stuck to it. I shrugged. "I don't know. Another keystone maybe? It's almost too much to hope the cane has the ability to dowse the location again." I carried it lightly in one hand, the weight of it so frail that I didn't even dare lean on it for fear that it would fall into little more than dust. It looked a little like Brian, as if it were becoming transparent and insubstantial. He strode beside me, though, with stronger steps than yesterday, but I had to blame his vigor on caffeine and sugar. Somebody had decimated the pack of cola overnight and seemed to be riding the wave into the daylight.

Central Park is gorgeous. Someone presented a project at

school once about how the older trees are dying out and it needed an aggressive replacement plan, but I couldn't tell as we strolled into the forested area. Pebbles lay across the rough asphalt here and there, followed by scatterings of grass bits and green leaves. We could see the obelisk pointing to the spring sky, fading in and out of sight as we approached it and the trees alternately revealed and then hid it. Because the pathway didn't go straight in, we had a chance to admire Cleopatra's Needle from several views, and although I thought it was striking, most people walked past without a second look. How could they? Here was a bit of ancient Egypt, misplaced though it was, taken apart and transported here, only to be resurrected. It might have been the center of mysterious rites when it stood by the Nile. Heck, maybe even here a hundred years ago.

A couple of midday joggers passed us, as did one screaming-fast messenger bike, taking a shortcut across town, his satchel banging against his side as his legs pumped the bicycle to new speeds. I pulled Brian out of the way, our hair blown to one side from the draft.

Brian murmured something I didn't catch as we centered ourselves on the path again. "New York," I explained.

His head bobbed in the affirmative. Unintelligible remarks made me think of the attack the day before. "What did M shout at you, by the way? Was that Latin or what?"

He stumbled a half step. "I don't recall."

"Maybe you don't, boy wonder, but how about you give the professor a nudge."

He made a quiet humph noise.

"Well?"

"Neither of us caught it."

"Nor," said Morty as he flanked us, "did I."

"It seemed important at the time."

Brian glanced at me. "So did staying alive."

"All I'm pointing out is that he's likely to yell that at us again sometime in the future so it might be helpful to know what kind of doom he's hurling at us. Maybe it could be blocked or nulled?"

"It could. However, it's just as likely he was calling on some ancient god to curse us."

I peered over at Morty. "Seriously? Old and forgotten gods? He has that much mojo?"

"The being in question has tons of mojo when he wishes."

"Again, I'd like to point out that he isn't emperor of Europe or Asia."

"Not that we know of."

"I stand by my assessment."

That brought a short guffaw from Morty. "Be sure to tell him when next we meet. It might put him off his game."

"Or so anger him that none of us will have a chance of surviving," Brian muttered. "He does have an ego."

We rounded a last corner and broke out into the open, taking a moment to stand and admire the structure. Nearby magnolia trees flowered, their branches laden with the early May blossoms, petals fallen brown about the benches. The Needle had been cleaned not too long ago and the hieroglyphs and runes on the whitish stone stood out after being nearly obscured by decades of New York grit and pollution. The obelisk stood nearly seventy feet high, not nearly as impressive as the Washington Monument, but then, it was a few thousand years older, too, and I gave it credit for that. It had been installed on not one but two platforms, which gave it quite a boost before the obelisk itself rose upward, but the ancient majesty reigned, circled by wrought-iron fencing and curving benches. While the Needle impressed me, the cane seemed entirely unaffected by it.

Morty sat down on the long bench. "Well?"

Brian and I looked up at the two stone platforms holding the obelisk, one on top of the other. A bronze crab perched in the crack between them, its weathering not nearly as old, its claws outstretched as if to protect the bases. I couldn't tell whether it had just been sculpted to fit into an odd crack or separation between the bases or if it had been designed to be there intentionally, like some turtle holding the world on its back. Peering at it didn't clarify the structure.

"That's freaky."

"It is, isn't it?" Brian shaded his eyes. "It wasn't stolen, by the way. It was a gift after the building of the Suez Canal, because the U.S. stayed neutral in the canal politics. It took a decade or so to get here, but it eventually made it. "

"Politics."

"Undoubtedly." He reached for the cane and removed it from my tight grip. With a look around to see if anybody watched, he stepped over the protective railing, holding the cane with outstretched arm at its greatest length, and tapped it gently about the bottom of the actual obelisk. Nothing.

Morty leaned back, folding his arms over his barrel chest, looking like he might slip back into tranquility.

I paced the perimeter of the object. Crabapple trees had finished blossoming and their faded flowers littered the ground as they turned into dust of their own. The hieroglyphs looked amazing, and I remembered, when I was little, wanting to be an archaeologist who could read things like that, thanks to reruns of Indiana Jones, Lara Croft, and my mother's own historical bent. I had even learned a few but didn't recognize any now. Except the eye. That seemed rather obvious. I ran into Brian on the other side.

"What do you suppose all this was about?"

"You didn't read up on it last night?"

"Not really. I decided to sleep instead."

"It regales one of the pharaohs, Ramses II. Hails him as the son of the sun and so forth."

"So you did Google it." I peered at his eyes, unable to tell who spoke to me just now. I hated that, frankly, because I wanted to get to know and understand Brian, but it felt odd to be getting close to the professor. I mean, he was not only old enough to be my grandfather, but he was dead. Or supposed to be. Or soon to be. Or maybe this whole reincarnation thing only meant that he would regress and start over. Who knew? A thought occurred.

"Hey. Maybe we're supposed to be at the London one."

"I scattered my things about, but not so far as to be unreachable in a crisis."

"Oh." Disappointed, I stopped in my tracks. That bronze crab. Kind of reminded me of the professor in his finer days. "Give me that." I reached for the cane.

He stretched it back over the railing.

I took it as I climbed over and took the three steps of the first base, getting close enough to put my nose to the stone. "Keep watch." No way did I intend to be arrested in the city for vandalism or whatever it would be called. A huge block of stone stood between the crab and me. I didn't think I could scale it, not without some tools and a fuss. But, if I stood on tippy-toe and stretched the cane up as far as I could . . .

The wood trembled in my hands. Or maybe I was shaking. I knocked on a crab claw tentatively, and said "Avaunt!"

That saying about letting sleeping dogs lie is undoubtedly one of the wisest things ever said in the history of mankind. The crab shot to life, grabbed the cane, jerked it out of my hand and scuttled away to disappear in the crack between the base and obelisk, leaving wood burns that stung like crazy on my palm.

CHAPTER FOURTEEN

BRIAN AND I both let out shocked squeaks, awakening Morty. He threw his head back with a "What? What?" to glare at us.

"It . . . it . . ." I pointed at the Needle. "It ate Brian's cane!" I scrubbed my sore palm carefully, trying to get the sting out.

"It what? What it?"

"There was a bronze crab, a sculpture, where the obelisk came to rest on its base." Brian explained to Morty without taking his eyes off the crevice where the giant beast and his perdition rod had gone from sight. "It tore the cane out of her hold and vanished." Ominous scraping sounds came from inside the shadowy nook.

"I'll find out why she was holding it instead of you later. Is it altogether gone or just hiding inside the stone?"

And could the frail, hollow-seeming cane survive anything that bronze crab might do to it? Like crunching it to bits? Raking noises continued. "The racket suggests it's still there." I swung on Morty, after hopping down the stone steps. "Get it back."

"Don't know if I can."

"This is your element, right?"

"Indeed, however . . ."

"However what?"

"Tessa, there is magic and then there is elemental magic. I can't do what the professor could do, not by a long shot. If I could, they would never have taken my Goldie."

I wanted to heed the sorrow in his eyes, but didn't. "But can't you make it spit the cane out?"

"Maybe." Morty put his hands on his knees and stood. "It might destroy the work altogether." He eyed it. "It spent hundreds of years in the dry Egyptian climate, and a hundred or so here, with rain and cold, wind and snow, eating at it. It was made to survive one but not necessarily the other. They've cleaned it up and tried to seal it against the pollution, but their efforts are not altogether successful. Stone is native to the earth where it is quarried."

"Oh."

Brian said, "Boost me up."

We both faced him.

He made a thumbs-up sign. "Boost me up, I'm getting my cane back."

"If it's not fallen into pixie dust by now. Or splinters. Or whatever old crabby has done to it."

"Just do it!"

I hopped out of Morty's way and let the big guy hoist Brian up onto his shoulder, after he first climbed the narrow steps and positioned himself. The gymnastics put Brian chest high at the crack where the crab sculpture had been, with Morty braced as the base of the human pyramid.

Stretching both arms out, Brian called for his cane. At least, I think that's what he did. As usual, I didn't know the language but I could feel the emotion behind it, and it had to have been the professor speaking. *Let it go. Give me what is mine, as I respect and need it, and it needs me.* The words died away, like a forgotten echo, and we all waited in silence. Faraway, the whoosh of traffic on streets could be heard, along with the occasional blaring horn. Closer, voices and footfalls as people walked, jogged, and pushed prams along the inner pathways. Even closer, the squawk of a bird or two and the answer of an outraged squirrel.

And then I heard it, the faintest of clicks, a whisper of stone on stone, as if the sculpture had suddenly become a shy creature and moved to peek out at us cautiously. If crustaceans could peek. Who knew? I didn't think they ate wooden canes either, and look what happened. I held my breath so that I could listen better.

Another furtive series of noises.

Brian repeated what he'd said before and put his right hand out authoritatively. The gold ring found at the Washington Monument glimmered at the base of his right thumb. I bit my lip, seeing in my mind's eyes the crab seizing his hand and making off with it, attached or not, sending an ewww of a thought.

I was at risk of turning purple from lack of air when the sculpture bolted out of the crevice and thrust the cane into Brian's hand before returning to its original position and freezing back into carved immortality. Brian hopped down from Morty's shoulder, and we all jumped the railings and tried to look innocent while I took several long breaths.

I watched as Brian turned the cane about in his hands. He handled it as though some weight had come back to it, and the burnished wood gleamed as it used to. It appeared to have gone through a rejuvenation of its own. He looked the length up and down, running his hands over the carved shaft, missing entirely what had happened to the curved handle.

I pointed. "What's that?"

"That?" He looked where I pointed. "Oh . . . ahhhhh." And a big smile spread across his face. "That is a gazing stone. Small but extremely powerful." He moved the cane upright and cradled the handle, rubbing his thumb over the crystal marble. "Once mine and now returned."

More than marble-sized, but far smaller than a traditional crystal ball, it winked in the bright sunlight, and Morty made a noise of satisfaction deep in his throat.

"Now that," he told us, "is a quality piece."

It looked as if it had always been embedded in the handle, but we all knew better, or at least I knew it hadn't been there the last week or so. Brian rubbed it again, and a glint of starry fire seemed to rise from it. A faint, chiming hum sounded, rather like the noise from a crystal wineglass.

"This," he said, "should make a great deal of difference."

"Well now. Ain't that just a bit of all right." A dapper figure unfolded himself from under a nearby crabapple tree, dusted off, and came to join us. "Progress. Soon the old chap will be himself again, instead of here an' there."

Steptoe shaded me.

"Speaking of which, how did you get here?"

Steptoe picked a bit of twig off his sleeve, ignoring Morty's belligerence. "Same way as you lot did. Sam drove me up last night and dropped me off to wait because it didn't seem as I'd get a proper invite, otherwise. Sam's a good man, 'e is, although I doubt 'e has many years left for chauffeuring after dark."

No wonder Sam's eyes had gone so baggy. He'd spent most of the night driving. I told myself he'd done it for the money, but I wouldn't have put it by Steptoe to have possibly threatened a bit. Or maybe the pay was honey enough to leave the family at home and drive all night, grab a few hours of sleep and do it all over again. I understood what it was to have a pile of bills on the kitchen table and not enough to pay them all off. I wouldn't blame Sam at all.

I edged over a bit, just in case someone thought of charging at someone else and causing harm in one way or another. I really didn't know what to expect from anyone anymore, but caution seemed to be the word of the day.

Steptoe eyed the cane. "Well done. Did you know it was there?"

"No."

Steptoe paused just a moment in case Brian wished to add anything, and then flashed a grin at me as it became obvious that Brian would not. "Did the pebbles help any, ducks?"

"Tremendously, thank you."

"Good. I've prepared a few more, but we'd have to arrange a trade."

I looked into his smiling face. "We're not giving you the cane or the crystal or the cane with the crystal."

"Course not! Wouldn't think of asking for it. There might be a little bit of something, help or whatnot, I could ask for though."

He had already helped us by finding a decent shuttle vehicle and Sam, although I could almost point out that it was in his self-interest too, but I could sense a debt there. I started to ask what he wanted when Morty thrust his arm across the front of me. I stopped talking in surprise.

"Make no deals."

"I wasn't. I just wanted to know what he had in mind."

"Bad bargains have come from few words. Our folk are tricksy, and sometimes have less than honorable intentions." Morty took a step closer and I, for one, couldn't miss it as his right hand curled into a fist.

Steptoe put his hand over his heart. "I 'ave been nothing but helpful. Haven't I? Like we was proper mates." He turned to me.

"When dealing one on one with me, yes, but I've overheard conversations with you and your minions that weren't so nice."

His hand over his heart doubled up as if reflecting an inner pain. "Now that 'urts, it does. I thought I explained all that."

"You never explained why the three of you thought you had to break in on the professor in the first place."

"Ah. That." He fell silent for a long moment, closing his eyes. Thinking, was he? When he opened them, however, he merely said, "Saw my minions, did you?"

"I did. I even saw your shit fit when you disintegrated one of them."

"Now, love, that wasn't a disintegration. Unpleasant yes, but the man deserved to be tweaked, didn't he, for not following orders and for being so damnably stupid about things. I sent him to limbo for a little rest." Steptoe interrupted himself with a shiver. "Much less unpleasant and permanent than punishments doled out by others. Definitely not permanent."

"Nice pivot. I still need an answer as to why you broke in on the professor."

"Needed his 'elp, didn't we? He wouldn't give it, and I thought that might be the case, so I sent my lads in with an order to be a bit forceful about getting what we needed. The professor panicked, unfortunately, and that's when my last order, to get his 'ead if he went up in smoke, should have been followed. I know I told you 'bout that, that someone could revive 'im all nice and proper even if all we 'ad was his head. But we didn't get it, and he panicked. It wasn't taken, so now we're all 'ere in this little dust-up."

"Self-protection!" Brian burst out, before clenching his jaw shut.

"Aye, it was, you thought, but need not 'ave been if you'd just listened to my lads before assuming the worst of their intentions. Now you have t'start all over again and construct your old rites, and nothing I can do but watch." Steptoe dropped his hand from his heart. "I know I ain't always been on the right side of matters, but we went in with the best of hopes, but 'e wouldn't listen. Prejudged and all that. I am on your side. Truly."

Morty snorted. I stood, pondering what someone it was who could have revived the professor from just his head and if we'd have to resort to finding them, after all, when Steptoe interrupted my thoughts.

"Now see? That's what I mean. Prejudged."

Our Iron Dwarf stomped a foot. "Judged based on past actions, and rightfully so."

"It's not wrong t' say we've been opposites before and likely will be again, but not now. Now we're all in the boat together, it's full of leaks and we're all likely to sink lessen we help one another."

"So we can just trust you now? And in what way would we have to be knowing that?" Morty ended with a harrumph of dissatisfaction.

"Because I'm 'ere, in broad daylight, and not skulkin' about in the shadows." Steptoe straightened his coat jacket. "I have my values, you know."

"Crooked though they might be." Brian straightened his shoulders. "I remember an alliance or two as well as a betrayal and more."

"Oh, now your brain is wakin' up," Steptoe said dryly.

"You should be pleased. If I were more awake, you'd probably be even less trusted. I tend to agree with my companion Mortimer, for he has been by my side through hard and lean times, and that I do remember."

"Something you cannot claim." Mortimer looked down his nose at his target, difficult to do at his height, but he managed. "You cannot bandy loyalty about."

"Oh?" Steptoe raised an eyebrow at him, before adding

smoothly, "I might have an idea where your wife is and who took her and why, but no one wants to ask me."

"Don't you be dragging Goldie into this!"

Brian glided swiftly in between them, and Morty shouted over his shoulder.

I waited for the fuss to die down a bit before asking, "Do you really?"

"I said I might. I'd 'ave to ask around about, 'ere and there, but it's not beyond the realm of imagination. I could find out."

"That's a favor I won't be making a bargain with you for!"

Steptoe shrugged at Mortimer. "Suit yourself. Not like he's going to be any help for a while," and nodded to Brian. "Not that I want to be dragged into this, but did you ever think she might have gone over, that she was never taken at all?"

Morty exploded, and I don't know how Brian held him back as the two of them scuffled but Brian did, or maybe the new crystal in the cane had an effect because it blazed white-hot when Brian threw his arms up to stop Morty in his tracks. Steptoe danced a quick two paces back.

Whatever it was, it worked, a little, although Morty's shoulders went tense and stayed that way. He made noises like an old train's steam engine while his ears blazed red, and I made a note to myself to stay out of his way if he ever got this angry again.

"Don't. Ever. Mention. My. Wife. Again."

Steptoe put his hands up in the air. "I'm not givin' away any secrets here, Master Broadstone. She comes from a tribe born on the dark side of the street, more oft than not, and 'er family, the sisters in particular, were none of them too 'appy when she took up with the likes of marrying you. That's to her credit, of course, choosing to follow a lighter side, but who knows? She might have regretted that decision later, and now that I've said my piece on that, I'll keep my tongue as you wish," he ended up, even as Morty shrugged one last mighty time against whatever hold Brian had on him.

"Now I sense that whatever 'elp I might have asked from any of you 'as up and gone. My fault, I know, but some words just need to be said."

"I'm still listening." Three heads turned to look at me. "Well, I am. I don't seem to have the same kind of baggage you guys have." I shrugged. Just a missing, presumed-dead father with gambling problems, not magic and alliances gone awry. Not that it wasn't fascinating trying to listen and try to read all that seemed to be going on between the lines, but if I had thought my reality was freaky, all I had to do was step into theirs. "I still don't know what it was you wanted from the professor in the first place."

"The library," said Steptoe. "I need a book from the professor's precious library." He wouldn't meet my eyes, so I wondered if there had been something more.

"Which you got burned. The entire house went up in flames," I reminded him.

He shook his head. "Not that room. Warded, it was, and inspectors have it taped off, but it stands, a little bit worse for smoke and some water, but the library stands. I can't get into it though, with the inspectors poking around and the professor not about to give permission."

"Does it stand? Really?" Brian's voice broke. I remembered vaguely that Carter had told me that. Events had chased it from my thoughts.

"It does, and all I'm askin' is a bit of wisdom from one o' the professor's valuable books. Not the whole book, mind you. Just a look-see at its precious pages. Won't touch the book, won't keep it, just a read."

That almost sounded innocent unless I remembered that his cohorts were willing to beat the permission out of Brandard in the first place. Still, it seemed doable, depending on the book and if the professor, once restored, would allow it. I traded looks with Brian. He gave a diffident twitch of his head.

"All right," I told him. "I'll do my best to get you an entrance into the library and a look at a specific book, if I get permission from the professor and authorities to do so."

"Best deal I've 'eard all day. Done." And Steptoe put his hand out for a shake.

We touched and I could feel a tingle across my palm, a little shocking and definitely surprising, and from the quick expression on Steptoe's swarthy face, he had been caught unaware, too. We dropped hands quickly.

"Now." He fished out ten or so of those explosive pebbles and dropped them into my palm. "Just a tad more powerful than the last batch, seeing as you might need them."

"Th—"

"Don't ever," Morty cut me off and stated, "thank one of us."

"Why ever not?"

"It leads to more complications."

"Ooohkay. That's very kind of you," I substituted.

"Better." Morty tugged his vest and shirt back into place, like a cat smoothing down his fur after a troubling patch, plaid coat wrinkling over massive shoulders, and motioned toward the street beyond. "We'd better head back."

"You're all done here?"

Brian hung back in doubt. "You think we're not?"

Steptoe drew his lips together and made a little face. "I grant that little bauble does light up the day, but . . ."

"It's not nearly all that's needed." Brian let out a sigh. "Keep a watch," and before any of us could say, "Don't do it!" he was back over the railing and up the steps to the block on top of it and this time, without a boost from Morty, he hitched himself up until he was nose to nose with the bronze crab again. Holding on by one elbow, he tossed the cane to me and then swept the crevice about the sculpture with his free hand. The only thing that came scuttling to life this time was an impressive orange and red autumn leaf, which had evidently been imprisoned between the stones since last fall. It had held onto its temporary glory, keeping its colors and suppleness despite the fact that its many peers had browned and gone to dust long ago. He let it drop and it wafted to the ground near my shoes, so I picked it up and pocketed it, Steptoe watching every movement. He smiled as I finished and began walking off to the street.

He called to Brian, "Wot now, professor?"

Brian jumped down and cast a look to the sky in thought. Then a slow smile came across his face. "I feel like a smoke."

"What?"

He dipped his head to the rest of us. "Quite. A bit of fine

tobacco while we're in the city, and I know just the place, on Broadway, not far from Columbia. A little cigar boutique. It may have lost some of its cachet now that we can trade with Cuba again, but it should still be doing business."

"Smoking?"

"Indeed."

It seemed to me like a little bit of power had gone to Brian's head, but he had a point. While we were in the city, now would be the time to visit a tobacconist. We headed toward the edge of the park, the ribbon of the street coming into view when they hit us, out of the sky, like a tornado.

Because I was in the front, I caught the brunt of the ambush, feeling a whoosh of foul-smelling air before a heavy object crashed into me, knocking me off my feet and into the brush, as a screeching tore the calm out of the afternoon and set my ears to bleeding. Senses reeling, it was the only thing I realized as I clapped my hands to my head and brought them away dribbling with blood.

CHAPTER FIFTEEN

THEY CAME SWOOPING in on big, angry gray wings that looked as though they rode on a storm, which caught us up and enveloped us. Strong winged women in full voice, their screeching battle cries clawing at my senses, as devastating as the clubs and blunt swords they swung, whirled about us. I rolled on the ground, recoiling out of their way, unable to even count how many of them came after us. A stench rolled in ahead of them, nasty and stinging to my nose, and my eyes ran with tears in response. Steptoe knelt beside me, shrugged off his dapper jacket and began to stretch it in his hands, pulling and expanding it, larger and larger, until at parachute size, he dropped it over both of us and we huddled under it. He gave me a wink as he tucked it into place. The sound dimmed, and that awful smell faded.

He put a finger to his lips and I nodded. An invisibility cloak of sorts, but we'd break the illusion if we spoke and gave our position away. He handed me a clean handkerchief, and I wiped off the trickles of blood from my eardrums and sent a prayer for good hearing. I tucked the kerchief away in a free pocket just in case, not too eager to give Steptoe a sample of my blood or DNA. I looked through the thin weave of the fabric, a smoky yet nearly transparent window, and watched the battle overhead.

The harpies circled about once, twice, searching, as Brian shouted words of power that sent a jolt of command through me, though they hurt the bird women far more. With high, eerie cries two dropped from the sky, bouncing to the ground, their wings disappearing, as they became nothing more than tall warriors with fierce scowls contorting their faces. Morty shoved them away from Brian as the cane swung in Brian's hands, trailing sparks of silvery-white all about.

The screeching and cackles grew louder. I got to my knees, ready to run if any of them blundered into us and we were found. One of the blunt swords slid across the ground as Morty pulled another woman out of the sky, and the weapon skidded until it stopped, protruding into our shelter. I reached out and quickly pulled it all the way in with us, and wrapped my hand about the handle, feeling a little better instantly. I was not a sword fighter but I knew what to do with a stick! I edged to the bottom of our cover, praying that Morty and Brian could handle it. The downed women flanked Brian and, as one, delivered leaping attacks, feet first, aimed at his head for the takedown.

Morty batted one out of the air and Brian's crystal flared wildly. The second leaper screamed out, twisting in midleap, falling prone to the ground and flailing in pain. I thought I saw a lick of white fire race along her body before she went still, burying her face in her arms with a sob.

That left four still in the air, as two broke off, lunging downward at their sisters, grabbing them about their thickly padded shoulders and bearing them off, back into the swirl of storm clouds that hung about all of us. I crept about, hunched over, counting those four diving about us, and the two standing on their feet.

Regardless of the cloud cover, the sounds of the battle could be heard. Someone had to be on their way, some civilian had to have called 911 after hearing the din of cries and battle yells, as Brian's voice grew hoarse and the howling shriller. Strange things happening in the city might not be all that strange, but an attack would bring help. Surely.

Knowing it hadn't arrived yet, I began to straighten, my hand tightening, white-knuckled, about the crude sword. It hadn't been made for slicing, but for bludgeoning. For bone-cracking hits. For head-numbing thumps. For ankle-snapping thwacks. I decided I was up for it and reached a hand to twitch aside our camouflaging cloak. Steptoe lashed out and caught me before I could. He shook his head violently.

"Coward!" I spat lowly.

He shook his head again.

"Flash bangs."

"They'd laugh at you." He lowered his whispery voice even more. "They'll take this too, ducks, if we reveal it." And he held tightly to my arm as if our lives depended on it. He pointed outward with his other hand.

I turned on one foot to see the four winged women circling in close about Brian, he standing with his arms akimbo, moving with them, alert but surrounded. The trail of snowflake-like sparks looked to be sputtering out, although the gazing crystal stayed alight. He wouldn't be able to hold them off much longer, and the attackers, as if sensing his weakening, swung lower and closer. What was Morty waiting for?

This, it seemed. With the back of his hand, he lashed about, and caught Brian on the side of the head. Brian grunted in pain and I tried to bolt out of our hiding spot but Steptoe still had his hand firmly holding me back. Brian dropped and one of the harpies dove down to seize his cane. She pulled and tugged and let out a scream worthy of a banshee but he held tight. A second harpy darted at him to pick him up by the ankles and the two played tightrope with him in midair. I twisted away from Steptoe and burst out of our cover, swinging my stick as Morty just stood and watched.

They flew out of my reach, now cackling with amusement and victory, the other two bird sisters getting a firmer hold on Brian. They carried him off as I flung their sword at them. Like a spear, it arrowed right at the last one only to thunk ineffectively off her leather corset, and they vanished into the storm.

I flung myself at Morty, fists knotted and landing but I might as well have been pelting a brick wall. "What did you do? What?"

He held me aside, his brow knotted tightly, his attention searching the skies as they cleared and went silent. "It seemed best to give them what they wanted, for now."

Steptoe emerged from hiding, his hands winding and winding the parachute-like blanket about, squeezing it down into the semblance of the old, dapper suit coat again. He tilted his head at Morty.

"Waiting, are you? Why? You made a deal but they're not meeting their part of the bargain, are they?"

I looked to Steptoe. "What kind of deal?"

Steptoe beckoned. "He's expectin' his wife back."

"Shut up."

"Don't 'ave to. You've betrayed us all. Given up the wizard and you've nothing. And you were telling th' miss here to be careful about the assurances she made! What about you? What 'ave you got now? Nothin', that's what."

Morty slashed his hand through the air and came about at Steptoe with a growl. Instead of mowing us over, he plowed to a halt, lifted his chin and let out a shout, in a voice that sounded of the earth itself, an avalanche of heavy boulders and stones grinding into each other as they slid into nothingness and the last notes disappeared into silence. Big, heavy tears ran down his cheeks. He put his hands to his face as he went down on his knees.

"She's not coming."

"Don't look like it, guv."

"I've done it, haven't I?"

"You've betrayed all of us," Steptoe said flatly. He shrugged into his suit coat and fidgeted until it fit him perfectly once more.

"What do we do now? We have to get him back."

Morty stayed silent. Sort of. I think I could detect a slight moan of grief.

"Might be time to get that smoke, after all."

I managed to close my mouth enough so I could ask, "Why?"

"Because it's likely that's where the biddies took him. So it seems. Since the professor seemed right intent on going there, and if they're lookin' for the same sort o' stuff we are."

"Are we taking him?"

The two of us considered Morty.

"Can't very well just leave 'im here, can we? He knows too much." Steptoe reached down to ratchet Morty up onto his feet.

"Oh." That did make sense, as I stepped onto the curb and looked for Sam and his shuttle.

And that's how the police found us on the edge of Central Park.

New York's finest seemed an efficient lot. I mostly kept my mouth shut because there wasn't anything I could say that 1) they would believe or 2) would get me out of trouble in any way. I was rather hoping, as the squad cars pulled up and the uniforms began to mill around, that it might be possible to get lost in the shuffle. They were asking questions and containing the scene, as police in uniforms do no matter where you are. Despite our troubles in Richmond, I kept a healthy respect for the police because that seemed the wisest course of action. We'd never been arrested, Mom and I, although we'd been in the station a few times to give statements, and then follow-up statements to our statements. That brought me back to what Carter had let drop at the train station, which kept me in frowning silence and busy, busy thoughts.

Then the fourth car rolled up, the doors opened, and out stepped our tall Virginia policeman as if summoned.

Luckily, he looked as surprised as I felt.

He wasn't alone, of course. He did do a double take and seemed to count noses. He said something to the head guy who climbed out of the front seat, and then pointed himself in my direction.

The uniformed cop stepped aside as we both said, nearly in unison, "What are you doing here?"

"I," I told Carter, "am evidently getting into trouble. You?"

"I'm up here starting two weeks of training ride-alongs, a liaison thing. That's why I came through DC yesterday. And what kind of trouble?"

I didn't intend on incriminating myself. I looked about. "Maybe disturbing the peace? Not quite sure."

The cop said helpfully, "We had calls about women screaming

and some sort of fight. No witnesses to the actual scuffle, but a lot of people heard the noise."

Carter looked me over, from toe to the top of my head. "You don't look any the worse for wear. Were you the one screaming?"

"No, sir. There were some ladies on the footpath back there," I jerked a thumb behind us, "had some words with each other about boyfriends and the like. You know the kind of catfight that can be. We booked soon as we heard them."

"Mmmm." He scanned my face closely again before looking to the other two. "Where's the other one?"

"Brian? We, ah, left him at a Starbucks. He didn't seem interested in Central Park. Now we just have to remember which one. Place is full of them."

"And these two were just here with you? I thought you were taking Brian sightseeing, and the Brit didn't seem part of the group." He took my elbow to steer me aside from everyone, as Morty and Steptoe told more or less the same story they had just heard me telling, and pitched his voice quietly. "Tessa, I think you're in over your head in something you know nothing about."

"Again?" I tried a shaky smile. "Does Mom know?"

"It's not funny. Now these gentlemen," and he gestured toward the New York troops, "probably won't book you or anything, but I know something else happened here."

I tried an innocent look. "You do?"

He wiped the ball of his thumb over my cheekbone and then showed me the faint smear of blood. "I do." Carter cleared his throat. "So. Anyone get hurt?"

"Um. Not on our side that I know about."

"Good. I can't begin to explain it to you, but you need to go home, and stay away from these . . . friends."

It felt, in a contrary way, really nice to be under his inspection. "And why would you care? You're not even here on official duty."

Carter shifted weight uneasily. "You're already under scrutiny. I mean, they're looking at you and your mom—"

"I know what scrutiny means."

He flushed a little. "There are things you don't know about that you could be getting mixed up in."

He seemed awfully earnest, did my tall and good-looking Carter Phillips. Awfully earnest and very conveniently turning up wherever I might be. An answer popped into my head, one I considered carefully and decided it might explain a few things. I paused a moment and then said, even quieter than we had been talking, "You mean magic?"

He jumped as if I had lit a fire under his feet.

I reacted. "Ohh. You're busted."

"Keep your voice down!"

"If we talk any quieter, only the dogs will be able to hear us." I waggled my eyebrows at him. "I've been wondering how you manage to keep an eye on me. It's almost, you know, supernatural."

"Cut that out."

"Because the rest of these guys aren't in on it." I waved my hand about at the uniforms and the few detectives that surrounded us, most of them talking with or listening to Morty and Steptoe. One of them enterprisingly asked Steptoe for his passport and got it, making notes before handing it back.

"No, they're not. And you shouldn't be either."

"It looks like we're both beyond common sense then." I folded my arms. "So what happened to you?"

He lifted a hand and rubbed the tiny bump that accented the bridge of his nose. "It's on a need to know basis."

"Sorry, but I think I need to know." I twisted on one heel, facing about, and cleared my throat to raise my voice.

"Don't!"

He was kind of fun to tease, but I didn't. "Show me yours and I'll show you mine."

"And don't be talking like that, either." Carter grumped at me. He took out a pen and notebook from an inside coat pocket and pretended to take notes. "There were strange things that happened when I was overseas."

Steptoe did a dance step and waved as if trying to get my attention, but I focused on Carter instead and gawked for a second. "Don't tell me you found a genie in a bottle?"

"For god's sake." He lowered his notebook. "Can we have this conversation somewhere else?"

"Nope."

"Not exactly," he answered me slowly. "But things exist that few people are aware of, and they influenced me. Saved my life, actually, and helped me save others. It leaves you with a sense of . . . well, kind of a sense of awe, and one of awareness." He looked into my eyes. "And I can tell you that you have this otherness all over you."

"Like a good perfume?"

Carter cocked his head in exasperation.

"You're just too straight for your own good."

Steptoe waved at me hastily, but secretly. I grinned at him, and then another intuition struck me. "Oh, no. Don't tell me. You're in the Society. That or you're a Fed."

This time he didn't jump but he fumbled his pen and it went flying over our heads and clattered onto the sidewalk. One of the cops scrambled to go get it and return it to Carter. The crooked cleft in his face had gone dead white.

"That sort of information can get you in a lot of trouble," he hissed and slammed his notebook and pen back in his suit pocket. I thought I heard fabric rip.

I pushed some more. "That would be a yes. Do you know Remy?"

"Not here and not now."

"Oh-kay. I'd set up a meeting place but you seem to know how to find me whenever you want, so I'll just move along with these two and you can catch up." I squeezed his wrist and walked around him. I raised my voice to normal. "Everything all clear?"

Voices murmured back at me but I didn't hear anything to the contrary, so I herded Morty and Steptoe along the street, then headed back to our shuttle in the museum lot where Sam sat, waiting for us. Carter didn't follow but I could feel his stare on my back the whole way.

Sam waited till we all snapped our belts into place. "Where is the young man?"

"Buying cigars. Would you happen to know a good shop on Broadway, not far from Columbia?"

Sam thought. "Two or three small boutiques," he said, before jamming the vehicle into gear, seemingly knowing exactly where to go.

But would we get there in time to save Brian?

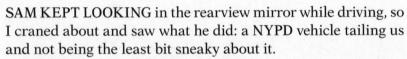

CHAPTER SIXTEEN

SAM KEPT LOOKING in the rearview mirror while driving, so I craned about and saw what he did: a NYPD vehicle tailing us and not being the least bit sneaky about it.

"It's okay, Sam, they're just keeping an eye on us, not you. One of the guys is from my hometown. He's trying to look out for me."

Sam's shoulders relaxed a bit and he stopped looking in the mirror every three seconds. Carter's deciding he should follow us would definitely cramp our style. Not that we really had one; we hadn't been a team long enough to plot our moves. Morty and Steptoe would be the muscle and I guessed I could be the coaxer, but we couldn't really pull off the good cop/bad cop routine. I slumped down in the back seat and pulled out my phone. Evelyn had texted me a couple of times already during lunch, which reminded my stomach that there hadn't *been* a lunch break, to my sorrow. I knew we'd forgotten something!

Evelyn sent snaps of a few dresses and asked for reviews, so I lost myself in auction fantasies for a few long minutes while we wove through New York traffic. I let her know what I thought was trending and what color would be the one for her and if she should show any leg or not—Evelyn had great legs, although I couldn't say if she inherited them from her mother or her father. Her father worked as a prominent local businessman and was just starting to get into Richmond politics, so I didn't have any memories of him wearing shorts around in the summer; he always seemed to be in business casual. Her mother swore in her quaint southern way about fair skin that burned at the slightest hint of sun, prone to freckles and wrinkles as well, so I didn't even know if she actually had legs, since hers were always covered.

Evelyn prodded at me to go dress hunting with her and it hit me that, with the things that had been happening lately, I wasn't at all sure what today would bring, let alone tomorrow. I made a vague appointment for two nights from now and hoped I could meet it. I shook my melancholy off. As Carter had pointed out, I seemed to be in over my head, and it was time to start treading water. Morty, Steptoe, and even Brian could take care of themselves. I needed to take care of me. As everyone tells you, this is the age of information, digital or not, and no one seemed inclined to tell me anything, so I decided to be proactive. I did a few searches for background on a good tobacco shop, found some interesting ideas as to what the professor might have been up to there, and then closed my browser.

I dropped the phone to my lap. And what was that all about, Carter being in the Society? It's not like I could Google them to find any information. Had he sought them out after encountering the weirdness he described in the Middle East, or had they come and found him after he returned home? Just how would that work? How would they know that he'd been exposed, for lack of better words, to magic? That he had been influenced and had an inkling of ability or whatever one needed to stay in the magic business? I bet that an invite hadn't come delivered by owl to a cupboard under the staircase, but it had come from someplace, and I felt an itch of envy with absolutely no idea how to scratch it. Until it occurred to me that, if magic carried a discernible trace, the Society might well come hunting me, not that Remy and Carter weren't already on my heels. I wondered if there was something there I could use to my advantage. I had no intention of letting it disadvantage me anymore.

Sam muttered something under his breath, and then repeated it, louder. "We're almost there."

I shoved my phone back into my backpack. Traffic moved along at a slow crawl, not much faster than I could walk. Chain stores stretched alongside small boutiques when a sign caught my attention: Fine Tobacco. Window art advertised cigarettes, pipes, cigars, leaf tobacco, and a big sign read: NO VAPING.

I pointed. "That's probably it."

"One of them, yes, yes. I can pull over, you all jump out and I will try to find parking around the corner. There are two more in the next block, but this is the oldest establishment."

Morty roused himself to say a few words. "Finding a garage?"

"Maybe," Sam answered evasively. "I have my secrets," he added, as if a little ashamed of himself for sounding short with us.

"You're fine," I soothed him. Imagine me, keeping the peace. "Okay, everyone get ready for a tuck and roll." I unsnapped my seat belt and prepared to run to the curb, snugging my backpack over my shoulder, determined not to leave it behind in the shuttle this time. There were things in it that I needed, especially if I got arrested.

He slid to a halt, narrowly missing a car pulling in at the same time, as if the two intended an epic battle for the one, undersized parking spot, and our doors flew open as we ejected ourselves.

"I'll call," I told Sam, and we regrouped on the sidewalk near the shop's front door.

New York runs at its own pace, generally quick and determined, and few things irritate a New Yorker more than unnecessarily blocking the sidewalk. I pulled Steptoe to the shop wall with me and left Morty on his own, knowing that anyone running into him would think they'd hit the building itself. Two or three pedestrians staggered away in just that illusion while I perused the front of the store, trying to decide what Brian had wanted with the place (maybe the professor did want a celebratory cigar) or if it was part of the treasure hunt. If it was, how would anyone hide anything in there?

Gleaming counters showed through the window, with the entire back half of the shop a glass-enclosed room, with shelves and drawers full of cigar boxes and other objects. Definitely looked like storage to me. "Is that what I think it is?"

Steptoe sniffed and straightened his coat for about the hundredth time since I'd met him. I decided it must be a nervous quirk, or maybe the invisibility cloak it morphed into had security needs or just fit awkwardly after having been all stretched out. "Humidors," he offered, seeing what I watched through the store windows. "An' storage drawers."

"Cigar containers?"

"Mostly. Looks like he maintains quite a few private collections here. There are cigar boxes, of course, which you can see, but he's also got custom humidors, quite pricey and unique. The room itself is temperature and humidity controlled. Cigars can dry out or they can even mold, so a true collector is concerned about keeping them prime."

"In addition to the stink? Ew."

"Now then, ducks, a good cigar or pipe is a grand thing."

"I'll take your word on that one. Thank god they don't allow vaping in there. I can only take so much patchouli or tutti frutti."

He shuddered in agreement. "Have you a plan?"

"Private collections? Sounds like we should see if he's keeping anything stored for the professor. It doesn't look like the others have been here yet."

Morty grunted. "They would have to beat it out of him first. We may just be half a step ahead of them, with no time to waste." He ran a hand through his silvery hair in worry and finished off by pulling on his goatee.

I glanced at Morty. "It's not a waste to wait and see if we can rescue Brian. But you are right—we want to get to whatever it is, first." I took a deep breath. "Okay, let's go."

A small shop, a narrow doorway, so we entered single file, and Morty balked. He looked over the area, eyes calculating, and I breathed a sigh of relief when Morty finally fit through it, but not before he turned sideways. Might have had a future as a ballerina, he tiptoed through so delicately.

The shopkeeper wore the turban of an adult Sikh and looked past me to the two gentlemen with a pleasant smile. His attention returned when I spoke up. "My grandfather asked me to get something from his storage while I was in town. I'm pretty sure I have the right shop, he described it as very well kept and professional."

"And who might the esteemed gentleman be?" The man had a deep, rich voice, accented with ancestry.

"Professor, well, he's a Doctor, actually, Brandard, of Richmond, Virginia."

"Ah yes. He's been with us a number of years. How is he?"

"A little under the weather, which is why he didn't come into the city with us. The train trip was a bit much for him at the moment."

The proprietor smiled, his teeth brilliant against the darkness of his skin. His hand slipped under the edge of the counter. "His is on the left, box 122, miss, and the door is unlocked. Please be kind enough to close the door after you. It's a bit chilly in there but you will be quite all right. Gentlemen, may I assist you with anything else while Miss Brandard is assessing the professor's collection?"

I didn't stay to hear. The ingenuity of the place struck me. Secure but nothing under actual lock and key with passwords and such to access. The door opened with a wave of cool air aromatic with a number of different smells, all exotic and familiar at the same time, and I looked around at a myriad of cigar boxes, most of them custom made from wood, some decorated with initials or gilt or even artwork. The canted shelves also held what looked to be funerary urns, but I decided those must be the humidors Steptoe had referred to, as this was no place to keep your family ashes. Bending over, I spotted the tiny and elegant tags that took me quickly to 122.

The wooden box looked plain indeed compared to the others, quiet and unassuming, but the wood gleamed with a handsome grain and color, and the little latch on it looked to be 18-karat gold and exquisite. I thumbed it open, feeling a frisson of energy go over my hand and down the back of my neck, wondering if I'd set off a protection spell or some such. I paused with my hand on the lock, trying to decide whether I should chance opening it or not. "Professor, this is for your own good," I whispered, and opened the wooden lid slowly.

A piece of vellum greeted me. Yellowed at the edges, crisp with the air temperature and humidity, it held both age and . . . nothingness. Blank. Waiting to be written upon, as pages were meant to be, and nothing there. I looked at it. Then I noticed that, like a box of chocolates, this box had a second layer. Maybe even a third one, like a secret drawer. I lifted out the tray carefully and found a few cigars waiting on the second layer, but they were arrayed in a symbol. Or, at least it looked like a symbol to me. A magical symbol? A word? A warning? Or information we needed to have? I stood there, stumped, and then thought, "D'oh, take a picture," so I fished my phone out and snapped the shot.

That drawer looked to be removable as well, so I lifted it out extremely carefully, trying not to rattle or displace its contents in any way. Underneath lay the velvety lining, nothing remarkable, except . . . hard to explain but the corners didn't tuck in quite right. Both my mom and Aunt April had a thing about tucking corners in tightly. Mom used to laugh and say she was taught to make a bed with sheets so prim and correct a quarter could be bounced off it, like a military requirement. The bottom lining for this box wouldn't even come close. I leaned forward to run my index fingernail about the corner, it being the longest, sharpest object I had at hand, and the velvet peeled away as I did. My nail encountered a corner of leather and I peered underneath the royal blue material.

A whisker-thin leather book met my eyes. Now this looked intriguing. I edged it out. It smelled of the cigars faintly, and the cover had been worn by much usage. I could see it held a number of delicate pages but decided I didn't have the time to stop and read it. It seemed best to keep it close, so I placed the blank parchment into it and tucked both into my waistband, at the small of my back, not wanting to entrust it to my backpack. I looked up to see Steptoe giving me a signal behind Morty's back. Time to go!

I put the box back into order and came out of the room, clicking the door behind me loud enough that it interrupted whatever discussion the three of them had been carrying on.

"Ah," smiled Steptoe. "All done then?"

"Yes. Grandfather always said a good cigar kept him young."

The Sikh bowed slightly to me. "We hold him in high regard. Send him our wishes, please, young miss."

"I will!"

We left, trying not to look in a hurry, and I said, "Where's the next shop?"

"Did you get what we needed?"

"I don't know, but I don't want to lead anybody here in case I didn't. Besides, he was nice. It wouldn't be fair to dump a load of trouble in his lap." I pointed down to the next block. "There's another smoke shop, and it has vaping." I grinned. "I think it only right that the harpies get a nose full of tutti frutti, don't you?"

We arrived at the same time as a gaggle of guys just out of high school for the day. They looked fine if terribly young, but my mind's eye seemed full of Carter Phillips, so I barely noticed the three as they came in just after us and lounged about at the counter and drink machine. One of them puffed like a steam engine, great wet clouds billowing up. He didn't smell like fruit, but something a little different that I didn't like any better. Butterscotch and vanilla, I think. I prefer to eat my candy, not smoke it. They made a little noise and jostled among themselves, trying to get my attention, but I ignored them as Steptoe and Morty inquired about cigar box storage and other business. He had a tiny corner of boxes, but nothing as elaborate as the first shop we'd found. I don't think he cared that much, but he stopped talking to us twice to yell at the boys before finishing with, "Get out of here, already, if you're not going to buy something!"

"We already bought something!" A freckled lad with tattoo sleeves on both arms sneered at him, and the other two laughed at him and passed the vape holder around. An incredibly over-scented and nauseating mist filled the shop. They howled at their wit and wrote words that were most definitely not PG rated in big looping letters with the vape mist.

The shop keep muttered to himself, and I wondered how much longer we should stall when the doors flew open in sound and fury, as the saying goes, and the harpies swooped in. The three bystanders let out yelps and fled as quickly as their feet could carry them. I mentioned sound and fury, but there would be no way I could forget their smell either. Wet chicken and dog, maybe? They stalled in midair, surprised as they saw us. I grabbed Morty by the arm. "Quick, before they get it!"

Thick as his body was, Morty's mind wasn't, and he nodded, powering himself toward the back of the shop, as determined as if the famed Holy Grail stood in the corner storage. The shop proprietor hit the floor behind his counter and rolled as far under it as he could get. Steptoe put his back to the front corner wall after pulling me into position with him, saying quietly, "Their wingspan keeps them from getting too close unless they land." Then, with a quirk of a smile, he added, "And you've a pocketful of help when they do put boots on the ground, as it were."

I'd forgotten about my flash-bangs and swore at my stupid self, although they wouldn't have helped when they picked up Brian, as the attackers had stayed mainly in the air for that one. I might have helped in the muddle when one or two touched ground, but they'd already been pulled out of the fray by then—and I saw no need to be hurting anyone more than I had to, especially if they might be related to Morty's wife. I hadn't met her either, but making enemies for the sake of it seemed like overkill. I still held no clear idea who was on whose side, and until the dust cleared, it seemed wise to not do any permanent damage. Neither Morty nor Steptoe seemed to hold the same compunction, but maybe they had a better idea of how things stood in their world of weirdness.

Morty found his corner and swung around to bat at two of the winged warriors diving down at him, his shovellike hands at the end of his thick arms coming within a feather of doing serious hurt. "Break your bargain with me, will you!" he crowed at them.

Their screeches seemed to be a main part of their weaponry, as the sound brought blood dribbling out of my ears again while my eyes felt as if they were playing ping-pong in my forehead. I dropped to one knee, sick with it, while Morty roared his defiance at his attackers. Steptoe put himself over me in protection while he grabbed, of all things, a humongous backscratcher from a sales dump display at the counter, the thing half as long as I stood, carved with an apt and fanged cobra head. He wielded it like a cricket bat, teeing off on anyone wheeling close to us, his teeth bared in a fearsome grin.

"'Ere's another stroke for you, love," he cried and swung up, underhand, sending his target flying backward out of the shop's still-open doors.

All the battle came to a halt when two harpies walked in, dragging Brian between them. "Desist!" called a third, tall one who followed at their heels, her stern face topped with steely gray hair, black and white magpie wings, and a ton of attitude. She folded her wings at her back as she came in, and I noted that if she'd flown in, they alone would have taken up half the store. Accordingly, they crowned the back of her head and the tips trailed behind her like a royal robe. I wondered if Morty's Goldie were half as impressive as this lady. I checked out Brian, who looked limp and barely aware, his cane stuck haphazardly through his belt and the gazing stone dimmed like obsidian rather than its crystal-clear silvery self. Not good.

"Move away, Mortimer Broadstone, or you will rue this day for more than one reason."

His lip curled. "Oathbreaker."

She shrugged. "Deals are not always possible to be carried out. Other personages hold an interest in your wife."

"Then you should have known better than to try to parley with her life!"

The woman stopped only a pace or two in front of him, and he half-lowered his head, brow furrowing, a bull readying to charge. "While I could not stop her from being appropriated," she said to him, "I did not approve, and I am approachable to working with you to free her from this new imprisonment. She is, after all, my sister as well as your wife."

"You lie. There are few who would dare to steal a prize from a harpy once taken."

"True. And equally true the one you might suspect who has done so."

"No." Morty's voice broke on a keening note.

"As I said, I would be amenable to assisting in a rescue from that one. If you could bring yourself to trust me again."

Steptoe shouted, "Quit fillin' his ears with poison! Do what you've come to do, take your bounty, drop Brian in our laps, and leave!"

Steel-hair looked over her shoulder at us, her expression marked with contempt. "Not so easily done as that. The boy stays with us. He has more secrets to spill."

Brian's head hung, with his chin touching his chest, but he managed to take a hoarse breath and look up. "Not meant for you, never, not my wizardry!"

She laughed at his thready protest. "Or you either, it seems, boy."

He slouched in their hold on either side of him, his slack weight keeping them on the floor with him. Steptoe moved away from me quickly, both distracting his captors and freeing my field. He brandished his cobra-headed scratching stick like a mighty baton.

I filled my hand with flash-bangs and tossed them, one at a time, strategically as I could place them at all the harpies. They exploded with sparks and smoke and an unholy loud noise, scattering everyone. Both Steptoe and Morty charged for Brian. Steptoe wrestled him free and Morty tackled them as they tried to snatch him back. With a shake of his mighty shoulders, he took down two of the women with one swipe and swung about, looking for his main adversary. Feathers flew as did banshee-shrill curses. I swear he gave a coughing growl, like some immense Bengal tiger, and set himself for another charge. He never saw the steel-haired woman pull her sword and plunge it into his back. It laid him low.

Steptoe and I had Brian bundled behind us when it happened. Morty let out a cry and rolled about, his hands digging at the blade buried between his shoulder blades as he did even as she swooped down on him. He pulled it out and stood up with a forward lunge before she even knew he moved on her, burying the sword into her stomach, just below her leather corset, a bared and vulnerable flank before her leather chaps began. They both went to their knees in a bellow of pain, and her hands went to his throat, determined to take him with her to death.

"Come on, come on!" Steptoe urged. "Before they trumpet

for reinforcements, like." He hauled Brian's limp body across my feet and out the door. I turned, and my eyes caught Morty's for a flash of a moment as the two of them thrashed in mortal combat.

I'm not sure—I'll never be sure—if he saw the tears that spilled from my own eyes and down my face, as I left him behind.

Maybe he thought he deserved that. Maybe he intended for us to go on without him, redeeming himself for his betrayal. Or maybe that was just the way it happened.

CHAPTER SEVENTEEN

I STOPPED AGAIN on the sidewalk. I *couldn't* leave Morty behind, not if there was a single chance he could still be alive. The harpies burst out of the tobacco shop with squawks and curses of fury, four of them hauling the queenly one between them, and crimson rained down from her body as they took to the air with a struggle, bedraggled sisters following after. Steptoe jumped and shook his fist at them, mostly in bluff I think, just in case one or two decided to hang back for bit of revenge. They dipped and flew in ragged formation, barely clearing the streetlights. None turned back and he danced a jig step in victory. I dodged the crimson drops after hearing the sidewalk sizzle as blood hit it.

I heard no cries of surprise or fear; although New Yorkers have seen a lot, I felt they must have surely not seen what just flew over them and off into the sky. Brian groaned and shuddered in my hold, the cane slithering out of his belt and clattering to the ground. I darted after it, but it seemed in one piece, even the dark crystal, as I gathered it up. He couldn't hold it, so I wrapped my hand more firmly in his shirt sleeve to keep a grip on him, curled my fingers tightly about the cane—gone light and nearly insubstantial again, unfortunately—and turned to say a final good-bye to Morty. Afraid to, but having to, I peered through the grimy window of the shop. The place looked as if tossed, but only mildly considering it had hosted a battle to the death. I searched without seeing him and then my gaze dropped to where Morty fell.

No body rested there. Instead, a massive heap of glittering stone, dust and ashes, gems and metal flakes. My jaw dropped. Steptoe saw where I looked and said, "Sorry, ducks, that's what happens sometimes," and he kicked the shop door open. Why, I could not understand.

A wind arose. Sharp and cold. Out of the nearly cloudless and bright warm sky, a stiff breeze swirled up and into the shop, spiraling round and round about the remains of the Iron Dwarf that bore no resemblance to the man I called friend. It filled, this metal and gem cyclone, it filled and swelled with all of his being. I'd had no chance to find out what he knew of my father, if anything. Nor would I see him grin when we brought his wife back to him. And I wouldn't have him about to tell me about the nature of the stone, brick and mortar, rebar and steel of the buildings that surrounded us. Gone, all gone. It left a very big hole.

The dervish or miniature tornado or whatever you might call it paused as it poured through the doorway. I looked into it, its beauty and its harshness and, for the briefest of moments, I could see a transparent Morty looking back at me. He waited until I realized it, and then inclined his head in a nod.

"All is forgiven," I whispered. "Every bit of it. You tried your best."

Like a mirror of a rainbow, the substance gained color and reflected beauty back at me. And then, unexpectedly, three things dropped from the cloud. A black credit card, a driver's license, and a brass token. I swept them up in my free hand and looked at Morty's ghost in confusion. "I'm to use these?"

Another nod.

"Thank you. And . . . and go in peace."

Morty smiled sadly before thinning away to nothingness as the winds began to churn again and then burst through the doorway, whirling away down the sidewalk heedless of pedestrians—I'd say it was heedless of all New York City—as it bore the atoms of his remains away.

The whirlwind gained air as it rose higher and higher, an indescribable cloud, glinting in the sun as it turned away from the city. I watched it disappear from view.

"Did you know that would happen?"

He nodded.

"Where—where is it going?"

"Home. Or, at least, where his family calls 'home.' Home to the mines and quarries thereabouts, and earth, and loved ones."

"He had them, didn't he? Loved ones."

"Of course, 'e did! The Broadstones are a family o' fame, and even without his Goldie, there is plenty of love waiting for 'im there." He let the door swing closed slowly. "We'd best be off."

"But—"

He waited.

"I don't know where to go."

"We did rescue the lad, after all. We still have a phoenix to deal with. And we need t' get inside that study of his. See what's left." Something glinted deep inside Steptoe's eyes. I didn't want to think it was greed but it might well be.

I put the credit card and license in my front pocket but fingered the token. This hadn't been Morty's. I turned it about and about, thinking that it looked like a lucky piece my dad used to carry about all the time. He used to tell me, when I was little and we still talked and I adored him, that he had been about to board the bus for work when my mom came running for him and pulled him off the bus to tell him that they were expecting a baby. Unused, the token went back in his pocket and he kept it for a remembrance of a joyful time. I tapped it with my fingernail before putting it away, and the cane I still held took the rest of my attention. It felt as light as a kitten's whisker, rattling with a familiar sound whenever I moved it, and it came to me slowly what it sounded like.

Not too many years ago, rain sticks had been a cute novelty item, hollow gourd tubes with seeds that showered back and forth inside from end to end, sounding like rain when moved or shaken. I wondered how long the cane could last if it had been hollowed like that, and what made the noise inside of it, shifting back and forth. I truly doubted it could ever shoot perdition lightning forth again, but I didn't want to throw it away nor did I think Brian could. The bright crystal looked smoky and bleak. I shoved the cane partway into my backpack and leaned down to get my arm wrapped about Brian's waist. Steptoe did the same and we both looked up as a car slid to a halt in the street, thinking it to be Sam.

Wrong. The police had caught up to us again.

Carter swung his long legs out of the car and leaned back in the window to say, "I've got this. I'll be along later" before joining us.

I let out a long sigh of relief but Steptoe muttered, "He'll haul our arses to the Society, see if 'e doesn't."

Brian gave a movement and a faint moan as if trying to straighten up. I squeezed him a little. "I won't let him."

Carter swept his cool gaze over us and into the store, where the proprietor had begun to crawl out on hands and knees from behind the counter. "Trouble?"

"Was. Isn't now, and we've got Brian back."

"But now you're missing the big guy."

"Yeah." I couldn't help it, my breath caught in my throat at that one, and I turned away so he couldn't see the tears brim in my eyes.

"Let me take care of this, whatever this is." Carter stepped into the shop and flashed his badge at the man who didn't want to get to his feet even when Carter put a hand down to him. He got up, finally, and they talked for a few moments and then Carter—I swear—did a Jedi wave of his hand and the proprietor stood stock still for a long moment. He didn't move until Carter rejoined us. Carter squeezed me briefly. "I'm sorry about Mortimer."

Feelings welled up that I tried to shove down. Even the one which gave me the sense that there was no one else in the world on this sidewalk but the two of us. I swallowed tightly.

"Did you know him? At all, I mean?"

"We'd met once or twice, though I doubt he remembered me."

"If he met you, he remembered you. He had a very sharp mind but kept his thoughts to himself."

"As a judge does. The Broadstone family is lessened by the loss. All of the Folks, really. I'm sorry this happened around you, too." He squinted out at the traffic as a horn or two sounded.

"There's your driver. Get in before I have to ticket him for double-parking."

"Seriously? This is the city."

"And that is an open car door." He helped steer Brian into it, got into the front seat himself and left the crowded rear seat to the three of us.

Steptoe glared at the back of his neck for five blocks while Carter gave directions and then had Sam pull into a wide alley. Then, with the motor turned off, we all looked at each other.

"I'm supposed to take you in."

"Under what jurisdiction?"

Carter shrugged at Steptoe. "Pick one, although I'd say the Society is by far the most interested party, and more likely to believe anything that you say."

I folded my arms. "I ain't talking."

"Didn't think you would, which is why we're here." Carter's sharp gaze came to rest on Brian. "He's the phoenix wizard once known as Dr. Brandard. He's a renegade. Some have even gone far enough to say he's been outlawed, which means he should be banned from all his powers, but that doesn't seem to be much of a problem right now."

"Outlawed?"

"Pshaw," returned Steptoe. "By those standards, I shoulda been put in limbo long ago."

"There's still a chance of that."

Steptoe drew back in his seat indignantly. "As if I'd ever stand in judgment in front of you lot."

"Better us than the other side."

The two traded a very long and hard look before Steptoe pursed his lips and waved a hand. "There's them that would differ."

"Just so you're aware. I don't like the way you're leading my girl around."

My ears burned. His girl! I didn't know whether to be insulted or pleased. On the other hand, he seemed worried about me. Maybe even a bit protective. Score!

"Me leading? Me? I've been on her heels the whole way about. She's the one 'eaded down the garden path!"

Carter tilted his head a little and they locked gazes again. A second time, Steptoe looked away first, with an unintelligible murmur.

"He did help," I pointed out. "His flash-bangs drove away Malender at the motel, and then—"

"You saw *him*? When? And where, again?"

"Late yesterday. And how could you not see him? About a million starlings died between the airport fields and Old Alexandria. I know the airport has a lot of nesters and they're trouble for the planes, but the birds stay anyway. Or did, until he called them."

"A million?"

"Well, you know. A lot."

"He's really here, then."

"Again, how could you not know?" I ticked off the facts on my fingers.

"Things do die off on their own. Even schools of fish. Sardines, for example, by the piers, can die for lack of oxygen in the water. Hundreds, thousands of them can go belly up."

"Or the guy could just step off a boat and suck their little fishy souls dry."

"Or that," Brian added in, sounding really, really drunk, his voice slurred and whispery. He tried to sit up, blinking his eyes.

We hadn't known he'd come to. I perched him up more comfortably between us, and he helped a little, reminding me of some overgrown three-year-old from the days when I used to babysit a lot. You know, back before people couldn't look us in the eyes any more. He patted the back of my hand as we settled the seat belt into a better position.

"I feel like a wet sack of grain."

"Noodles," I told him. "A bowl of well-cooked noodles is more like it. Do you hurt?"

"Everywhere. But I live. And I've kept my head." This last, with eyebrows knotted, and eyes narrowed, at Steptoe.

Steptoe grinned back at him. "Always someone about who will take care o' that little problem, guv."

Carter cleared his throat. "I'd like to return to the matter at hand. You all were attacked yesterday by Malender?"

"By himself, in the flesh. I weren't there, understand, but I had given the little lady 'ere some ammo and 'eard they was most useful. Glad to be of service." He tipped his hat to me.

"He's the most beautiful person I've ever seen. Is he some kind of Fallen Angel or something?"

Shaking his head at me, Carter answered, "Not even close. That's just a projection, for him, and he's more than a little vain about it, but you would have, should have, seen more."

"He brought the tar pit with him."

Startled, Carter repeated, "Tar pit?"

"A big cloud of stinky, gooey awfulness. I think maybe that gunk was more dangerous than he is."

"You know more than you should," Brian said to me. "And he saw you?"

"Don't you remember?" Brian stared down at his toes in slight embarrassment. I patted him on the shoulder. "We were mano a mano. Or nearly."

"Gods. How could the two of you allow that?" Carter frowned at the others.

Brian stiffened up a little. "You've known her longer. Does she take direction well?"

"Not from what I can gather, but you'd have to ask her mother about that."

"My observation would say that she is fiercely independent and—"

"Sitting right here, guys."

"Mouthy," the professor finished. "Definitely has a mouth on her."

"Heeey!"

From the front seat, Sam offered, "America is a great country where women can speak freely."

Carter pointed at me. "Letting him get a good look at you wasn't wise."

"Nobody said I should hide under the bed while they fought the good fight."

"Well, they should have. And, you're very intuitive. That cloud of gunk is essence that he could not or wasn't willing to glamour, for any number of reasons. He may be too weak still from crossing the Atlantic, or he may just be flat-out mean and uncaring of what he touches. In any case—"

"Salt."

He stopped at the interruption. Then, "What?"

"Salt. Salt disintegrated the gunk, or at least its leading edge, when he tried to slither into my room. Made the rest of him very uncomfortable."

"Kosher salt? Sea salt? Any idea what kind? And how much?"

"Regular, ordinary, in-the-tiny-white-paper-packet salt, although a heck of a lot of it. We were shredding paper everywhere trying to get them open. Next time, just get the big, kitchen-sized shaker."

Carter's eyes sparkled. "That's incredible news. It means he's vulnerable, at least for now, and we've got an ordinary weapon that could work wonders."

"So take that to your Society and tell them to leave us alone."

"It doesn't work quite like that." Carter scratched his chin uneasily. "I will report the good news, however, and attribute it appropriately." He unclicked his seat belt. "I'm going to leave this as it is, and let Sam take you back to Richmond. I should be here for a full two weeks for training, but it sounds like you could use my help."

"We could," Brian said cautiously.

Carter put his hands up in the air. "No strings attached."

"It would have to be under those circumstances." The professor sounded forceful.

"I'll get released and get back as soon as possible. My postings are fairly flexible." His glance flicked to me as if I might interrupt with a "Fed!" but I kept my silence. "You need to . . . well, you need to remember what you can and get a protection spell for Tessa. Our opponent always goes for the weak link."

"I fear he already found it in our departed companion."

"Mortimer?"

Brian and Steptoe nodded in unison. Eerie.

"He betrayed you? Why . . . and how?"

"He reached out to the harpies, trying to get his wife released because he thought they had taken her, and they wanted Brian to even an old score. They took Brian at the park but they didn't bring Goldie back."

"And now we've got trouble with the harpy alliance, too? I shouldn't be surprised. Well, work on keeping Tessa safe."

"We'll do what we can."

"I assume you're trying to complete a ritual which failed?"

"Yes, but that's not the cause of the arson. That came about as a result of self-defense against an attack." Brian went stiff-necked trying not to look at Steptoe.

"I'll keep that in mind." Carter leaned toward Sam and did the Jedi wave again, murmuring a few words, which I almost, but not quite, made out.

"I'll leave you all here. Get home safe."

Steptoe slid into the vacant front seat, and I moved over to a window, as did Brian, while Sam took a few moments to wake up from whatever reverie he'd just been in.

"Home?"

Steptoe patted Sam on the shoulder, "Back to DC and then we've another journey. Hopefully a lot quieter than this one has been."

"Quieter? You guys are so dull I keep falling asleep!" Sam snorted as he began to back the shuttle out of the NYC alley.

The ticket agent at the station made adjustments to our tickets and we just made the train south. He hadn't even asked for ID for me to use Morty's card, but I'd had it and a story to go along with it if needed. The ride home did not restore our energy or our hopes, and it was dark by the time we traipsed up the sidewalk to my house, the porch light on, gleaming a faint gold against the night.

Remy sat on the front steps awaiting us.

CHAPTER EIGHTEEN

THE HAIRS AT THE BACK of my neck went all prickly and I moved in front of Brian, but it was Steptoe who got to her first. He swept his bowler hat off and gave a deep bow.

"Lady Remy. What a joy 'tis to see you again."

She looked down her nose at him, a nose that was slightly longer than fashionable and thinner than trendy. She'd swept her hair up, although a soft curl or two dangled down, and I thought I had finally placed that look about her: she was French. No wonder she was looking at him like she'd ordered caviar and gotten coal.

"Steptoe."

"You remember." Cheer infused his voice. He took a pace closer as he resettled his hat with a pat. "Then remember this. I beat you off the last time we met, and I'll do it again if you interfere with any one of us. From what I 'ear, you can't 'ide behind the Society's cloak anymore, so you are, dear lady, fair game." He didn't sound at all as if he meant dear lady.

Remy stood. She topped him by a hand's width, but he didn't seem the least bit intimidated. In fact, she was the one who looked a bit unsteady. "Bygones," she began, and he cut her off.

"No excuses. You are what you are, just as I'm wot I am. But I don't go lyin' about it. Now bug off."

"Child." She looked to me.

"Not a child and I'm not too fond of you either. Or trusting."

Lastly, she considered Brian. She pivoted away when his

voice, a little rusty and hoarse, stopped her. "You didn't think to come to me."

"No. No, I didn't. I couldn't."

"Despite what we'd been through."

Remy sighed. "Especially because of that. You don't remember all, not yet, in fact you don't even remember most—but you will . . . and there's no apology I can make that you will accept. You never have."

"I'm not the forgiving sort?"

"No. Not at all." She shook her head and another, single curl fell loose from her hairdo to join other tendrils along her bare neck. "You should be, but you're not." She held her hand out to him. "I am indentured to him. A foolish thing that I did, not being wary enough. Binding, but not permanent. Just enough to put us at odds. I have very little wiggle room, but what I can find, I will use. I don't want to lose you." Her gaze swept the group and her eyes widened as she realized we were short a man. "Broadstone. Was he taken?"

"Died in battle honestly."

She exhaled. "Protect yourselves, all of you." With a wave of her arm, a pirouette, and a shadow that reached out to swallow her, Remy disappeared. Something, leaflike, drifted to the porch steps in her wake.

Brian bent over and picked up a scroll. He tapped it against his fingers. "This might be just what we were looking for."

"What is it?"

"Guardian scroll, if I'm not mistaken."

"Could you be mistaken?"

"Not with this, no. I wrote it." He smiled crookedly. "Wiggle room, as she called it, might be quite helpful."

Steptoe made a noise at the back of his throat as he walked up the porch and waited for us. "I wonder," he noted, "what deal she made, and if she expects us to help her break it."

"That would be typical, wouldn't it?"

"Very," he agreed with me. "Very."

Mom heard us and threw the door open, almost clocking Steptoe in the face, but he jumped back nimbly before it hit. "Goodness. Back at last. Tessa, you have two days to make up on campus and I expect no excuses." Her professorial voice hung on the air.

"Yes, Mom."

"As for the rest of you. What trouble did you bring back with you?" Her gaze swept them.

"We have no idea."

Steptoe left us after introducing himself and then doffing his hat to my mother, going off to wherever he went to, which I suspected was somewhere nearby that his minions held safe for him. Brian trudged up to bed but not before demolishing a salad and huge bowl of leftover stew. I picked at mine as I listened to his weary footfalls up the stairs.

Mom wiped down the counter. "So Mortimer left all of you? Was that why you brought home another one?"

I wasn't quite sure what she meant by that. Another one what? I decided to be a little dumb on the subject. "Yup." I chased around a chunk of carrot, speared it, and chewed. I hoped she wasn't expecting more of an answer, since I had my mouth full.

Her hands made thoughtful swipes in circles, cleaning old linoleum counters that probably were original from when the house was built. Here and there, all the brown speckled spots had patches worn away to colorless. I watched, thinking that old houses didn't get wrinkles, they just faded away. Finally, Mom looked up. "That's not the sort of thing I'd expect from him, so I imagine there's more than either of you have told me. Mortimer wouldn't have just left. I don't like what's going on, and I don't like not knowing the whole truth." She seemed to expect an answer so I swallowed.

"You worry too much."

"Thank you. That seems to be one of my main jobs now. I used to be right there on the front lines with you, but now I'm relegated to just watching." She rinsed off her sponge and stowed it away, her face crinkled in a frown. I didn't like seeing the lines, old and new, in her face.

"And I'm not lying."

"But you've omitted a ton of facts. Do you think I can't tell?"

"I can't explain everything that happened."

"Then tell me about Mortimer."

A chunk of potato looked inviting but she lowered her head a bit to look into my face, and I decided there wasn't any use in further avoiding answering her. I put my fork down. "He's gone. He died trying to protect all of us from an attack, an attack that won't show in any newspaper or police report or anything else. And he didn't leave a body. He . . . I don't know how to explain it. He was an Iron Dwarf, akin to stone and metal, right out of the earth, and his body returned." My throat dried and I took a big gulp of water, trying to force down a sudden lump. "He was there and then he wasn't, kind of. Not that fast, but in front of my eyes. He wasn't human, Mom, not like us and yet he was." My hand shook as I lowered my drinking glass. "How do you explain that?"

"It seems to be one of the things in life that are better felt than explained." She put her arm around my shoulder. "What attack and why? If he was killed, this whole thing has become lethal. I can't bear that. No one else was hurt?"

"Brian got a little pushed around but, no." I took a deep breath. "He knew stuff about Dad. He was going to tell me but he didn't have a chance. It might have been important, and now it's as gone as he is. But the lethal stuff, yes, there was a fight and he lost, but it was between him and the attackers, mostly. It had nothing to do with us."

"I know you've heard of collateral damage. I've had my hands full trying to keep us on an even keel financially, but emotionally, I can't accept this. I can't accept the friends you're making or the trouble they're bringing with them."

"But what if it leads us to Dad?"

Somewhere in the kitchen, pots and pans rattled loudly. We both started at the sound.

I could feel the tension in her arm. "I want you out of this, Tessa."

"Mom. Brian needs my help."

"He seems to have friends and enemies enough of his own and you shouldn't be a part of this. We don't deal with magic, this isn't our world, and I'm not sure it even exists, except if Mortimer is gone, then it can be deadly whether we believe in it or not. Tessa, think. I don't want to lose you, too. I couldn't bear it."

"You won't lose me."

"You don't know that! You can't promise me what neither of us understands or can anticipate. And you shouldn't have to. What you should be doing is planning your life, college, friends, the ordinary stuff that you spin into your own kind of magic, human magic. Not this . . . this . . ."

"Stuff that dreams are made of?" Brian said dryly from behind and above us, from the stairwell.

"Nightmares are more likely," she said without missing a beat. "How did you ever live to be an old man?"

"I only wish I could remember. It seems unlikely that this body will enjoy the same lifespan."

"And you dragged Tessa into this?"

He looked at both of us. "I doubt anyone drags Tessa anywhere. But she has been invaluable to me, in both lives, that I do remember." He held up the tightly wound scroll that Remy had dropped and he claimed he had written. "This, when I enact it, should give coverage to all those within hearing range."

"Should."

"The operative word, yes."

He took the last few steps down and walked into the kitchen, unrolling it as he did. A tiny flake of red skittered off the parchment and floated down to the floor. Paper? Blood? Wax from a seal? He stepped over it, unnoticing. "Do we have everyone here we want protected?"

"What about Steptoe?" I asked.

Brian flicked a finger. "He should be amply protected on his own. We're the vulnerable ones that need whatever I can conjure up." He flattened out the ancient paper carefully on the kitchen counter to scan it. He cleared his throat two or three times. "I should be able to handle this." He looked pale and too weary to even stand up on his own, but I didn't dare contradict him. I should, however, question him.

"Should?"

"It's simple enough. It's one of those spells that merely needs the proper words said—and I have them written down—and a force of will. I should have that. And you can assist me."

"I can?"

"Of course. You are obstinate as well as intuitive. Both apply."

I threw a grin at my mother who seemed far from delighted.

"Now then." Brian straightened his youthful body, smothered a groan as he did so, and woefully rubbed his rib cage. "My mind says it's not that sore, but my body protests."

"You came through better than Morty," I pointed out.

"Indeed. My dear friend. I have no cause for complaints. I shall miss him more than he will ever know. Now I have to take care of the business at hand as he gave his life for this endeavor." He stretched for a moment and Brian came back with a yelp. "Man, if he doesn't take better care of us, I am never letting him into my mind again." He shook his head vigorously, ample hair ruffling. "Back." He read the paper again. "Ready?"

About to say yes, the house suddenly swayed and creaked, timbers straining, and my mom looked about wildly as if ready to catch dishes jolted out of the cabinets.

"What was that?"

Brian stared about. "Earthquake? We don't get earthquakes, do we?"

"Not generally, although there was the one that damaged the Washington Monument. We didn't feel it much, though." Mom stayed alert, hands out, ready to catch falling items if another shock hit. "Stay put. This is a fairly sturdy room of the house."

I felt another shiver through the floorboards and looked at Brian. "It couldn't be." I started for the front door when something heavy pounded on it.

Brian joined me, Mom trailing in behind, as I threw the door open.

An Iron Dwarf stood there. Not as broad as Morty, and a bit taller, and definitely far younger, his auburn hair curled down to his collar, a floppy hat in his big hands and his miner's boots with a shiny black polish to them. The porch light gave a kind of halo reflection to him.

"This be the Andrews' residence?"

"It is."

"I am Hiram Broadstone, here to fulfill my father's obligations to you. May I enter?"

While I tried to think coherently, my mother reached around to open the door wide, saying, "Of course you can. And please, call me Mary. Our condolences on your father. We all liked him quite a lot."

"Aye, he was a good man." Hiram entered, and although his presence did not quite make the building protest as it had when Morty trod through it, he still raised groans and sighs from the construction. He moved a little slowly as if expecting that and giving the house time to absorb his bulk. "I take it none of you were expecting me."

"Not really."

"A sad, sad thing that would be, not to know that a man's honor would be upheld by his family in his stead. But then, times have changed." He stopped at the kitchen's edge. "Would it be any trouble to have a glass of anything cold and wet?"

My mom hustled to the fridge, pulling out that pitcher of sweet tea that never seemed to empty, filling a glass for Hiram and one for Brian, who seemed to be studying the dwarf closely. That's when it occurred to me that there might be a problem. Hiram might not be who he said he was, though I had little doubt he was what he claimed from his effect on our home. I hadn't known Morty well enough to know he had a son, and surely Goldie hadn't been a mother to this one. I shot Brian a sideways glance. He caught it and shrugged back at me. He had no idea either? Surely the professor would. I tapped an index finger to my head, hinting to Brian that someone with knowledge, even if it had gaps in it, should maybe be in charge.

Hiram, meanwhile, drained his glass with a smack of his lips and thanked my mother for the hospitality. The glass hit

the counter with a ring as he turned to face both of us squarely.
"Now then," he declared. "It seems we have a task ahead of us.
Where do we stand in the gathering of the relics and objects
needed to rejuv you successfully?"

"Would that I knew."

"Don't be glum. I am here to help however I can, as my father would have."

"He gave his life for us. I think that's enough, don't you?"

Hiram smiled thinly at me. "He made that sacrifice because
he had betrayed the two of you. His love for my stepmother had
proven unwise on several occasions. I hope to hold your trust in
firmer hands. You've given me sustenance and shelter, and I am
beholden to you, in addition to the burden my father placed
upon me. You may know that I will do whatever is in my ability
to be of aid."

"Wow." Everyone swung about to look at me. I spread my
hands. "I mean, chivalrous, right? Sounds like something from
the Round Table."

"Referring to Arthur the king, are you? He goes far, far back
in our ancestry but some of the manners of loyalty and debt
remain the same. Now, it's evening and perhaps late for you,
but I am willing to carry out a task if necessary."

"Actually," and I nudged Brian, "we were just preparing a
little something."

"We were? Oh! Oh, yes, indeed. All right everyone, hold your
tongues till I am quite finished."

Hiram raised an eyebrow as Brian spread his feet and took
a steadying pose, raised one hand in the air, and began to recite
from his scroll.

Words filled the air with a physical presence, suggesting
shields and bucklers, and trees with stout branches to cover
us, and the sun conspiring to keep us hidden from both glare
and dangerous shadow, and yet I could not repeat a single
syllable of what I heard, as if it were entirely foreign to me. I
understood it but I could not voice it. The words held a power
but also a plea, as if asking for this protection, not forcing it,
from the nature about us. And it was natural. Not a thing

about it came from modern man, no weaponry or technology. This was something Brian coaxed out of the earth itself with his asking.

And then it settled about us, all of us, a recognizable weight on our shoulders, and I thought for a moment I could smell the fresh, green scent of some vast primeval forest. He didn't have to tell me he was done, and I don't think he could have anyway, as he reeled back, spent, and leaned upon the kitchen counter to stay on his feet.

"Wow."

"Indeed, and well said." Hiram scratched his chin through his beard, a neat and short beard, trimmed nicely, and he hummed a moment, before flexing. "Substantial."

"Good." Brian reached for his drink and finished it in two long gulps. "Bed."

He staggered off.

"And you, Hiram?"

"A couch, good mistress, if you have one that will hold me."

"Right this way." She led him off, and I stayed behind to straighten up the kitchen, thinking. Wondering if we had just accepted an enemy into our midst, side by side with us, and had given him all the protection we gave ourselves.

There wasn't anyone I could ask who had an answer.

Unless Steptoe could. But how far did I really trust him?

I closed the top cabinet door firmly, shutting away my thoughts even as I shut away the clean glasses. Or tried to. Some things linger.

The doorbell rang, a very soft version of its usual jangling chime, almost as though the utility knew the hour and that people could be asleep. Drying my hands, I went to the door, expecting to see Steptoe, hat in hand, asking for shelter. I glanced through the peephole.

A young man stood there, very well dressed and groomed, in a suit that might well have been worn to the Academy Awards or other society doings. And inside the suit, a very fit and polished Japanese guy who could give Carter and Brian a run for the money in the handsome race. I opened the door cautiously because he held a red envelope in his hands and not a ninja weapon like nunchucks or a throwing star.

He smiled as the porch light fell over him. "Miss Tessa?"

"Yes."

"Permit me. My employer has asked me to deliver this invitation to you and await your answer if possible. I am sorry the hour is late."

I took the envelope. It smelled faintly of cherries. Thinking of Joanna, and who else could the man represent but her father, I slipped a finger into the crease and then shook out the letter.

It was a smaller version of the invitation Evelyn had answered, framed on a larger sheet of paper upon which senior had penned: "It has come to my attention that Joanna has overlooked a most important personage in her plans for auction night. We therefore, my daughter and I, would now like to extend our hopes that you will join her and her date. The fun and pleasure of two girls will only multiply bountifully if you agree. Partners for all will be supplied. If you send your answer back with my employee, Joanna will have a suite of dresses sent to your home upon the morrow for your approval. Yours.

"Hironori Hashimoto."

And he'd signed it with a flourish, very American, and in the corner a brushed symbol.

Wow. I took a quavering breath. He'd even anticipated that our budget might make me turn down the invite, and neatly bypassed that. Did I want to go?

Hell yeah. Although I couldn't put it in those terms out loud. I pulled my phone up and decided that Evelyn would possibly be awake. I put a finger up to the messenger in Armani haberdashery to indicate I needed a moment, texted Evelyn, and waited.

She was. I told her what I had in my hand. She responded. *OMG. Joanna said she would ask! Come! We will have an amazing time!*

I put the phone away and smiled at the paragon of patience on the doorstep. "Thank you, and I definitely accept. It sounds awesome."

He smiled again and bowed. Though he might be in America, Japan flowed deep in his veins. I watched him retreat to a limo sitting in deep shadows at the curb. It roared away smoothly into the night. I hugged the letter to my chest.

The auction, after all. I wondered if Morty had worked a little earth magic for me in his ghostly form. Whether he had, or not, I intended to take advantage of it.

CHAPTER NINETEEN

MORNING BROUGHT DELICIOUS smells floating up to my room, along with the sound of voices, all of which I thought I recognized before realizing, sadly, that the deep tones came from Hiram, not Morty. I sat on the edge of my bed a moment, saddened by that realization. Then I hurried to my bathroom where I got to mourn the lack of hot water for my shower. Guests had evidently put a strain on the old house's plumbing, which it couldn't quite meet. In and out in a hurry and shivering while I dressed, I went through my clothes of DC and New York before throwing them in the hamper. I found the autumn leaf I'd kept and put it on the nightstand nearest the window where it blazed in the rays of an early sun. Maybe it had come from Faerie too, where everything lived close to forever, if such a place existed. I propped up Brian's leather journal there. I'd have to tell him about it, the object we'd found that Morty had given his life for, as well as his rescue, but I wasn't quite ready yet. I couldn't explain why. Steptoe didn't need to know about what I'd found, and I wasn't sure about Hiram yet. Definitely Carter couldn't know about it because he might have to tell the Society. So I would wait for the moment. I lined up the remaining flash-bangs, only five left, thought a second, and then put two in my pocket. Be prepared, right? The items joined a collection of a few other things I'd picked up and kept because there was no calculating their worth or worthlessness. The brass token I slipped under my pillow. I ought to ask Mom about it, but with things going the way they were, I thought it might be like adding salt to an open wound. I decided to keep it, though. I hated to throw anything away. Lastly, I meant to set my invitation there, but couldn't find it.

My stomach growled. Breakfast couldn't wait any longer. Dressed and geared up mentally, I trotted downstairs.

Mom pushed a full plate at me and said, "Classes."

"But—"

"Classes. We both have them, you to attend and me to teach."

"Right." I sat down on a tall stool as the chairs were mostly taken, the last one by Carter Phillips to my surprise, one hand filled with a coffee mug and the other holding my invitation. The aroma of coffee blended nicely with his leather and cedar scent and I inhaled to enjoy them.

He waved the mislaid invitation. "Going?"

"Yes."

"Good. There are some memories of youth everyone should have."

"Tell that to the guy they put in the college dumpster last week." I grabbed a spare, clean fork from the table. Mom had opted for scrambled eggs, easy to fix in bulk, and she'd mixed cheese, some chopped chives, and diced tomatoes in with them, so they looked like colorful confetti had spit up in them. I dug in.

Steptoe had taken his hat off and kept it off for once, it sitting on the small desk in the corner where women were supposed to do the budget, write notes on their recipes, and other quaint activities. His dark hair waved nicely, with only a slight indentation from the bowler. He passed a teacup to me, filled to the brim with the most heavenly smelling brew. "Have a cuppa."

"You made it?"

He gave a slight bow in my direction. "Of course, ducks. Wouldn't drink it any other way. Though how you lot can have it without milk is beyond me. Sticks in me throat, it does."

I grinned at him and took a sip. It was, indeed, heavenly, if sugarless. I promptly remedied that before taking another gulp. Yup. Worthy of paradise. "I think we should keep you around."

"Thanks, but you know. I have things t' do and places t'be."

Steptoe blushed slightly and looked away, obviously not used to compliments.

"I see you've met Hiram Broadstone," I noted to Carter.

Carter nodded with a murmur, "I am familiar with all his clan, but it's a pleasure to know Hiram better."

"He understands the honor I uphold." Hiram returned the nod and held his plate out for seconds. Or possibly thirds or fourths. Mom beamed and dished out the last from her enormous frying pan, the one we only used for family dinners on major holidays, the one that held bulk quantities. In those days, we used to have Great-Aunt April and Dad and some miscellaneous cousins that no longer lived in the area, but who we heard from at the holidays. I stared at the fryer, thinking of how things had changed. She set the pan in the sink. "You're going to have to run to catch the bus or bicycle and you need to—" She checked the kitchen clock. "You need to get a move on."

"You're not driving me?"

"I have a faculty meeting this morning. More nagging about publishing or perishing, I imagine." The corner of her mouth quirked. "Good thing I have an article coming out in July."

"You do? Hey, Mom, that's terrific. Not about the not driving, though."

"I can take you." Carter set both the invitation and his mug down. "I've got an undercover car today."

"Oh goody."

He colored a bit too, but not in a pleased way, and pushed back a little in his chair as I mopped up the last of my breakfast. I would have liked another half serving but that had gone the way of the Iron Dwarf. I dusted my hands off. "Brushing my teeth and I'll be ready."

He opened the front door for me when I joined him, backpack and toothpaste breath in place, and we both froze in surprise as we caught Joanna in midknock.

"So sorry. Did I interrupt?"

"Just leaving for campus."

Petite and immaculately dressed, casual to a tee, she had three garment bags that nearly capsized her over one slender arm. "I brought these early. I thought we could come over after and see what worked."

"Great." I carefully took them from her.

She stood on one foot and then the other, not coming inside, but then Carter was in the doorway, blocking her. I nudged past him and stowed the bags in my room, laying them out more or less carefully across my bed. My fingers itched to pull the plastic aside and see what they concealed, but no time. I settled for pushing a finger into the plumpest bag. It concealed chiffon, unless I was greatly mistaken.

Downstairs, Mom had let Joanna in, and they were chatting amicably, when a pan began to rattle on its hook and then fell down with a loud crash to the floor, just missing Joanna's toes. Mom hurriedly picked the pot up, but didn't rehang it, setting it at the back of the counter.

Steptoe and Hiram both watched the pot as if it had grown legs.

Joanna recovered and held a hand out. "Come to campus with me. I've a car waiting."

I was so gone, if it was anything like the sleek limo I'd seen last night. We waved and left. I didn't even look back to see if I'd disappointed Carter.

At Skyhawk, Evelyn heaped a ton of notes onto me and wished me luck. I made the rounds, listening and learning, and wondering what any of these teachers would say if they'd seen what I'd seen over the last few days. What rules of chemistry and physics and mathematics could explain and support magic? Unless, of course, I'd taken a spill down the stairs and lay in a coma somewhere, imagining everything. I lifted a hand to my head and probed here and there to see if I could find an injury of any kind.

"What are you doing?" Evelyn looked over her bottled tea at me, her sandwich only half-eaten in the tradition of dieting.

"Checking for injuries."

"OMG, did you get hurt?"

"No."

"Riiiight. So, Joanna told me she brought some dresses over."

"Yup."

"And we're coming over to help you decide?"

"Yup again."

"You don't sound excited."

"I am! Just tired and maybe comatose."

"Tess-aaaah."

"It's been an interesting week."

"Missing two days doesn't help. Don't lose those notes! We've got finals coming up in four weeks."

I took her iced tea from her and downed half of it. Then I eyed her sandwich. Despite having eaten my own lunch, I felt starved. Without a word, she pushed it over. Actually, she had a word or two but didn't deliver them until after I finished her lunch.

"I hope those dresses will fit."

I wiped my mouth on her napkin. "They'd better. You know my size."

Evelyn smiled smugly. "I used to know your size." She waved at the luncheon debris. "Now I'm not sure."

I shot a wayward potato chip at her and it hit midtorso. "Score!"

"Honestly."

"I know. I'm just tired of being demure."

Evelyn leaned across the table on her forearms. "You have never been demure a day of your life, for which I'm grateful."

"Thanks. I think." A bell rang. We swept up our trash in a hurry, readying for the next slate of classes. My coma faded enough so that I could absorb the afternoon of teachings, though I was so ready to get home.

Joanna, limo and all, waited for us as we left the hallways.

The house seemed ultra-empty with none of the guys in it. I had no idea where Steptoe and Hiram and Brian had gone, but I knew Carter had gone to work. The key rack jangled noisily as we passed it, and I threw out a hand to steady it even as I hung up my keys on it. It fairly quivered like a live thing under my touch. What was wrong with this house?

Joanna gave it a wide berth as she went by it in the hallway.

My key ring sprang off its hook. I caught it before it hit the floor, but Joanna and Evelyn never saw a thing. I put it back on the hook. "Now, stay."

Upstairs, by the time I got to my room, the girls had opened the garment bag cocoons and laid the resulting butterflies out for my approval. I stopped in amazement. These were not dresses. They were stunning rainbows of material and color, style ranging from fun to elegant to simply outrageous. "Wow."

Joanna gave a shy smile. "You like them?"

"Wow," I repeated. Evelyn nodded to Joanna.

For the next hour I slipped in and out of silk, satin, and chiffon, and back again, turning about to see in the mirror, laced or open, off the shoulder or slit up the leg, twirling to see which one I liked best. Although there were only three garment bags, five dresses had been pulled out of them and every one of them looked awesome. Not necessarily on me, but in themselves. I felt both silly and royal at the same time watching myself pose in an ocean of pink chiffon or peach-colored satin. I must have tried on each one of them three times. You know, just to thoroughly check them out.

Evelyn perched on a corner of the bed, cheering me on, while Joanna paced back and forth a little, as if eying me on a catwalk, trying to decide what the best perspective would be. She paused by my nightstand. Her gaze fell on the journal, and for some reason I felt very uneasy, as it seemed to catch and hold her attention. I sashayed over in her direction, swishing my extravagant skirt about, and managed to knock the journal onto the floor. One quick kick and it scooted under the bed out of sight. Joanna gave me a sideways look when she noticed it missing and then a little shrug. We hooked arms and sashayed about the bedroom some more, making Evelyn laugh until she cried at our silliness.

I finally picked up the silk one, in a sea glass green with a side leg slit, although a modest one, ruched over the bosom and dipping nicely at the back. Nothing scandalous but daring in its own quiet way. I held it up for about the fourth time, just holding it against me and looking at the mirror that covered the back of my bedroom door. With it, my freckles seemed less, my hair richer in color and lustrous, and I knew the side slit would accent my legs nicely. Field hockey and bicycling had definitely given me killer legs.

"That one," Joanna stated.

"I think so."

"I knew it!" Evelyn bounced on her corner of the bed. Joanna looked at her.

"You were right."

"Don't get me wrong, the others are great, but this one, well, it's awesome but . . . I don't know. You can still see me, while I'm wearing it, you're not just looking at dress, you know?"

"Absolutely." Quick and efficient, Joanna began to repack the other dresses, while Evelyn found a suitable hanger for my choice. "I don't even think it needs alterations if you wear heels."

"And why wouldn't I?"

Joanna's gaze swept the side of my room, where a pile of sneakers, sandals and flip-flops partially blocked the closet. "Oh, I don't know. Just a hunch."

When we left my room, though, Joanna cast one long and thoughtful look behind her. I decided I'd better move the journal somewhere safer. Evelyn punched her in the arm for being slow and the two dissolved in giggles while I put my gown on the acquired hanger and tried, loftily, to ignore the hilarity before joining them in the hall. The moment seemed blissfully normal. I delivered meals, did assignments, and slept in my own bed.

That normalcy flew out the window a day later when I handed Brian the journal. I'd tried to do it once or twice before but got interrupted, and then it would slip my thoughts entirely. Self-defense on the book's part, so I wouldn't reveal it? Was it still, somehow, in hiding mode until delivered to Brian? I determined not to wait another moment, in case I forgot again and it became too late. I whispered to him, "I found a book."

"A book?"

"At the tobacco shop. Not the one where we rescued you, but an older, nicer place up the street. An establishment, a fine tobacconist. There was a cigar box stored there, with your name on it, and under the second layer, I found a small leather journal. No one else saw it."

His hand trembled in mine. "Could you read it?"

"Haven't tried. I've kept it hidden."

"Very wise of you. I wonder what it might be. I wrote several journals about this and that."

"Hopefully it's a very important that." I slipped it into his hands.

He staggered back a step, as if I'd hit him with a two-by-four. I grabbed for his shoulder to steady him. "Hey!"

"I thought I'd never see this again."

"But it's yours, right?"

"Oh, yes." He tapped an index finger on the cover, on words I couldn't begin to read. "Of all the things I thought you might hand to me, I never thought of this. It says 'How to Burn,' and only I and a few others could have written it."

"It's a recipe book for phoenix wizards? DIY? For the regen process?"

He nodded. His hands shook a little, and he made no attempt to open the journal further. Finally, he looked up at me to break a long silence. "I made notes, you see, on the best and most painless ways to accomplish what is a necessary if nasty transition." He rubbed his thumb over it several times, the thick gold ring gleaming as he did.

What could I say to that? "Wow" didn't seem suitable.

"A snake sheds its skin. A cat gives up its nine lives to insatiable curiosity, hopefully gaining enough in wisdom to live long and full the last incarnation. The rest of us go rather blundering through, don't we? But not I. I have to build a pyre, prepare myself and . . . drop a match."

"Technically, they didn't have matches back then."

Brian's gaze shot up to meet mine, belligerent, and then he caught the joke. He did give a soft laugh. "Technically. Also, some of the essential herbs and spices have changed a lot throughout the centuries. I've had to substitute some and manipulate others, but I can't complain about the results. I've made it this far, haven't I?"

"Or almost."

"Indeed." He stuffed the journal in his waistband. "Thank you, most deeply. I'll be studying it closely to see how much of this quest we have before us." He returned to his room, and the house lapsed into quiet. Hiram napping. Steptoe gone to check on his minions. Mom in her study, working on her class grading and another new article. Brian didn't know it, but it seemed only a matter of time until Practical Urban Wizardry crept into her work as she absorbed the influence.

I decided on a nap. The quiet seemed perfect for it.

It couldn't last. An hour or two later, I stood with the guys in the professor's backyard, trying to determine the best way to enter the charred wreckage of his home.

CHAPTER TWENTY

BRIAN SIGHED. His skin, now so pale it looked translucent, accented the veins showing at his wrists and purpling under his eyes. He looked tired beyond the extreme, and I knew he wanted nothing more than to be at a home, any home, preferably resting and reading. We both wore empty shopping satchels over one shoulder, in case we could actually retrieve something.

Yellow plastic tape wavered a little in the early evening breeze, a welcome bit of coolness against the heat and humidity. Summer to come hung in the air, hot and heavy, with a tang of maybe a sprinkle of rain in the next day or two, but it would be a warm rain. I patted Brian on the shoulder, hoping to interrupt the thoughts that held him in place.

He looked at Hiram. "I don't think the foundation will hold him."

Hiram wagged an eyebrow. He leaned over and put his palm down on what was left of the solar porch across the back before nodding to Brian. "You'd be correct. The fire has left little of the bones of this place."

"Okay, just the three of us, then."

"I will stand guard."

My mouth opened to tell him we wouldn't need one, but then I closed it. Stranger things had happened and probably would happen again. Frankly, I expected Remy to be a half step behind us. Or ahead of us.

Hiram nodded to me. "You'll be the easiest on the ruins."

"Weight, right."

"That, and other considerations."

Steptoe and Brian traded looks but said nothing. Great. I stepped forward and bent under the tape cautiously, my shoes sending up a puff of loose ash. I moved cautiously over wood eaten away by fire damage, the whole porch leaning drunkenly to one side, the screening gone, while my memories of rushing in to try and find the professor filled me.

Behind me, Brian gave out a small noise and I imagine some of the same memories filled him. Had it been painful to burn as a phoenix? Did he fear going through it all over again? I slowed and put a hand out behind me. He caught it and held on tightly.

I smiled encouragingly at him over my shoulder. That confidence that had been the professor and eager innocence of young Brian no longer rested in his blue-green eyes. Something important ate away at him, or perhaps it was a lack of that something important, and every day he looked lesser.

He looked through the burned-out doorway and into the interior of his ruined former home. "I'm hopeful there will be some things we can salvage here."

"There might be smoke and water damage, even if there wasn't any burning."

"I understand. Forward, then."

Steptoe stepped onto the porch behind us and even though I didn't have the senses of a Broadstone, I could feel the home giving way. I quickly hustled inside, hauling Brian in at my heels.

Inside, the smoke smell still hung on the air so thick it became difficult to breathe. I could, but my nose and lungs seemed to fill with the pungent aroma. My shoe soles crunched over char and debris, and the water damage made things here and there very squishy. Once completely inside, Brian released my hand and made his way quickly to the threshold of his library.

Steptoe's source had spoken true. This room stood almost inviolate of the fire itself. Water had permeated the first three or four feet beyond the door, but the rest of the room looked untouched, except for the smoke itself. These books would all

hold the scent of a campfire cookout unless sprayed with something that smelled cleaner, maybe pine or cedar or eucalyptus,
to be bearable. Years might filter the cloying scent away eventually without help.

Brian stood running his hand over a shelf, but when he
pulled it back with a book in hand, it literally melted in wet
clumps, falling to the ground at his feet. He pulled another out,
and it too collapsed in a soggy mess. I'd never seen anything
like it. He let out a stifled cry.

"That can't be normal."

"Normal or not, it doesn't matter, it's in ruins." He stood and
spun slowly about in a circle, hands extended. "All ruined."

"Never say never, guv," Steptoe remarked as he moved in.
"That lot on the far wall seems dry enough."

"Seems is the operative word." I steered Brian to the desk,
which had char marks on one side as if the fire's tongue had
entered the room just long enough to give it a lick or two before
the wards stifled it. Steptoe's eyes had glittered a little too
brightly as he'd spotted the desk and its relatively untouched
condition. I didn't expect any of the truly important relics
or artifacts to be in any desk drawers, for how hidden would
that be? But I didn't want our dubious friend to be close
enough to go hunting. He'd come just to hold the bags once
filled and knotted closed. Brian said he could "lock" the bags
with a personal ward, or thought he could. If not, I'd play pack
mule.

I tapped the desktop. "Search here and I'll see how bad the
damage is in this bookcase." Brian nodded numbly.

Unfortunately, I could see most of the tomes in the case were
relevant to his years as a professor and doctor on campus. At
least ten had been written by him, and he might well want to
keep them, but they could wait. I knelt on one knee on the floor
to look at the lowermost shelf. It looked ordinary but slightly
out of kilter. I blinked at it. The alignment moved even as I
stared at it. Just a hair's width or so, and just a degree offside,
but . . . very odd. I rubbed one eye. Was it the smoke hanging in
the air that blurred my sight?

Rubbing didn't make staring at the lower shelf any more

focused. Finally, I grinned. "Professor, you've got a secret book-case. Or shelf." I began running my hands about the side and foot molding of the case, looking for a release or latch.

Brian joined me while Steptoe hummed. The tune seemed to be out of the chimney sweep songbook of street ditties, and it jarred my thoughts a little. I shot a look at him.

"Stop that."

"Stop wot?"

"Look, you and I both know you'd sneak back here to find what we couldn't if we don't, so stop trying to magic the search." Words tumbled out of me before I'd thought them through but they sounded accurate, so I let it stand.

Steptoe's apple cheeks got a wee bit redder and he immediately dropped the tune. "Righto," he said, and made a little hand gesture. "Sorry."

I turned back as Brian found the right carving and depressed it. A click rewarded him, and the bookshelf swung ajar. He carefully finished swinging it open and behind it, a solitary lineup of very old-looking books met our eyes.

"That is cool." I put my hand out. "We want these, right?"

"Right. Sadly, they can't fix my current situation but they are invaluable for study later on. It never hurts to relearn important lessons. And I may have to do it the hard way."

I filled my shopping bag, and Brian pinched it shut with three muttered words. The top of the canvas bag fastened tightly and did not answer to my attempted tug. "Good job."

Dryly, "Thanks."

We both stood, and oddly, Oliver Twist filled my first thoughts. Pickpockets and cutpurses. The top of the bag seemed secure but anyone with a sharp knife, and who moved fast enough, could cut the bottom out. I secured my burden closer to my flank. Brian put the swinging door back into place with a solid click.

"Anything else?"

"A few papers in the desk, probably." He moved to it and began to open doors and such, his hands riffling through old possessions so quickly and confidently I knew the professor was in charge again. He came up with a few items, including a checkbook, which he stowed away in his bag. He scanned the study. "In light of the water damage, I think we've found all we can. Drying fans might or might not help what's left. I can't depend on that."

Steptoe cleared his throat. Brian arched a brow at him.

"Oh, right. He wanted something."

Brian looked at me briefly. "What?"

"I don't know. Ask him."

"What?"

Steptoe quailed a bit under our combined stare. "A small book. A pamphlet, actually, even if the water got to it. Just to read, understand, mate. But I might be able to save it."

"And that book would be . . ."

"Chaos and How to Tame It."

"Taming chaos? And you reckon that would be a small, insignificant pamphlet?"

"To you, perhaps, but not to such as myself."

"I know."

"She offered it, but I know she 'asn't got the right, so I'm asking you. I 'ave been a help, haven't I?"

Brian stood silent for a very long moment. Then he nodded. "You have. Without our asking. You offered." He waved across the room. "If I still have it, it should be over there, I think I remember. Not certain."

Steptoe started in that direction. Stopped. "May I?"

"Yes."

Beaming, he went to the indicated bookcase, running his fingers along spines. He came to a book, a massive book, and pulled it forth carefully. Damp, it dripped slowly on the floor, but did not disintegrate into pulp.

"Insignificant?" I repeated.

"Wait an' see." Steptoe returned to the desktop and opened the book carefully. Within, three smaller books nested in relative safety. He plucked the middle one out, showed the title to both of us, and then tucked it away in his suit coat. "Clever."

Brian took the other two without a word or revealing their subjects and titles. Equally as carefully, he placed them in his sack and locked them away. "Cleverer than I obviously recall. I shall insist they dry this room out, if they can, and return to explore more such options."

"Good idea, guv."

Brian and I traded looks behind Steptoe's back. How did he know what the professor hadn't remembered, about three books hidden inside the greater one? I doubted we'd get any answer, let alone a straight one if we asked.

Outside, Hiram reported no skulkers or problems, but he took guard behind us as we walked home. We hadn't been inside long, and the sun lingered in the sky as it did in late spring. It wouldn't be dark until nearly eight o'clock. My stomach growled a bit. Not nighttime, but definitely close to supper. Mom's car sat in the driveway, so she probably could be found fussing in the kitchen. I heard the pots, pans, and key rack rattle lightly as I walked in, and she poked her head out.

"Full house?"

"Yup, please."

She wrinkled her nose. "Where on earth have you—oh, you went to the professor's house."

"I know, we all smell like an old fire pit. Except for Hiram. He stood guard."

"Any trouble?"

"None, and a patch of success, too," Brian told her as he took up a kitchen chair. He liked watching people cook and had even learned to pitch in with setup and cleanup. With the Broadstone family attending, that aid meant a great deal. I dropped my bag in his lap.

"Do I smell fried chicken?"

"You do, and I used Mamaw's recipe."

"Wow! Thanks, guys. That's a company-only menu." Pleasure filled me at the thought. "I'll start peeling potatoes if you've got the water boiling. Are the green beans simmering?"

"Yes, I do, they are, and you're all set up in the corner." Mom pointed with her tongs.

I began washing and peeling and doubled the amount we usually made for big holiday dinners after sizing up the expression on Hiram's face. Like his dad, he looked to be a big eater.

Unlike his dad, he wore plaid suits that were a tad easier on the eyes, in soft greens and blues, rather than the oranges, yellows, and reds Morty preferred. And his forehead didn't look like you could bounce a boulder off it, unlike his dad. I didn't know where Goldie figured in his history, but she obviously hadn't been his mother, as she was Mortimer's second wife and he'd called her stepmother. So the first wife must have been Iron Dwarf too, from the looks of Hiram, or at least in the Dwarf family somewhere. It would be crass to ask what had happened to her, but if he asked about my father, we could trade misfortunes. He seated himself carefully as Brian stowed his precious cargo and mine under his chair.

The backburner smelled of bacon and onions and garden-fresh beans, simmered by now for probably a good hour or so and steeping over a very low flame. My mouth watered.

I looked around, peeled potato in hand. No sign of Steptoe. "Where'd Steptoe go?"

"Simon wanted to drop off his pamphlet. He may or may not be back."

"He told you that?"

"No, but it stands to reason."

Hiram intoned, "He will likely only stand with us as long as it serves his purpose. My father had little trust of him."

"Well, I do." I pushed my potatoes aside and reached for more. "I'd hoped for at least a good-bye."

"You'll get that, ducks, and more when I decide to move on!" Steptoe filled the doorway, doffed his hat to my mother, and narrowed his dark eyes at the others. "Rumors of my demise and resignation are premature."

"Great. You'll love Mom's chicken."

"It smells loverly." He pulled a chair out and sat in it, rocking it back on its two rear legs and keeping it balanced somehow.

Even using a whole sack of potatoes, we almost didn't have enough mashies for everyone to have seconds, but we managed after scraping the bowl. Brian jumped up to clear the table with me while the others retired to the living room. I could hear what sounded like a hushed argument, even with the clatter of cleaning dishes.

Then came a faint chime of my keys on the board in the hallway. I sighed. Mom glanced my way.

"It's been really noisy the past few days."

"I know. And what was that the other night?" Mom wiped her hands dry.

"When Joanna was here? I have no way of knowing, but it was spectacular. Almost as if our ghost didn't like her at all."

A hanging pot rattled off its hook and crashed to the floor between us. Mom swore. "Dammit. Another bent pot the lid won't fit." She hung it back up with a sigh.

"See what I mean?"

"I do, but I don't understand it, and I don't think I ever will."

"How did the faculty meeting go?"

"Good." That brought a tired smile to her face. "Really good. Word of my publication was well received, and someone had even obtained an advance review, and it garnered four stars out of four."

"That's great. I bet that set old Flankinshaw on his defense." I held little liking for her department head.

"Yes, Flank was more than a tad disappointed."

"Academia."

She shook her head at the scorn in my voice. "Wherever you work, there is always a pecking order and rivalries that can seem petty or serious. It's a fact of life. We're all competitive."

"Well, he should retire."

"He doesn't want to, if it looks like I'd replace him when I finish my doctorate. I think he's trying to wait me out. He's an old dinosaur with regards to women. I couldn't replace him anyway, I haven't the seniority."

I poked a finger in her shoulder. "Don't give him a choice."

"I don't intend to!" She wiped her hands on her apron again, an anxious tell. "I suppose they're all staying the night again?"

"Probably."

"All right. I'm going upstairs. I think I'll read a bit and turn in." She looked back in the kitchen at me. "Make some more sweet tea, if you wouldn't mind."

I nodded. Good thing tea is relatively cheap and easy.

Steptoe looked asleep in his corner, while Brian and Hiram sat practically nose-to-nose, quiet but intense.

I sat down on the coffee table. "What did I miss?"

"Hiram is of the opinion that Malender is not actually here but is projecting strongly. After some persuasion, I'm inclined to agree."

"We were attacked by him."

"Yes and no. He could have done us a lot of damage, but if he'd been at full force and habitation, he would have made mincemeat of us, I think."

I watched Brian a moment before saying, "But Hiram didn't see the attack."

Hiram put his hand on my knee. "My father had the ability to transmit much of his recent history to me."

"So you know what Morty did? How far back?"

His young face frowned a bit in calculation. "You would say . . . perhaps a decade?"

Wow. So Hiram might be able to tell me what Morty hadn't! My pulse drummed in my throat for a few quick beats. "How did he do that?"

"He sent it through the stone."

Stone keeps its promise. It touched me, and for a little while I absolutely could not speak. My eyes brimmed and I felt helpless for a long moment.

Hiram squeezed my knee gently. "I know."

That could only make me bob my head up and down quickly as tears threatened to fall. I coughed. "But Malender had to have been close."

"Yes, but not likely here in Virginia. He's made land, but that journey should have exhausted him and his resources. He can threaten but he can't attack directly."

"That was only a threat?" I swallowed tightly.

"He's powerful," Brian agreed. "We've a lot to fear once he gains the strength he needs. If he's the Great Deceiver we think he is."

"And how will he do that? I mean, I know he preys off smaller life forces, but sooner or later, someone like the Society is bound to notice."

"He can also tap into the souls who live on the edges of our cities and are forgotten."

"The homeless."

"And the criminal. Yes."

"What do we do now?"

"We prepare defenses." Hiram stood and frowned slightly. "Tessa, are you aware your father occupied this house, if only briefly."

"What?" I sat back in shock. "Did the police know?"

"I doubt if anyone knew. His vibrations here are very faint."

"There are still vibrations?" Vibrations! A thought spun its wild way into my mind. "Can you find them? Identify them?" Mom would shit if she knew who I suddenly thought our ghost might be.

Hiram answered slowly. "Yes. Still." He stood and turned his head as if sussing them out. "Stronger than they should be, actually." He began to move through the parlor. "Odd."

I jumped up. "How odd?" I ran my hand across my face, dashing away tears I couldn't afford.

"Very."

"Where? Can you find them?"

"Maybe."

As if awakened by his steps, the house began to creak and moan in its joints. I wondered if it was simply his weight on the flooring—or if something else added to the voice of the home.

Upstairs, I could hear Mom's door opening and shutting, and then she stood poised at the top of the stairs, alert, and looking down at us. "What is it?"

I waved a signal at her to calm her down. "Nothing."

"It's not nothing. The whole house sounds like it's threatening to collapse."

"Nothing like that at all, missus," Steptoe called back in his most reassuring tones.

"Now that I absolutely don't believe." She came lightly and quickly down the stairs as Steptoe put his hand over his heart and tried to look offended. I'd seen that look before and still didn't know if I thought it was genuine.

Hiram kept moving. He ended up at the mudroom door, a side entry we never used, because of the clutter there and also because we just didn't. He opened the door that closed it off and entered.

With a crash, he abruptly fell through the floor.

CHAPTER TWENTY-ONE

WHAT WAS LEFT of the mudroom avalanched into the gaping hole as I threw myself flat and hung my head over to see what had happened to Hiram.

The fall landed him on one knee, his knuckled hands balancing him on either side, his head down to avoid the flakes of debris drifting downward.

"Are you all right?"

"Right enough."

He and I looked about. The space into which he'd plunged took up far more than below the mudroom. It stretched at least under the kitchen and maybe even Mom's study.

"What was that?"

I yelled back at my mother, "Hiram's fallen through the floor into the basement."

"We have a basement?" Mom asked in amazement as she appeared nearby.

I answered, "We do now."

Hiram rumbled, "I'll repair the damage, miss. So sorry."

"Don't worry about that." I wanted down there in the worst way. What had Hiram sensed? Were my father's bones down there somewhere? How else could Hiram have been led there? "Look for a ladder or stairs. There's got to be an entrance."

"It's a tad dark down here."

And it looked to be, especially in the corners not easy to see behind the edges of the hole. I thought about the extra light switches in the kitchen, the ones Mom and I could never quite figure out what, if anything, they lit up. I got up, raced to the room, and flipped them all on, every single switch. The kitchen blazed into glory.

"That's done it!" Hiram called up triumphantly. "There's a rickety staircase in the corner." I could hear him move around and the floor under my feet vibrated a bit. "Tessa, I calculate it's where the pantry is."

"The pantry?"

"Aye."

I turned on one heel. We had no pantry, just an open shelving unit. Unless . . .

Paint, thickened by many years and many coats, rippled along molding that I'd always thought just decorative. I knocked on it. It could be hollow. A walk-in closet or pantry or just a big ole hole in the wall could be hidden there. I grabbed an old steak knife and began to run it down the seams, peeling the thickness away.

"What—oh dear." Mom joined me, at first bewildered, and then finding a knife of her own to work on the other side, muttering, "We'll have to paint again or Aunt April will have fits."

I thought of Dad staying here, for however long, after he'd left us. On the sly, or had she known? "She's Dad's aunt, right? We all look alike."

"Honestly, Tessa, I thought you paid attention. She's your father's aunt on his mother's side. You know that."

I did. Seriously. It's just as though it had intentionally slipped my mind. As if that wasn't complicated. "Riiight." The blade in my knife wobbled a bit and turned, slicing at a fingertip. I let out a cuss word, apologized and then looked at where my blood seeped into the opening crack. "I think I've got an opening here."

"A door?" Mom said from her side.

"Maybe. It's going to be a tough haul, though. I bet it hasn't been opened in decades." And, it looked it. So if that was true, how did my father get into the unknown basement . . . if he did? Mom pulled up a kitchen chair and worked on the top, which went much quicker. Who painted the top of a pantry door where no one could see? Few people, evidently.

Brian and Steptoe leaned on the doorway, fascinated.

"I could use some manly muscle right about now."

"Oh. A-course, ducks. Coming along."

As soon as I had the seam completely cleared, I bowed and indicated the revealed edging to a doorway. The two moved in and with quite a bit of straining and grunts, got the pantry door swung about an inch away from the wall. Mom knelt down with a rag and put vegetable oil on the floor to aid any sliding. Of course, that made it extremely tricky for anyone trying to stand there and exert any great force on the stubborn wood-work. It squeaked and complained and opened another inch before Brian took a slippery fall.

Before he could do more than get up with a hand from Step-toe (who then looked at his hand in disgust and went to the sink to wash and dry himself off), the door suddenly heaved wide open.

Hiram waved his meaty hand from the hidden stairway as he looked up from the basement, halfway up the steps. I hopped over the oily spots to peer down. The staircase did indeed look rickety and unsubstantial, particularly its upper portion. If I went down, I could get back up—probably. Hiram looked stuck.

"Coming down!"

Hiram hopped back and held his arms out as if he thought to catch me. Not that I didn't trust him, but I took the steps down, jumping two at a time, listening to the boards complain as I did. I thought that I had never lived in such a noisy old house. It was almost like living inside a huge pipe organ at an old-time theater or church.

Dusting myself off, I looked around. Ancient mason jars lined one wall, but I was pretty sure whatever had been pickled in them, even by archaeological standards, had not survived. Cobwebs decorated everything in abundance. I yelled upstairs, "Mom, don't come down. I think we just invaded Spiderland."

"Oh, God!" I could hear her scurry overhead and knew she'd dived for the cupboard under the sink where several bottles of insect spray reigned, next to the dishwasher soap container. Her hatred of spiders echoed throughout the kitchen.

Hiram wiped a large web off his shoulder and elbow before eying me. "That was both considerate and a little mean."

"I know. Couldn't help myself though. Seriously? How much bigger is she than a spider?" I paced around him. A stack of three big trunks in the corner held who knew what. Probably clothes and other items most people stored in an attic. We didn't have much of one upstairs, so I figured I knew what were in these three. Evelyn loved haunting vintage clothing stores, so I knew who I'd volunteer to help me go through these. If Aunt April let us. She might have skeletons hidden away down here that she didn't want anyone to know about, although from the paint layers I'd skinned through, she'd have been my age when they were stored.

"First things first. How do we get you out of here?" I paced about the basement, searching the walls. Finally I found a grimed and almost totally obscured window. It looked up into the garden from the soil banked against it, with white, spindly roots pressing against the dirty glass. "I'd say that led into the side garden."

Hiram tilted his head to eye the window, long but not high, and gave a grunt. "I doubt I could get through there."

"Well, you're not going up that staircase."

"I made it up three steps."

"Yeah, but I bet the next four or five can't hold you."

"I can pull myself up on the rim of the doorway."

"Really?"

"Like doing a pull-up." He nodded confidently. "I am more agile than I look."

Like his father, he looked like a ton of bricks. "Oh-kay. Worth a try. And if that doesn't work, we'll go back to the window and see if we can enlarge it without collapsing the side of the house."

Hiram laughed, a gentle rumbling sound. I liked it.

Brian and Steptoe lay on the hole's edge, heads down, watching our every move. I called up, "No bones or anything yet."

"I don't believe you're going to find any." Brian ran his hand through his red-gold hair, trying to keep it out of his eyes in vain.

"Good to know."

Steptoe reminded us. "Hiram had some sensin' of 'im though."

"True," Hiram agreed. He started casting about again, reminding me of a good hound winding a scent. I hadn't felt it before, but now the hairs at the back of my neck danced about uneasily. I scrubbed a hand over them but it didn't help much. Plus, the tip of my finger still hurt, slightly more than a bad paper cut but less than a bad slice. I sucked on it, tasting the copper on my tongue.

To add to my uneasiness, Brian called down, "Be careful. There is an energy I'm sensing that I don't like."

And Steptoe added, "It gives me a fair roil to my gut, it does. Something's about."

We both stood still a moment and assessed the shadows of the basement. Nothing looked too dark or obscured from the dangling lightbulbs overhead. Something did squeak and skitter away as Hiram took a step, heard if not seen, so probably a very tiny mouse.

"What was that?" Mom's head, haloed by kitchen light, appeared at the doorway to the cellar.

"A mouse. One of those itty-bitty field mice. I think."

"Oh, fantastic." I could hear her retreat back to the sink cabinet and a moment later something clattered down the stairwell steps. "Set that before you come back up."

I bent over to retrieve a mousetrap, the old wood and spring kind. "Okay." I stuffed it in a pocket, not at all certain I wanted to set a trap that would probably cut the little thing in two. If it managed an existence down here, more power to it. I assessed the area. "No pentagrams on the floor or wall or anything dire like that."

Hiram nodded absently, lost in his thoughts or whatever he was doing. A tall wardrobe cabinet stood near one corner, warped a little to one side from sitting forever on a down-sloping base, so its doors did not quite meet or hang right. Its ivory paint, yellowed with age, flaked at the corners, and its latch swung open, useless. I reached out and pried it wide, curious what it might hold.

A crimson drop fell from my finger as I did, into the depths of the wardrobe, my hand reaching inside.

"Tessa!" screamed Brian.

Too late. Something leaped from the hidden shelf and sunk its teeth deep into my left palm. It, and the pain, knocked me on my ass.

Hiram knocked the cabinet doors shut and bent over me, reaching out in concern. I could hear a racket upstairs, three voices in loud confusion but not sensible.

I looked up through sudden tears, clutching my left hand and saw—

Nothing.

The thing, whatever it was, had burrowed into my flesh on the other side, into my palm.

Jaw clenched as the waves of agony slowly ebbed about, I peeled my fingers open, bracing the back of my hand on my knee, determined to see what ravaged me.

An oval piece of what looked to be marble, and very beautiful marble at that, lay buried in my flesh. Its swirls of caramel, ivory, gold and ebony reminded me of the very nice marble in Evelyn Statler's mansion counters and floors. Quality. Cool. Inanimate. Beautiful to look upon.

But this seemed anything but inanimate or stonelike. It pulsed in time to my racing heartbeat as its icy being burned in its cold. Even as I watched it, my heart calmed. The burn receded. I flexed my hand.

It felt liked it looked—something immovable embedded in my palm. A dollar piece welded into place. A bit of marble permanently attached to me.

Brian tumbled down the stairs. "What is it? What's happened?"

"It—it's stuck in me." I held my hand up for him to see. He stopped dead in his tracks. Steptoe bounded down after him, and he said, softly, "Oh, Tessa."

"What is it?"

"I d-don't know," Brian stammered. "That is to say, I'm not certain."

"Well, I am. That's a maelstrom stone." Steptoe approached me cautiously, his sharp gaze with a speculative glitter that he shuttered away quickly by closing his eyes tightly a moment before looking on me again.

"What does that mean?"

"It means," Brian told me, "you could be very, very dangerous."

His words jolted me. They had to be wrong. He meant I could be in a lot of danger, right? Surely.

"I'm . . . I'm in trouble."

He shook his head slowly. "No. I meant what I said. You could be very dangerous. It harnesses chaotic energy, but it doesn't stay neutral. It all depends on you, and how long it takes you to master it, and keep control of it."

"Get it out!"

"Not possible. It's symbiotic."

"Symbiotic. Like a parasite? A partnership?"

Brian nodded.

It would live in partnership with me. But it was stone, marble, albeit very handsome marble, not living! And yet I had felt it move with my rhythm and warm to my temperature. I dropped my hand in my lap and looked at the miserable thing. I wasn't magic. I might have luck but that wasn't magic, and I didn't want to be magic. Look at all the trouble it caused Morty and the professor! "It's got to come out."

"When it's done with you."

"And what do you mean by that!"

"He means," Steptoe said kindly, "it has a purpose, and when it's fulfilled that, it'll loosen, drop out, an' wait for another for a different purpose."

"Seriously? How long will that take?"

"No one knows. Some quests are lifelong. Some are generational. And some might be completed in a few days."

I stared at it. "I guess I could wear gloves to the auction." I looked up at Brian. "Is this the item you gave to my father? The business arrangement you had with him that didn't go well?"

Brian blinked. Then he pursed his lips in thought. "No, no it's not. And how did you—" He paused. "Morty talked too much."

"Nailed it." I got to my feet, leaning on Hiram. For a moment my head swam in dizzy circles and I held onto his arm for dear life. Everything went haywire and sparkles flooded the basement. Then everything steadied although the room seemed much, much dimmer. I narrowed my eyes to see better.

It was then I saw it.

Or rather, not an "it."

A figure in the corner of the basement. An apparition, layered over the reality of where we all stood. A ghost watching me with an ineffable look of complete sadness.

I had found my father.

CHAPTER TWENTY-TWO

I DIDN'T KNOW if anybody else could see him, and he certainly wasn't looking at anyone but me, not even Mom when she appeared at the top of the shaky staircase, afraid to come down but more worried about me. "Tessa, are you all right?"

"Sort of." I looked at the ghost. He wasn't all white and misty but himself, although one dimensional and sepia colored, as though there had been colors to him once but something had leached them all out before flattening him. He looked almost like a vintage photograph back in the early days, one of those tintype thingies. When he realized I saw him, he gave a weary and crooked smile and lifted a hand.

I lifted a hand back.

"We *thought* the house was haunted. It was you, all this time. All the rattles and pots and pans."

He inclined his head.

Mom came down a shaky step or two. "What is it? Who are you talking to?"

She knew something happened to me before anyone else did. The men around me stood stock still, but she fairly quivered with anticipation and worry. But then, she was my mom. I craned my head around to tell her.

"I can see him. They can't."

She didn't ask who. She put shaking fingers to her mouth instead. "Is he . . . Is he . . ."

"Dead? I don't know. Are you?"

Mom took another slow step down. "John?"

He glanced at her, and then away quickly, as if the sight of her burned him. He stared at the floor a moment. I saw his lips move long before the words reached me. "I don't think so. But I can't really tell. I've been trying to let you know I'm here somewhere."

She didn't react but I stepped back with a gasp.

"What is it?"

"I can hear him." I whirled around to face her. "You didn't hear that?"

She shook her head, blonde curls tumbling about her shoulders. "Not a thing."

"He answered you. And I heard him."

Steptoe drew himself up. "It's the stone. We can't perceive wot she does. Well, perhaps Hiram did, slightly. But she's on 'er own."

Brian put his hand on my arm. "Tell me, us, what's happening?"

"The room got all wonky, but that might have been shock. Then it filled with sparkles and kind of dimmed. Hazy-like. And then I saw my father, only it's not, he's not quite real. He's near transparent."

My father's lips moved again and a few seconds later, I got the sense of what he said. "Tell the professor I still have it."

"And he says to tell you he still has it."

"Does he now? Well, that's good, that's good." Brian frowned. "If I could only think of what it might have been."

That caught my father's full attention. He moved, wavering a bit, as if walking across the bottom of a swimming pool. "What happened to the old man?"

"It's a long story," I returned. "If you're sticking around this time, I might be able to tell you." My throat stung. I wanted to hug him and cry and then get mad all over again, then hug him again. I had missed him. I had.

My mother whispered, "How does he look?" as if afraid to draw attention.

I shrugged at Mom. "Not like Casper the Ghost or anything. It's . . . strange. Like an old-timey picture. And his words come across slowly, out of synch."

"Aha!" Brian jumped a step. "It might be, of course I can't be certain, and it's rare, but it can happen. He's caught between dimensions. How on earth he managed that, I've no idea."

"Then he's not dead?"

"No, not yet." Brian scratched the side of his jaw. "He'll eventually fade away though to the other side if we can't draw him back. I have to remember . . ."

"Is he carrying a relic you need?"

After a long, thoughtful moment, Brian shook his head. "I don't believe so. An item of great importance. I remember being very distressed when he disappeared with it, but just what it is . . ." He sighed. "I can't bring it to mind."

My father said, "I never opened the box. I have no idea what it is, either." His form rippled suddenly, winked out, and came back. He held shaking hands out to me. "What's happening?"

"I have no idea!" I cried to the others, "He's winking in and out. Are we losing him?" Not again. Not yet. I wasn't ready. I know Mom wasn't.

Both Brian and Steptoe said as one, "Not good."

Steptoe added, "He's weakening. It's willpower that keeps him on the edge of this reality. But it draws on him, it has to."

I grabbed for him before he could wink away totally. The stone in my hand went ice-hot and as I touched him, I felt him, the cloth of his shirt's sleeve, the slightness of his shoulder, the smell of his old-fashioned after-shave, the warmth of his body.

Everyone else in the room gasped as they saw him. Just for a moment. Just for a flash. Then my stone cooled and he faded back to his sepia self and I let go.

I didn't know how he got to where he was, but I knew that my stone might have the power to bring him back if we'd all seen him. Somehow, I'd brought him in line with us, just for that brief moment. So it gave me the power for that, among other uses. Would that be a dark thing to do? Would I be upsetting the worlds between here and wherever *there* was? Life and death?

I suddenly didn't care.

"I'll get you back, Dad. I will."

The stone flared again and as I held my hand out, palm up, to look at it, a tiny flame danced over the surface, and then the marble absorbed it. I could feel a coldness go through my body.

"Ah, no, ducks, you shouldn't have done that. Never make a vow with a maelstrom stone."

I'd meant to do what I did, but a mantle of fear tried to settle over my shoulders, and I shook it off impatiently. "Too late now."

"Too right that is." Steptoe sighed again.

We left him there, in the basement. I tried to coax him upstairs with me, but it seemed he couldn't cross the boundary. He had used all his energy strength over the past many months poltergeisting. He might cross later, Brian told me, if he gained it back.

Brian and Steptoe fastened a kind of rope hoist, a block and tackle, to get Hiram up the stairs, at his instruction, and it worked, more or less. The first thing he did was get his phone out and notify the family that he needed a small construction crew, and then he told us that he would get repairs and remodels done punctually. They'd arrive in a day or two. After that, we ordered pizzas.

I wouldn't let anyone slide the pantry back into place. I wanted to be able to pop down and talk to him if I needed to, or if he needed me. Mom didn't say much, but she cried quietly and clung to my right hand, the one without the maelstrom stone.

She, the pert and blonde one, cried enough that her nose finally turned red and her eyes looked a little bloodshot. I sat down with her, side-by-side on the couch, our bodies close from ankle to shoulder, and realized how much I'd grown to look like my father in the last two years. Tall, lanky, thick tangle of hair. I couldn't remember if he had freckles too. I must remind her of him every single day, and I'd had no real idea. I'd been thinking of myself, mostly.

And I decided that I'd become as much of an adrenaline junkie as he was, searching for that surge of excitement, only I didn't gamble for it. I played with magic.

I put my head back and waited for the doorbell to announce the delivery guy. I listened to three men who'd been absolute strangers just days ago, argue about what to do with my life. I wanted to object but suddenly felt too exhausted to join in.

I barely heard the last sentence: "I still don't see how it could have bonded so strongly with her."

A quiet fell among the three as they contemplated the meaning of that.

After many long moments, I lifted my chin. "I bled on it."

"You what?"

"I'd cut my finger trying to get the pantry seam open, and I bled on it. Or on something on the cabinet shelves when I reached in." Of course, I'd bled on it later too, when it dug itself in, but that didn't seem quite as significant. It was almost as if I'd baited it, and it had responded.

Brian's mouth fell open. He snapped it shut. "That is not good at all."

"What does it matter?" I pushed away from my mother. "It's done. Now all we have to worry about is undoing it."

"No. What we have to do is make certain you stay strong enough to control it. Its bond with you will be that much more formidable. Because it is, it will take considerable effort to undo anything regarding the stone."

"What do you mean, strong?" My mother's voice took an edge.

"The stone has a mind of its own, in many ways. Although it looks like a static object, it can tap into other things." Steptoe took the folded pamphlet out of his suit coat. "Give me a few hours to peruse this and I might be able t' tell the lot of you more. If the stone embodies anything, it certainly does chaos." He rattled a page as he opened it and the first sound out of his mouth was an "Uh-oh," which didn't give me much confidence.

The door knocker sounded. I stumbled to my feet, grabbed the wallet Mom tossed to me, and went to retrieve the pizzas. She couldn't foot the bill for five pizzas (Hiram alone would eat two full ones and maybe a slice or two more), so I still carried Morty's black credit card, but she insisted on leaving the tip. I opened our door to a frazzled looking Carter Phillips.

His mouth twisted and so did that off-center cleft scar.

"Someone reported screams and a crash. Or maybe it was a crash and then screams."

I quickly closed my left hand so I couldn't flash him the maelstrom stone. I had the sudden thought that the Society would be less than thrilled. "We—ah—well, that would be us, because Hiram fell through the floor in the mudroom and Mom and I let out a yell. It was very traumatic at the time, but everyone's okay."

"He fell through the floor?"

"It's an old house. There's a basement we didn't know about. And, you know, Iron Dwarves are weighty."

"Wow." He managed to look impressed despite being tired.

"Tessa, is that someone you're going to let in or do we need to come help you throw him out?" Mom called from the living room.

"It's Carter Phillips."

"Oh. Then do let him in. There's pizza, when it gets here."

Carter followed me to the living room and dropped in a wing chair. "That sounds good."

"What flavor?"

He gave a diffident gesture. "Any. All."

"That's my man." Hiram smiled widely at him.

Everyone lapsed into silence. I stayed on my feet and decided to pull paper plates and napkins out of the kitchen in preparation. Stumbling a bit, I kicked a lower cabinet and made the pot on the stove rattle ever so slightly. That pulled me into a dead stop.

Yes, my father had been trying to alert us. Yes, we hadn't understood for months and months. But none of that explained the absolutely berserk rattles and crashes and clanking when Joanna was here, and I'd forgotten to ask him.

I dropped my pile of paper goodies on the kitchen table. Making sure no one saw me from the living room, I crept to the hole in the mudroom, lay down, and hung my head in, upside down.

We'd taken out two of the bulbs to reduce the lighting from a brilliant glare to muted, and it looked even dimmer through my inverted vision. Not the rest of the house, just here. Wherever it was my dad occupied.

"Dad!" I pitched my whisper sharply. If he lived in a dimension that was darker, who knew how well sound projected?

A waver, like a mirage, rippled below me. His head and shoulders appeared. Nothing else. I swallowed tightly, wondering if our meeting had drained him of valuable and necessary energy. I couldn't back out now.

"I forgot to ask you, but . . . well, you got really noisy when I had a friend come over the other day."

"A friend? Who? And when?"

"Joanna Hashimoto. She goes to college with me and Evelyn."

"Statler's daughter? Her, I remember. You're friends now? She used to shun you in middle school. Hashimoto. That would be Hironori Hashimoto? Businessman, important, getting political, country club? Statler surprises me though."

"More friends than not, now." I calculated and told him exactly when the two had come over, for the dress try-on. He frowned and I realized that time quite possibly didn't pass for him as it did for us.

Then he scowled. "I remember now. You have to stay away from her, Tessa!"

His voice thundered in my ears and I drew back a little, thinking that slim, quiet Joanna looked far from dangerous compared to her ninja drivers. I thought a moment before saying, "After what we've been through, I think I deserve more than a heated warning. Like some evidence."

He rippled. The anger had cost him. "I'm in a place of darkness, where the light only reaches a little, and all I can tell you is that the darkness appreciates him. Her. Reaches for them. Don't let it come for you, too."

I licked lips suddenly gone dry but the doorbell rang, and blood had gone to my ears making them buzz, and I knew from the sight of him that our conversation had finished, for now.

"All right. I've got to go."

I went and gathered the pizzas and made the delivery boy very happy with his tip.

Everyone else devoured the pizzas as though they were the most important things on earth at the moment, and I guess they must have been. I picked a little at mine and wondered if I should confide in Carter, if he would agree not to share it with the Society. My mom gave me a sideways glance, noticing me playing with my pizza slice, so I rolled and demolished it, deciding that Brian and the others would have to tackle me to keep me silent. Except about the stone. That still seemed to be something we wouldn't want the Society to know about. They might demand to remove it, and failing that, take the whole hand. I shuddered.

Mom rubbed my shoulder. "You all right, honey?"

"Long couple of days." I took a deep breath. "Carter, what do you know about ghosts? Or, better yet, people who are neither here nor there."

He choked on his last bite, coughed heartily a few times, and took a big swig of his tea. "What?"

"The hole in the floor?"

He cleared his throat and nodded.

"There's a cellar under half the house we didn't know was there."

"That is interesting."

"It is. Because a ghost came with it, and that ghost is my dad."

He wiped his hands off and sat back, crossing his arms. "I should get CSU out here. Did you find remains of any kind?"

"No. And he says he isn't dead. Exactly. So there's nothing to investigate because there's no evidence, no body."

"You spoke to him?" The corner of one hazel eye twitched.

"Yes."

"But you don't think he's dead?"

I shook my head. "He seems to be in between, caught. Maybe he can come back, maybe we have to send him on. I don't know. I'm not asking the Society to help, just you. I think," and I twisted my fingers together. "I think bringing the Society in might just cause more trouble."

"You'd be right!" Steptoe insisted. Brian stopped him from saying anything else by putting a hand on his arm, watching me alertly.

"Did he know what happened? Or where? Or who?"

"Not that he said. He's weak, so it's not like I can interrogate him for half the day or something."

That made Carter wince. I added quickly, "Not that I think you work like that."

A grateful expression flashed across his face so quickly I almost wondered if I'd imagined it. It hit me that he cared what I thought. He unfolded from his chair and dropped his napkin to the table. "Let me go home. Think about it. Do a little discreet studying. I'll see what I can figure out."

"Great!" I walked him to the door while behind us I could hear Steptoe angrily muttering to Brian, with Hiram giving off soothing, low tones of placation.

Carter turned on the porch step. I stood just inside and a moment came I didn't want to resist, so I didn't. I leaned forward slightly and cupped my right hand along the side of his face. I could feel bristles that needed shaving, and the measured drumbeat of his pulse, and the glow of his skin. His bone structure felt chiseled. His eyes widened. His personal aroma, that scent of pine and leather and something else I couldn't identify, wrapped around me.

More than that. It wasn't the proper hand, but the maelstrom stone awoke sharply. It knew him, sensed a deep and dark core buried inside him, and woke something in me to answer. We'd both seen things we shouldn't have. Knew things beyond mortal knowledge. Could reach for and use power in any, and all, of its forms. We could pull in whatever strength we needed from whatever source, and mold it to our command. Together. Without remorse or hesitation. We could be a force worth reckoning with, a force that could shape our world.

I dropped my hand suddenly, shaken.

"What was that?"

"I—I don't know."

"Tessa, what have they done to you?"

"Nothing." True. I'd done it to myself. I wasn't lying to him, exactly.

"You don't get power from nothing."

"You can't tell anyone."

"I can't do that. Not if anything threatens you."

He stood, tall as one of the stately alder trees on the boulevard.

Slowly, I turned my left hand over and showed him the maelstrom stone.

CHAPTER TWENTY-THREE

HE GRABBED MY HAND. "Which one of them did this to you?" His words sounded heated, leaving me with the distinct feeling he'd kill whoever it was.

"Nobody. I was alone in the basement when it attached." Hiram had been there, but I didn't intend to get him in trouble.

"It attached itself? Where did it come from?"

"An old wardrobe that my great-aunt had sitting down there. The cellar's got trunks and boxes and junk in it, like an old attic. It attacked me. I swear I thought a pit bull or something had grabbed onto me. But it was this. It burrowed in. I can't get it out. They told me it won't come out until it's ready." I took a quick breath. "That's how I saw my father, and no one else can, or hear him either. Just me. So whatever it is, and I gather it can go good or bad, it's got some worth."

"It's worth a king's ransom. The only good thing about it is it just can't be ripped out of you, not if the one taking it wants it to still be viable, so that protects you a little. But . . ." and his words faded. "It will call *him*, just as it will the Society. It's a thing of power that can see into the shadows, and it will reach out to him. You're not going to be able to keep this hidden for long."

"I think I guessed that." My voice went a little shaky, and he cupped my hand in both of his. He had big hands. Not mitts like the Broadstones, but big, strong hands. I liked the feel of them, except my left palm did not. The stone grew nasty hot and I thought I might have to pull away quickly or get horribly burnt, but then it stopped. Slowly, with each heartbeat, it cooled. Was I doing it or was Carter? "Please don't tell them."

He closed his eyes a long moment. "I don't know if I can avoid telling them. What's wisest? I have to think."

He squeezed my hands together and let go. "I'm wrecked. I need to go consult some sources and get some sleep. I have to report to the department tomorrow morning, but I'll come find you later in the day."

"Oh, yeah. We're finishing up courses. The auction is next weekend. Then reviewing. Finals. End of semester stuff coming out of my ears. You remember." Surely he did. Surely there wasn't that big a gulf between us. Everyone else might think so, but I didn't and I hoped he didn't.

"I'd tell you to wear a glove, but—" He eyed my hand. "Conspicuous."

Thoughts skittered through my mind like an alley cat with a hound dog on its tail. "Wait. I have a wrist brace I can wear, and it wraps around my hand too. Used it when I sprained my hand in field hockey. Everyone will just think I popped it again."

"Good idea." He leaned forward slightly, the line of his jaw softening, and then abruptly stepped back. "Nite, Tessa. You take care."

"And you."

We'd had a moment, there. I knew it. Hadn't we? I had no idea what had pulled him back, but I wanted to call out to him, to make him return and finish.

I watched as he trudged down the street, tiredness in every step, and wished him a good rest even though I figured he'd spend half the night trying to understand what had happened and what could happen. And had he almost kissed me good night? Even if it was aimed for the forehead or my cheek? Had there been more than concern gleaming in his eyes as he talked to me, held my hands? Woah.

My fingers itched to get my phone and text Evelyn.

My common sense warred with that. If she let it slip to either her mom or dad, Carter would be in serious trouble. But I needed to tell *someone* as it bubbled up inside me, warm and cheery, as though I'd drunk a glass of champagne. Good champagne. I'd had some cheap, awful stuff at a wedding reception last year for one of Mom's college colleagues that frankly was little better than sucking a lemon. Ugh. But it had definitely bubbled. Or maybe curdled.

This was so superior to anything I could imagine. I rubbed my hands together. How long would it be before he held my hands again? Leaned in again? Maybe would not change his mind next time?

A voice sliced through my dreams. "Assignments, Tessa!"

Oh, yeah. And a lot of them, too. Not to mention digging up that old brace from the corner of my closet. It probably smelled like old shoes and gym socks. I'd have to do something about that or nobody would ever think about coming closer to me.

I closed and locked the door behind me and retreated to my room. Maybe I'd tell Mom. On the other hand, maybe I wouldn't.

Evelyn waited by the quad. She gave a little bounce, her pert skirt flouncing with her. "You're back. Again." She either had a new purse that looked like a shopping bag hanging from her arm, or it was a shopping bag.

"Well, yeah. Did you think I'd flake on you? Grab the dress and run?"

"You've been a bit odd lately. I thought maybe you'd ditch again today. Three days out of five." She shrugged and then her nose wrinkled. "That brace is gross."

"Yes, but I have it on good authority it smells like lilac toilette water. I put enough on, anyway."

"The stuff you got from one of the old ladies on your route?"

"That would be it."

With many paper rattles, she pulled her purse out of the bag and shoved the bag at me.

"What's this?"

"Shoes! I have the perfect silver ones."

I peered into the depths. Yes, two silver five-inch heels lay on their sides at the bottom of the bag, as if they'd gone to sleep there, nestled like little, sparkly silver reptiles. Definitely not for running anywhere. "Huh."

"Seriously. Silver will go perfect with your dress."

"True." I lifted one of the heels out. "Good god. I can change bulbs on the streetlights wearing these."

"They're not that tall!"

"Really?" I put my free hand up to measure. "Yup, five inches. I think the shoemakers stopped at six, didn't they? With platforms?" I turned the shoe about. "These must hurt."

Evelyn tossed her head. "It's not like you have to wear them all day. Anyway, practice in them. Remember to keep your knees straight, don't walk all crouched down."

I dropped the shoe back in the bag and deposited all in my backpack. "I'll try not to let my knuckles drag."

"That's my girl!" We walked through the crowded corridors toward class, one of several we shared. "Still excited about Joanna's girls-only invite?"

"Can't wait! It's going to be glorious. Like princesses."

"With paid escorts."

She bumped her hip into me. Evelyn is skinny, so her hipbones can be sharp. I grunted an "ow," but she didn't apologize. Never had and never would. She is sprung from the stock of "can't be too rich or too thin."

"I've met one or two. They're formal but have a sense of humor, and they're devastatingly quiet."

"I wonder if they're Yakuza and have taken vows of criminal silence." I dodged her hip bump and she laughed as she staggered a bit, trying to recover.

"Mr. Hashimoto is a gentleman. You know he wants to run for state congress in a few years."

"Really? I thought your dad had that on tap."

She shook her head, and her dark blonde hair fell in silken, disturbed waves about her shoulders. "No, he's planning on DC once he's mayor here a term or two."

"Wow. I had no idea."

"It's in our blood. My uncle was a congressman. Representative for almost twenty years." She waved her hand. "A while back. He's a lot older than my dad. Can you imagine my father being the baby of a large family?"

"I have trouble seeing your dad as a baby of any kind."

She laughed.

I swung into our classroom, catching the closing door with my elbow, and wedging it open with the rest of my body for the two of us, and about a half a dozen others, to enter.

Taking my seat, I thought about lines of power, those born to it and those determined to gain it. I didn't think either of my parents was ever interested in any of that. Mom's commitment now was keeping us healthy, fed, educated, and housed. Was that the same? I didn't know exactly what I saw in the professor or Brian, or Morty and his son, but I recognized the gleam of ambition in Steptoe's eyes, at constant war with decency. That could have been what made him chaotic. Or not. I didn't want to think of Carter with that same gleam, but he did have a glimmer, a flame inside him that I thought meant he warred with himself between helping and bringing the Society in on happenings.

I did make some notes, and not a few doodles in my notebook, before class drew to an end.

I ambled to independent computer lab. My brace made it difficult to keyboard and I almost just unlaced it and shoved it to one side, but I didn't dare. The stone kept making hot little sparks in my palm as if agitated.

Joanna, sitting opposite me, narrowed her eyes. She leaned forward, indicating I should pull my earphones aside, too. "What is going on? You keep jumping as if someone is sticking a pin into you."

An apt analogy. I shrugged. "Wrist is hurting."

"I hope you're better by auction."

"I should be, you know?"

She flashed her very white teeth. "I can hook you up with my masseuse. She's terrific."

"Shiatsu? That sounds wonderful."

"I'll give you a text later, see when we can slip you in."

It would be expensive. I shook my head. "Thanks, but I probably shouldn't."

"Why not? It will help!"

I didn't want to say it, but there it was. "Our budget is pretty tight."

Joanna wrinkled her nose. "Forget about it! My treat. In fact, I know my father will insist. All you have to do is show up."

"That's . . . that's really nice of you. I'll check with my mom and let you know, okay?" I didn't feel like accepting but I could throw that on my mom. She didn't like living on the kindness of strangers any more than I did. Friendship was one thing. Sympathy quite another.

"Deal!" She gave me a thumbs-up before turning back to her monitor, replacing her earphones and catching up with her lesson.

I returned to my monitor, pausing every now and then to slip an index finger inside the brace to rub my palm where sparks danced, itching and burning like crazy. After a particularly long scratching session, I looked up to see Joanna glancing away quickly, not to be caught staring.

She seemed like any other normal teen. Yet my father had warned me about her. Why?

I remembered her brief interest in Brian's journal. Had she had that same ambitious gleam in her eye that flickered in Steptoe? And how would my father know?

I caught the bus home, Evelyn having an appointment with the administration over something or other, and the day wrapped around me hot and sweaty. I was busy pfoofing damp curls from my forehead when I spied Carter sitting on the front steps waiting for me.

I wiped my face off as delicately as I could, nearly impossible, and said, "You couldn't come to campus and pick me up?"

"I'm not a mind reader. Besides, you always hated me showing up with the patrol car."

"That was before I had to walk in eighty percent humidity." I pfoofed again. "The guys didn't let you in?"

"The guys," and he beckoned to two pickup trucks and one utility truck parked along the street, "are busy."

"Wow. The work crew is here?"

"You bet."

I would have blushed but the heat had already set my face glowing. I hadn't even noticed the various service units; I'd only seen him. "Did you learn anything?"

He looked unhappy. "I'd say that. How about we go inside, find a quiet place—if that's possible—and talk. Where's your mother?"

"Office hours." I checked my phone for the time. "She won't be home for at least two hours."

He frowned even more. "I should wait till she's here."

"So she can enjoy the bad news, too?"

He shuffled inside behind me, the house instantly growing cooler as the noise level ratcheted up to deafening. Saws, nail guns, pounding, shouting. I would have gone right back out immediately but I needed something cold to drink. Hopefully there was a refrigerated can of soda with my name on it. Plus, my mom would kill me if I didn't play hostess to the crew, so there was tea to brew and sugar syrup to make. Again. And ice cubes to fetch from the freezer in the garage, which held little in storage these days but ice cubes.

A singleton can remained on the fridge shelf, so we split it, and he helped me transfer ice from the garage to the kitchen. Then he watched solemnly as I located two containers for tea, big glass canisters. His eyes widened as I put them out on the kitchen counter.

"Church potlucks," I said to him. "Thirsty crowds. Same difference as one of those big punch bowls."

"Ah."

"I can't talk long. My meals should be here soon for distribution." I shucked my wrist brace and began boiling water for tea and syrup.

Brian wandered through, a tool belt fastened low around his hips. He grinned and grabbed a tomato from a basket, washed it and walked back, sinking his teeth into it. We both lifted an eyebrow at that. Steptoe, as I went through the rooms to count heads, could not be seen anywhere. Somehow I hadn't expected him to be found anywhere near hard labor.

I eyed Carter. "Did you know my dad was here?"

"No, not a hint, either at the department or the Society." He paused. "We have your Aunt April on our radar, but she lives on the other side of town, even though she owns this property, too."

I perked an eyebrow. "Whose radar? And why?"

"Society. April has a modicum of talent."

"What?" I skewed around to face him in astonishment.

He shrugged. "Nothing noticeable to the average person. Not even enough to qualify as a hedge witch, per se, but she has luck. Good fortune. Enough that she's listed as an attractor."

I tried to imagine Great-Aunt April as attracting anything but couldn't. In fact, it made my head hurt. "Interesting."

"Yes, particularly that she gambles a lot."

Another startling reveal. Did it run in my father's heritage? "Really?"

"Absolutely. We think that's part of what started your father on his own streak. Luck, however, never holds."

I rubbed at the stone again. He looked at my hand.

"It bothers you."

"No kidding." That, and hearing family secrets I'd had no idea about. I decided to shrug it off by going back to work. I headed back to the tea-making after counting five heads in addition to Hiram and Brian: one bald-headed dwarf, two gingers, and two more seal-brown, albeit with very high foreheads. They all shouted and gave me a wave as I told them cold drinks were on the way shortly. They'd taken up the entirety of the mudroom floor except the extreme edges, which held some built-in shelves, and seemed to me to be demolishing everything rather than repairing, but they were the experts. I just prayed Aunt April wouldn't show up unexpectedly and have a heart attack at the construction. Two batches brewing, I stood back and crossed my arms, no longer certain I really wanted to hear. "Tell me more."

"I want to wait for Mary."

"There are some things I'd just as soon she not know. It's not like she doesn't have enough to worry about." Despite all the repair noise, I lowered my voice. "It reacts now and then, I just don't know why. Or what to do about it." Even as I said it, I reflected in relief that it stayed quiet around him, unlike my pulse.

"How?"

"It sparks. Gets heated. Sends me a shooting pain. I feel like one of those voodoo dolls sometimes."

Carter rubbed his brow in a tired, futile way.

"Don't tell me. Not good."

"No, not that. Well, yes, sort of, but—" He pulled up a kitchen chair and sat in it, sucking on the ice cubes left in his emptied glass. "It can be used for defense, from what I've read, and it might be reacting to a perceived threat. What were you doing at the time?"

I thought of Joanna. Slim, graceful, smart, and quick, and probably able to down me with some kind of Japanese martial arts, but would she? Seriously? "Just stuff." I shook my head in dismissal. "What else?"

"It responds to chaos. Feeds on it, it's believed, but no one is quite sure about that. It's possible it feeds on other energies and then creates chaos."

"Wun-der-ful." The tea held a good color now, so I lined up mason jars and filled them with ice and drink, put them on a tray, and took them out to deliver them. The crew emptied the jars in two gulps, so I made seconds and set the tray on a safe part of the living room floor, hopefully not destined for demolition, so they could reach them.

We sat on the top step upstairs with our own sweet teas, and I finally felt quenched. Carter took my hand and laid it open on his knee to examine the stone.

"It is beautiful," he said reluctantly.

"I think it is. I saw marble counters like this in Evelyn's home and loved them. All the rich caramels and gold sparks, and the brown and even the ebony swirled up with the ivory. Looks like a really good ice cream."

Carter laughed.

"Of course, I could break my teeth on it." I curled my fingers up, hiding the maelstrom.

"Is there training for it?"

"Does it come with a manual? Not that I could tell."

I thought of the pamphlet Steptoe had recovered from the professor's library. "You might be wrong on that."

"I can be wrong on nearly everything. I can find out more, but in doing so, the Society is going to notice the questions I'm asking, and they will not hesitate to contact you."

"Put me under dungeon arrest?"

"Maybe."

He ducked his head as I punched him lightly in the shoulder. I know I couldn't have hurt him—there were muscles galore there.

"So there's no real good news and bad news."

"Some bad news."

"Then tell me."

"The stone probably isn't going to leave you as long as you're alive."

"Oh." I blinked. "So if anybody wants to take it from me . . ."

"Exactly."

CHAPTER TWENTY-FOUR

"OF COURSE," Carter added, "there is another scenario. The stone uses you for whatever it wants, and then it moves on by itself."

That didn't take away the sudden chill at the back of my neck at my imagined vision of the wreckage left in its wake. "It—it can do that?"

"Historically, that's exactly what it's done. It's far more likely to choose its next partner than it is to be acquired. It has a mind of its own."

"I don't want to be the chosen one." I felt as though I'd been trapped in a hobbity storyline.

He looked like he wanted to take hold of my hand again but didn't reach for it. "No. The only good thing about it is, you've found your father."

"Sort of. He doesn't think he's dead, but he doesn't know. Brian and Steptoe think he might be transitioning or caught between this place and another dimension. Do you have to be dead to do that?"

"Not all the time."

"What could have forced him between?"

"No way of knowing, but if we could find out, then we'd have a better idea how to get him back. Or." He stopped.

"Help him go forward."

"I wasn't going to say that."

I twisted my fingers together. "You didn't have to, because it stands to reason he can't just hang where he is. We have to find a way to get him free, and that means going forward if that's what it takes, right? It's not like I haven't already thought of him as dead these past few years anyway. But, if we have to do that, I don't know how I'm going to explain it to my mom." My words choked up in my throat and I stopped talking because I ached and my voice went mute on me. He still didn't take my hand back in his, but he leaned against me a little. His body was both strong and warm, and I drew comfort from it. I glared at my hand in case the stone started sparking but it didn't. If Carter Phillips were dangerous, the stone was not reacting.

That didn't stop me from thinking he *was* dangerous, just a different sort of threat than the stone might sense.

"You might be about telling 'er the whole truth."

I twisted about, to see Steptoe standing in the shadowed end of the upstairs hallway, stepping out of the darkness as if he'd manifested himself there, rather than coming in the front door like everyone else. He walked toward us, snapping a rolled-up paper in one hand against the other. Carter's jaw tightened.

"That's the truth as far as I know it."

"No, it ain't, and don't let him tell you it is, ducks." Steptoe lowered himself to sit, not quite next to us, but back against the corner of the hallway.

"Maybe I haven't had access to the same sources you have." Carter pointed at the rolled-up paper.

"Well, now that might be a bit true, although I would think your lot had a copy or two of this in its study, eh? Maybe you just weren't allowed to see it."

Carter made a muffled noise, rather like a muted snort.

I craned my head at Steptoe. "What truth would that be?"

He eyed me solemnly. "It's possible the man you greeted as your father is not him. We know Malender can project if he gathers enough power, rather than greet us in person, like. Maybe he's stretching his influence here."

I made a funny sound from deep in my throat, words that stuck and wouldn't come out.

"How would he even know anything about John Graham

Andrews? Why would you be telling her something like that, Simon?"

"Because it's the truth." He sighed. "Not that I ain't above twistin' it now and then to my advantage, but Tessa 'ere has been nothing but kind to me. After our first meeting. I call us friends. It's not like that with most folks, is it? You can't call just anybody your mates." He unrolled the pamphlet. "The stone is chaos. Not lawful or unlawful, just simple chaos. It can reach for whatever it wishes and who's to say that it didn't jump into our girl here because that one ordered it to?" He underlined a paragraph with his finger as he spoke. "Says 'ere it doesn't 'ave to be attached to do its user's bidding."

"One would have to be very strong in using magical energy." Carter's voice went flat.

"Oh, and our guy wouldn't be? C'mon." Steptoe poked him in the chest with his pamphlet.

Carter put a hand up as if to snatch it before stopping, and his gaze never left the pamphlet. I could almost feel the itch in his fingers to grab it.

"Wot? Got to see it yourself? Here then." He pushed the fragile missive forward.

Carter spread it out carefully and began to read. I watched his face, my throat still a bit knotted up from that momentary jump of fear. I felt it melt away entirely as I took note of his lips moving slightly while he read. The schoolboy concentration rounded some of the hard edges off him.

"So," Steptoe said, as he hooked his arms about his knees companionably. "I heard you got exposed while you were in th' Middle East. What's that about? Got a touch of the djinn, did you?"

"I don't talk about it."

"Never? Now that's a right injustice, that is. People want to know. I want to know."

Carter turned his head slowly to meet Steptoe's stare.

"It's private."

"Sure, and I wouldn't wonder, 'cause it puts you on the same rung as me. Your power is just as chancy as it can be, init?"

"If it came from a djinn." Carter turned back to his paragraph. "It did not."

"Well, that's wot you might say, right?"

Carter grabbed him. Then he took up my hand. "I don't talk about it, but I'll show you."

In the blink of an eye, we stood in a desert. That wink hit me in the gut with a whirling sensation that made me think my head might pop off, but deposited me neatly on my feet under a velvet, starlit sky. Sand crunched under my sneakers. Dry air reached down and tried to suck my breath away the way only a desert could.

Nighttime had cooled it down but not all the way, never all the way I was guessing, and the desert held sandy dunes and far away, dun-colored hills. The silence—so complete. I realized that the city I inhabited buzzed crazily with noise, barely heard but always there, intruding, and here—nothing but the sound of our breathing. Out here, nothing distorted or took the stars' shine away. They hung, crystal clear and in force, overhead. I felt a sense of awe and knew why early man must have seen godlike forces in them, fates that operated for and against us, the ordinary. The night began to fade and lift. The sand we inhabited looked almost pink, its hue coming from the sun on the horizon as it started to crown, and far away misty shreds of cloud and night pulled away. I lifted my face to the sun and felt as many had before, I'm certain, awe and fear of the power shifting to the sky. The sun brought life. It chased away fear. It could also melt you down into a mere greasy spot on the ground. As it rose, I could feel its beams angle across my body, draining away hopelessness and cold.

Carter spoke, his voice wrapping around me. "I died in Afghanistan. Under attack, trying to save what I could of our patrol, but my buddy and I, we got hit. Hard. I woke in Egypt."

This was Egypt? Woah. I wanted to see the Sphinx. The pyramids. The great museum in Cairo. I twitched with all the wants. Then I caught what he'd said. "You . . . died?"

"I did. Maybe just for a second or two, but I died. And when I opened my eyes again, I was here. Cradled in Amel's elbow, he on his knees in pain. We were bathed in sunlight."

"You were gifted by Ra?" Steptoe murmured.

"My buddy was Egyptian-American. He brought us here. It took less than a heartbeat, and then I felt myself breathing—and bleeding—again. He didn't move. He held me in what was . . . I don't have words for it . . . a corona of sunlight. And blessing. And an otherworldly interest, as if we'd caught the attention of something so vast, there were no words available. Another blast of sun-heat and we were back in Afghanistan, with the med-evac chopper landing next to us. I made it. He didn't."

But the rest of his patrol had, too. That had been the whole hero incident for which we knew him when he came back home to Richmond.

"As bright as the sun is, it casts mighty shadows."

Carter took a deep breath, echoed by Steptoe. I think I kept holding my breath until something growled at me, from behind.

"Don't look back." Carter's fingers tightened about mine.

My stone grew very warm in my left hand, but Carter couldn't know that as he held tight to my right. I didn't want to look, but neither did I want to have my spine ripped out of my body by whatever growled back there. Without more thought than that, I began to turn my head. Sand crunched under a stealthy footfall or paw step.

Carter pulled us close into his hold and the scene whirled again, going absolutely black, and sending my stomach into a whirlpool before our feet thudded down on carpet and we were home again. Sitting, even, on the stairs.

I wanted to tell him how awesome it looked and felt, but my stomach revolted. I pitched to my feet and barely made it down the hall in time.

When I came back, wiping my mouth and cringing at the taste of mouthwash, Steptoe and Carter were more or less ignoring each other at the top of the stairs. I knew why the two of them sulked: Steptoe thought he'd had an ally even if Carter didn't want to be one; Carter didn't like having his secrets pried out of him. Of course, maybe the prowler at our backs had been more in sync with Carter than he wanted us to know. Bright sun, dark shadows. Sounded rather chaotic to me, so maybe

Steptoe was right after all. The lesser demon would know all about the flip side to good things. Carter wouldn't give him the satisfaction, naturally.

I sat down. "That can't be all that happened."

"Well, no. But I won't talk about the rest. It's different for each and every one of us, unless you're born into it."

"Was Brian born into it, you think? The professor, I mean."

"I couldn't say. He's not talked about much, except for now, of course, with all that's been going on around him. I won't even venture to say how much power his last incarnation had or didn't have, though I know his influence could have been great."

"Could have been?"

"He refused to play politics. Said it demeaned all those who should have been working toward a common cause. It's one of the reasons Remy left him. She thought he was both impractical and arrogant. She is ambitious. Some would say too much so."

I considered my professor. Impractical, sometimes—but arrogant? No. If I would put that label on anyone, I'd put it on her first. So maybe she'd wanted to rise through the ranks to become, what, Imperial Overall Wizard or something? Would that have given her more power? Or did power come out of study and learning, not greedy acquisition? I had no way of knowing. "So how does one go up the ladder? Is there one?"

"Yes, and no. There are always those who like to lead, but they're not necessarily the most powerful in the Society when it comes to their personal magic. Sometimes the detail oriented and the diplomatic are more valuable. And then there's the Enforcers."

"Enforcers?"

"Right up your alley, eh guv?"

Carter sniffed. "Not me, unless I've been cornered into it. Frankly, I've little time for the Society. I'm building a career here that is important to me, and they know they're on the backburner as far as I'm concerned. They helped place me here, but had no idea how much I wanted to be where I am. So they've lost a bit of their hold on me."

"You'll boil that pot when you come to it?"

"Exactly. Which reminds me." He gathered himself. "I've got chores waiting at home."

"Yeah?"

"Yeah. Clothes don't get cleaned and pressed on their own."

"You can't wave a wand?"

He nudged me. "Say good night, Tessa."

I nodded. He carefully handed back the pamphlet to Steptoe. "Keep an eye on her."

"Always."

The two nodded in silent agreement at one another, which frankly gave me the creeps. What had Carter picked up in those papers that Steptoe also knew, and all of a sudden, made the two coconspirators?

Plus, I wanted that pamphlet myself. The stone contaminated me. Might control me. I had a right to know as much as they did. I peered at what I could see of the booklet in Steptoe's hands. "I could use that."

"For wot?"

"Knowledge, Simon. Shouldn't I be in on all this?"

Steptoe looked, really looked, at me, his dark eyes narrowing a bit as if he had to bring me into focus. Then he shook his head vigorously. "I don't want that mark on th' soul I've got left. You want educated, you talk t' Brian." He stood up and tucked the mystical tome inside his suit coat pocket, away from sight, as he left.

His words didn't change things much, but my brief look at the pages not hidden by his handhold did. I hadn't recognized a symbol. Maybe one needed special eyesight to get past the gibberish or illusion? Or translation into a modern language? That was ridiculous. I needed to know. I'd have to hope the professor thought so, too. I didn't like being kept in the dark, but it looked like I didn't have much choice at the moment. When Brian felt stronger, Brandard might be easier to convince. Or not.

I decided I'd had enough of magical thinking and went down the hall to my room to practice wearing insanely tall high heels. They slipped onto my bare feet as if they'd been made for me. Cobbled for me? Whatever. They fit. And they did hurt when I stood up on them, all my weight sinking down to my toes and pinching them tightly. That and the loss of mobility was why I didn't like wearing heels. Others did because they liked being taller. Me, not so much.

I didn't set my phone up to video until I could glide confidently across the floor. Tough to do with pounding and muted shouting downstairs as the crew worked. It seemed that Hiram and the boys made the decision not just to repair but improve the whole basement floor of the house, ceiling, floor, and Wi-Fi included. Not that it wouldn't be nice having an entertainment room all to ourselves, but a resident ghost would frankly creep most people out. Mom had told me to be thankful we didn't have to pay for it, but she hadn't seen the remodel up close. Yet. When they finished and cleared out, then I'd take Mom down and see if I could help Dad manifest for her. I didn't know if that was a wise thing to do or not, given the circumstances, but it seemed like I had to try. If it was truly Dad, she needed to see him again and he needed to know that there might be a way back. If he got back.

I only hoped he'd kicked the gambling habit for good wherever he'd been stuck all those years. If he hadn't, I'd be tempted to lose him again. I think I have this terrible character flaw of being unforgiving.

I crossed the floor twice, looked at the phone, decided I didn't look like an idiot and texted it to Evelyn.

I swear her phone was grafted to her. Worst case of phone dependency I had ever known. She shot back, *Well done, grasshopper.*

I sent back a grin with the tongue out emoji before heading downstairs to start a dinner of sorts, because Mom would be home.

The kitchen table stood piled with ten, I kid you not, ten extra-large pizza boxes. Nine of them were demolished and empty. The tenth stood, steaming and inviolate, waiting for Mom and me. Steptoe too, I guess, but he'd disappeared again. I opened the lid to smell the delicious combo flavors.

Mom came in, purse in one hand and computer bag in the other. She took a whiff. "Pizza? Again? Though it does smell delicious."

"Roll with it, Mom."

"Guess I'm going to have to. They're all still here?"

Hiram shouted up from the bottom of the kitchen ramp. "Packing up now, Mrs. Andrews. Left you some dinner."

"Bless your heart," she shouted back, "Yes, I saw, thank you." She perched on a kitchen chair. "And how was your day?"

"Fine. Assignments all caught up, and I really don't think anyone missed me. I wore my wrist brace in case anybody asks how I'm feeling." I flashed her the stone. "Seemed best to hide this, all things considered."

She peeled a slice up and began to eat it. "What does that do, exactly?"

It's not easy to lie with a great pizza in front of you. I picked a black olive off it and nibbled it. "Think of it like a protective shield."

"Oh, so when you're biking down the street, I don't have to worry about your getting hit. Or hijacked on the bus."

"Nooo. More like a barrier against errant magic."

"Ah. So next time Brian yells 'Avaunt!' and breaks something, I don't have to worry about you being in the way or getting caught by a ricochet."

"Yeah. Like that." Maybe. I pried off a mushroom and chewed. I decided I had better get to eating and finished a slice to be safe.

The front door opened and someone called, "Yoo-hoo" gently. Mom jumped to her feet. "Aunt April! We're in the kitchen."

We traded looks frantically. She hadn't been told about the mudroom floor yet, but there'd be no missing it as she came in. Not to mention the dust and noise of the wrecking crew in the cellar. Mom washed her hands at the sink and had a glass of sweet tea ready for my aunt as she came in, puzzlement all over her.

"What on earth happened?"

"The mudroom gave way. Did you know you had a basement down there?"

"Oh my." Aunt April took a sip as she sat down carefully. "I had truly forgotten. First things first—was anyone hurt? Do I have to make an insurance claim?"

"Nobody hurt, and the man who fell through brought his family in to make the repairs. He's in construction. It won't cost you a nickel."

Up to his neck in construction, at the moment, I thought. I wrangled a paper plate. "Pizza, Aunt April?"

"Don't mind if I do. No pepperoni though, gives me dyspepsia."

"Right." I served her a Canadian bacon and pineapple slice. She beamed when I handed it to her. Pizza fed crowds. I wondered when she'd last had any on her own. She'd dressed in prim navy slacks and a navy and white pinstriped blouse today and looked not a bit wilted from the warm weather, her hair swept back and pinned neatly in place.

"The basement?" I prompted. For good measure, I added, "Did Dad stay here after he left?"

"Oh, no. Not that I know about. He had keys so he might have. I don't come here often anymore. I was lucky to keep this place when the Great Recession hit, but I managed."

"Why did you hold onto it?"

"Because I thought someone might need it, dear." Aunt April neatly bit off a bite. "I was born in hard times and remember them well. I wasn't necessarily thinking of y'all but I knew someone might need it, some day. A lot of my friends are widows now. I wasn't sure if they would have a place when their husbands passed. I'd been lucky to own several properties, and it didn't hurt me to keep holding on."

"But you had to sell the great house," Mom said.

"True, but that place was grandiose, wasn't it? A manor and a half. I rattled around in there like a dust bunny. The summer place is fine for me, and I do love it. Gardens and my sun porch."

Mom and Aunt April laughed while I tried not to choke on a meatball at the mental picture of her as disheveled as a dust ball.

When I could swallow and breathe decently, I pressed. "But Dad . . ."

"Well now." She went very still for a moment, thinking. "As I said, he did have keys, but he never mentioned it to me. I always thought he'd have come home in a few days, but then it became weeks, and then . . ."

We all went silent. Aunt April cleaned her hands on her napkin. "Mind if I have a look? They're certainly making a racket."

I jumped up to pull the pantry door open. She looked amazed for the tiniest moment.

"My. I had forgotten all about that door. It must have been painted over four, five times. Always was the coolest place in the house. My brothers used to sleep down there when it got hot as blue blazes." She leaned in the doorway and looked down. One of the gingers and the bald dwarf waved to her. "They're working to beat the band down there. Renovating everything?"

Mom shrugged. "They insisted. Hiram, the young fellow in the blue and green plaid shirt and jeans, felt awful when he fell through. It should look really nice when they're done. They're saving the goods that were stored down there."

"My, my. I should imagine we'll have some fun opening them up." Aunt April backed out of the stairwell. "That should be something." She gave me a glance as she sat down to finish her pizza. "Now, my brothers would be your father's uncles, so they'd be your great-uncles."

"But gone now."

"Yes." Her mouth turned down. "World War for one of them, and road racing for another."

"Road racing?"

"Died running moonshine, trying to outrace a treasury agent." She winked at me. "We have a bit of a history, young lady."

"I'll say. Wow." Not much of one when they ran out of luck, it seemed, or maybe she'd just inherited all of it. Moonshiners. Huh. I still had no idea why my dad had been trapped here, but it seemed neither did she.

I was cleaning up my plate when the doorbell rang twice. The meals for delivery now sat on the porch. I wiped my hands off. "Save me another. Got to go."

"Okay. Watch yourself on the streets, please." Mom arched an eyebrow at me, meaning more than she said.

"Always." I kissed her on the cheek. She looked perky today, always a nice thing to see. I hugged Aunt April, who looked pleased that I did, and I bolted off.

The food envelopes smelled meaty. They hadn't taken the professor off my route yet, so I decided to double up one of my regulars in case they had a friend. Someone had oiled the bike and chariot for me, probably someone on the wrecking crew, and the set waited for me in the driveway next to Mom's car. Her vehicle makes creaking noises as it cools down, and I figured it was due for some kind of maintenance work and would probably get it before nightfall, as Hiram's guys seemed to be the Obsessive Fix-It types. I pulled my brace on and set off.

My legs had caught a bit of a tan, too, the last few weeks in shorts under the sun, freckling a bit as I tended to, but I looked okay. That dress for the auction wouldn't entirely go to waste on me. Nice to know. I biked along relatively happy until I got to Mrs. Sherman's. She always waited for me, peeking from her snow-white curtains, her Texas-red bouffant hair easy to spot through her drapes, her lipstick to match her hair gracing a generous smile. The spot at the window looked empty.

I put the kickstand down in her driveway and pulled an envelope free, as it leaked a warm but unidentifiable smell into the air. What dinner was tonight, I had no earthly idea. Approaching Mrs. Sherman's door, I noticed the absolute quiet. It reminded me of the blazing moment when I'd stood in the desert with Carter, surrounded by wilderness and silence. Especially that second when I'd thought something awful stood behind us. Right now, it felt like something waited in front of me.

Where was she? Had she fallen? Was she really sick? Each step I took dragged a bit, because I didn't want to know. The league had told me I'd lose a few route members if I did this long enough and tried to prepare me for it. Most moved in with relatives for support and a few went to residential homes, and a very few, well, died. What had happened to the professor went beyond a technicality of life.

I balanced the food envelope on my left arm and knocked hesitantly on the front door, totally unused to not having Mrs. Sherman there, smiling and waving me on in before I'd even taken the last step onto the porch. Uncannily, the door swung open before me with no one apparently waiting on the other side. It missed the chance to creak ominously.

"Mrs. Sherman? Dinner's here." My voice went a little hoarse and thinned too much to be louder. I swallowed tightly and took two steps inside. My presence echoed in the too-quiet house. My heart thumped a quick "Oh, no" and my feet wanted to turn around and head back through the doorway. Surely nothing could have happened to her, but my tingling nerves told me *something* had happened here. Or maybe my nerves were just shot from the past few days, which I could hardly be blamed for, considering everything that had happened.

"Mrs. Sherman?" I tried again, thinking I really couldn't bear just one more thing. I slid rather than walked toward the kitchen, my sneaker soles squeaking just a little, as if someone dragged me. The hairs on my arms stood up even as I thought I'd feel really stupid if she walked in from the garden now, arms full of early summer corn and green tomatoes, and a big ol' smile on her face. Whatever aroma wafted up from the insulated envelope began to smell less and less inviting, and my stomach knotted.

No one sat in the sunny kitchen. The morning dishes hadn't been done, either, a first for the vivacious redhead. I sat the meal down and knew then I'd have to go through the house, room by room, and then the yard, until I had an idea what had become of Mrs. Sherman. I thought of calling for backup. Mom would come. I might need more help than that. I should tell her to bring the wrecking crew with her. You know. Just in case.

I sashayed quietly out of the kitchen, past the little laundry room and side door, which might have qualified as a mudroom once upon a time, but it was really too small. The whole house was much smaller than ours, Aunt April's, that is, and only one story. I should be able to go through it quickly, if I could just get my body to move.

I rubbed my left palm under my brace but the stone stayed quiet and neither warm nor chill. "Big help you are," I muttered and retraced my steps through the entry, wishing I had those sky-high silver heels. Not on my feet, but in my hands where I could wield them in my defense like sharp, shiny little daggers, drop 'em and run.

My physical ed classes had been filled with field hockey the last few years, with off-season fitness like cross country. Now the idea came to me that I should take a martial arts class and learn some serious moves instead. Maybe they taught stiletto heels right alongside nunchucks and morning stars. I should take the time to learn some awesome martial arts defense. Right?

Mrs. Sherman's house had a small, tidy front bedroom, which she'd turned into a crafter's room. I could see homemade quilts she'd hung on the wall, two sewing machines, tubs of fabric against another wall, and a table for measuring and cutting. A chair in the corner came with a diminutive and ruffled footstool, and a pair of those antique knitting needles she'd bragged about once, or maybe those were crochet hooks, wrapped in yarn and waiting on the seat. It all looked and felt as though she'd just stepped out for a moment. I grabbed one of objects, sliding it out of the yarn, IDing it definitely as a knitting needle, and it did look fairly sturdy and sharp, despite its ancient and yellowing ivory color. I ran my hand down it. Seriously, bone? Could it be? Feeling lethal, I wrapped my fingers about it tightly.

Nerves tighter than strings on a family fiddle, I backed out of the crafting room and headed toward the living room, the center of this small but neat house. That's when the sight of her hit my vision.

If she'd gone, she'd gone sitting up, straight as a board on the far end of the divan, near the fireplace and hearth. Her bouffant red hair sat in her lap with her natural head nearly as bald as an egg under thin and wispy strands of gray, a sight I knew the public had never been meant to see. Her Texas-red wig must have been her glory. "Mrs. Sherman?" She didn't move a muscle as I came through the arch.

"She's occupied, dear." Remy glided up at my flank, smiling and smelling like a perfumery of Paris. She managed to make those three words sound sinister.

"You didn't kill her, did you?"

"Oh, no. No. She's enjoying a memory, if you will, fond thoughts of the past."

"Then why did her hair fall off?"

"I had a bit of a tussle getting her to sit down and relax. It's just a wig."

Since Mrs. Sherman wore it every single waking moment, I knew it was more than a wig; it was an age-defying act and a matter of dignity. But I had a feeling this elegant woman talking to me wouldn't appreciate any of that one bit. Wait until she was old and lost her hair, if magicians ever got that old before someone bumped them off. No wonder the professor didn't consort with the Society. Along the way, members must—at least this one had—lose their moral compass. I knew she'd probably sold it off. I closed my eyes a moment, thinking I really didn't want to see that happen to Carter.

"She'll be all right?"

"I give you my word, depending on you, of course."

"I'd rather have a string-free commitment."

Remy laughed. "Of course, you would, clever girl. But that's not the way it works."

"What are you doing here? Besides meddling with Mrs. Sherman?"

"Waiting for you, of course. You have something I need."

"I thought Brian held all the goodies you wanted."

She smiled sadly. "Not this time. It fell upon me to single you out."

I leaned a little against the end of the couch, the knitting needle tucked alongside my forearm and, hopefully, out of sight. My hip thoughtfully pushed my cell phone against the furniture and, I also hoped, butt dialed. After having been embarrassed once or twice, I'd programmed the thing not to dial so easily, except for one number. Home. "I'm a little confused," I told her. "Are you or are you not a member of the Society? Or with the other guy?"

"Yes."

"That's not the answer I wanted. So, another question: what is it I have that you want?" I had that one figured out, but confirmation would be nice.

"The maelstrom stone. There are some of us who felt it, quite keenly, activate, so there is no sense in your lying about it or saying that it hasn't attuned to you. I'm not asking if you have it. What I know, I know well."

She almost came around to face me head on, but not quite. Why, I wasn't sure. I took a glance at Mrs. Sherman, who seemed oblivious. I shucked the brace and lifted my hand, palm out, toward her. "That would be this."

"Precisely." A longing filled her expression and I shifted my weight, thinking that I'd once thought her beautiful in a way, and elegant, but the naked want now glistening through her expression erased all that. It etched heavy lines in her face. Left purpling puffiness under her eyes. Creases across her forehead. When she got old, she was going to need a lot more than a bouffant wig to look presentable.

"It seems rather attached to me but even if it wasn't, I don't think I'd be giving it to you."

"You really have no choice." She angled toward me now and I straightened, my right fingers curled about the knitting needle. "I will take it, one way or the other."

"Meaning you'd kill for it."

"If I must. I'm sorry to say that, but he gives me little recourse. If I take it from you, it goes straight to him and that—" She paused sharply. "Well, that is unacceptable. If you knew him, you'd know why."

"I've seen him."

"You have?" That stopped her in her tracks, her eyes widening and her complexion paling delicately. "I'm sorry for that. Before or after, this," and she indicated my hand.

"Before."

Remy nodded. "I didn't think he would let you live if he'd seen it."

"And you don't intend to, either."

"But that's not the only option, Tessa. If you give it to me, then I'm the one who has it and I can keep it from him. I can fr—well, that's no matter. It is a better choice, trust me."

"You were going to say you could free yourself."

Remy tilted her head slightly, and her hair fell in a silken wave down her cheek and about her shoulder. "I was. Clever, clever girl."

Now she had me feeling like a velociraptor in a classic movie. I flexed my hand. "I can't give it to you. Or won't. Either way."

She sighed. "Such pain this will cause your mother. I have to stage a crime scene here, you and Mrs. Sherman. It won't be pretty." She reached for me.

Like that velociraptor, I struck, the bone knitting needle sinking deep into her side and up into the ribcage. It felt almost as if the needle knew the way. Remy let out a scream of pain.

She unleashed a violent wave of force, grazing me as I pitched myself in the other direction and frying a bit of my own formerly silken hair. I rolled on the floor and came up under the coffee table as a shield, to catch another high-power bolt. She yowled a second time, throwing the needle to the floor. It spun my way on Mrs. Sherman's spotless plank flooring. I scrambled to grab it and lunged, stabbing Remy down and through the foot as I bowled past her.

She screamed a second time just as the front door burst into splinters.

CHAPTER TWENTY-FIVE

THE FORCE OF THE ENTRY knocked me over. From the commotion just beyond the door, I figured the guys had arrived in answer to my butt-dialed call for help. Remy swooped down on me, her voice strained with pain and anger. "You stupid, stupid girl. But this is not over. I need you, and you need me, or *he* will devour us both. You don't know the stakes. If I can't beat you, you've got to accept my help. It's the only hope I have. Do you understand?" She shoved a bracelet off her arm. "Summon me and I will come." She pushed her face next to mine, eyes wild, the skin pinched white about her nose and mouth. "Don't fail or we both shall lose horribly!"

And then Remy dissolved in a puff of smoke, all shimmery and smelling of her expensive perfume and the copper of her wounds before it went to nothingness. The knitting needle balanced on its point, twirling in an unseen whirlwind before it clattered to the floor onto a small bloodstain, the only evidence left of Remy's presence. I rested on my back for a split second to catch my breath, the bracelet at my throat, and blinked.

The crew burst in as Mrs. Sherman said, "Oh my goodness. I must have been daydreaming." She lifted a hand to her eyes and rubbed gently, without noticing her wig in her lap.

My jaw dropped but I could not think of anything, not one thing, to explain to her why her house suddenly began filling up with boot-stomping Iron Dwarves wearing tool belts and reducing her door to splinters.

Brian dashed around them. He caught the situation with a single glance. "Latius! Extend!" he cried and flung a hand toward Mrs. Sherman, who responded with a dainty yawn and sagged back against her flowery divan, asleep once more. "A good guess," he finished, pleased with himself, as he gave a hand to me and hoisted me on my feet. "What happened?"

We leaned together to talk, because the boys at the door immediately set to repairing the damage, hammering, nailing, with one heading back to my house for wood and another to her garage looking for matching paint. "Remy. She wanted the stone, in the worst way, and took Mrs. Sherman hostage. Remy put her to sleep. Is she . . . will she be all right?"

Brian squeezed my shoulder. "She won't remember a thing, hopefully."

"Hopefully?"

He shrugged. "I have no idea what thoughts Remy might have put into her."

"Memories, she told me. Good, past memories."

"Well, then. Everything ought to turn out just right." He bent over to pick up the bracelet. "You dropped this."

"Oh. Right." I slipped it on, the metal and small gems having already lost their warmth from Remy's body heat. I wanted to ask him how safe it would be to wear it, and even more, to summon her, but something held me back. If I wanted an unbiased opinion about Remy's actions, past, present, or future, I doubt if I'd get one from the professor. Brian might be even worse, all those guy hormones leaping at her obvious allure. Men. Can't trust 'em even when you can trust 'em.

"It bothers me that Remy would target you."

"She's caught in some kind of deal with M, wants out, and I guess she plans to use the stone, either as payment or a weapon." I decided not to tell him about the bracelet, although he might have recognized it when he handed it to me.

"Interesting. Even more interesting is how she might have learned about the stone at all, or that you have it now."

I hadn't thought of that. "She told me she felt it activate."

He snorted at that. "She's never had that kind of talent before. It seems more logical she learned it."

"But only a few . . ."

"Precisely. Carter or Steptoe would be my best guesses."

"Oh." That sounded even worse. "Why would either of them tell her?"

"Remy is evidently operating as an independent now, despite the fact that both the Society and he can put a claim on her. She's got a lot of power, or she had when I knew her, and she can be quite advantageous if she picks a side."

"Do you think she can move about that freely?"

"As I said, she has a lot of power. I doubt even Malender could subdue her for long if she fought him on it. It would be too much trouble for him."

"What would he do? Just let her go?"

A pause. Then, "He'd merely eliminate her."

"Awkward."

We lapsed into silence to observe the remaking of Mrs. Sherman's entry.

All the nailing stopped within minutes while we watched, and then the air filled with the noise of sanders, followed by the smell of fresh paint, the door finished before anyone could even say abracadabra, and all the guys but Hiram slipped out the open front door.

I looked at Brian. "How will I explain wet paint?"

"No need." He stepped to the door and flicked a hand. A blast of hot air came through the house, concentrated on the door and then gusted on its way out to the yard.

"Remind me to call you if my hair dryer ever breaks."

He winked. Stepped to the door. "Coming?"

"Yeah. She'll wake up in a few?"

"As soon as we're on the sidewalk. My spells don't last very long. The ones that I can remember, at any rate."

If at all, I thought, knowing that his guardian spell on me had done little. Or maybe it had done a lot, and I just hadn't felt it. Pondering the thought that I might be fried if not for his enchantment, I followed him outside. I grabbed my bicycle, after putting a hand into the chariot and checking to see the remaining meals were all reasonably warm. They were.

"I've got to finish my run." I didn't want to disappoint anyone waiting for a meal. Then, I was going to have a talk with the senior center and quit. I couldn't jeopardize anyone else.

"See you at home then. We're nearly done with the basement."

"Oh, good. My ears could use the silence."

He nodded, now somewhat absently, and I had no idea what he could be thinking, him or Brian.

"Professor?"

"Hmmm?"

"How close are we to getting all the things you need?"

"Very, very close."

"Are you worried?"

His gaze met mine. "Very, very worried." He waved good-bye and I set off, meals to be delivered, things to be considered.

Mom waited for me, arms folded across her chest, feet braced, and chin up. I knew that look. Petite, blond, and determined. She watched as I stowed the bike and chariot away and then pounced as soon as I came back around to the front door.

"What in God's name was all that about?"

"Remy ambushed me at Mrs. Sherman's house."

"Is this the way it's to be? I can't let you go anywhere anymore."

"I don't know. You'd have to ask Brian or Carter or Steptoe—"

"The truth helps."

I took her by the hand and led her to the old swing at the edge of the porch. It made little noises as we sat down on it. My legs were more than long enough to reach the ground, but I noticed my mom had to stretch hers out and point her toes. We set the swing to rocking gently.

"I really don't know what's going to happen. It seems to be escalating but the professor says he's very close to having all the ingredients for his ritual. I think once he transforms, things will settle down. Like, everyone will be back in their place where all this is concerned. He's a phoenix wizard, right?"

Her face paled.

I couldn't remember if my mother had been told all the details. I proceeded carefully, keeping my tone light. "That means he lives many lives, so he regenerates through flame, and he has to build a pyre and say the right stuff, and then we light him on fire again."

"Good God!" She seized my wrist. "Tessa, you can't be serious. You can't help set a man on fire!"

"Hey. It's not *my* idea. Everyone says that's what it takes. Brian made it through once; he should make it through again. I hope." Her fingers were going to leave bruises on my arm if she clutched me any tighter. I gently pried her hand away. "I know it sounds awful and unexplainable."

"Inexplicable. It sounds crazy and homicidal." Mom took a deep breath. "Don't fight me on this—three weeks ago, you would have thought this to be the creepiest thing you'd ever heard. I don't want you there when it happens."

"I'm not sure if I can do that. He might need me."

"He's lived, what, centuries to this day without you. I'm sure he can manage. Tessa, I want you to promise me you won't be there."

"I will do my best not to be." I held my breath, hoping she'd accept that, and she did, patting my arm.

"Good." She inhaled. "Am I feeding that army again tomorrow?"

"I think they've ordered a wagon full of tacos already."

"Okay, that's out of the way then." She rubbed that spot between her eyebrows that she always rubs when she's tense, tired, and at her wit's end. "I think I'll stay in my study, working."

"I'll fix you a plate and bring it in. I hid some Cokes. The dwarves aren't much for coke but I think Brian is addicted. Want one or sweet tea?"

"A Coke sounds good."

She left me swinging on the porch. I was not going to abandon the professor if he needed me, that much I knew. We'd come too far. On the other hand, I'd try to stay out of the final ritual, just to make my mother happy. Was this a win-win or a lose-lose? I didn't look forward to being proven right one way or the other.

As for Remy, her desperate words left an icy feeling in the pit of my stomach. She hadn't always been on the wrong side of awful, according to everyone who knew her. She didn't sound like she wanted to be on it this time, except that *he* had her up a tree, it seemed. In my neck of the woods, though, that's when a critter became truly dangerous, when it was treed and didn't want to be brought down. She hadn't been entirely ruthless dealing with me, and I had the feeling that if he didn't have a hold on her, she would be square with the Society. Now I had no idea of the laws or philosophies of said Society but they hadn't gone after her, so maybe they were hanging back, waiting to see if she could free herself or if she needed to be dealt with along with M. They'd given the professor a pretty long leash, after all, although I hadn't come across anything he might have done (or not done) that would offend them.

I decided I would deal with Remy along the same lines. Live and let live, unless I thought M had me in a death grip, and then you can bet I was going to be rubbing my bracelet and yelling, "Remy, Remy, Remy!" until she showed. Along with hollering for anybody else I could remember. I'd better learn the wrecking crew by name because they looked immensely helpful, quick, and handy, although I had the feeling they might be a package deal with Hiram. Then there was Simon Steptoe, of course, and the stone. I walked into the house to wash up for supper, mentally ticking off whatever support I might be able to call upon if I needed it.

Saturday, the wrecking crew showed up in fine fettle, sensing an end, and hopefully a successful one, to the project. We stayed out of their way: I worked on a term paper and Mom did the laundry. Halfway through the day, we swapped. Mom is great as a proofreader, and I don't mind ironing the stuff that's supposed to be permanent press but never quite seems to look that way. The day ground to a halt in the late afternoon as I did some dishes by hand and got ready for dinner.

The taco delivery, actually a catering truck, pulled up as I finished. For the next hour, we were all busy munching crunchy tacos, passing refried beans (I made a note not to go visit the basement until long after the crew left and the gas dissipated), rice, and even some fairly good guacamole. Guacamole is not a southern delicacy, but my parents had developed a fondness for it in their college years, and it was more or less a staple around our house when avocadoes were imported and in season. Mom knew just how to ripen those alligator pears and whip up a batch for chips and dip. Some moms made cocoa and cookies for football season, we had guac. The cool thing about that was, every once in a while, a friend would invest in a handful or so of avocadoes and not know a thing about ripening or preparing them. I'd get the leftover green gems when they gave them away in disgust after discovering how hard and bitter they could be. Dude. Like a peach, it has to mature to a nice but firm softness to have that taste. At any rate, the wrecking crew approached the guacamole cautiously before jumping in and demolishing it. No leftovers for us, which kind of sucked, but I'd put away plenty before they'd decided they liked it. The Cokes I'd hidden in the vegetable bin of the fridge, and it wasn't like anyone else was going to go looking in there, so they were safe. Brian gave me a mournful look so I split mine with him, but Mom got a cold can all to herself.

After dinner, Brian beckoned me off to the living room while the crew finished up the job. He pulled his journal out of his waistband at the small of his back, with me for just a tiny moment there thinking he pulled a gun. After all, not impossible, right?

He tapped it.

"Two more items," he said, "And I'll have all I need for the pyre."

"What about the ritual itself?"

"Got it. Several versions, but I'll go with the latest one."

"What do you need?"

"Frankincense and myrrh."

"Seriously?"

"Very seriously. Two rare, tough items . . ." His voice trailed off. "And rowan wood."

"Stay right here." I clumped upstairs to get my laptop. Back down and I flipped it open and pulled up Amazon. He frowned at it. "You can buy just about anything."

"I don't remember much, but I do remember the last time I had to procure them, it was the very devil. They're made from sap of trees along the African coast, and what with colonialism and independence struggles . . ." He shook his head.

I typed in the items. They came up almost immediately, and I turned the laptop so the screen faced him.

"That's it?"

"Just that easy. Available for all sorts of aromatherapy and face washes and whatnot. The world has changed, Professor." I dug out Morty's credit card. "Say the word and I'll order them right now. We should have them in the mail in, oh, three to five business days."

He swallowed hard and then nodded.

I filled in the pertinent information and got him two bottles of essential oils, both flavors, for a pittance compared to what they might have cost him a hundred years or more ago.

After a stunned moment, he raised an eyebrow. "Rowan wood?"

I put that in search too. We found whole pieces of furniture comprised of the stuff, but he needed wood or twigs. Finally, on one of the craft consortiums we found bundles of twigs. He leaned forward, almost nose to the screen, examining the website description.

"Looks like rowan wood," he allowed. "And she's taken Wiccan steps in harvesting it. If it isn't what it professes to be, there will be a disaster."

I ordered two bundles, but they wouldn't arrive for at least a week. "That's the best we can do. You don't need any artifacts or relics?"

"I need to restore my gazing crystal, and I'm working on that. Other items are superfluous, and the more of a hunt we go on, the more we seem to be exposed. I'll make do with the cane and gazer."

I closed my laptop. "So, what are you going to do?"

"I build a circle of the items. Perform a ritual. Then drop a match." A shudder ran through him, despite the lightness of his tone.

"Will it be awful?"

"I don't know. It wasn't so bad this last time, but of course I didn't have anything prepared. It could be excruciating. I have . . . there's the weight of centuries that I need to remember and absorb. Memories."

"Both good and bad."

Brian nodded. "Some, I expect, are terrible. As a witness to human history, how could they not be? We are a striving and contentious people, often wrongheaded in our philosophies and ambitions. Yet we do try. We can reach out."

"So you're going to go through with it?"

"I must, I think." He gave me a tired smile. "And Brian would say, man, just go with the flow."

"He's definitely picked up some of the attitude."

But the professor didn't seem quite finished. I waited. After a very long moment, he said, "I need a witness or two."

"Really?"

"Yes. Morty would have been there for me, but." And his words stopped.

I had just given my word to my mother. But then, he wasn't quite ready yet, and we had three to five business days before the stuff came in the mail. A lot could happen in that time, especially if there was any delay. Like, for instance, the auction. "If you need me," I answered. "I'll be there."

He smiled. "Cool."

I laughed to see both the professor and Brian shining through.

CHAPTER TWENTY-SIX

THE WRECKING CREW lined up to say good-bye with tired grins and big hugs. The bald-headed foreman gave me a stout embrace first, saying "I am Len Broadstone, cousin to Mortimer and second cousin to Hiram, here." I hugged him back after I caught my breath.

"I appreciate everything so much!"

The two gingers got me both at once before letting go and going for my mom. "Kent and Lyle Kettlestone!" they cried enthusiastically. "Please send home your recipe for sweet tea. Almost as good as ale it is, and easier to get more work done after drinking it!"

The two seal-brown and curly-headed men shook my hand solemnly, one after the other.

"Brownstone Gemcracker and Jackson Gemcracker, father and son, related by marriage to the Broadstones."

They waited politely while Mom dusted herself off after the gingers' hug, and took her hand as well, while I made mental notes as to who was who, for future reference.

She clasped her hands and gave them all a fond look. "I can't say how thankful I am, because I haven't all the words. But come back whenever you wish for dinner, and tell your family they are fortunate to have you! And I'll see that Tessa passes along her recipe."

They all gave a shout and then, with a mighty clomping of

thick-soled work boots, left our house, piled into their trucks, and were gone. Silence engulfed the house in their wake.

"Well," said Mom. "Wasn't that something?" Still in her workday outfit from a Saturday meeting, a faint dusting of sawdust covered her here and there, so she brushed herself off before saying to me, "I'll be in my study. I have the beginning of a new article in my head."

That meant I probably wouldn't see her till breakfast, although she'd stick her head in to say good night, but I often slept through that. I caught her by the elbow as she turned away.

"Wait a minute. We need to see how Dad is doing."

She stood frozen, her body so rigid I thought she might shatter if I forced her. Then, she said, "I already know he's there."

"But you haven't really talked to him."

"You can do that?"

I opened my palm and let the stone shine up at her. "I can try. It depends on how much energy he has, but he's had several days' rest." I pulled at her a little, and the thought flashed through my mind that it used to be her tugging at me, my childish and reluctant body unwilling to go to new places and try new things as I grew up. The flip-flopped image boggled my mind for a minute or two before my mother sighed.

"All right. Do we have to . . . do anything? Take precautions?"

"Just one." I went to the kitchen, got what I needed, and put my head out after swinging the pantry open. "Ready."

The wrecking crew had built a magnificent new basement room which looked odd in all its gleaming modern glory, with Aunt April's trunks and boxes, yellowed with age, put back against one wall. The shelves full of miscellaneous jarred goodies had sadly disappeared, although I'm not at all sure I could have talked Evelyn into exploring their contents with me. Too much potential to be a kind of horror show. I hoped Aunt April hadn't gotten a good look at them and would miss them. The cabinet, on a straight and solid floor, still stood a little warped and slumped to one side, doors hanging slightly ajar, its wood and structure shaped by decades of being atilt. The lights, which could be set to any level, from blindingly bright to romantically hazy, stood at medium. It smelled fresh and neat and I wondered if the tiny little mouse had survived the makeover. With any luck, it had escaped to the garden where the garage might be a more suitable haven. The spiders had definitely been banished. The crew had also added a side door, quite sturdy, locked and barred against intruders, but useful if someone wanted to get out of the house without going up through the kitchen. It replaced the window with its delightful view of how things grew from below ground to upward. I'd miss that window.

I took a deep breath. "Dad? Dad, if you can make it, show up for a few minutes, okay?"

The basement held a different kind of silence than the quiet house upstairs had held. It almost felt as though it were listening, actively, but for what I couldn't tell. Me, I hoped. Mom and me. Even if he couldn't respond, we now knew from the poltergeist activity that he'd been around, reacting to our comings and goings, voices and presence. I couldn't see malevolence in that, although knowing it definitely seemed more than a little odd.

Mom's hand felt a little chilled in mine, despite my holding tight. Maybe too tight. I relaxed a bit and she squeezed my fingers back encouragingly.

I tried again. "Dad? It's okay if you can't show up. We'll try again. We're not giving up on you."

I'd already done that once and was determined not to do it again. Not unless he gave me cause. The room felt a little cool around us, a nice break from what would be a hot and humid summer. I could see hanging down here, ghost or not, for comfort.

"Tessa."

He sounded out of breath and very far away, but I heard him clearly, and from Mom's slight gasp, she did too. I put my hand with the stone out and could feel myself grasping an unseen shoulder.

"We're here." I pulled Mom a little closer to me as she'd been hanging back slightly, and she touched the back of my wrist as if to let me know she stood with me.

He materialized slowly, mostly the upper torso, and his face looked a little strained.

"Hey! You had a couple of days off to soak in the rays and stuff. We were hoping you might like a little company."

A shiver rain through my father's transparent apparition. It was like seeing a ripple run across a pond of still water. "Mary?"

"It's me." She trembled in time with his ripple.

"Can you see me?"

"Mostly. I mean . . . you're not all there, honey."

A short burst of sound that might have been a laugh. "No, I'm not."

Not discounting his lack of energy, I waited for one of his dry quips, because Dad had always been a man with a quick answer. Nothing else came through. I shifted weight from one foot to the other. Strange thoughts filtered through my mind.

"Dad, where's my dog? Where's Baxter? Do you know?"

Mom started to open her mouth and I yanked on her hand. She closed her lips but looked at me funny. Why would I be asking about the dog? A couple of reasons, none of which I had shared with her yet.

That strange difference in time stretched out between us before he finally answered slowly, "Baxter's gone on."

I heard my mother suck a breath in and hold it. Under my hold, the stone pulsed a little, giving me spiky little jolts. I wondered if he could feel it, too, or just me. His sepia gaze slid past me. "Mary. You look good."

"I think you mean tired." She smiled faintly. "It's good to see you, too. I thought—I thought we'd lost you. We've been busy. Tessa growing and me teaching. My paper is almost done."

"About time." Another ripple and my father's image turned toward me. "And you're learning, too."

"I am. In leaps and bounds." I dropped Mom's hand and pulled a bundle out of my shirt with both hands, a large cardboard box of crystal goodness, as I let go of him, too. "Sorry, Dad." I dumped the container of salt, pouring it all over the ghost.

Mom couldn't see what happened, and for that I was grateful. The image split in two, one a great dark bulk of spitting fury and the other a barely visible, wavering reflection of my dad. He faded rapidly, a proud smile on his face, until he was barely there, seen only by the thinnest of existence.

I, however, stayed in the black gob's face. "My dog's not named Baxter. So, whatever you're doing in our basement and to my father won't work, because I'm onto you, M. Get out and stay out! You're not getting the stone if I can help it, or the professor."

"Foolish one. You've no real power."

"Maybe not, but I held Remy off. Maybe common sense is better than magic."

"She will pay for this."

"Whatever. This room is part of my house, and you've crossed my threshold without being invited. The stone is mine, bonded to me, and here it stays. Get out. Now."

The blob reared up and roared in anger, my mom scrambling backward to the staircase, while I stood my ground and gave him a nasty grin. It shrank into an ugly stain on the floor and curled in on itself until it could be seen no more. I took the salt shaker out of my jeans pocket, popped the lid off it, and dumped the last two tablespoons on the invisible but undoubtedly still there presence.

A squawk answered me, and the house shook to its rafters and then fell silent.

I looked at Mom. "Just making sure."

"What was that?"

"A who, not a what, and it's about what you think it is. Evil slime."

Dad hadn't faded completely away. He raised a hand to me. "Smarts run in the family." His voice quavered. "And Barney did pass over, very peacefully," and then he disappeared as well.

She came back to get me and pull me to the pantry staircase. "Is he gone?"

"Dad? Mostly."

"He was there too?"

"Yeah, that was Dad. Possessed, I guess. Free now but that left him weak."

"How did you know?"

"Just an uneasy feeling, like when you get an itchy back with no way to scratch it." I sighed. "We're not going to be able to talk to him for a few weeks, I think." If ever. I had no way of knowing if what I'd just done had pushed him forward or not. Would I ever see him again? I hoped the power of the stone might keep him nearby until Brian and I could figure out what to do, but I had no idea. Magic had a lot more limitations than hinted at.

We hugged each other, and then Mom led the way upstairs, stopping now and then to look back over her shoulder as if making sure I followed and hadn't disappeared behind her.

Brian cursed. Fluidly. In several languages before taking a deep breath and saying to me, "That could have gone quite badly." No one needed a translation to know that he'd been as profane as he knew how, and I knew exactly who scowled at me from that young face.

"No kidding. Actually, I'm really just amazed at how good ordinary salt is at getting rid of the bad things." I pulled my sneakers off and wiggled my toes. Free at last. "I had to do something, especially when I confirmed that it wasn't my dad. Not entirely."

"And now you're overconfident. A fortuitous response leading to an unfortunate expectation."

"Professor. It's not like any of you are sitting down to teach me anything. I'm having to improvise here, and it worked once, so." I shrugged. "And I can't believe anybody would be happy if I'd just let something like that hang in the basement all he wanted."

He sputtered a bit. Then he stood up straighter. "Has it ever occurred to you that he's just crossed a great salted ocean and might be temporarily vulnerable to that particular substance? That it won't last and using salt could fail you just when you need it most?"

"No, but now that you've told me, I'll keep it in mind. Should I switch to holy water or silver?"

"Gah!" Brian flung his hands into the air. "Maybe and no."

"See? Now I know even more than I did. Are Catholics the only ones with holy water?"

"Mostly." Brian forced himself to relax enough to lean a shoulder against the door jamb. "He could have taken your hand."

"Seriously?" I looked at my left hand, safe and secure at the end of my arm. "You mean lopped it off. But he didn't."

"Because he didn't know he'd been exposed. Next time, he'll be on the offensive, all the angrier for having underestimated you. He doesn't like failures, even small ones. We've no chance if he decides to mount a full-scale attack with whatever strength he can muster. If he does that, he will punch through until he has what he wants, and when we're all destroyed, he can rest."

"Then teach me."

His jaw tightened and I thought I could hear teeth grinding. "I can't."

"You said yourself that I found most of the relics for you. That I had the luck or something. Maybe I've a recessive gene hidden in here that knows how to work magic." I tapped my chest.

He shook his head.

I measured a tiny distance between my thumb and forefinger. "Just a pinch."

"Tessa. You don't."

"Maybe you don't and can't know. I mean, just like my dad, you're not all there. Not yet, anyway."

I looked across my bedroom at him and watched him chase thoughts through his mind like moths dancing around a flame before he told me, "You don't want to be in this world. My world."

"Maybe not, but I seemed to be up to my neck in it already. And if I am, knowledge would be a great thing. Teaching. Scholarly applications. Books. Instructors. Knowing stuff."

He put a hand up. "All right, all right. I get it."

"Do you? Good. When do we start?"

"When I'm restored."

I picked my phone up and slid it to the calendar, reading it. "Mmmm, that's no good for me. My life could be in danger at almost any time prior to that, and I need an immediate and firm date, I think."

He shifted his weight from one leg to the other. "Not willing to wait till next week when our shipments get here?"

"They could be out of stock. Stolen from the front porch by Remy. Waylaid by zombie postal bandits. Who knows what could happen?"

"All right then. We'll start tomorrow." He began to back out of my doorway and looked in briefly. "Good enough for you?"

"Yes."

He made a muffled noise and I could hear him trudge down the hallway, feeling sorry for Brian who seemed to be almost permanently locked away behind the professor's gruff nature. I wasn't sure who would win out when all the dust settled. I didn't think he knew either.

CHAPTER TWENTY-SEVEN

IF THINGS BEING NORMAL meant boring, we slogged through by the barrelful for the next few days. I, for one, was really happy I'd gotten that paper done early, because Brian dumped five hefty books on me, three from back in the day when bookmakers didn't have typesetting equipment, and said "Read these."

He should have said, "Get these translated and then see if you can read them."

I blessed the Internet gods who managed to make that odious task a little easier. Not easy. Never that. But easier. And it was tedious, like trying to pour molasses in the dead of winter. Eventually it works, but your arms might feel like they're going to break off before gravity finally takes hold. I have to admit I asked for it. And by the time I'd waded through the first book, I almost believed the professor might be right. Maybe it was something you had to be born to, leaving me with quite possibly no talent at all. I gritted my teeth as I finally shut the first book, thinking I hadn't learned a thing. Not one single thing.

The doorbell rang downstairs. I ran down to get it, wondering if Steptoe had decided to come back now that all the hard labor seemed done, or maybe Brian's packages had come. Meal deliveries would continue, since we needed the free rent, despite my heartfelt plea to my mother to let me transition out, but it was Tuesday and not a delivery day. No packages or bowler hat and coal-dark eyes looked back at me through the peephole. I lowered my gaze and saw Joanna, standing there demurely, while one of those limos sat at the curbside, with two of those incredibly handsome and impeccably suited escorts waiting for her. I shoved my left hand into my pocket.

I opened the door.

She smiled widely. "I couldn't believe the video Evelyn forwarded me, so I came to see myself."

I drew a blank. "Video?"

"The high heel walk! Take me upstairs and show me." In that quaint way she had, she hid her smile behind her hand in a show of modesty.

Odder things had definitely happened to me over the past few weeks, so I said "Sure!" and let her in. The midafternoon sun ushered her through the door and for just a minute, a freaky moment, she had two very distinct shadows. One followed at her heels, a perfectly ordinary silhouette of my friend, but the other gave me a start to see, hunched over and skulking, with sharp and cutting edges. As it flowed over my feet and flip-flops, a distinct chill crossed over. I blinked hard but it stayed, points and all. Joanna smoothed the line of her skirt and the shadows both copied her, falling into line with what they should have been. I rubbed the corner of one eye, trying to decide if I'd seen what I thought I'd seen, as far from normal as I could imagine. I began to regret inviting her across my threshold. Brian was upstairs too, sleeping the sleep of the dead tired, but he'd hear me if I screamed loud enough. Right? Maybe he could find enough zing to get a sputter out of his perdition rod if necessary.

Joanna led the way up the stairs confidently as though she'd been there a million times. "This is quite an old place. I didn't get a chance to ask you about it when we brought the dresses."

"Yeah. My Aunt April says it was the original home on this part of the land they turned into the tract, so it's decades older than most of the places around us."

"Got any secret passages?"

"No, right? I wish." And I did, sincerely. I felt like I might need one.

"Your mom doesn't own it?"

"No, we're renting. You know we lost our house when my dad disappeared?"

She nodded and waited for me by the bedroom door. "I'm sorry."

Shrugging, I opened the door. "Nothing you did. For a long time, I didn't even want him back, but now I wish he could come home."

"You know half the school said your mom did him in."

"I know, and the other half said I did it but to feel sorry for us. But we didn't. He had an addiction and couldn't deal with it."

"Wow. Prescription drugs?"

"No, but that is what everybody talks about today. It's almost even understandable, but not my dad. He went crazy for gambling."

"Oh. Sad."

She said sad but I heard pathetic in her tone. I'd never thought of Joanna as being judgmental, that had always been Evelyn's take, but I revised my opinion. "Not as sad as the idiot who keeps updating my picture ID and stuff on the Internet. It's everywhere I look. I'd like to just forget everything and move on."

"Social media can be the worst," Joanna agreed, not meeting my eyes. I looked at her slender hands, always so quick and sure on computer keyboards in the labs. "Bullying."

"Anonymous." I added, "Stay out here and I'll walk up and down the hallway for you. My room's a little messy today."

"How about you put on the dress too? No sense waiting until the last minute."

"You think? Okay." I did want to have an idea how they went together. I grabbed my brace while she looked behind her and slipped it on. She followed me in and perched on the edge of the bed while I changed.

The gown slipped over me like silken water, flowing into place and pooling around my ankles. It felt so good that I made a mental note to ask Santa for a silk nightgown when the season rolled around. I had to search the corner of my closet to recover the shoes with no idea how they'd gotten there. I stood up, dangling them by their silver straps. "Got 'em."

"You are not going to wear that brace, are you?"

"Hell to the no. My wrist should be pretty well healed by Saturday. My mom's got a pair of silver iridescent long gloves she wants me to wear. Old fashioned and formal, from back in the day."

"That should be awesome." She had moved to my night-stand. "Didn't you have a journal here?" She flashed me a side-ways look. "I bet you write poetry in it."

"Do I look like my soul is tortured? No, don't answer that. It doesn't belong to me anyway; the professor's nephew left it here. I've given it back."

"He's still staying with you guys?"

"Until we contact his parents. They're like lost in Peru or the Amazon or something."

"Interesting. I didn't know people could be off the grid like that." She ran a finger over my Central Park leaf, still brilliant and supple. "Pretty."

It felt as though someone had run a buzz saw down my spine. I slipped my shoes on, leaned over to hook her by the elbow, and dragged her out the door with me. I paraded up and down several times, feeling graceful and scared.

She applauded. I did a little curtsy and told her, "I've got as-signments to finish or we could go for a frappé." The lie floated off my tongue easily.

"Oh, right. Me too actually. I hope you don't mind my just showing up." She gave that bashful little smile again. Waved. I escorted her down the stairs and out the door before my heart-beat got back to normal and I stood there, back to the door, silver shoes on my feet and fabulous sea-glass gown on my body and wondered what the hell had just happened. A hot burn streaked up my left hand. I hissed at pain I hadn't felt earlier.

I wanted to bolt upstairs, wake Brian, and pry into his brain for answers, but a knock sounded and I jumped high enough to half-climb a tree. I peered through the peephole, expecting Jo-anna again, but Steptoe stood there instead, looking expectant. I let him in.

He tipped his hat. "'Ello, 'ello. All the hard work and noise done?"

"Yes, and no thanks to you."

"Ow, that wounds me, it does." He familiarly put his hand over his heart, and then gave me a look up and down. "Got a date?"

"Yes, but not now. Stay here, I'll go change."

"You don't 'ave to do that on my account."

"Oh, yeah, I do." I nudged him before going and changing. Feeling slightly more like myself in jeans, T-shirt, and barefoot, I walked him into the kitchen. My toes finally warmed up from the iciness of Joanna's shadow. "What brings you here? Bored with the minions?"

He rolled his eyes. "That lot. Well-meaning but not the sharpest knives in th' drawer. No, actually, I came to return this." And he held out the booklet on the maelstrom stone and chaos.

"I'll go get Brian."

"No. This is between the two of us."

I took it slowly. "Why?"

"You need it more than 'e does, and a wizard is like a dragon. He hoards his things, 'e does. A true wizard. Brian is not all he has been or could be, but it's still in 'im to want to keep his things to himself. I figure you might need this more, at the moment." Coal-dark eyes sincere, ruddy cheeks glowing a bit from the near-summer sun, he watched my expression to see if I accepted his words. He nodded when he realized I did.

"I'm not supposed to say thank you, right? So, this is nice of you."

"It is, isn't it!" He beamed at that. "Got any tea, luv?"

"Always." I fetched him a glass and made myself one as well, and we settled at the kitchen table. I watched as he drank it slowly, savoring it.

"You make a decent cuppa," he said.

"I'll take that as thanks."

He laughed, but a short one. One eyebrow lowered a bit. "Something's on your mind."

"Wellll." I traced my initials on the condensation of my glass.

"Not a personal question, is it? I don't talk about meself much."

"No, no. Nothing like that. At least, I don't think so." I thought back on the book I'd just labored to finish, and some quaint ideas about the philosophy of self, among other things I didn't think I'd ever understand. But it nudged me toward the question I wanted to ask. "What do you know about shadows?"

"Everybody 'as one but vampires."

"Vampires!"

"They don't run around in the sunlight, now, do they?"

"Steptoe!"

He waved a hand, laughing. "No, no, vampires don't exist. At least, not that I know about." He took another drink. "Shadows. That was a serious question?"

"Very."

"Well then. Speaking from my side o' the magical street, shadows are rather like a mirror. They can reveal a person, like? If you've the eyes to see with. Most of us never really look. Children do, sometimes. And sometimes that's why they disappear."

"That sounds awful."

"It is. Make no bones about it, 'tis bloody horrid. Look, if I stepped outside and stood in that blazing sun, and lost control o' myself, you'd see a handful of shadows. That's me, chaotic, never quite in line with the rules of time and space, see?"

"That's perspective though, and angle of the light, and science. Sometimes we all throw multiple shadows."

"I'll give you that. But they're all the same, right? As science applies."

"Right."

"A person like me, they're not. It's quick, it's fleeting, but you can spot it all the same."

I refilled his glass, thinking. "So if I met a person and they had, for just a minute or so, two shadows, and one of them was really, really different, that might reveal something."

His drink stopped halfway to his mouth. "What kind of different?"

I gestured with my hands. "All sharp and spiky. Cold, too. Very, very cold."

"Both shadows?"

"Just one. And then it smoothed down and got normal."

"I think you need to ask th' professor about that one."

I narrowed my eyes and he fidgeted a little. "I asked you."

The glass made it to his lips and he took a big gulp. Then, words tumbling out in a rush, he said, "Might be a twinned soul. Not bloody good."

"Twinned soul?" Something from that tedious book I'd just finished reading bounced around in my skull for a moment even as I talked. "Two souls, one body, and generally neither is up to any good?"

"That would be it. Sorry, ducks. I 'ope it wasn't a friend."

I didn't answer. She was a friend, although not a close one. And, the longer I thought about it, the more I realized I really knew very little about Joanna Hashimoto, and wasn't sure I wanted to know more. But I needed to. Like, why was she suddenly so interested in Evelyn and me? I settled. "I know her."

He tapped the back of my wrist brace. "This should have told you something."

"I didn't notice it was burning my hand until after she left."

He frowned. "Could have put a damper on it, somehow. You let her in after all, right?"

I nodded.

"Then the stone is not quite sure. You let her in, but she might be a menace. What's a stone to do, eh?" He put his glass down firmly. "Which is why I brought th' booklet to you. You're needin' it now, not him." He looked up at the ceiling. "Not sure if he woulda told you proper anyway."

"He'd hide it from me?"

"No, no, just part of the wizarding way is t' let the young ones learn as they go. Lesson earned and done is more dear than one handed you. Old-fashioned way of teachin', but it works, mind you."

That much was true. I'd probably learned more from that blasted book Brian had given me by translating it myself than by sitting at his feet and having him drone it at me. That thought bouncing around inside my skull finally came to a halt and I caught it. "A twinned soul, sometimes they need to take on a second body, don't they? And then they're twice as powerful, side by side, right?"

"Some 'ave it that way, yeah."

"And Brian has no soul. Or two very, very weak ones."

Steptoe nodded. "Right again."

"So M might not necessarily want Brian dead, just . . . occupied."

Steptoe grimaced. "Oh, that's a bloody nasty thought."

"All the more reason we get him rejuvved as soon as possible." I stood up. "I appreciate the information."

He stood too, and hesitated a moment, before turning and starting toward the front door. "Nothing I can do around here tonight?"

"Not really. I've got stuff to do and this to study."

"A'right then. You know how to get ahold of me. You do, right?"

"Call your name three times."

"That's my girl!" He beamed then, tipped his hat and let himself out. I went and locked the door behind him, just in case. It didn't get unlocked until the postman came.

She knocked lightly and was down the street by the time I got to the door and found the smiling package on the steps.

"Hey, Brian!" I yelled, knowing from the noise upstairs that he no longer napped. "Some of the stuff is here!"

He came downstairs, combing his damp hair back with his fingers, the muted red-gold color more of a soft brown when wet. "Is it?"

"It is." I put the parcel into his hands.

He looked at it. I could sense a subtle fear in him, and felt it myself. It meant he drew that much closer to a ritual that was about as daunting as any I could imagine. Who looked forward to going up in flames, even if you had the best DIY handbook in existence? Plus one had to wonder just how many lifetimes a phoenix wizard could count on. What was the lucky number? Seven? Eight? One hundred? Any miscalculation could end up in a pile of ashes.

"You should check and make sure the bottles didn't break in shipment or something."

He looked up from the box. "I think," and he gave a wry smile, "we could smell them if they had. They are very aromatic."

"Oh. Right. Well then. All we need are the rowan sticks?"

He put the box on the foyer entrance table and absently rubbed the thick gold ring on his thumb. "I believe so."

"They've shipped. They should be here any time." I put on a smile and started an end run around him.

Brian put a hand out. "Did I hear Steptoe down here earlier?"

"Briefly. He was wondering if it was safe to visit or if we'd shanghai him into the work force. Imagine his relief when he found out the wrecking crew had finished up and left." I wanted to tell him about Joanna, but I didn't. The decision not to, though, knotted in my chest like a really awful lie or a medium-sized betrayal.

"Mmm."

I took another step and stopped when he added, "Tessa."

"Yeah?"

"The two of you seem to be fast friends."

"I think he's proven himself, don't you? He's been quite helpful."

"And yet, he is who he is."

"Do the two of you have a checkered past?"

"Easily. I would say so."

I tilted my head a little. "Why do you think he changed?" Or maybe it was the professor who'd changed. I hadn't forgotten that both Carter and Remy called him an outlaw.

"I think he's an opportunist. He changed just as much as it serves him to change, which is why I'd urge caution with Simon."

"Take what he says with a grain of salt?"

"At the very least. Chaos," and his gaze dropped to rest briefly on my wrist brace, "tends to act for itself, and only for itself, and for the general disruption."

"Maybe the status quo needs a little rebellion now and then." I didn't like hearing what I heard. I knew lying liars and I knew friends, and Steptoe had, after that first rocky start, been a friend.

He gave a half nod. "Such has been the thought of youth from the very beginning. It's in your hot blood, unfiltered by things like consequences. Striving for change is necessary and sometimes only the young are brave enough to attempt it. I'm not unaware that people of my age and experience have a comfort zone they don't wish to leave."

I wasn't sure where that put him on rebellion. For or against? Or youth either, for that matter. I decided to change the subject. "Finished the first book. Which one do you want me to start next?" I knew which one I wanted to start, although there might be a reading problem. I hadn't had a chance to look at what Steptoe left me just yet, although my hands itched to pick it up.

My having finished startled him. "Already?"

"The internet is a wonderful thing."

"It must be. I would suggest two titles: *Matter and Immutability* or perhaps *The Spirit Way*. But it depends on you, my dear. Look at them and find the one that speaks to you."

The one speaking to me stood spread wide open on my bedroom desk, the treatise on chaos, and I almost said as much, but Steptoe's caution against telling him he'd returned it stopped me. I wondered if one of the five books the professor had given me was titled, *Wizards and Their Dragon Hoards*. I should check. "I'll do that."

"Good, good. No hurry."

"But shouldn't I be ready for the ritual?"

"Tessa, your only role in my ritual is to be there for me, as a friend and witness. In case something should go wrong, or even if I succeed." He paused. "I don't think either of us is looking forward to this."

"Not really. I mean, I know you have to do it, you're weaker every day, so something is *not* right, but . . ."

"It seems like a drastic cure?"

"Exactly!"

"I understand. Believe me. But the actions of both Remy and

Steptoe have convinced me that a confrontation of monumental proportions is coming, and I need to be ready for it, or we will lose a great deal."

"A war of wizards?"

"That sounds a bit glamorous for it, but something in that neighborhood, yes. I am not looking forward to any such conflict, but it seems it will be thrust upon us, and we should be ready to brace ourselves."

"You think we need to be heroic?"

"No. But I do think we need to be wise." Brian suddenly looked very tired and rubbed each eye gently.

"I think being wise is harder," I told him. At least it was for me.

"Oh?"

"Anybody can react to a situation, but to figure out what should be done and the best way to do it, and how things will look on the other side of the action—that's going to be hard."

"That's what it is to be human, isn't it? Knowing that sometimes we have to do things the hard way." He placed his hand on top of his box.

I reached out and gave him a comforting pat, uncertain as I felt inside myself. Neither of Brian's personalities seemed at peace, and I didn't like thinking about the future that would give that to them.

CHAPTER TWENTY-EIGHT

REMY DIDN'T SHOW UP at my next meal run, thankfully, although Mrs. Sherman seemed a little hesitant when I gave her
hers. She held the tray carefully between her two palms, standing quietly in the doorway, almost afraid to turn away while I
stood on the porch.

"Is everything all right?"

"Oh, fine, dear, fine. I was just thinking." She giggled a bit.
"Stopped to smell the roses and got a bit lost, isn't that what
they say?" Her wig had returned to its proper place on her head,
though it seemed to sit a bit askew.

Did she remember being held hostage? I told her gently, "I
can stay and talk a while, if you want to."

"Oh, no. No, I'm fine. Just filled with old memories, some of
them so vivid, it's like being there again."

Had Remy done that to her? "Good memories, I hope."

"The best, the very best, when I and Arturo were young. He
was quite a dashing young man, you know. Came from one of
the families with money in Cuba. They got out before all the
trouble and did well for themselves." She gave a wistful smile
and tucked a curl of vigorously red hair behind her ear. "He
didn't believe in saving for tomorrow though, and when he died,
I had just enough to move to Richmond and buy a modest
house. He never lived here, but in my memories, it's almost as
if he'd come home."

"That's adorable, but your dinner is going to get cold if you stand around dreaming about him, right? So go in and enjoy the stroganoff while it's piping hot, then go sit out back in the shade and wait for the moon to rise!"

"Quite right." She nodded briskly. "Off to it then. Give the others my regards. I'll be at bridge on Thursday."

I watched her march back into the house and shut the door behind her firmly. Then the click as the dead bolt snapped into place, the sound echoing through me sadly. She'd never locked the door after me before. She seemed all right but wasn't, not quite, and all I could do was hope time would make her feel safe again.

When Remy and I met next, we were going to have some words.

By the time I pedaled back to the house, a dewy sheen covered me. We don't like to sweat in the south. We shine. I was shining a lot and maybe even stinking a little, with a whole summer of heat and humidity awaiting me. I came out of the shower and dressed with as little as I could wear and get away with, which was actually pretty conservative because my mom has rules. Most of them have to do with her feeling like a good parent when she enforces them, but a few also reflect on her standing as a college professor in a certain layer of society and the responsibility to project an image, blah blah blah. So I stay pretty hot because I can't wear a string bikini around the house. Not that I even own one. Or would anyway, but it's the protest that counts.

Brian's eyes widened a bit as I came downstairs.

"You've seen legs before!" I told him.

"Not that long. Did you spend some time on a rack while you were out?"

"Very funny. Deal with the short-shorts." I opened the fridge and didn't see what I wanted. So I went to the pantry. "I'm going downstairs."

"By yourself?"

"Unless this is some slasher movie and I shouldn't do that, yeah. We have a second refrigerator down there now, remember? It's where I hide the Cokes from you."

He brightened. "I knew they had to be around here somewhere." He hung around the top step as I went to fetch a couple.

My momentum slowed near the bottom of the steps. I hadn't been down here since exorcising my dad and finding out that part of him, a substantial part of him, seemed to consist of bad guy. I rubbed my wrist brace, but the stone under it remained cool and calm. The lack of salt slowed me down even more. Even though I'd vowed never to go anyplace ever again without a pound on me, my pockets were empty.

The old fridge stood in the corner. The wrecking crew had dragged it out of the garage, checked it out, and plugged it in before finishing the new cellar door that led up through the side yard. It hummed invitingly. I approached it, yanked open the door, got the Cokes, and bolted back to the exit. At the bottom, before I could take the stairs two at a time, a warm current passed over me. A warm and soothing current, with a feeling of being loved.

I turned around to see nothing unusual. The stone stayed quiet in my palm. There was only one thing I could think of, so I said, "Thanks, Dad."

Nothing more happened. I guessed I couldn't expect any more, but I waited a few heartbeats before I finally took the stairs, Cokes icy in my hands but the rest of me welcomed and reassured. It had to have been my father. Not that I wouldn't put it past Malender to yank my chain, but frankly, I think he had more important conquests in the works than to stop for a minute and give me the equivalent of a mystical hug just to spook me. Brian gave me a look as I pressed both cans into his hands. "One of these is mine," I warned him. "Go on, I'll be up in a few."

I shut the door and went back down to sit on the bottom step. "Don't materialize, Dad. You need the rest. But if you could talk a bit, that would be nice. I need some advice that Mom can't give me."

Like a tropical ocean current, warmth eddied up and swirled around me, ever so gently.

"Thanks. I need to understand, if you can tell me, why Joanna Hashimoto upset you. She's a friend, not a close one, but I know her and, well, she's getting spooky. I think she has a foot in the magical world, if not both feet, and I don't know if I can trust her."

"Hironori runs gambling dens." His answer, breathy and uneven, came after a long silence.

"Oh." So that might explain some of her interest in my long-gone father and me. Not magic at all, just malice. "He was part of the trap, huh?"

"No. I tried to find evidence on him."

I blinked. "You . . . were you working with the police?"

"Feds. After I got in too deep. They were going to help me out."

"Dad. You should have told us."

"Trouble for everyone."

"Mom could have helped, you know that. She loves you." I crossed my arms, thinking. Carter might have known, too. Was that why he'd been so secretly protective all these months?

"Hironori uses power."

That skipped off my thoughts. "Power. Influence? Bribery? Or do you mean something more?"

"Unnatural."

"Then the Hashimotos are into more than money." And that bounced back to my first fears. The Hashimoto luck came from more than hard work and education, never to knock that, but if they'd tapped into magic to reinforce it, they had to have education and relics to refine their talent, and with that came the inevitable thirst for more. I hadn't imagined Joanna's keen interest in the journal, and in me, augmented by the stone, which she hadn't seen but might be able to feel, like a magnet. Magic seemed to be an ever-expanding force. Their strength might be attracting Malender, and his them, a mutually beneficial partnership if Hashimoto brought strong allies to the table. And if Hironori had uncovered the fact that my dad had gone to work for the Feds, he could be the very reason my dad existed as little more than a ghost of himself. I stood up. "I've got to stop whatever Joanna has planned."

"Danger."

"Oh, I got that." I pulled my bracer off to see my stone glowing softly in the dim light of the basement. It didn't like organization. Plans. Power that depended on thinking within a box. I knew that much from a little reading. Some things in creation lived beyond explanation and boundaries. Like love. "A little chaos should unravel anything she has scheduled."

"Tessa. Take care."

"If they put you here, I intend to take everything back that I can from them. And that includes you." Before the warmth could disappear, I bolted up the basement stairs, shut the door behind me, and began to make plans.

One thing I didn't have to worry about: I had already been invited over the Hashimoto threshold. I could get in. I just had to be concerned about the options for getting out.

Brian waylaid me in the foyer. "Problem?"

I took in his ever-paling skin, with the bluish bruises of fatigue growing under his eyes. The robust young man of days ago could barely be seen now. I might have been looking at some junkie just about to sink back into rehab. Whatever strength he had left, he needed for his own ritual. "Just some private family stuff."

He rubbed the thick gold ring about his right thumb. "If you say so."

"I do." I started to step around him and then stopped. "Do you have any idea how weird it is to have the ghost of your father living in the cellar?"

"Can't say that I ever had the privilege." Brian smiled slightly. "But then, I am old enough that my parents are extremely difficult to remember in any way at all. I envy you, a bit."

"That makes odd sense, because I don't envy your forgetting them at all, even though it might be a little easier that way."

He thrust a glass of ice and my can at me. "Thanks. I'm going to need the caffeine." He stared after me, openmouthed, as I bounded back upstairs to work some more on those plans.

Saturday night needed to be spectacular. If I had anything to do with it, and the Andrews family luck, it would be.

No doorbell but a firm knock started it off, and I opened the door for the limo driver.

The driver took my garment bag from me and hung it carefully from the back passenger hook as I sat on the other side. He gave an odd look at the lumps at the bottom. "My shoes," I told him. "And gloves and purse." He smiled as he closed the car door. I wondered if he would be one of the provided escorts for the evening. Not too much older than me, I guessed his age some-where between seventeen and Carter's twenty-three years. He wore his hair shaved very close at the back of the neck and over the ears, like a Marine, but unlike a Marine, he had a big wave of dark hair on top in a trendy look. He looked good in a suit and would look even better in a tux. I scanned the car interior as the locks clicked down and we pulled away from the curb.

"Just me?"

"You are a bit late, miss, so the car is for you alone." He gave me another short smile before turning back to the business of driving. As I watched the back of his neck, repeating in my mind all that I'd learned over the past three days of intense study, I saw a blur of color creep up his neckline. I hooked a thumb over my seat belt, prepared to bolt if the worst happened. I froze, transfixed, sighting a tattooed dragon just revealed above the collar line, its scales a pattern of beautiful, vibrant color, the whiskered snout elaborate, with white fangs. Sap-phire eyes watched me, a sight as beautiful as it was incredible. I sat speechless.

My thoughts began clawing through my mind and every-thing I'd read in my entire life for a clue, even a worthless one.

I hadn't studied tattoos, had I? And why not? Maybe because I had to find some time to sleep, go to campus, deliver meals and . . . oh yeah, breathe. I pulled my phone out, fingers flying over the search bar. After long minutes, the screen filled with answers.

Japanese dragons. Meaning: wisdom, strength, wind or water, and force for good.

I let the phone drop in my lap. This guy worked for Hironori Hashimoto and twin-souled Joanna. Maybe working for good was only a matter of perspective, and that put me on the wrong side.

Wonderful.

Of course, no one ever said the Internet is only full of truth and honesty.

This was not for myself. This was to find out what might have happened to my father, which the powers that evidently be around here either ignored or didn't see in time, but I needed to straighten out. If I waited until I got permission, the opportunity to infiltrate could be gone. I had a few friends to guard my back, and that would have to be enough. I put my phone away and watched the cityscape of Richmond flow by as we drove out into the country toward the private club, with its own river access, while I planned for dealing with contingencies like dragons bolstering the Hashimoto abilities.

The Hashimoto grounds lay not too far outside town, with a white-railed fence with Japanese gates at the main drive, and a little guardhouse complete with a guard who watched us enter. Beyond that was an acre or so of immaculately groomed grass, signaling to golfers that a heavenly paradise of eighteen holes awaited on the other side of the country club, and even more manicured acres. The clubhouse stood in all-American flag-stone beauty, expansive and tailored to its clientele. We went to the right, to the shops and spa, which looked tastefully Asian. The river connected both, a brilliant blue ribbon of man-made goodness, complete with bobbing barges vaguely like junks but with much more class and river worthiness docked on the shore. Joanna pounced on the car door as soon as we pulled to a stop in the parking lot. Her eyes and nose wrinkled disapprovingly as soon as she saw the brace. Both she and Evelyn walked wrapped in kimonos and wearing flip-flops as they pulled me out of the backseat.

"I thought you were ditching that."

"I am, I am. My gloves are in the garment bag." I grabbed for it as the driver retrieved it and started to make away with it. "Wait a minute!"

He stopped with an apologetic nod as I unzipped the bottom and retrieved my purse for the evening. It shimmered in silver iridescent glory as I hung the strap over my shoulder. "Borrowed," I told Evelyn.

"Well, it's gorgeous. Come on! The masseuses—is that a word? Many massagers—are waiting."

Joanna looked over Evelyn's shoulder. Her gaze assessed my necklace, earrings, and focused on my bracelet, just for the sparkling, I hoped. "Nice jewelry. You'll have to take it off for the massage and the sauna though."

"No prob. I'm sure they'll be safe here."

"We have lockers for personal items."

And I intended to circle my items with a sprinkle of holy water, courtesy of one of the two vials in my purse. If that didn't work, then I didn't have much hope of surviving the evening anyway. Evelyn locked elbows with each of us. "I can hardly wait!"

I lowered an eyebrow at her. "Someone has teriyaki breath, so I'm guessing you already didn't wait."

She blushed. "A girl has to eat."

Never-thin-enough Evelyn eating? I bumped hips with her. She did eat, but usually on her own convoluted diet. We laughed at her now.

"Are you hungry?"

I shook my head at Joanna. "I'll make it till dinner. We're having it at your restaurant, right?"

"That's the idea, with everyone else, just before the catwalking and bidding starts. If Evelyn can wait."

Evelyn smothered a delicate burp before adding, "I'm waiting, I'm waiting!"

"Paragon of patience." Joanna mocked her with a fake burp of her own.

I threw a look back over my shoulder at our shadows trailing behind us. We each had two, from the sun's slanted angle. Joanna's second shadow grew a little as I observed it, and spikes crowned its head and . . . tails. I looked away as soon as I saw it, and any warmth in me faded despite the hot Virginia almost-summer sun. Auction night. Evelyn looked forward to fun and games, while I anticipated trouble and Joanna. I gather she expected easy prey.

CHAPTER TWENTY-NINE

GOLD AND IVORY marble swirled about the lobby, and complementing pillars reached elegantly to the ceiling, the room sweeping and impressive. It spoke of money, not in a whisper, but with a shout. No one sat at the reception desk, a curved piece of highly polished cherry wood as imposing as a baby grand piano, a gateway to all the magnificence beyond. It seemed the spa stood open today only for our private party. Our footsteps seemed to glide over the flooring, echoes off walls muted by swags of ivory silk painted with sweeping branches of cherry blossoms, an echo of Joanna's elaborate kimono. A faint perfume drifted through the air, so light and delicate I could barely place what it was, except for a touch of both pear and ginger.

Evelyn had evidently already been through the staging area, for she did not stop to gawk in awe as I did. I had heard of the opulent yet tasteful Hashimoto resort and spa but never thought to see it, and here I stood. A little voice inside me kept yelling "it's a trap!" and another little voice argued back "but what a way to go!" In a slow twirl, I took in the fact that the driver and my garment bag didn't follow us in. Not that I blamed him, this place obviously seemed to be the domain of everything female on the property, concentrated into a few glorious rooms.

I spun on one heel. "Where are my clothes going?"

"Akira is taking them around back to a private entrance and hanging them up there. Massage and sauna first!"

Ah. Another entrance and exit. I could have stood there all day, bathed in the glory of the vision while my voices argued about the wisdom of my plan, or any plan at all, but Evelyn trotted back to hook my arm.

"Come on, silly. Quit staring."

"But it's beautiful!"

"Isn't it?" Joanna agreed. "My mother helped design it."

"She's talented."

"Yes. She was." Joanna stepped ahead and opened the doors leading to the treatment rooms. Her words sounded as glacial as the marble, reminding me that she came from a single-parent family, too. It had happened so long ago that I had forgotten about it, and felt my cheeks warm in an apologetic blush. Joanna beckoned me onward.

Under my brace, the stone began to heat in warning. I curled my fingers in acknowledgment, praying that it would not get so hot that it scorched me. Thanks to Steptoe, I'd gained a rudimentary idea of how it worked and what it might and might not do for me, but I hoped to keep it under wraps until the actual happenings began. Whatever they would be. I expected fireworks but hoped they might be duds.

Outside a flock—no, a murder of crows—peeked in through the windows at me, windows showcasing the private river and peaceful greens and pines beyond. At night, the barges would take guests to the restaurant and country club venue, with paper lanterns swaying with the movement of the rowers and kimono-clad hostesses attending to the various groups on board. Hironori had planned the experience as no less than a trip to a fantasyland, as exotic as he could make it. No BBQ here. The moon hung in the spring sky as it does sometimes, silvery and partial, unafraid to invade the sun's empire. As if Joanna disliked my view, she pulled a sash and the shutters closed, leaving us entirely immersed in the spa atmosphere.

I thought I heard a caw of disagreement as she did.

Evelyn escorted me into the group massage room where three beds had been set up. A fountain in the corner flowed into a room-long pool—or perhaps it was a miniature river, burbling quietly as it streamed slowly past, disappeared down a drain in the far corner somewhere, and circled back around to cascade downward again. It not only looked beautiful but it sounded that way, too. On the adjacent wall stood the bank of lockers, this time in a tasteful, almost Scandinavian light wood, very minimal and efficient looking. "Put your clothes in here, and there's a kimono for you, too."

"Great." There was also a racquet of some kind, left behind I presumed, so I ignored it. I stripped down as much as I intended to while the two of them, distracted as their masseuses entered, turned about. I wrapped a towel around myself, covering up my athlete's running bra and shorts. I had no intention of running around in the altogether while throwing salt or tossing one of Steptoe's flash-bangs. My brace came off, and I held my bracelet in my curled hand, hiding both it and the stone as my masseuse entered and motioned me to my table, parallel to the wall fountain and brook. I climbed up on my stomach and found myself looking down at the floor through the head brace. She said nothing as she loosened my towel and began to oil down my shoulders.

My ears muffled, I managed to hear Joanna leave as someone came to the door and asked softly for her. Evelyn switched her joyful chatter from that target to me and didn't seem to mind when I just managed a soft murmur now and then. Evelyn in talk-mode is like a freight train barreling down the tracks: you don't stand a chance and should never get in the way. I did gather that my driver was likely to be my escort, and he was the tallest of the three volunteered for the jobs tonight. Evelyn seemed pleased over the moon about it, and I thought of telling her that not all was as it looked, but decided against it. Some things just have to be experienced in person.

In the middle of a sentence, Evelyn said "Oh!" and then went rambling on as though she hadn't interrupted herself. In the next minute she let out a big yawn. "I'm soooo sleepy," her words nearly hidden by the soft drumming of hands against flesh.

I started to turn my head as she drifted into total silence, but then something sharp bit into my shoulder. "Hey!"

The masseuse continued working on my upper back and

neck as if nothing had happened, talking in Japanese to the other masseuse, their rhythm lulling, and my eyelids drooped. I found myself echoing Evelyn's yawn. My stone began to grow heated, sending sparks through my hand as though we'd been short-circuited and my eyes flew open. Footsteps circled my platform.

"Come help me!"

"She's not asleep yet."

I could sense my masseuse pausing over my form and looking to her teammate before slapping me once, hard. Biting my lip, I kept from jumping and deepened my breathing.

"That one is light. What's your problem?"

"My back hurts. Come on, let's get her out. Joanna-san is waiting. I'll help you with that one, she looks taller and heavier."

"No kidding. A lot of muscle though. All right, but only if you help."

"What? You don't trust me?"

"Never." And the two voices blurred into Japanese as the two debated what was obviously an argument as old as the hills: not everyone did their share of the work.

I could not turn my head to see what was happening, but I got a view of two pairs of feet shod in white canvas shoes and legs in white pants dragging a bare-legged and footed person between them, and from the bright red polish on the toes, I knew it had to be Evelyn. From the silence I also knew she had to be out like a light or she would have been all over them with questions and protests.

She seemed to be as unconscious as I was meant to be if the stone hadn't been throwing a hissy fit in my palm. My head worked and my arm worked but the rest of me felt like lead. As the room cleared, I tried to roll onto my side and nothing happened. They'd be back for me as soon as they disposed of Evelyn. I got my arm under my torso and pushed. With a grunt and a roll, I managed to get on my side. Not great, but some improvement. That spot on my shoulder ached like a bee sting. It seemed a little early to call for help, but since I had no idea what they had planned for us, I decided to let out a shout.

But my face didn't work right. Or rather my mouth and voice

box, the important parts of it, didn't work, although I have had flirty guys suggest that my eyes and freckles are my best features. A string of drool managed to escape my lips but that was the extent of it. Maybe a ghoulish-sounding moan did as well.

I tried to sit up. Nada. Move a toe. Zilch. Turn my head to stare at the ceiling. Nope. Except for one arm, and a slight ability to move my head, ever so little, my body had frozen solid.

I stared at my arm. I couldn't even uncurl my hand. Brian's weighty book on one's self suggested that I was only imprisoned inasmuch as I thought I was. But whoever wrote it in the Dark Ages had obviously not had a poison dart stabbed into their body. The author wouldn't dispute that I had to use whatever came to hand and that was, well, my right hand.

It felt like doing a one-armed push-up, but I got it straight under me and pushed, hard as I could. Rather like tipping a cow.

Again! I held my breath and tensed my body, pushing with muscles that I couldn't feel respond, but I knew I couldn't afford to fail.

I went over backward, prepared to hit the floor, hard.

Instead, I nearly drowned. I fell into the ornamental river backside first in a spray of foam that rushed in to cover me.

That very slight movement of head came in handy. Rather than drowning in the bubbling brook edging the room, I managed to keep my head above water. Bracing, very cold water. Water that shocked me to my toes and back to my head with wetness. And a lot deeper than it looked, too. I floated down toward the drain while prickling sensations of feeling returned to me in lightning, stabbing pain, but by the time my feet bumped against the recycling drain in the corner, I could move and hauled myself out.

Sorta. Let's just say if a zombie (one of the slow ones) came after me in a fifty-yard dash, it would win. But I'd be hobbling as fast as I could go, and I did now to the lockers. Jeans. Check. T-shirt, check. Shoes, double check. Fancy purse with a pound of crystal salt in it, triple check. It is really difficult to dress yourself when you've been numbed within an inch of your life. I managed somehow though the inside of me didn't seem to be waking up as fast as the outside. If it had, I'd have thought to grab my clothes and run rather than stand there, hopping around in front of the locker, trying to get dressed.

Seriously. Hindsight and all that. The door burst open and a very angry woman charged in. Luckily that ignored handball racquet in my locker looked useful, and I could swing it when my masseuse came after me with a shout and a string of colorful curses. I unloaded my best field hockey goal shot on her. She staggered back from the racquet, slipped on the wet floor where I'd climbed out of the riverbed, went down, clipped her head on the edge of the fountain and lay still when she finished. Most of that, I thought, had nothing to do with me, but I'd take whatever fortunate accidents came my way.

I kept the racquet. Took the main door out of the room and moved slowly down the hallway in the opposite direction of voices I could now hear.

My shoes squelched. I was neither as dry or stealthy as I wanted to be. Had to be. Whoever found the masseuse wouldn't know how I took her down, but they were bound to be better equipped and trained for hand-to-hand than I was. So, I needed to find Evelyn and Joanna, determine what they were up to, stop them, and get the hell out of Dodge before things got worse. And I'd found a second door out that would aid in that endeavor. Opened it and hobbled swiftly right into the janitorial closet.

I'd expected that. Steptoe had mapped out the place for me, and I pulled his map out of my jeans pocket only to find the ink running together messily. Don't ask what favors we traded, but I ended up with the map and another handful of flash-bangs and I think I might have given him a book of his choice out of Brian's library. I exhaled gustily over the map to dry it, but did manage to locate my position. I'd tried to get his magic invisibility coat off him to use myself, but he'd insisted only he had the talent to wield it and subsequently insisted on doing the recon. Running ink told me that not all bargains were good ones. I waved it a little in hopes of clearing it up. My room stood out. It was the rest of the spa that looked blurred. The location of the casino, a separate building just off the country club, had disappeared altogether in an interesting blob of smeared ink. I might not need to break in there, however, depending on what I found here. Offices needed bosses, and I doubt Hironori trusted more people than he had to. Joanna was surely one of the highest on the list.

I squinted and turned the map in a few directions, getting an idea just where I was as well as where I had been, followed by the reason maps were created: deciding where to go. What Steptoe had detected as a very tech-oriented room had to be an office of some sort at the spa, and if it was, I knew I had to get in there. I blew on the map a few more times to get it dry, folded it back up and put it away, put my ear to the door, and listened.

The nice thing about upset people is that their voices get high, loud, and shrill, i.e., easy to hear. I heard nothing. I did three stretches to confirm my body could now move and opened the door carefully. Out and to the left, then a quick right, keeping to the walls and praying that Steptoe's observation about the cameras had been correct also. I shouldn't be in their range if I hugged the walls. That handled the tech aspect. What I couldn't guess for sure would be the magical element. The corridors had to be warded. I couldn't see them, but my palm let me know when something stirred or snagged or broke as I moved through the building. The stone, if it worked, should be nulling whatever signals the wards attempted to send. If I'd done my part correctly. I had only the two books read under my belt, but what I'd learned so far signified that will had a great deal to do with magic. I didn't know if the Hashimotos were on the good side or bad side of Malender, but I was convinced they'd spirited my dad away, leaving grief and estrangement in their wake. They owed me. For that, I intended to own them. I would bring them down and my father back.

As always, easier said than done. The spirit might be willing but my flesh basically gave up. Sapped of energy, I barely moved. Huddling against the wall kept me on my feet as I raced an imaginary sloth down the corridor, and lost. That's when I realized that magic has a very real, very definite price, and I had gone bankrupt. Or perhaps the stone took its power from my core, and the more I depended on it, the lower my body functioned. If it couldn't feed on chaos, it fed on me. Not a pretty thought.

I made it to the tech room door and slipped inside, panting. The room stood empty of personnel but not equipment, and the computers, two of them, were up and running. I hooked a chair with my foot and pulled it to me, collapsing in the seat. I rolled back over to the desk and began searching the drawers for whatever I could find. I struck gold. A handful of candy bars and a can of caffeinated soda goodness. I ate two bars and washed them down hastily before my eyes crossed so badly I couldn't see the computer monitor. Powering myself up should only take a few minutes. Tapping the keyboard experimentally, I pulled up the command screen and began looking for programs or documents. The stone hissed and fizzed a little as I did, deflecting whatever safeguards they'd put on the machine. It took a moment to focus, no fault of the computer, I was the one who needed rebooting. As soon as the snacks hit my stomach and then my bloodstream, I began to hum along with the computer.

This one had a few hidden files. I didn't bother to decipher the name or open them up to see what they were. I figured if they were hidden, that was reason enough to copy them. I didn't have time to rifle through the files now. Opening my purse carefully, to keep the salt from spilling out, I found the small plastic baggie holding my flash drive and extracted it.

If my life was a thriller movie, I'd be frozen in the seat waiting for the download to finish while a werewolf tore away at the closed door and I feared for my life. Luckily my greatest danger at the moment was falling asleep. I unwrapped and gulped down another candy bar. I finished with all I could see to steal from that computer and wheeled over to the second one. The first had been a PC but this was a slim, sleek laptop.

It sat reigning over the middle of the desk, like a prince or a king on its throne, and from the heat in my stone and the spats growing louder, wards were wrapped around this computer like a spiderweb. This was the one I should have hit first.

I stood up and leaned over the laptop and dangled my arm over it, hand down, and began to make circles around it, counterclockwise, as though I were spinning cotton candy. In actuality, I hoped I was unwinding all the wards and spells that had locked this computer in place, the stone doing all the hard work in its job as protector and shield of *moi*. As a relic and as I worked it, the value of the maelstrom stone struck me. Practically idiot proof, it could do almost anything defensive. How had the professor not grabbed this up and utilized it? Tried to convince me to give it over to him? No wonder Remy wanted it so badly. Steptoe not so much because, as he'd explained it to me, he wasn't that far from the stone itself with regards to chaos, and it wouldn't function the same with him, but he'd wanted to learn about it to control his own forces. Its value though, seemed clear. I understand why people might kill to possess it. Even the lowliest magic user could be a wizard with the maelstrom in his hand.

My palm let out a loud crackle and hiss, and then the web cocooning the laptop disappeared.

"Bingo."

Now all I had to worry about was passwords. Hit the wrong one enough times and the laptop would either lock up or maybe even fry, if set to react to that way. I could possibly just put it on my body somewhere and smuggle it out, but the drive seemed much easier to hide, not to mention transport. I opened the lid, turned it on and sure enough, the password prompt came up. I thought for a second, or rather the soda and candy bars chased themselves around in my brain like a hamster in a wheel. A sleek, fast hamster.

Then I typed in "cherry blossom" and held my breath, praying that the password was not in Japanese. But since the keyboard was a standard US QWERTY, I had hopes.

The laptop opened up. My jaw dropped. That easy? Surely not.

And it wasn't. I hadn't disarmed all the wards, just the easy ones. This one felt lethal. As I dropped my fingers to the board to do some searching, it fought back. White lightning flashed through my hands and up to my shoulder. My mouth clamped shut and my teeth ground. I think only my sneakers kept me from being fried.

The stone lit up. It glowed buttercup gold and pulsed as if it swallowed the curse, wave after wave after wave. My ears stopped buzzing. My jaws relaxed. Then I could swallow and stretch my neck a bit. Another moment and the shock and pain disappeared into the palm of my left hand. I examined the maelstrom. The surface I had thought to be immutable marble danced in beautiful color and swirls, folding over and over on itself, bringing fresh and rich new brilliance to itself. When it cooled, it returned to its stony finish, but its pattern had changed, although the richness of the ivory, gold, caramel, and obsidian stayed. Now it had flecks of red-gold copper studding it. I stared at it, lost for a few long heartbeats in its glory.

It let out a tiny spit, like an irritated kitten. I jumped in surprise and then returned to my hacking. Let me say that hacking is not a skill taught in class. Not officially. But frankly, in any computer lab on any campus, there are ways to learn whatever you might want to know about computer systems. Just not endorsed. And let me add, that while I'm not a criminal, I am curious about a lot of things in life, including technology. Not a lot, but I do have some game. I plugged in my drive and prepared to steal whatever evidence I could.

I didn't need a lot. As I explored the laptop, I knew instantly who it belonged to and what she could do with it. More than myself, surely, but not enough to keep me out of the folders I wanted. She had protected it very well, but once past that, Joanna obviously hadn't expected anyone to get past her firewalls, and left it wide open to navigate and use. She probably utilized this laptop every day and had no patience for a laundry list of safeguards and passwords. I looked at the icons and folders waiting to open for me. The contents seemed legion.

Ledgers for the casino, both books. Lists of the whales, the big-time players. A list of the perpetual debtors. Emails concerning their handling. Files on the bribes paid locally to keep some of Richmond's finest out of their way. Not many of those, I was glad to note, and I did take enough time to see if Carter made their lists and was relieved to see he hadn't. In fact, he'd been tagged as someone to be wary about. My flash drive gobbled down copies as quickly as it could. Somewhere in there should be mention of my father and what they'd decided to do with him.

I thought I'd finished when I stumbled across another folder, simply labeled as "Kitsune." An avatar of a fox-woman decorated it, pretty cool looking even if she did have three tails. It brought to mind her very odd shadow and the possibility of being twin-souled. I couldn't resist that.

I should have.

CHAPTER THIRTY

THE CURSOR BLINKED over the folder and its odd little illustration even as I popped the jump drive out and tucked it in my shoe. You know that thought that tickles the back of your mind, the one that says, you don't have time for this, you should just run? Always pay attention. It's usually right. I ignored it and clicked on the folder, pages spreading open to reveal their secrets.

The Kitsune is a Japanese deity, which I should have guessed, for what self-respecting fox would have three tails? The number of tails indicated its magical strength and prowess, all the way up to nine, which went beyond interesting to just plain gross. At least in the illustration I viewed. It held Joanna's face, disturbing behind the vixen features, but strangely appropriate, sly and crafty, covetous even as she peered out at me. A Kitsune is meant to be on the good side of things but I already knew better than that.

Before I had a chance to see if she had a page and graph titled Plan for World Domination, the door opened. I slammed the laptop closed and sprang out of the chair, but Joanna moved quicker, leaping over the table and blocking me into the corner. She didn't even take a breath as she boxed me in.

She smiled. "You are so much smarter than you've looked."

"Thanks. I think. And you, so much meaner."

"In the so-called real world? Who has time for that? I've been poking at you for years, wondering what it took to make you wake up and totter to the dark side. Did you just now realize that I'm the one who's been posting all the Internet updates on your sorry lot in life? Reminding people to pity and isolate you? That you couldn't be trusted, perhaps? Doing everything I could to drive you sideways? So much easier to recruit that way."

I hadn't, actually, but events to date had gone so much farther than that. I shrugged it off, even though it stung that she'd been tormenting me all along. "I have bigger things to think about, like that second soul of yours."

Surprise flickered across her face. Then she smiled. Slowly. "Why don't I just show you?"

She flicked a hand at me. Before I could blink, let alone dodge, white lightning hit me and I remember flying through the air before the wall stopped me. And that was the easy part.

Waking hurt. All over. My stomach bobbed up and down, threatening horrible consequences in the future if the earth didn't stop moving. Things looked brighter than they should, and the backs of my eyeballs felt fried, not to mention all the bones in my body complained about their treatment. They complained so loudly that I was prepared to find them stacked in a heap in a back alley somewhere, rather than still connected (more or less) and functional. Not as functional as I might hope. While I could sit up, standing seemed absolutely beyond possible, but that might have something to do with the bungee-like cords twisted around my limbs. I peered down at myself. Strike bungee cords. These appeared to be colorful serpents of one kind or another, making me even less likely to try and break free, especially when one lifted its head and hissed at me. Forget zombies. In this state, I couldn't even outrun a slithering snake. I spared a moment to be disappointed that the maelstrom stone hadn't saved me this indignity.

Narrowing my eyes, I peered out at the current view. I sat on the deck of one of those imperial barges I had admired earlier, minus the cocktail crowd and accompanying band. It sailed near empty. Evelyn stood slumped near me, her body half-wound around one of the masts, hanging on for her inebriated life. At least she looked drunk. Sounded it, too, when she waved a finger at me. She had her kimono back on but it kept flapping in the wind, and I could only pray for her that no one was taking a video and posting it. Most interestingly, she hadn't been tied in place. Too loopy to take advantage of it, but that might not last.

"S'hello, Tesha."

"Evelyn." My voice creaked as I answered. "Are you all right?"

She grinned. "I'm fiiiine."

And feeling no pain, although I figured that would end shortly.

A tall, furry figure slipped in between us, Joanna in fox and human form, barely recognizable as a Kitsune, her tails wagging the air. Evelyn tried to catch one and, failing, giggled at herself before trying again, and giggling again. Joanna swung about and slapped her wrist. "Stop that!"

"So fuzzzzzzy." Evelyn rolled her head a bit. "Oh, hi, Tesha."

She'd forgotten me already. "And hi, again."

She snorted, as unladylike as I'd ever heard her, and certain to have appalled her mother. I almost grinned except my face still hurt.

The boat rocked as someone joined us, or rather three someones, two tall bodyguard/driver types and Hironori himself, dressed in what I could only identify as samurai garb, complete with a helmet and a sheathed sword at his hip. It might not have been, but that was the best description I could give from my brief dive into Japanese culture. Kitsune Joanna bowed before her father. His sharp gaze swept over us.

"You've done well thus far."

"Thank you, Father."

He lifted my chin with his index finger and gave a satisfied smile. "We have plans for you."

"Got to catch me first."

He had a fan in his left hand and gestured it over me. "I believe we already have."

"Looks can be deceiving."

"And here my daughter reported to me that you lacked spirit."

"That was then," Joanna told him. "Now we contend with this." She grabbed at my left wrist, my arm snake-bound high and tight, and pried open my fist to show him the maelstrom stone. When it didn't spit or crackle at either of them, I felt a little more betrayed. Hironori let out a slow hiss of interest as he leaned close to examine my palm.

"You have unknown depths," he told me. To Joanna, he said, "This is well done. Have you prepared for this?"

"Only what the goddess has shared with me. The chaos stone has many rumors surrounding it but few enough facts. I have learned that it can only be given away, unless its possessor is killed and it is taken."

Hironori assessed me. "I doubt she will give it up willingly."

"Damn straight!"

He turned, snapped his fingers, and told his honor guard to depart. They did, quickly and efficiently. He evidently wanted no witnesses. Joanna went to one knee. "I know we had plans for Statler's daughter, Father, but if I can possess the one with the stone, not only will my second soul be released to our use but chaos would come under my dominion. I will still be twice the power I am now, as we wished."

One of his eyebrows lowered. "My goals depend on more than you, Joanna. You know that."

"Congress," she answered reluctantly, her fox's face twisting in displeasure.

"It is one of the roads we have chosen, you and I, planned for many years. And chaos is . . . chaos. I believe the path we forge is better in many ways. We have trained long for this and we are prepared for it."

Joanna looked to Evelyn and then to me. I could see the calculations in her eyes. *Be careful, Dad. Someday this daughter is going to outfox you.* Her tails swished from side to side as she rose from her knee and stood, humanlike, despite the fur and form. "Innovation should not be brushed aside, if opportunities present themselves."

"And I'm not suggesting we do so." He nodded to his daughter. "If you cannot persuade her to release her stone to you, there are other methods we can use."

"Kill her?"

"Or simply lop her hand off. The appendage would function much like a monkey's paw, except that we could be in command of its uses and deviations."

Okay, that was cringe-worthy. I had been preparing myself for some defiant bravado if they threatened Evelyn to get me to relinquish my prized possession, but this went beyond that. I glared at the stone inhabiting my hand, feeling deceived by its inactivity. I would have to do this the hard way. Their mild disagreement had revealed a few things to me: Evelyn's possession was definitely a step Hironori did not wish to skip on his way to more power. And Joanna did not wish to give me up either.

I didn't intend for them to have either of us.

I had one small advantage. They had a lot of guests coming at eight pm for the dinner and charity bidding and Monte Carlo night, and all these plans had to be wrapped up neatly and put away without a hint of carnage.

Snake bindings or not, I managed to get to my feet, slow and steady, eliciting only a solitary forked tongue hissing from my right ankle. The snake gave me a lazy eye before putting its head back into place. My head pounded, my temples line dancing in time to my heartbeat, and I took a deep breath to steady myself. After this pair went through me, they were going to go after Brian, with only Steptoe (maybe) and Carter (maybe) to slow them down. The professor in his boyish form might sling a spell or two, but he couldn't face them for long, not in his current state, and outside of me, I couldn't be sure of what allies he might have left. Hiram perhaps, although I didn't know how far his father's vows of loyalty might extend. This was about more than Brian, though, this was about my dad, and if the flash drive in my sneaker hadn't fried along with the rest of me, I might have what I needed to exonerate him, maybe even bring him back. That, I did not intend to give up on easily.

As if reading my thoughts, fox Joanna smirked down at my feet—my bare feet. She shrugged as my jaw dropped in disbelief. "Missing something?"

I would just have to make certain that I 1) survived and 2) got that laptop from the office. And if the laptop had the files I needed, chances were that another computer elsewhere had the same information. I had no intention of quitting. I let my shoulders slump and my mouth curve down in defeat. No sense letting Joanna know she'd just poked the bear one time too many. I looked up to meet her gaze. "Just counting my toes." I peeled my lip back in a half smile.

Hironori chopped his fan through the air. "Enough. We waste time. I do not wish to give Malender warning of what we hope to accomplish. When we're done, Daughter, we should have the strength we need to be worthy allies. And then . . ." His dark eyes glittered.

And then Malender had best watch his back, I guessed, and it almost tempted me to let them succeed and watch the power struggle to see whether the mighty Mal or the cunning Hironori was victorious with only one little hitch. We'd get devoured first.

I threw Joanna a look. "So. What does it take to split a soul out of you? More than a social media post from a mean girl, I'm betting."

"I'd like to surprise you, but since it involves you intimately . . ." She stepped toward me and without my volition, my left arm snapped up, free of its serpentine bond. Joanna's face curved as she leaned in to have a look at the stone she coveted. Her fox ears perked with her keen interest and her whiskers flared. My palm warmed as she moved close and a sense of hope ran through me. I wasn't all alone after all.

Just as she moved near enough that I felt pretty confident of an effective strike, Evelyn groaned. Joanna's attention jerked around.

"My head hurts." She put one hand out, seemingly aware that she clung to the boat's mast to stay on her feet. "Oh gawd. Did I miss the auction altogether? What were we drinking? My father is going to *kill* me."

"Evelyn, run!"

"What? Where?"

"Just RUN," I yelled at her, and she took three wobbly steps in answer, a good effort but not nearly good enough.

Hironori pivoted and snapped his closed fan down on her

shoulder, and she collapsed like she'd been hit with a two-by-four. Joanna and I stared down at the heap of blonde hair and light blue kimono.

"Now," he said to his daughter, and tucked his fan into his belt sash, reached a hand over, and withdrew his curved sword.

Joanna's face, what could be seen through the auburn fur of her fox guise, paled slightly, but she faced him and threw her shoulders back and her pointed chin up. I had no idea what Hironori planned until he raised his sword high over his head, chanting in Japanese. She confirmed my fear when she braced herself.

His blade came down. The lantern lights on the boat caught its silvery blaze as it fiercely descended upon Kitsune/Joanna. His voice rose and she called out, her voice laced in pain and obedience. Both seemed a little busy with the ritual.

It would be a good time to call on whatever strengths I had.

I flexed my left hand and ran it over me, over the writhing snakes that fell apart as the stone grazed over each one. Scales and serpent heads fell to the deck, and I danced my bare feet away from snapping fangs and forked tongues as they flopped about, dying. Joanna had left my bracelet dangling on my wrist, probably hoping to claim it when she got the stone. I ran my fingers over it.

"Remy! Remy! Remy!"

Fog boiled up over the river until I could see nothing but the barge itself, in a halo of muted light, as Hironori stood over his daughter and sliced her in two. The parts stood as one for a moment as the blade hit the deck, Hironori bowed with the effort.

Remy appeared just in time to see Kitsune/Joanna fall in two different directions.

She let out a startled cry before dropping into a balanced stance, hands up, her own shield sparkling into place, and I conveniently stood behind her as she faced the Hashimotos. All of them. For the two fox figures curled and thrashed, halves, and we could see them sprouting the missing legs and arms, new paws, whiskers and skulls writhing as they attempted to become whole again. Hironori let out a cry of triumph. I thought he might have been premature. One shaped into Joanna as she'd stood before, but the other grew not in vulpine curves, but sharp spikes and angles, a travesty of the Kitsune silhouette but an echo of the shadow I'd see before. It moved in jerks and fits until it crouched over Evelyn's unknowing body.

"Leave her be," Remy ordered, and crossed the deck carefully, one foot over another, and I followed in her shadow.

Hironori drew himself up to face us, nostrils flared in his narrow face. "You are too late."

"It appears I may be just in time."

He curled a lip. "Perhaps if you came as a guardian of the Society, with your fellows as backup, you might survive me. But not now. Not as you are. Your new master holds no sway here. I have not one but two daughters here before me, and together our power is trifold. Retreat now while I allow you."

I could see the spiky figure bent over Evelyn, prying and poking at her as if trying to find a weak spot. With each prod, Evelyn let out a weak gasp. The sound of her distress tore at me. I sidled over behind Remy's shield, and with each step closer, my palm grew hotter. I didn't know what I could do, but I knew I had to do something, anything, as Evelyn's cries grew weaker and more pitiful. In front of me, Hironori pulled his sword back into position and began to advance on Remy.

He, dressed in full samurai gear, and she—well, I must have pulled her out of a cozy evening with a book in front of a fireplace, because she wore stockings instead of shoes, stonewashed jeans, the kind with those artsy tears in them, a slouchy sweater top, and her hair tied back in a swinging ponytail. She still looked gorgeous enough to make Brian and Steptoe pant, maybe even Carter, although I hoped panting was beyond him.

And she looked ready to duel Hironori to the death, balanced on the balls of her feet, her arms leanly muscled and tensed as she maintained her shield, her face tight in concentration. I hoped she could hold her own. As I watched, she pursed her lips and whistled, and those slender white and red hounds of hers began to leap out of the fog and onto the deck with clicks of their nails and sinister rumbles.

Her hounds flowed around us, flanking their mistress, jumping now and then with nips and yips at their targets, bounding back and forth.

I thrust my hand between the spiked shadow and Evelyn, peeling it away, hoping it would go the way of the shredding snakes—and it did hiss. Coiling backward on its haunches, it bared its teeth and came at me. It grew more and more solid with every hissing breath as it gained strength. It snagged a paw at me and I could feel its claws, like ice, raking over the back of my wrist. It burned like fire and stung like a thousand bees and worse, it felt like sheer evil. I twisted my wrist over and grabbed that paw, crushing it against my stone. I heard it sizzle like scalding water falling on cold stone. The spiky thing let out a squeal and shuffled away from me, out of range, and its voice settled into a low growl. Two hounds bounded in, teeth flashing, and yelped as they caught the shadow's edges. They retreated abruptly, back by my feet, stomachs to the deck as they still dared to growl in menace.

I reached out and caught Evelyn by an ankle, determined to pull her out of reach. The hounds, deciding that this might not be as painful as attacking, grabbed the kimono by its sleeves and helped. It would be a close one as to whether we'd disrobe Evelyn completely or get her to safety first.

Hironori slashed with his sword. Remy whirled out of range, her shield catching the edge of the katana and responding in a swirl of sparks. Joanna the first came in at Remy's side with a vicious high kick that missed Remy's temple but caught her in the elbow with a sharp crack, and her arm flailed helplessly in response. Remy tried to shake it off only to reel to one side in pain, her limb useless. Her defensive shield shattered.

I skipped back with a high squeak, pulling Evelyn out of the way again, and seriously considering dumping her overboard— surely with those boobs she'd float. But I had no idea what, if anything, lay waiting in the gray fog roiling about us. It could only be there to hide our movements, or perhaps we'd transitioned to another plane, just as my father had—anything might be possible.

Remy spat out, "Cease and desist, Hironori." She tucked the hand of her useless arm into the waistband of her jeans and put her left hand up, and another shield shimmered into place. Not as wide, not as brilliant, not as dense but undoubtedly still powerful. All six of her red and white hounds gathered at her heels, jaws gaping.

"By what authority?"

Her lips thinned as they locked gazes. "By whichever authority scares you the most."

"Neither the Society nor Malender can touch me now."

"But they already have. Where is your sacrifice?"

Hironori looked at me. "Neither is safe by any degree." And before he finished speaking, he lunged.

Not at us. Not at Remy. His sword swept out and to the side, and took out three of her hounds with one shrieking cut. Their blood splattered out in a wave of crimson and, like their bodies, disappeared in midair.

Remy threw me a look, her face pale, deep etches by the sides of her mouth, pain or worry, I couldn't tell. I pulled Evelyn back another foot or so as the spiky fox figure began to advance on us again. Joanna Two opened her fox jaws in a wolfish grin, tongue lolling out, looking less like Joanna or her twin with every step. I could feel the evil rolling off her like an oily stream of malice.

"You can't save both. I will have one or the other," it said, rolling the last "r" as if savoring its flavor and warning me to pick one.

I put my palm up, and in the midnight flow of the fog and mist and lantern light around us, the stone glowed, a miniature sun beaming in golds and ivories. The obsidian flecks that inhabited it only shaded the rays of its light, making them that much stronger.

Spike shrank away from me, throwing a paw over her face, showing me her hindquarters, and her tails lashed out. They flipped across me, full of shards, sharp and burning, and I shook them off, aiming my palm at them. One of the furry tails shriveled in on itself and turned into black crumbs, falling like ash to the deck. Joanna let out a scream of fury, and threw herself at us, her original self missing a foxtail as well. I'd managed to wound both of them.

Hironori threw his katana at Remy. It whipped end over end

before straightening out and thudding deep into her chest, as true as any arrow. She dropped to her knees, her good arm flung up, her lips moving, but her voice cut from her throat. Her hounds melted into the air.

I stepped into Spike, throwing a left hook I'd only seen thrown in the movies but praying I could land it. Openhanded, I missed her jaw, catching Spike in the throat with the stone full-force. With a guttural choke, Spike tumbled backward, heels over head, across the narrow boat and then going over the side with a squeal, splashing into water and fog that hissed and spat with the fury of a boiling cauldron. I waited half a moment to see if she'd boomerang out of the river, but the fog and water swallowed Spike down.

Evelyn croaked, "Look out!"

I got half a turn in as Joanna jumped me.

Hand-to-hand we grappled, my stone quiet as though emptied of power, her fox form and girl form fading in and out. One moment I had paws and teeth gnashing at me, the next Joanna in high martial art form, with me bobbing, weaving, and scrambling for all I was worth.

Remy wrapped her hand around the hilt of the katana, looking up at Hironori, attempting to keep him from pulling the sword out. Froth bubbled from the side of her mouth, staining her chin crimson. He closed on her with slow, deliberate steps, leaned down and, with a grunt, wrenched his blade out of her. It came free with an awful sucking noise that reached my ears even as I rolled to the deck and away from one of Joanna's lethal kicks. I also heard the last, keening sound Remy would ever make as she sank to her side, curled in agony as blood pumped from her chest and soaked her slouchy sweater dark.

I kicked back as Joanna crouched low over me, looking for the same killing blow as her father had delivered, but I connected, bare heel to her temple. I'd been in some field hockey brawls and knew some moves so dirty that I'd been removed from games. It knocked her down with a whoosh of breathy surprise. I launched myself onto her, grabbed her by her ears, and began to knock the back of her head to the deck again and again.

I couldn't do it hard enough to hurt her the way I wanted or had to, and before I could hit her a fourth time, Hironori socked me in the jaw with a fist wrapped about the handle of his katana.

Stars burst inside my eyes and nailed me flat. Quiet followed. When my vision cleared, I saw Hironori standing over me, sword held high over his head, Joanna at his feet, her arms wrapped around his knees as if to anchor him. I found myself down on one knee and looking up at the two of them.

"Relinquish the stone willingly, Tessa Andrews, or I will cut it from you."

CHAPTER THIRTY-ONE

BEFORE I COULD MOVE, dodge, or even roll overboard to what had to be a nicer fate than what I looked at, Joanna wrenched herself from her father and grabbed Evelyn. She bared her teeth at me, her foxy self shining through again.

"Do not move."

I didn't want to surrender. The thought of it rose in my throat like bitter bile and I spat it out. The katana curved across my vision, shining silvery keen except where smeared with Remy's blood.

"Let her go!" My throat went raw with vehemence.

Hironori looked to his daughter.

"No, Father! Not yet. I have not failed you yet."

"No," he answered softly. "Not yet. But we may make a bargain and still gain what we want." He looked back to me, considering.

"I want the flash drive back. My father exonerated. And my friend safe."

"That might be difficult. His proclivities were well known. He could not stay away from a gamble. A sad story, his, following in his aunt's footsteps. She was the first to owe me much, much money. He came in to make good on her losses, and he did. He saved her paltry pension and properties, and she swore off her favorite vice, but by then, we had him hooked. He'd forgotten that the house always wins." Hironori smiled thinly. "Gambling is like an opiate to many people, as sure an addiction, and generally

legal. I cannot bargain the drive with you. You mean our downfall. The only thing I can offer is her life and yours." A moonlight
from beyond the fog glittered on the upheld blade.

Did he mean Aunt April? My great-aunt with the rigid spine?
Like the moon filtering through, some sense of my father's actions came to me. I looked up at Hironori. "Businesses can be
moved."

"As can stones."

His eyes, dark and shadowed, gave away nothing more. If I
relinquished the maelstrom to him, he didn't have to keep to
any deal we'd make. I knew that but pretended to be considering his offer, weighing my options.

Joanna held none of the patience her father did. "Don't treat
her like an equal! She has no options, and I have my souls!"
Joanna shook Evelyn like a limp doll. Evelyn responded by
vomiting on the two of them even as Joanna raised her fist and
a second shadow, watery and blurred, twinned the first. Insubstantial. Barely visible, but there. So much for falling overboard, I thought sadly. The Hashimotos skipped back a step or
two from the spew.

I had only slowed them down. I hadn't stopped them. I didn't
know if I could.

But then . . . I wouldn't know if I didn't try.

Evelyn wiped her mouth on the back of her hand and gave
me a sideways smile. She knew me from the field hockey fields
as well as the classroom. Her gaze slanted across the deck behind me, and she arched an eyebrow.

I hazarded a quick look and saw, lying in the shadows of the
rim between deck and railing, a rusted golf club. A three-iron,
if I wasn't mistaken, forgotten by golfer and crew and left to the
elements, tucked almost out of sight. But it took a long time for
a good golf club, even abused, to go bad. I rolled to my right,
grabbed the club, and came up swinging at Joanna. Hironori
moved as one with me, and the edge of his sword caught the
shaft of the golf club. We hooked, and metal against metal sang
in a high-pitched squeal as my club slid off the katana.

Joanna ducked away, and as she did, Evelyn disappeared into
thin air. Off-balance, Joanna staggered to the rail and stared,

wide-eyed and openmouthed at the hole in reality. Evelyn was just . . . gone.

I shouted, "It's about time!" I spun about to free my golf club and got ready for another hit. I heard a soft chuckle behind me and made a note not to back up. Hironori closed in with a soft hiss, his lips thinning in concentration, his wrists flexing slightly as he waved his sword in intimidation. He didn't intend to be parried off the club this time; I could see his focus on my hands. My wrists, one of which he intended to slice through, freeing the maelstrom stone. I had an ace up that sleeve, though, and kept the club head down, ready to swing up with all the driving power I could manage. I wasn't feared on the field hockey team for nothing. Settling my feet on the deck, I could feel the vibrations of the boat as the seen and the unseen moved upon it.

Hironori twitched as he began his drive toward me. I tightened my grip. Two little marbles rolled past me and thumped into his samurai-sandaled feet, exploding with all the smoke and fury of a great flash-bang. He pirouetted, missing me entirely, and I grabbed his hand, deflecting the blade toward Joanna. It swooped downward, burying itself in wood and splinters and severing that spiky shadow entirely from her. One-handed, I clubbed it a number of times, ending up with a nice slice to knock it overboard into the fog and sizzling river waters surrounding us. I didn't know if it would surface yet again, reattached to her, but I didn't have time to worry as the smoke cleared and Hironori homed in on me once more.

This time I swung first, a backhanded slash to the knees. I connected but he didn't buckle like I'd planned. With a swish of his samurai robes, Hironori sidestepped the brunt of my hit, grinned, and came back swinging, the edge of the blade so close as I ducked that I could count two new notches in its silvery steel. He drove me back to the deck, on one knee again.

I couldn't shake the feeling that he was toying with me or the instinct that said Joanna would attack at my blind spot at any moment. My unseen ally had his hands full of shielding Evelyn so I couldn't hope that we could double-team them, plus we had the disadvantage of Remy's fallen body in the middle of the action. For a flicker of a moment, I thought I saw Remy flinch but knew that couldn't be possible. Hashimoto felt my hesitation, I think, and leaped at me, sword lowered for an upward swing, and I put my hand up to stop him.

And then I realized that I had very obligingly given him a clean shot at cleaving my hand from my wrist, freeing the stone.

My palm flared in scorching pulses and I let out a cry. Joanna let out a low, derisive laugh and vaulted Remy's body to close on me, to finish off whatever her father left in his wake. Like a mirage, searing waves flowed out of my hand, rippling across the front of me, and my father's image rose in the midst of the torch. I don't know how he got there but he had. He brought his hands up, a shield spreading out, halting the Hashimotos in their tracks. I let out a startled gasp and heard a muffled one behind me as well.

"Call the name," he said, and added in warning, "I can't hold them long, Tessa."

And I knew he couldn't because although he used whatever ghostly power he could summon, the stone itself drew from me, and I could feel what little strength I had left rapidly draining away. Its heat and light pulsed in time with my heartbeat. But what name did he want me to call? Brian? Hiram? Steptoe was already here, and hiding with Evelyn under that suit coat of his. To bring him forth would put Evelyn out in the open as a pawn again, and about all Simon could do was lob more flash-bangs. Carter? It was the only other name I knew I might be able to count upon.

He must mean Carter Phillips, and if he came as a member of the Society, he could bring some heavyweight backup. I drew a quavering breath to name him.

The broken hulk that was Remy moved in her puddle of crimson. In a valiant, death-dying move, she arched upward, straightening. Her lips fell open. With breath she should no longer have held, she cried, "Malender! Malender! Malender!"

Oh holy, no.

That was so not the name I would have summoned.

The fog that had been roiling about the boat grew darker and dense, and then black as a starless and moonless sky. It crawled over the railings onto the boat, carrying a weight with it that made the boat shiver and dance on the river. In fact, I think the whole world shuddered. I scrambled to my feet, keeping the shield deployed, and backed up until I heard Steptoe grunt softly in warning and thought I could feel the heat of their two bodies against my bare feet. I wanted to take our leave, but the now oily cloud settling about us looked about as easy to get through as a brick wall. I would be stuck here until Malender was through with all of us.

Hironori Hashimoto dropped with a thud to one knee, released his sword, and pushed one fist into his open hand in salute, dropping his chin in obedience. Joanna froze next to him until her father hissed and she quickly copied him. Too late, if I were a judge, because Malender had already materialized, although his now-human form appeared out of the nothing, and he stood as handsome as ever, taking his time to sweep his gaze over me, the deck behind me, and all corners of the party barge until it at last fell upon Hironori and Joanna. I couldn't see much of his face from my angle, but it looked to me as though his eyes had narrowed and his mouth tightened and his teeth ground before he spoke.

"Hashimoto."

"Saikōshidō-sha."

"Supreme leader, eh? Yet somehow I do not feel as though you concede my supremacy. Or my leadership. This—" and he spread his hands about him, "feels like a ritual. One intended for elevation. Perhaps one even meant to surpass my own station. You have a sacrifice. You've taken down one of my best lieutenants." Malender paused, looking both sadly and fondly at Remy before waving a hand, and a bloody stain was all that remained of her. "You've even cast covetous eyes on a valuable relic." He looked directly at me, and the maelstrom stone crackled, its power driving my father into an unsteady reel. He disappeared as Malender beckoned at him, but the stone's shield stayed, although thinner and lighter than before. "What am I to think?"

I froze as I lost my father again, but then felt a swirl of warmth about me that told me he still existed and had only been sent back to his shelter. I managed a breath as I felt that touch.

Hironori grasped at words to satisfy Malender. "I would have you think that, as allies, we strive to be more powerful and thus more worthy to serve you." Hironori did not look up as he lied through his teeth. Joanna's two remaining foxtails swished twice in agitation.

"Commendable if true. I don't feel truth in the night air, however." He looked again to me. "Do you?"

I opened my mouth and the first sound out didn't quite make it. I cleared my throat. "Far from it."

He pointed at my palm. "Did you intend to relinquish that to them? Or to me?"

"No. Not if I can help it."

"Was it you who summoned Remy?"

My mouth had dried again but I managed a "Yes."

"Why?"

"She told me she could, and would, help me."

"Ahhh." He leaned over, touched a fingertip to the blood, and lifted it to his lips where he tasted it. "Ah, Remy. I think we must have words."

"She's dead now, or must be."

Malender shrugged at me. "Perhaps. Perhaps not entirely. I am disappointed in her actions even as I am intrigued by yours." He returned his attention to the Hashimotos, and I found myself grateful. Handsome yes, and brilliant against his darker self, and altogether the scariest thing I'd ever hoped to see, because I had the impression that even though he looked human, he couldn't be farther from it. I felt sincerely sorry for Remy's sacrifice and prayed that she had slipped away from his grasp.

The three of them began to argue in Japanese, fast and loud. I wet my lips and managed a whisper, three times. I had no way of knowing if it could even be heard, let alone answered, through Malender's looming presence.

I felt a hand on my ankle. Steptoe whispered, "Sorry, ducks, we're all full under here."

"It's okay." I thought. "Did you manage to grab up any of my things Joanna took off me?"

"Just your evening purse. Pardon me, but that thing feels like you've a cannonball in it."

I grinned. "Not quite. Shove it out, will you?" The purse bowled up against my ankle and I stooped to recover it. Then, as quietly as I could, I opened it and let its contents seep out in a circle around us, white crystals shining in a thick line that not even the evening wind off the river could disturb.

Joanna snarled. Or maybe that was a foxy snap. Hard to tell, I still wasn't quite versed in speaking Kitsune. She leveled a hand at me and loosed a few scornful words in Japanese.

The two men swung about on me.

Malender tilted his head. "Tessa, Tessa, what am I to do with you?"

I shrugged. "Salt," I told him.

"I can tell." The handsome creature took a deep breath. "I am not finished with you two," he said. He clapped his hands and the Hashimotos disappeared, the boat rocking with the force of their exit.

I blinked. "How long will they be gone?"

"If I let them return, it will be quite a while from now."

I had a feeling his timeline stretched very differently from mine. "Long enough that I don't have to worry about them?"

Malender's eyes smiled though his expression did not. He had very small laugh wrinkles at the corners of his lids as if that had been different, once. "It can be if you wish to give me the stone."

"Mmmm . . . no. It seems to want to stay with me."

"For now. It has a history, if you didn't know, of picking its owners. Perhaps I will appeal to it in the future."

"Que sera, sera."

"Indeed." Malender threw his head up, like a stag sniffing the air and discovering a pack of hounds approaching. "You continue to surprise me. You have friends approaching."

"And I'll bet they're your enemies."

"There are many who have yet to see the wisdom of following me or even what I am. I've been gone for too many decades. Rumors arise. Truth twists. I can see I've much work waiting." He arched an eyebrow. "Tell me, Tessa of the Salt. Would you listen if I return to speak with you?"

I didn't know. I really, really didn't. He scared the bejeebers out of me, but was that only because of his strangeness? His total impossibility? Or did I know evil when I felt it, a greater evil than I'd ever thought I could encounter? I settled for a shrug. "Everyone deserves the benefit of the doubt, I guess."

"Good enough." Malender began to wind his wrists about each other, his black cloud coming to him and collecting about his hands. "Next time," he added, "Salt will not likely hold me back."

"What will?"

That brought a crooked grin to his handsome face. "That's for you to discover. As for your father . . ." He stood very still. Then he nodded. "Recover the laptop and you should have some idea of how to restore him. If not, we can always make a deal." He winked and then he disappeared in a puff of white, clean smoke, as aromatic as a virgin spring day. The oily stuff slinked after.

Carter stumbled as he hit the deck in the emptiness left behind. "Tessa! What's going on?" He straightened and spun about to ascertain his bearings. Four others hit the deck as well, three guys and a really badass looking woman. The Society, I'd guess.

"Ummm . . . attempted human sacrifice by the Hashimotos and Malender was here but now he's not and, oh, there's a laptop in the spa that the FBI will want, but I need to get a flash drive and copy some files first, and Steptoe, come out from under there, and see if you can keep Evelyn calm."

He did, and she did, although she cried a lot first.

Carter did one of his Jedi mind-wipes, though, and Evelyn collected herself like a trooper as we returned to the spa. I helped get her into her gown and repair her makeup. Then I changed into my party clothes, and we escorted Evelyn over to be the star of the auction. With so many bidders, I thought an old-fashioned brawl would break out. Oddly, her father turned out to be the highest bidder. Carter, standing by me at the back of the room, agreed with me that he'd probably done it strictly out of fear of some of the prospective dates. A few words were said about the missing host and hostess, but the party went on, staffed by the charity, and nothing else seemed to go amiss.

Nobody noticed us much, and I thought maybe it was because

I stood in the aura of his radiance and we weren't supposed to be noticed. I had on my sea-glass gown and stood barefoot, my hair down about my shoulders, and felt like I sported a good-sized shiner. Carter had let me slide my fingers into his hand because I'd told him I still felt a bit wobbly. When everyone else surged like an incoming tide to the buffet and gambling tables, we turned and left.

A police cruiser is not a car for a romantic drive home. It smells. Faintly, because I'm sure someone cleans it diligently every day, but a lot of stuff, not the least of which can be an aromatic police dog, happens in the back seat. I didn't mind it much though, my thoughts drifting to the flash drive in my possession and what Malender had said about it, and about the guy driving the cruiser.

Although we'd left the auction early, night had fallen truly and thoroughly, and the only things lighting the neighborhood as we glided through were the streetlights and an occasional porch light here and there. How nice, I thought, to have a welcome waiting for you whenever you were ready to come home. Had my father looked for that at first? Before becoming trapped in limbo? Had my mother kept the lights on for him at first? I didn't remember. Maybe I would put a small light in the basement and turn it on, for when the shadows fell down there. Just to let him know we remembered and waited.

Carter led me to the front steps, my garment bag over one arm and the other still keeping me steady. He looked down at me. "It's a shame not many saw you in that dress."

"It is, huh." I looked down at myself. "That just means I can wear it again someday."

"True." He handed me my bag and then slowly slid his hand away from mine. The moment he let go, I could feel his warmth retreat and I leaned into it, not wanting to relinquish it.

Carter moved his hand up and cupped the side of my face, gently, and his thumb smoothed over the tender spots. "Those should heal quickly."

I looked into his eyes. He leaned down a smidgen more and my heart leaped because I knew what was going to happen. My whole body trembled with a kind of "Yes! Finally!" tingle.

His lips brushed my forehead softly.

"Night, Tessa."

And then he was gone.

I stood, wavering, for just a second before my mother pulled the door open, and the cruiser drove off.

"Tessa?"

I just stayed there, grinning, until she pulled me inside our home.

CHAPTER THIRTY-TWO

Days Later

"THE ROWAN WOOD is not good," Brian said mournfully as he took stock of all the items he'd spread out on the picnic table.

I picked up the bundle of twigs. They looked just like their picture on Google. "What's wrong with them?"

"Not rowan."

"Are you sure?"

"Fairly certain. Similar but in a ritual like mine, I can't use substitutes."

"I'd think not." I dropped the bundle. "I can order from a different source."

He sighed. "Tonight's a blue moon. A most auspicious sign for me."

"And you're tired of waiting."

He held out a hand to me. He wasn't the strapping young man who'd appeared in Professor Brandard's backyard like magic. His hand looked nearly transparent and he shook. "I'm not sure how much longer I'll have the ability to wait." I covered his hand with mine.

"Where else can we get it?"

"My perdition rod. It's rowan."

"But you'd have to burn it! And then, it's gone. It's a relic, Brian, you have to hold onto it."

"I can, if I recover, make another. A trip to England, a bit of hosteling, a bit of luck . . ."

"With Malender on the prowl, gathering up wizards and such like they're bread crumbs on his trail back to domination?"

He wrinkled his nose. "You make him sound so predatory."

"And he isn't?"

"Oh, he is. Definitely."

We pulled our hands back and thought for a minute about Remy's fate, and those of the Hashimotos. I echoed Brian's earlier sigh.

I reached for his cane. He'd been using it more and more not for magical protection but just as the necessary means to keep him steady while walking. It made that rain stick sound as I lifted it to me, the noise it had begun to make ever since the crab at Cleopatra's Needle had stolen it. I shook it again. Something at the back of my mind itched.

I pulled out my phone.

"Calling Carter?"

"Heavens no. What would I say to him? Excuse me, Detective Carter, but Brian and I are trying to find out the best way to set him on fire and can you ask the Society if they have any ideas?" Fingers flew over my keyboard rapidly and I looked at the Wikipedia entries in offering. I picked one.

Rain stick. Hollow. With seeds or thorns or pebbles inside that tumble and fall as the cylinder is rotated.

I grabbed up the foot of it and began to twist off the heavy rubber cap. Old and stubborn, like the professor had been, it didn't want to be removed. Forcing it on the picnic table's edge, I finally wedged it off and held it out.

A shower of thorns cascaded onto the patio, bouncing about until the cane felt emptied. It was as though the heart of the perdition rod had morphed into what he needed.

Brian looked at them thoughtfully, and then leaned close to examine them. "Good heavens. Those are rowan wood twigs."

"Less than twigs, but hey, kindling is kindling, right?" I muscled the cap back into place. "How much do you need?"

"A handful, more or less to stand within and that—that is

exactly what we've got." He swallowed, hard. "I think . . . I think I have all I need."

Except courage, and I didn't think him a wuss for hesitating, not one bit. Who wanted to go up in flames again? But that was the path he'd chosen centuries ago, and he'd not live to see another year if he didn't follow it again. We both knew that. Brian and the professor needed to be one whole person, with his knowledge behind him and his destiny in front of him. He rubbed the thick gold ring on his thumb for comfort and reassurance, a gesture he did more and more frequently now. It seemed to steady him and give him resolve.

I looked up to see him watching me as if he could read my thoughts. "I'll be here."

"I know."

"Anyone else? Hiram? Steptoe?"

He shook his head.

"My mom?"

"No." He gave a rueful smile. "A set of clothes?"

"Oh, right. Get them now or are we waiting till sunset or midnight or something?"

He threw his head back. He still had a full and glorious head of hair, red-gold in the sun, and he looked to the sky. He pointed. "The moon is up now."

And it was, shining as brightly in the blue sky as it would at night. "Wow." I inhaled. "Well, I'll run and get some clothes and we're good to go?"

He put his palm over his store of goods. Frankincense and myrrh. Rowan wood. Stick cinnamon and a few other things, among them a shed snakeskin and a bird feather I did not recognize but looked as if it must have belonged to a glorious bird at one time. A phoenix? He'd never told me.

I left him to run upstairs to the closet holding my father's things. Suddenly, I wasn't too keen about giving them away. The files I'd been allowed to copy took hard study, and I'd even downloaded my own dictionary to decipher the Japanese sprinkled throughout, and I figured that one day I'd find the key that would set him free. He'd need a wardrobe. That was then,

though, and this was now, and if Brian reincarnated, he'd definitely need a set too.

I picked out a worn pair of jeans, another old pair of sneakers that Barney hadn't chewed on, and a henley style T-shirt
that I didn't like on my father—he wasn't a teen any more, after
all—but that Brian would look okay in.

Outside the kitchen entry, I hesitated. Then I went to the
pantry door and opened it to the basement, sitting on the top
step. I hadn't talked to Dad since that evening days ago when
he'd nearly shredded himself protecting me. I don't know how
he'd done it through the stone, but he had found a way, just
when I needed it. I didn't think of him as unreliable anymore. I
had put one of those electric candles halfway down the staircase and turned it on every night.

I called down the cellar steps. "Dad. Thanks for everything.
I don't know if you heard anything, you know, through the
stone, but Hironori said you'd started gambling to clear Aunt
April's debt. So. There's that. And you did it. And the other
stuff, too, but . . . well, I forgive you. I want you home and
I'm working on it. Hang on, okay? For Mom and me. Just—
hang on."

I didn't get an answer. I wanted one, but he could still be
really drained of energy. I know I'd been, for days. I stood up
to leave. Then, very faintly, I heard words. "I love the two
of you."

The sound caught on my heart. "I'm getting you out!"

Hugging my bundles of clothes, I left the basement and hurried outside.

Waiting for me, Brian had arranged his little pyre with herbs
and fragrances interwoven with the fragile rowan thorns. He
managed a feeble smile when he saw me.

"All done?" I plunked his stuff down on the now-empty patio
table. I wished Morty were here, his big broad frame as sturdy
as an oak tree, his hands broad as a shovel, one of them holding
onto mine. Hiram would come in his stead if we asked, but it
wouldn't be the same.

"One last thing." He fetched a cigar out of nowhere, twisted
it open and began to sprinkle tobacco leaf all over the mound.

"Tobacco? Seriously?"

"Hey. Why do you think men starting smoking it to begin with? They saw the wizardly things we were doing with good leaf."

How gullible did he think I was? I pursed my lips in disbelief but didn't say anything. Brian laughed as he dusted his hands off, a thin and nervous sound.

"Well, this is it."

"If it doesn't work . . ."

"I left a note upstairs in my room. You guys are absolved of everything because I'm delusional." He winked.

"Yeah, but I can't . . . I can't just stand here and watch you if anything goes . . . Well, you know."

He brought an empty vial from his pocket and tapped it. "This is an accelerant. I'm covered in it. Supposed to be, but, well, it should be quick. Whatever happens."

The stone in my palm began to throb in time with my pulse, quickening a little. "Okay. Good luck—wait, should I not say that? Break a leg, maybe?"

Brian took a position in the middle of his small pyre. It only spread out maybe three inches further than the length of his feet. "Thank you, Tessa, for everything. The meals, the friendship, the help, the belief, the rescue. Everything and more."

"And thank you, Professor, for believing in me."

He rubbed his fingers on his thumb ring. Then he opened the matchbox and struck his match.

I looked at the ring, thinking of all we'd gone through to get him his ritual necessities. Where would we be if Remy hadn't dropped that by accident at the Washington Monument? It had helped to restore him enough to remember what else he needed.

My stone throbbed.

What was it Malender had said about her? *"One of my best lieutenants."* Since when had Remy done anything by accident? Like dropping a valuable she'd been sent to retrieve? Thoughts tumbled through me.

Something felt terribly wrong. Even my stone knew it.

"Professor! Wait!"

Too late. He released the flaming match. It dropped, sizzling as it fell. The tiny flame bloomed larger, blue and yellow. I reached out with both hands, one aiming for the thumb ring, the other to bat the match away.

Time slowed. The match seemed to fall forever and the gold ring gleamed at me, just out of reach. I strained to do the impossible.

I could feel the phoenix power rising to greet both of us as I stepped into his circle.

I could see, just for a split second of a moment, why one would want to be a wizard and own the world, see it, sense it, use it with the giddy power of all the elements just aching to be recognized and released. It swept through me, and I felt it as a rainbow, colliding with and then gathering me up, carrying me with it, and I realized that I held both the match and the ring, each in opposite hands. That Brian's mouth contorted in a sound of dismay which hadn't reached me just yet as I stood, the sole impediment on the bridge he'd built to get from here to there. I could sense the arc of his very long life, the wisdom he'd gathered and the knowledge he'd lost, bit by bit, as his mortality failed him.

I knew why he wanted it all returned to him.

I knew that he couldn't get it this way. An abyss yawned in his bridge, a chasm that would swallow him up, plunging him into depths I couldn't comprehend from where I stood, but I could see it. It chilled my bones and stopped my heart for a beat or two to contemplate the mistake. Whatever waited at the bottom for him boiled with evil and impatience, anticipating his fall.

As dark as the abyss loomed, and even though Malender and Remy had been in my thoughts, I didn't think he was the one who waited. Something worse occupied that void.

The match sizzled red hot against my flesh. I squeezed my hand shut to put it out as I fell out of the circle, overwhelmed, and landed on my hip as Brian finished crying out, "No!"

"Sorry, Professor. It's the ring. I don't know how or what, but the ring is no good."

He clawed at the hand that grasped the lump of gold, his eyes wild, his feet and legs practically dancing in upset. "Give it back!"

"I can't." I opened my hand slowly and we could both see the maelstrom stone absorbing the remains of the thick, golden band. It flared hotly in my palm as the ring slowly melted into its undeniable force. The stone absorbed it totally.

We stood, wordless for a moment or two longer as one magic ate the other. Then the professor ran his hand through Brian's wavy, copper-tinged hair.

"Well," he said. "I would be madder than a boiled owl, but I can feel the difference already. I had no idea. How did you?"

"How different?"

"More substantial. Stronger. Less scattered in my thoughts." He looked down at his feet. "It's a good pyre, but that's not all that I will need. Whatever made me think it might be?" He gave me a hand up and then bent over to look closer. He made a tsking sound. "Not good at all. This might have wreaked some havoc. I shall have to salvage what I might."

"What kind of ritual did you build?"

"Oh, it looks like a summoning for a greater demon."

I choked, swallowing my own spit. Absentmindedly, he pounded on my back for a few minutes. "Good work, Tessa. I don't like repeating myself, but what made you suspicious?"

"It just didn't feel right, and I thought of Remy. She doesn't seem the careless type of person. Dropping a ring like that, just when we thought we needed it—well, the coincidence gave it away."

"If only you'd thought that earlier."

"We might have saved Morty?"

"No, no, not that. I'm not sure anyone could have saved Morty from his folly. I just could have saved myself some time searching for the correct artifacts, instead of the wrong ones with a muddled mind. As it stands now, we're still not done. Another day, another treasure hunt it seems." He dusted his hands off as he straightened. "Still in this with me?"

"Did the possum cross the road? I might ask the same question

back at you—this stone just ate a malevolent bit of jewelry. I think
I might need you as much as you need me."

"Indeed."

The professor stepped out of his little nest of phoenix wizardry and clasped my hands, both of them, in promise.